THE
KILLER
COLLECTIVE

Center Point
Large Print

**This Large Print Book carries the
Seal of Approval of N.A.V.H.**

THE
KILLER
COLLECTIVE

BARRY EISLER

CENTER POINT LARGE PRINT
THORNDIKE, MAINE

This Center Point Large Print edition
is published in the year 2019 by arrangement with
Amazon Publishing, www.apub.com.

Originally published in the United States
by Amazon Publishing, 2019.

The text of this Large Print edition is unabridged.
In other aspects, this book may vary
from the original edition.
Printed in the United States of America
on permanent paper.
Set in 16-point Times New Roman type.

ISBN: 978-1-64358-249-8

Library of Congress Cataloging-in-Publication Data

Names: Eisler, Barry, author.
Title: The killer collective / Barry Eisler.
Description: Center Point Large Print edition. | Thorndike, Maine :
    Center Point Large Print, 2019.
Identifiers: LCCN 2019017947 | ISBN 9781643582498 (hardcover :
    alk. paper)
Subjects: LCSH: Large type books. | GSAFD: Adventure fiction. |
    Suspense fiction.
Classification: LCC PS3605.I85 K53 2019 | DDC 813/.6—dc23
LC record available at https://lccn.loc.gov/2019017947

For Alice and Andrew Vachss, whose work has inspired Livia and Rain—and their author.

The months and days are the travelers of eternity.

—*Bashō*

PROLOGUE

Arrington smoked in the dark. Smoking meant so much, not just for its intrinsic pleasure, but because he knew what it did to him. Accepting the inherent risks involved, the price of the pleasure, elevated the activity from what might have been a mere indulgence to something more akin to a passion. After all, a man had to genuinely love—had to be *committed* to something—if he was willing to sacrifice himself for it.

Still, he didn't do it all the time. He never wanted smoking to become rote or routine. It had to have impact. Mark the moment. Signify something special, even something extreme.

Tonight, it did all those things.

In some ways, what he had just learned defied reason, because how could something so awful also contain something so impossibly good? He had experienced a similar dynamic only once before: 9/11, when the news came at CIA about the Pentagon hit, and his first thought had been *Kelly is there.* Kelly, who only a month earlier had told him she wanted a divorce, and that she hoped they could do it amicably, with reasonable visitation rights so he could continue to be a father to their two small daughters, and with no more child support than what the law would require anyway.

9

And then she was gone. Extinguished. Suddenly, instead of a sad, impoverished divorcé, he was the widower of a martyred Defense Department employee, sanctified by her death, recipient of a six-figure life-insurance payout and a seven-figure September 11th Victim Compensation Fund settlement. Rich instead of poor. Celebrated instead of scorned.

That was the dirty little secret of 9/11, he thought. Not the conspiracy theories—the accusations about advance knowledge and controlled demolition and inside jobs. The real secret was that within the overall loss, there were also winners. After all, it was just a matter of statistics that half of marriages ended in divorce. And divorce was the chemotherapy of marriage, so expensive and toxic that only couples in extremis would attempt it as a cure. And if half of marriages were so cancerous that they justified treatment with the equivalent of chemotherapy, what did that say about the others? How many of the nondivorced had just learned to live with the illness because the cure seemed even worse than the disease?

And all those unhappy unions, the bad and the worse, ended that morning. With the widows and widowers consecrated by the nation and showered with cash.

He had sensed today's similarity immediately, but the full ramifications were so vast that he needed this moment in his town house living room, the lights off, the tendrils of tobacco smoke curling up past his fingers and the nicotine sharpening his focus, to try to fully understand.

He'd initially thought it would be just another scandal for the Secret Service. He didn't care about that, beyond the value he thought he might extract politically. And then he had a hunch. A long shot, he'd thought. But it turned out he'd been right. Spectacularly so.

On the one hand, the whole thing confirmed his deepest fears. The fears the Agency shrinks had pronounced as "overblown"—as though a psychiatrist had any basis to opine on geopolitics. The fears he knew his complacent colleagues laughed about behind his back. The ones they had used to derail his career.

But on the other hand . . . hadn't it been discovered by exactly the right person? Who else would have known how to leverage it to protect the country? Who else would have had the will, and the insight, that all the people who had laughed at him, and marginalized him, and in the end jettisoned him, had lacked?

Doing it right would require some . . . difficult decisions. But when the health of an entire forest was at stake, you couldn't afford to focus too much on individual trees. In fact, to protect the forest, sometimes firebreaks needed to be constructed, and certain trees removed.

The first step would be the least pleasant. There were security risks to eliminate. Information integrity to protect. Too many people knew, and the longer he waited, the worse the problem would become. Within a matter of days, in fact, if not sooner, it might already be too late.

Obviously, none of it could be done from within the government. Because the problem *was* the government. It had already been penetrated, as he'd always suspected. The only surprise was that the disease was even more advanced and widespread than he had imagined. But Arrington knew exactly how to ensure that things were taken care of the way they needed to be. An outside force. A kind of . . . supplement to the immune system of the body politic.

He stubbed out his cigarette and closed his eyes, his heart pounding as hard as the first time he'd jumped from a plane. Which, of course, made sense. Because the stakes were that high, the margin for error that narrow. But he was going to do this. He would make sure to follow through. And then they would see. They would all see.

He picked up the phone and made the call that would set everything in motion.

PART 1

CHAPTER ONE
RAIN

I told them no. But I might as well have said yes. The killing business has its own gravitational pull, and if you get too close, or stay too long, you'll never break free.

Or maybe it's just more comfortable to blame circumstances, or fate, or some other outside factor for results in fact engineered by ourselves. After all, I could have taken down the secure site. I could have severed that link. I could have roamed the earth as Bashō did, unmoored, untethered, as remote and untouchable as one of the solitary clouds that inspired the seventeenth-century poet in his ceaseless wanderings.

But I didn't.

They used Larison to make the initial contact. Larison, one of the most dangerous and volatile men I'd ever known. And, following the detachment we'd assembled to stop a series of false-flag attacks designed to instigate a coup in America, one of the few I trusted.

I was living in Kamakura, clear of Tokyo at last. Flush with an unexpected fortune in uncut diamonds from the job with Larison and the detachment, I'd bought property—a plot of hilltop land with a view of Sagami Bay, obtained via a painstaking series of cutouts and a lot of laundered money. Through further cutouts and at even greater expense, I'd hired a specialist in such matters, a man named Takishita, who found me a *minka*, a traditional Japanese farmhouse, standing derelict in Gifu province, the snow country sometimes known as the Japanese Alps. Takishita purchased the three-hundred-year-old structure on my behalf and had it disassembled and transported to my land in Kamakura, where he reassembled it, building in electricity, plumbing, large windows, and other modern conveniences, but in all material respects maintaining and, indeed, enhancing the design's original beauty. He even created a modest but lovely *karesansui*—a traditional rock garden—outside the living-room window, which would take on different hues with each change of the seasons: autumn colors, winter snow, spring rains, summer sun.

The work took over three years, but I was in no hurry. I told myself a home was worth waiting for, and worth getting right. But when the project was finally done, I grew restless again, and I realized the *minka*'s purpose had been more to keep me busy than to provide a place to live. I would sit on a cushion by the *irori*, the open-air hearth in the middle of the living room, reading Bashō's travel memoir, *Oku no Hosomichi*— *The Narrow Road to the Interior*—in Japanese

16

and English, occasionally correcting what I felt was an inelegant line of translation, and I would feel like an artful forgery. Half-Japanese and half-American had always meant neither, and no amount of mastery—whether of judo, of language, of culture—would ever change that.

The distractions of the project behind me, I came to understand that building something of value was a way of sublimating, of suppressing my torment about having ruined things with Delilah—a bizarre act of self-sabotage, considering all the forces that had previously tried and failed to set us against each other. Every day, I wanted to contact her. Every day, I knew I should. And every day, I didn't. My *minka* was beautiful, but it came to feel more a fortress than a home. A fortress of solitude.

So Larison's contact, when it came, felt like a relief. I should have taken it instead as a warning.

I used an encrypted satellite phone to call the number he'd posted on the secure site. That I even maintained the untraceable unit was, of course, at odds with the notion of my "retirement." But we rarely see what we prefer to overlook.

He picked up on the first buzz, his gravelly whisper instantly recognizable. "You just won me a bet with myself."

I imagined it was just a crack, but I didn't like it. In my business, being predictable is one step from being dead.

Of course, I wasn't in the business. I was retired.

"What do you mean?"

"I bet that you wouldn't have taken down the site. And that you'd still be checking it."

"Should I be wishing you'd lost?"

"I doubt it. You kept it intact because it's better to know if someone's looking than to make him find you another way. I was betting on you being smart."

I liked his explanation better than what I was beginning to suspect myself—that maybe I just *wanted* to be found.

"How are you?" I said, surprised and a little discomfited at how pleased I was to be talking to him. "Getting any sleep?" Once, in Vienna, he'd told me he was plagued by bad dreams. The things he'd done in SpecOps to cause those dreams, he wouldn't speak of at all.

"Sometimes," he said. "It's never going to be good. But . . . sometimes it's better. You?"

"I'm retired."

He laughed.

I felt a touch of irritation. "Why's that funny?"

"Hey, it's not me you have to convince. It seems Hort has someone in need of your services."

The "services" I'd been known for were jobs demanding the appearance of natural causes. When a bullet, a blade, or a bomb would do, you could hire anyone. But when it absolutely had to look like something other than a contract hit, I'd pretty much had the market to myself.

"Horton?" I said. "I half expected you would have killed him by now."

Once upon a time, Colonel Scott "Hort" Horton had been a legend in SpecOps. He was the one who'd tapped me to lead the detachment through which I'd met Larison. But his endless manipulations and deceit had made him a lot of enemies—Larison foremost among them.

"I might still. But I like imagining him smoking an after-dinner cigar on the porch of his little cabin outside Lynchburg, wondering every time if tonight's the night I ghost up out of the woods and punch his ticket."

"So he reached out to you, what, as a way of keeping his enemies close?"

"One possibility, sure."

"What are the others? He's retired, isn't he?"

Larison laughed. "Yeah, same as you."

I let it go. Whether he was right about me or not, his meaning was clear enough. Horton might have been out. But he was looking for a way back in.

"All right," I said. "If Horton's the broker, who's the client?"

"I asked the same question. Hort wouldn't tell me. For your ears only. But if you want to share, I'm a good listener."

I said nothing. Playing it reluctant was an old

habit. Maybe I should have been alarmed at how easily I slipped back into it. But the main thing I noticed was that it felt as comfortable as a second skin.

Or even a first one.

"I didn't tell him I knew how to contact you," Larison said after a moment. "Even though I was pretty sure I did. Anyway, I don't know where you are. I couldn't tell anyone if I wanted to. Or if they tried to make me. You're safe. Still retired, if that's what you want."

Again I said nothing, and after another pause, he went on. "But you know how it works. You don't call Hort, they'll keep looking for another way to get to you. And maybe the next way they find won't be as friendly as I am."

CHAPTER TWO
LIVIA

"It looks like you were right about Malaysia," Trahan called out by way of greeting. "I think we got him."

Livia felt her heart kick with an adrenaline hit at the news. She locked the door behind her, and walked down the corridor into the loft the Bureau had rented. It was gray outside, but the place was nothing but tall windows on three sides with some brick in between, and even with the lights off, it was well illuminated.

Trahan was sitting at the end of a wooden table in the center of the room, staring at one of the monitors in front of him. Livia stood at the long end of the table and watched him silently for a moment, then said, "Kool Kat?"

"Yeah. The camera, just like you said. I created a spider to search in and around Kuala Lumpur. I found only thirteen expats posting photos on social media with D5 metadata, the same as the photos Kool Kat posts on the site."

She'd told him the Nikon D5 was too expensive for most locals, and that he should concentrate on expats—particularly expats with jobs in education, childcare, and other professions that offered access to children. Even a top hacker had to know what he was looking for, and no one knew the freaks and predators like Livia did.

"Thirteen?" she said. "Can you narrow it down further?"

"Already have. Three were traveling during the week when Kool Kat didn't post any new photos. Two Brits and a Kiwi. I just sent you their particulars—I bet you'll know who's Kool Kat just by looking. Just like you knew the kids in his photos were Malaysian. Speaking of which, how *did* you know?"

There were so many ways to answer that. She might have told him that having grown up as a little Lahu girl named Labee in the hills of Thailand's Chiang Rai province gave her an eye for nuances Westerners generally missed. Or that after watching countless hours of children being sexually abused, she had become attuned to cultural differences. The children of some cultures screamed. Others were more stoic. When she herself had been trafficked to America, at thirteen, she had veered from one to the other, stoic when the men had done it to her, screaming when it had happened to her little sister, Nason.

"A hunch," she said, willing away the images from Kool Kat's video posts. She was good at dissociating while she watched—ignoring the terror and the anguish, focusing instead on what language the children were screaming in, and

22

what she could learn from the appearance of their tormentors despite the masks they wore, and whether anything in the background could provide a clue to the location.

Afterward, though, the dissociation always broke down. Leaving her to live as a person with whatever she'd seen as a cop.

"What cops call hunches," Trahan said, "FBI hackers call pattern recognition."

It felt like he was fishing for something. "Is that right, Terry?"

He nodded. "But to make sense of patterns, you need data. The more, the better."

She looked at him, not sure where he was going with the commentary. Trahan, with his shoulder-length brown hair and matching beard, had a vibe so mellow he seemed perpetually stoned. But he was obviously an exceptional hacker—Livia had seen that herself, and besides, if he weren't good at what he did, the Bureau wouldn't have put him on the Child's Play joint task force. So maybe computer networks weren't the only things he could see into.

When she didn't respond, he said, "I'm sorry I can't help with that. The photos, I mean. The videos. I tried, but . . . I can't look at them anymore. I don't know how you can."

So that's what he'd been getting at. She might have told him most cops couldn't look, either. She didn't blame them. People reacted to horror in different ways. She dealt with her own by an obsession with protecting. A never-ending attempt to save poor doomed Nason by proxy.

She suspected the Seattle PD brass understood the psychology. She'd put enough rapists behind bars for the pattern to be obvious. What the brass didn't know—what no one knew—was that she also needed to avenge. In her mind, the only thing better than a rapist in prison was a rapist in the ground, and starting fifteen years earlier, when she was still in high school, she'd killed over a dozen.

"Don't worry about it," she said. "I can't do what you do, either."

"I mean, I don't know how you can see that stuff and not just kill the people behind it."

He was looking at her closely, and for a moment, she wondered if the comment had been a probe. But no, it wasn't that kind of look, and anyway, it wasn't the first time she'd caught his eyes lingering. He'd tried to flirt with her a few times, too, and while she never responded in kind, she didn't mind, either. A little flirtation was the least of what an attractive Asian female cop had to deal with. Besides, Trahan was harmless. A young guy with a good heart. A weak stomach for what got shared on a ring like Child's Play, sure, but that just meant he was human.

Still . . . his stare was a little more intense than usual.

"What is it?" she said.

"Your cheek," he said, squinting slightly. "It's
. . . did somebody hit you?"

She raised a finger to the bruise, which she'd
forgotten. "You could say that."

"Are you serious? Is it . . . are you okay?"

She laughed, touched despite herself that this
skinny hacker felt some latent urge, no matter
how silly, to protect her.

"I teach women's self-defense. Last night, I
caught an elbow. It's nothing."

Trahan raised his eyebrows. "A woman did
that?"

If someone else had made the comment, it
might have irritated her. Maybe even made her
want to teach him a lesson. Coming from Trahan,
though, it only made her smile.

"You don't think a woman can throw an elbow?
Though as it happened, this one came from a
man."

"Oh. You said women's self-defense, so I
figured . . ."

"A women's self-defense class that doesn't
train against men isn't going to be much use."

"No, I guess . . . I hadn't really thought about
it."

She waved a hand in a *no big deal* gesture.
"Don't worry about it. Women's self-defense is
my thing. Hacking is yours."

"Yeah, well, I wish I were getting you more,"

he said, looking relieved to be on familiar ground again. "How are we doing on time? You said we're running out."

"We are. The Bureau played it smart suppressing news of the administrator's arrest, and they've been doing a great job impersonating him on the site. But at some point, one of the members is going to notice something isn't right. At which point, he'll post a warning and go to ground, and a second later all the other Child's Play rats will have scurried off into the darkness."

"That would suck. We've got only five names so far. Out of a hundred and seven members."

"Well, the more we uncover before we're blown, the more arrests get made right after. So let's keep going."

He glanced at the paper coffee cup she was holding—Uptown Espresso, two blocks away in Seattle's South Lake Union district. The Bureau had installed Trahan in a loft in the neighborhood because it was reasonably close to police headquarters. But Trahan was a homebody, and Livia found it more efficient to drop in on him here than to try to arrange a meeting at HQ.

She walked over to his end of the table. "Here," she said, extending him the coffee. "Extra-large cappuccino. Your favorite."

He took it and smiled. "To keep me going?"

She might have returned the smile, but she didn't want him to get the wrong idea. So she walked back to the other end of the table, sat, and fired up the laptop she used while working in the loft. "Something like that," she said. "Now let's see what I make of those KL expats you like."

"Okay. And I'm going to follow up on an anomaly I came across while my spider was searching for Kool Kat's metadata."

"An anomaly?" she said, deliberately mirroring his words the way she did when interrogating a suspect. It worked especially well in conjunction with the typical male urge to explain things to women.

"Yeah," Trahan said, responding unconsciously to the technique. "These people all use encryption to mask their identities. But it's usually commercial stuff."

"Usually commercial?"

"Yeah, off the shelf. Nothing you can tell about the user from the software other than that he's security conscious. But this one app I came across . . . I know this sounds weird, but I think it's mine."

That threw her. "What do you mean?"

"So, these days most of what I do is contract white-hat hacking for the Bureau, but back in the day, I used to do a lot of work for different agencies. The Secret Service once hired me to design an encrypted communications suite. Pretty cool project, actually."

"Couldn't they get something like that off the shelf?"

He shrugged. "You know how it is with the government. They think if it's available to civilians, too, it must be not as good as what you can custom order. Hence thousand-dollar coffeepots and toilet seats and the rest. It's all insane, but hey, it makes every day into Christmas for contractors like me."

Livia was indeed familiar with the mindset. Websites selling police gear loved to tout their wares as *law enforcement only* because they knew the perceived exclusivity made cops eager to buy.

She decided to hold off on Kool Kat for the moment. "So the Secret Service hired you."

"Yeah, they needed a way for any agent to communicate with any agent without ever being singled out as an individual. An anonymization app."

"Meaning . . . ?"

"Well, if you could identify the members of a protective detail, before long you'd start acquiring actionable intelligence about the protectee, too. So in a way, shielding the agents was almost as important as shielding the principals. At least online."

"And you're saying you think one of the Child's Play members is using that application? The one you designed for the Secret Service?"

"Well, it sure looks like my work. But I don't know how one of these bottom feeders would have gotten a hold of it."

She shook her head in amazement. It wasn't his fault. This wasn't his world. So his comforting notion that child rapists were all "bottom feeders," some alien species divorced from the rest of humanity, had never been punctured.

"The obvious inference," she said slowly, "is that the Child's Play member who's using your custom application is connected to the Secret Service."

A long beat went by. Trahan shook his head and said, "Yeah, but . . ."

She waited, letting him work through the cognitive dissonance. After a moment, he said, "But those guys . . . I mean, there are a ton of psychological tests. Background checks. Polygraphs. Everything."

"No test is perfect. Besides, I doubt any of the tests was aimed at uncovering a sexual interest in children."

"I guess. But . . . what if it *is* someone in the Secret Service?"

"What do you mean?"

"I mean, what happens?"

She felt herself getting irritated. "The same thing that happens to anyone arrested for child exploitation. If the prosecutor does her job, he goes to prison, and then is kept away from children for the rest of his life."

"I get that. But the Secret Service . . . I got to know some of them, when I was developing the app. Those guys have a mystique. You know, esprit de corps. It would be a big black eye for them if one of their agents gets frog-marched out of the White House on child-pornography charges."

"Why is that our problem?"

"I'm not saying it is. It's just—"

"I'll never understand it. Really, I never will. People who care more about protecting an institution than they do about protecting children."

He reddened. "That's not fair. You know I care. And I'm not trying to protect anyone. Any institution, I mean. I'm just telling you, if it turns out a Secret Service agent is part of this Child's Play ring, you're in for some static when you try to get an arrest warrant. If you don't want to hear that, if you want to pretend it's not true, fine, it's your party."

She took in a long breath, then blew it out, giving herself a moment to calm down. She'd worked so hard to hide her buttons. And yet sometimes they were right there on the surface, waiting to be pushed.

"I'm sorry," she said. "I've just seen the pattern so many times, and it's maddening. But I shouldn't have slotted you into it. You're right, it wasn't fair."

He shook his head. "Don't worry about it. I can see where it would have come across that way."

He smiled. "Pattern recognition isn't a science. You have to allow for the exceptions."

She nodded. "Anyway. If one of the Child's Play members is a Secret Service agent, I might have a few bureaucratic battles to fight. It wouldn't be the first time. But right now, it's too early to say. You still have to confirm the anonymization app is yours. And then we'd need to unmask the person who's using it on Child's Play."

About twenty minutes later, as she was sifting through data to determine which of the three Kuala Lumpur expats was the member who called himself Kool Kat, Trahan said, "Oh, man. This is bad."

She leaned to the side so she could see him behind his screen. He looked slightly ill.

"The app is yours?"

He nodded, still looking at his screen. "It's mine."

She didn't understand his distress. He must have really lionized the agents he'd met while developing the app.

"Okay," she said. "So it's what you thought. We have a suspected Secret Service agent member of Child's Play."

He looked at her and shook his head slowly.

"No," he said. "We have six."

CHAPTER THREE
RAIN

I waited a day to call Horton. I told myself it was because I hadn't made up my mind. But I knew I was just playing it reluctant again.

I decided to keep it brief. The former colonel and I hadn't parted on the best terms, and if I'd been overly solicitous, he would have recognized the behavior as an attempt to lull him, which would have been counterproductive.

"I understand you wanted to talk to me," I said by way of greeting.

"I'm glad you called," he said in his unmistakable Mississippi Delta baritone. "How've you been?"

I was surprised at the warmth in his tone, and I wondered if maybe he was the one trying to lull me.

"No complaints. Enjoying my retirement. You?"

"Oh, the same, I suppose. I didn't realize how much I'd come to hate Washington until I retired and moved out to my place in the country."

"The place in Virginia you mentioned. Lynchburg, right?"

He'd once told me Virginia, nothing more specific than that. But I doubted he'd be surprised that I—or more likely Larison—would know more than just the state.

"Close," he said. "Northwest of Lynchburg, in point of fact. Little town called Coleman Falls. I work on Mondays with the volunteer fire department and fish every weekend in the James River. My place is a cabin on Cove Creek Farm Road, with a long gravel driveway, surrounding woods, and a lovely porch out back where most evenings I like to enjoy a whisky and sometimes a cigar."

Not for the first time, I had to admire the man's balls. He was practically daring me.

On the other hand, if Larison really wanted him dead, there probably wasn't a lot he could do to stop it. Might as well enjoy his time fishing and volunteering until that fateful day, and not give us the satisfaction.

"It sounds nice," I said. "I'm not much for cigars, but I've been known to enjoy a whisky from time to time."

"You ought to come visit. I've got an '81 Glenlivet I haven't opened yet. I keep waiting for a special occasion."

"I'll let you know if I'm out that way."

There was a pause while he took in my meaning. "I appreciate that. I know we've had our differences."

That was one way to put it. But at this point, probably the less said, the better.

"Anyway. I understand you know someone who wants me to do a job."

"That's correct."

"You know what the job is?"

"I didn't ask."

"All right. Who wants the work done?"

"Other than confirming that the individual in question is a man to be taken seriously, it's not for me to say. I'll give you a number. You can call it if you're interested."

I considered for a moment. Then I said, "Why?"

"Why what?"

"I thought you said you were retired."

"I thought you said the same."

"I did."

"Then why are you talking to me?"

I didn't respond, and after a moment he said, "Come visit sometime. We can enjoy that Glenlivet and compare notes about the joys of retirement."

CHAPTER FOUR
LIVIA

Livia spent the next few days on her typical caseload. Testifying in a domestic-abuse trial. Reviewing CCTV video footage related to a peeper in Ballard. Interviewing the victim of a sexual assault—a morning jogger in Discovery Park, the attack worryingly similar to one in Lincoln Park one week earlier. Both women had been wearing earbuds—one of the many things Livia taught her self-defense students never to do, because demonstrating both that you can't hear and that you're too naïve to know better is a beacon to predators. Both women had been tackled from behind before they were even aware of anyone near them. In both instances a knife under the chin; the same whispered threat—*Move or scream and I will cut your throat;* wrists zip-tied behind the back; running pants cut away; the attack over in minutes. The first victim saw nothing. The latest had the presence of mind to look back as the attacker climbed off her, but the man had been wearing running clothes himself and the woman hadn't managed to see his face.

The second attack confirmed what Livia had suspected even after the first: this was no neophyte rapist. This man had spent time honing his craft, discarding what proved unworkable, improving his efficiency, practicing to the point of professionalism. The victims' pants, for example—the nature of the cuts indicated they had been sliced open not with the knife, but with a pair of scissors. Probably high-quality EMT trauma shears. Of course, she couldn't know, but Livia could imagine the man initially cutting away a victim's clothes with the knife, finding it required too much effort and time, and transitioning to the shears instead. Refining his rape kit. Fetishizing the tools and fantasizing about the tactics.

Above all, planning meticulously. To ensure he could go on enjoying his hobby for a long, long time.

All of which almost certainly meant Livia was dealing with someone who had arrived in Seattle recently, after deciding it was too dangerous to continue his hobby in some other place. In theory, ViCAP—the FBI's Violent Criminal Apprehension Program database—would be a good way to zero in on crimes outside Seattle similar to the two park attacks. In practice, over-burdened local cops weren't nearly as diligent as they might be in entering information into the database. And even when they made the time to enter it, they didn't always include the relevant details.

Both attacks had taken place in the rain, for example. In Seattle, that could easily be coincidence. On the other hand, rain muffled sound and ruined evidence. It would also reduce the number of joggers to a more desirable victim-to-witness ratio. And it would provide a congruent setting for a man to go out in his own top-to-bottom nylon or Gore-Tex running clothes, clothes that themselves would hinder DNA collection while making witness identification more difficult as well. The problem was, would a cop entering data into ViCAP think to mention the weather?

But she was in luck, and ViCAP offered a solid lead: an attack in Bridgeport, Connecticut, eight months earlier. The same victim profile: a morning jogger. The same MO: the blitzkrieg attack from behind, the knife, the zip tie, the practiced efficiency. No mention of the likely implement used to cut away the clothes, but it had been raining, confirming for Livia that the weather the man was operating in was choice, not coincidence. And the setting was similar, too—a place called Seaside Park, another spot popular with joggers and situated on the water, this time Long Island Sound. There had been other attacks in the past, she was certain of it—as certain as she was that there would be more in the future, unless this man was stopped.

She put Child's Play out of her mind, knowing

that for the moment, at least, Trahan was on it, and that whatever arrests she might make in connection with the site were months away regardless. She stayed at her desk, working every local database she could access, calling police departments up and down the Connecticut coast. But she turned up nothing.

Two attacks already. She was guessing one more—probably the next time it rained, which in Seattle would almost certainly be soon—before this rapist moved on to new hunting grounds, where she might lose track of him forever.

She wasn't going to let that happen. One way or the other, she was going to stop him here.

CHAPTER FIVE
RAIN

I called the number Horton gave me. The voice that answered was male and spoke in undifferentiated American-accented English. It said, "That took a while. We now have one day fewer than we otherwise would have."

The grammatically correct *fewer*, I noted, not the more common *less*. And the delivery was crisp, the tone a mild rebuke. An officer, maybe, accustomed to addressing subordinates. When I was younger and something of a hothead, that kind of peremptory treatment would have gotten my back up. But if you live long enough, you gain perspective, and maybe some self-control. So instead of getting irritated, I responded as though bored.

"Is that the royal 'we'? Because your time constraints have nothing to do with me."

"Then why are you calling me?"

Maybe because Horton had challenged me with something similar, and maybe because the question wasn't completely without merit, I felt myself getting annoyed.

"To hear you out," I said. "And for someone purporting to be concerned about time, you sure take a lot of it getting to the point."

I congratulated myself on demonstrating wisdom and tactical restraint by not finishing the sentence with *asshole*.

There was a pause, probably while he recalibrated his approach. Then he said, "Three jobs, all requiring immediate attention, all needing to look natural. If my information is correct, the kind of work at which you excel."

First was the *fewer,* not *less*. Now it was the care in avoiding a preposition at the end of a sentence. An educated man, presumably. Precise. Apparently fussy about small-minded rules, perhaps to compensate for a willingness to ignore large ones.

I placed the observation in the mental file I was building and considered. He would tell me who. Probably where. Certainly how much.

All critical topics, obviously. But after a long string of manipulations and betrayals, I'd learned that nothing was more important to my own protection than *why*. And maybe the question had become important for other reasons, reasons of conscience or clarity or other areas I tried to obscure with a more practical focus on my own survival.

Of course, *why* was the one question the people handing out the jobs least wanted to answer. Which meant it had to be approached obliquely, the truth discerned like a shadow cast by the lies surrounding it.

So I started with the easy part—the part he'd be expecting, and that would most suggest I was interested. "Who are we talking about?"

"Are you in?"

"Are you high?"

"What?"

"You expect me to say yes to a job—no, three jobs—I don't know anything about? What kind of amateur outfit am I dealing with?"

The insult was calculated. Whether this guy was an amateur or a professional, he would perceive himself as the latter, and would now be invested in proving it to me. Interrogators call the technique *ego down*.

"I assure you," the guy said, a touch of indignation creeping into his tone, "you've heard of me."

"Government?"

"I was government. I left because the amateurs were impeding my efforts. Now I get things done."

"Then who are the three jobs?"

There was a pause. Then, "Three people in law enforcement—a Fed, a local, a consultant. Is that a problem?"

I didn't need the money. I didn't like the guy. And anyway, I was retired.

But it couldn't hurt to learn a little more.

"Not so far."

"Let's start with the local. A Seattle cop. A woman. You okay with that?"

41

"If you know the guy who brokered this introduction, you know I'm not. No women. No children. No acts against non-principals. And no B-teams."

I didn't like the way it came out. Like a parameter instead of a protest.

"Yes, he mentioned you're squeamish that way, but I didn't believe it. Aren't we all special snowflakes? You'll melt some snowflakes, but not others?"

I was beginning to dislike the guy sufficiently to have some fun with him. I said, "Some snowflakes are more expensive than others."

"We'll get to that. Now, as I said, the time frame is tight. Maybe three days, given that we've lost one already—but the intel is extensive, and we can help you control the environment as much as you need to make it look natural."

"That's good of you, but I work alone."

"That's not what I heard."

I didn't know if Horton would have mentioned the detachment. It didn't matter. Either way, I didn't like the comment. Not because it was false. But because it had become true. Yes, I was alone now. Aloof, like once upon a time. But even before the detachment, there had been Dox. And Delilah, and a couple of her Mossad colleagues. And Kanezaki at CIA. And Larison, and Treven, the guy Larison had brought with him. Hell, the last time I could honestly say I only worked alone

. . . . it was longer ago than I cared to think about.

I wondered if that was why I had talked to Larison. And then Horton. And now this guy. Maybe being alone didn't suit me the way it once had. Maybe I wanted a connection, even if the connection in question was to this shitty world I'd told myself I was trying to get clear of.

"I'm not responsible for what you've heard," I said, the evenness in my tone now slightly more of an effort. "And if you think that speculating about me while revealing nothing about yourself is the right approach here, you're not just ignorant. You're incompetent, too."

There was a pause, maybe while the guy digested the truth of that, maybe while he struggled not to respond with an insult of his own.

"You don't need to know who I am," the guy said. "And maybe more importantly from your perspective, you don't want to."

"I'm pretty sure I do."

"No, you don't. All you need to know is that my money is green, and there's plenty of it. If you don't know more than that, you can't be a threat to me. If you're no threat to me, I'm not one to you."

The suggested symmetry was glib, but I let it go. "I'll take my chances."

"Enough. The fee is one million US. Half up front, half upon completion. Don't pretend it's too little—we both know it's too much. Are you in? Or do you want to waste the rest of your life in Tokyo pretending you're retired?"

I'd been careful to lay down some clues before leaving Tokyo. An apartment I continued to pay for through a cutout. Jazz clubs I'd drop in on from time to time. That kind of thing. The measures all subtle enough to seem genuine, and all designed to be pieced together only with difficulty. That this guy had spotted the head-fake suggested he had resources. That he'd gone for the fake suggested those resources weren't quite as good as he might have believed.

Beyond which, the low-key *I know where to find you* threat suggested his ego was driving him more than sound tactics. Otherwise, he would have seen that what he'd said earlier—about not being a threat to me as long as I was no threat to him—went both ways. An officer, I thought again. Or former officer, more accustomed to issuing orders to subordinates than to negotiating with freelancers.

What he didn't know was, I like threats. Threats clarify. And with clarity comes calm. So it required no effort at all to take a moment before responding, the pause intended to suggest the quality of his information had me off-balance, even worried.

"Good luck with those jobs," I said. "I can't help with the staffing."

I clicked off, powered down the phone and removed the battery, and placed a fresh log on the *irori*. The seasoned wood crackled and ignited almost instantly. Then I sat on the cushions in front of the fire, watching the flames slowly dying, the wood turning to glowing coals, the warmth good against the soles of my feet.

The guy had told me little. More likely a blowhard than a threat.

More likely. But how much was I willing to bet on that?

Beyond the perimeter of the *irori*, the *minka* tended to be chilly. Which made the warmth of the cushions before the hearth even more welcome by contrast.

I placed another log on the coals. I watched it burn, wondering what it was that made fire so hypnotic.

Life is full of paradoxes, I decided. Certainly I hadn't foreseen how much work retirement might involve. I put the battery back in the phone and called Larison.

CHAPTER SIX
LIVIA

Livia knew she'd been neglecting Child's Play, but that operation depended more on Trahan's hacking skills than on her detective work. Still, she needed to check in. Maybe in the intervening days, Trahan had made progress on that "anomaly," as he called it—the use of the encryption app he had designed for the Secret Service.

She picked up a cappuccino at Uptown Espresso and headed over to the loft, holding the paper cup under her fleece to keep it out of the morning drizzle. She reminded herself that even with the rain, it was too soon—the park rapist would still be in his lair, waiting.

But he wouldn't wait forever.

Stepping out of the elevator on the loft level, she noted a wet umbrella propped outside Trahan's door. She hadn't seen him use one before, and Seattleites tended to eschew them in favor of hooded jackets. Was someone else in there? She let herself in and immediately heard a voice alongside Trahan's—female, with an authoritative tone. It sounded like they were arguing, but they stopped at the sound of the door closing.

She walked down the corridor. Trahan was standing behind the table, a tall brunette in a gray pantsuit and a lightweight down jacket across from him. FBI, Livia decided. The lightweight down looked like something that would pack up well for traveling. A male agent would have lost the suit jacket, but women dressing that casually risked being taken less seriously than their male counterparts. Beyond which, something in her stance, her posture, suggested authority over Trahan, though to his credit it had sounded as though he'd been arguing gamely before Livia came in.

Trahan's laptop was closed—the first time Livia had ever seen that. She didn't like it.

They both looked at her, their expressions grim. "Livia," Trahan said. He gestured to the woman. "This is Special Agent Smith, head of VCAC."

VCAC was the FBI's Violent Crimes Against Children program, part of the Criminal Investigative Division. Livia knew of Smith but had never dealt with her. Counterpart interactions with heads of federal divisions typically happened at higher pay grades. She said nothing, wondering what the hell was going on.

Smith nodded an acknowledgment. "Detective Lone. I wish I were meeting you with better news. I'm afraid this operation has been terminated."

Livia walked over to the end of the table, creating a moment to collect herself before responding, knowing the pause would come across as confidence, though in fact it was the product of confusion. She set down the cappuccino and looked at Trahan. Aware of the potential for political pushback, she had told him to keep the encryption app between the two of them until they'd had a chance to investigate further. He'd told her he would. She'd thought it was understood their agreement would hold until they had a chance to discuss it again. Now she realized that not checking in with him sooner had been a mistake.

She looked at Trahan. "You told them, didn't you?"

He could barely look at her. "I had to."

"Trahan reports to me," Agent Smith said. "He has a duty—"

"He has a contract."

"Whatever you want to call it. He's required to keep me in the loop about all important operational developments."

"You're telling me the Secret Service is shutting down a child-pornography investigation."

Smith's eyes narrowed. "That is not what I'm telling you. I'm telling you the *FBI* is shutting down this investigation."

"Why?"

"It has been determined that the images being posted on the site as bona fides—"

Livia couldn't believe what she was hearing. "Posted by the FBI!"

"—could themselves be construed to be child pornography. And as you know, in the United States, posting such images is illegal even for a law-enforcement agency in the course of an investigation."

Livia took a deep breath, knowing she was running too hot. Still, it was maddening. Presumably because of the rules Smith had just mentioned, Child's Play required that all members post new video of child porn at least once a month. The requirement was canny, as it tended to prevent law enforcement from infiltrating the site. But the FBI had gotten around it by hiring a Hollywood green-screen specialist to doctor existing videos to make them look like new ones.

"Those images aren't real," Livia said, knowing she'd already lost, but determined to try to salvage what she could.

Smith nodded. "Parts of them are real, as I understand it. Look, we should both acknowledge that this was a legal call. And I don't think either of us is in a good position to second-guess the lawyers at the Justice Department."

Livia leaned forward, her palms on the table to either side of the laptop she used while working in the loft. She wasn't going to leave without it—it was her only way of logging in to Child's Play, and her only record of the members they'd managed to uncover so far.

"Agent Smith. Do me a favor. Don't piss down my back and tell me it's raining. This is about the Secret Service. Terry knows it. I know it. And you know it."

Smith glanced at the laptop. "If you're thinking about walking off with that laptop, I can guarantee you'd be prosecuted for theft of Bureau property."

Strangely, Smith looked almost sad when she said it. Less issuing a dire threat than describing an unfortunate fact.

Livia looked in her eyes, trying to find an opening. "We've uncovered five members—identified them by name—already. We can at least make those arrests. All we need is—"

"The suspects you've identified won't be arrested. Or prosecuted. At least not in connection with this operation."

Livia realized she should have seen that coming. Still, it shocked her. "We've made a case—a fucking good case—against five degenerates trafficking in child porn—in child *torture*—and you're going to let them go on preying on children?"

"This is not my decision."

"Do you know what *hurtcore* is, Agent Smith?"

Smith didn't respond.

"It's a pedophile subculture. The point isn't just to cause pain. It's to cause *damage*. Not just to break a child's body, but to destroy the child's soul. Terry couldn't watch it. Most people can't. Do you want me to show you some? Just so you'll understand what you're enabling by shutting down this operation."

Trahan said nothing. He was looking down as though ashamed.

"I'm not 'enabling' anything," Smith said. "I'm following the rules. As for the 'hurtcore' itself . . . I can imagine."

"I doubt it. If you could, you wouldn't shut us down."

Smith said nothing.

"Do you have children, Agent Smith?"

A little color crept into Smith's cheeks. "My personal life has nothing to do with this. Beyond which—"

"Nieces? Nephews? Were you ever even a child yourself?"

"— it's none of your business. As I said, this is not my decision."

"It is your decision, if you make yourself complicit in it."

"It is a Bureau decision. It is above my pay grade. And yours. And it is final."

"Fuck you. I have a case against those traffickers. I'm going to have them arrested. And I'll find a way to have them prosecuted."

She knew she wasn't being tactical. She knew she was showing too much. She didn't care. And she couldn't have reined it in regardless.

Smith looked down. "Detective Lone." She seemed to be struggling for words. "Livia."

"Detective Lone."

She nodded. "Detective Lone. My understanding . . . there is some exposure here for everyone who participated in this operation."

"What does that mean?"

"The videos being posted as bona fides themselves could be the basis for prosecution."

Livia shook her head as though to clear it. She felt buffeted by currents she hadn't sensed and couldn't see.

"You can't be serious," she said. "You just can't."

"Let it go, Detective Lone. Just let it go. Keep doing your good work in all the other ways you do it. There are some fights you just can't win."

"That doesn't mean you don't fight."

"It does if you want to live to fight another day."

Livia wanted to stride over and sweep Agent Smith's ass to the floor. But that would have solved nothing. Beyond which, she recognized on some level that the woman wasn't threatening her. Not even warning. Advising, if anything. Maybe even trying to signal a sympathy Livia was resisting because being the object of sympathy was abhorrent to her.

She looked down for a moment and took a deep breath. Then another. When she felt calmer, she looked up. "I'd like to speak with your superior. Whoever made the decision to pull the plug. Or I could have my lieutenant make the call, if she would be the right pay grade. Hell, if you prefer, we'll get Seattle's chief of police on the phone."

Agent Smith shook her head. "You can have anyone call anyone at the Bureau. I'm just telling you, you'll be wasting your time. Or worse." She inclined her head toward Trahan. "Terry and I have to be back in Washington ASAP. We're leaving on a red-eye. Tonight."

Trahan looked at Livia and shrugged helplessly. "I'm sorry, Livia."

Livia stared at both of them, knowing she'd lost but determined to make this just a round, not the fight.

She picked up the laptop. *Fuck them.* If they wanted to prosecute her, let them try.

"You're both cowards," she said, and walked out.

CHAPTER SEVEN
RAIN

Larison wasn't able to shed much light on the identity of my mystery caller. "Hort knows everyone," he told me. "You know that. You thought the guy was a former officer of some type? Colonel or higher? Well, that narrows it down to about a hundred and seventy possibilities. You want more, you're going to have to ask Hort."

"I already did."

"Well, maybe you didn't ask him the right way."

I'd seen Larison in action. No one would ever want to be on the wrong end of what he considered the right way.

"Here's the question," I said. "Why is Horton protecting this guy?"

"No. The question is, Who is Hort more afraid of? This guy? Or us?"

"Oh, it's 'us' now?"

"Up to you. I told you after what you did for me I'd have your back. You think I say that kind of thing lightly?"

All I'd done was show him trust when the smart thing would have been to kill him. Still, having

once been on the other end of that equation—
with Dox—I knew it could be mind blowing.

"No," I said. "I don't think that."

"Then say the word and we'll pay Hort a visit.
Make sure he's got the right fear priorities."

CHAPTER EIGHT
LIVIA

Livia headed from the loft to Lake Union Park and strode along the water, her footfalls reverberating against the wooden planks of the walkway. The rain had stopped, but the sky was still gray, the air cold and wet, and the park nearly empty.

She was seething, and she knew that until she got past it she wouldn't be able to think tactically. The worst part was, so much of it was her fault. She should have been clearer in telling Trahan to keep quiet about the Secret Service angle until she and he had learned more. Maybe he would have gone around her anyway, but at least she wouldn't have been left with the feeling that the shutdown was her fault.

And Smith's threat—that if Livia didn't stand down, she herself might face prosecution—was making her positively apoplectic. Not just because of the insane injustice of it. But because she hadn't seen it coming. Sure, the woman seemed to take no joy in what she'd said. But someone had foreseen how Livia might resist, and had prepared a counter accordingly. If this were a judo match, Livia would already be down

56

by points and fighting off her back. All because of an entry she hadn't anticipated and a throw she hadn't blocked.

She paused to tighten her ponytail against the wind, then started walking again, needing to burn off the rage. A flock of pigeons took flight as she approached, alighting on the grass to her right. For a moment she thought of Nason, who she had called "little bird" when they were girls because of Nason's uncanny ability to imitate the songs of forest birds. She had gotten better at disconnecting those sorts of thoughts from an immediate emotional response, but this morning the echo of *little bird* in her mind produced a strong surge of guilt and grief, and she had to work for a moment to push it away.

What she needed was information. Insight into who was really behind the shutdown of the Child's Play operation, and why. She didn't know anyone at the Bureau well enough to reach out. But maybe . . . maybe B. D. Little at Homeland Security Investigations could help. Especially with the Secret Service angle, because since 2003, the Secret Service had been part of Homeland Security.

She didn't trust him. He'd used her in Thailand, dangling a chance for her to go after the men who had trafficked and assaulted her and Nason. And then telling her afterward that he knew she had killed every one of them—the traffickers and the US senator the traffickers had been working with. But he understood. He had his own tragedy. A teenage daughter. He'd shown Livia a faded photo of a beautiful black girl—a radiant smile, arms tight around her beaming father's neck—abducted and disappeared a decade earlier. He had as much motivation as Livia to eliminate predators, he'd claimed. Whatever it took. All he wanted was a partner.

A lot of what he knew he wouldn't be able to prove. And he'd assured her he would never pressure her. But circumstances changed. Just like people.

She kept walking, the cold and the exertion slowly clearing her head. She came to a collection of wooden houseboats swaying and creaking in their moorings, and walked faster. She didn't like boats. Or ports. Or cargo containers, even the ones safely across the river from her loft in Georgetown. Nearly two decades later, the smell of curry still made her sick. She'd taken all the psych courses in college and knew about stimulus generalization. But understanding the phenomenon scarcely lessened its impact.

It would be safer not to contact Little, no doubt. But now she had five monsters in her sights. She could protect herself, or she could protect the children those monsters would continue to prey on if they weren't taken down.

When she felt sufficiently calm, she stopped.

The walk had warmed her, and she unzipped the collar of her fleece. The cold air was bracing on the skin of her throat. She looked out across the lake. The rusted relics of Gas Works Park were just visible on the northern shore. Behind her, she could hear the dull cacophony of construction at a half dozen South Lake Union building sites. A cluster of ducklings approached on the water to her left, their mother glancing at Livia and then leading the small ones farther into the lake, away from Livia.

She sighed and took out her cellphone. One ring. Then the friendly baritone: "Livia Lone. You must have felt me thinking of you."

Little liked games, and she'd been expecting his voicemail, or at least a delay. He really must have been hoping to hear from her.

"I need your help," she said. "But I'm not going to promise anything in return."

There was a pause. She knew how pleased he must have been that she needed him, and she hated it.

"All right," he said. "But that doesn't mean I can't ask. Fair enough?"

Fair enough. Cops used the phrase all the time on gullible suspects. *Just help me out here, so I can make a good impression for you with the prosecutor, fair enough?*

She hoped she wasn't being the gullible one now.

She told him about the Child's Play op. The

59

Secret Service angle. The shutdown. All of it.

"Ass-covering assholes," he said when she was done. His outrage seemed genuine. But of course he knew what she'd want to hear.

"Can you find out where the pressure is coming from?" she asked.

"Maybe. But, much as I'd like to think otherwise, I doubt I have nearly enough juice to restart your operation. The Bureau doesn't take kindly to interference from DHS."

"I know."

"Then what do you want?"

"I want to know who at the Secret Service is part of a child-torture pornography ring. Who at DHS or the Bureau or both is protecting them. And why."

"What are you going to do with that kind of information?"

She'd expected him to press. Fine, let him. "Get me the information, and we'll discuss it."

"That's my girl."

"I am not your fucking girl."

"Look, it's just a figure of—"

"Forget it. Forget I asked. This is stupid."

She clicked off. Then stood there in agony, waiting for him to call back, fearing she'd miscalculated, sensing that she hadn't been calculating at all, that she'd just reacted viscerally to the notion of someone being in control of her. She was horrified that she could default so quickly to protecting herself and forgetting, even if only momentarily, the other stakes.

Call back, she thought, staring at the phone, hating how much she needed him. *Call back.*

A minute went by. Another.

The phone buzzed. Little. She let out a huge sigh of relief and forced herself to let it buzz a second time. A third.

She clicked "Answer" and held the phone to her ear, saying nothing.

"I didn't mean it the way you took it," he said. "I just meant I'm glad we're working together. We want the same thing, you know that."

She realized how lucky she'd been. If he hadn't blinked first, she would have had to go crawling back, with even less leverage than she'd initially surrendered by reaching out to him. As it was, though, she'd demonstrated that she was willing to walk away.

"I'm not doing this for you," she said. "I'm doing it despite you."

"I'm just glad you're doing it."

I'll bet you are, she thought.

"Find out what I'm up against," she said. "And we'll go from there."

She retrieved her Jeep from the lot where she'd parked it and drove back to headquarters, wondering what to tell her lieutenant, Donna Strangeland, about the Child's Play operation shutdown. A Brooklyn transplant with a regional accent wildly incongruous in Seattle, Strangeland was a good cop, a straight shooter, and as much of a friend as Livia could reasonably expect from someone she reported to. Even so, this situation was fraught enough to make Livia want to go slowly, to see what she could learn from Little before looping in the lieutenant.

But no, she would have to tell Strangeland eventually, and it would look odd if she waited. In fact, Strangeland, who had an uncanny knack for knowing everything, would probably have learned already—whether directly from Agent Smith or otherwise. Besides, whoever was behind the shutdown knew Livia was going to react. It was why Smith had come prepared with her warning, or whatever it had been. If Livia didn't tell Strangeland, someone might wonder whether she was up to something else. Better to make it look like she was complaining through channels as expected.

She parked in the underground garage and took the stairs to the sixth floor. She didn't like enclosed spaces, and besides, eschewing the elevator meant an automatic half mile or so of stair walking every day. It was a good supplement to her formal workouts.

Strangeland was at her desk, a lieutenant-level pile of paperwork in front of her. The door was open, as was Strangeland's custom. She looked up over her reading glasses when she saw Livia standing in the doorway.

Livia cracked a knuckle. "You got a minute?"

Strangeland leaned back, pulled off the glasses, and motioned to the seat on the other side of the desk. One of the things Livia had learned from the lieutenant was the power of silence. Even when you knew the technique, it could make you want to talk.

Livia closed the door and sat. "The Child's Play operation. It got shut down."

Strangeland looked at her for a long beat, and Livia knew this was the first she'd heard.

"What do you mean?"

Livia told her everything—other than her call to Little. Strangeland didn't trust Little—partly because she didn't want to lose Livia to the Feds, and partly because she just had good instincts—and for the moment, Livia saw no upside to letting her know they were back in touch.

Strangeland listened intently, as she always did, sometimes grunting or nodding in encouragement, occasionally requesting an additional fact or a clarification. So much of being a good interrogator was just knowing how to actively *listen* to someone, and Strangeland was among the best.

When Livia was done, Strangeland glanced off to the side and drummed her fingers together for a moment. Then she looked at Livia again. "It is beyond fucked up that I'm hearing this from you, and not direct from the Bureau. Or down from the chief."

"What do you think it means?"

"That someone didn't want us to know the operation was being shut down until after it was an accomplished fact."

"And what do you think that means?"

Strangeland gave her a tight smile, maybe in recognition that Livia was using open-ended questions and subtly appealing to Strangeland's ego—techniques she had learned from the lieutenant herself.

"My guess?" she said. "This is coming from way above our pay grades. Director of the Bureau, maybe. Or the Justice Department. Or Homeland Security, which would certainly want to protect the Secret Service. Especially after all the scandals over there, it would be natural for someone to decide they couldn't afford another."

"Scandals?"

"Yeah, a few years ago. Multiple revelations about strippers and sex workers and the president's security detail, a couple drunk agents driving their vehicle into a White House barrier . . . then some of the higher-ups got caught trying to under-cut the congressman investigating, by leaking information about him to the press. And then another prostitute thing and the vice president's detail. So yeah, pretty easy to imagine someone over there deciding the organization couldn't afford another black eye."

"I didn't know about that."

Strangeland smiled. "Because it didn't involve kids. But now maybe it does. Anyway, whatever channels the shutdown order went through, they were all too scared to do anything other than click their heels. Otherwise, someone would have called me, even if just to ask what the hell was going on. The Feds sometimes treat us like we're peons, okay. But a fait accompli shutdown . . . that's a lot."

"What do we do?"

"Probably get ready to eat a shit sandwich. But let me make a few phone calls. See if I can get some sense of what this is all about, beyond the obvious. Any progress on our park rapist?"

Livia told her about the lead in Connecticut, her developing sense of what they were dealing with, her belief that the man liked to operate in the rain.

"If that's so," Strangeland said, "we're going to have a real problem in Seattle."

"The rain seems necessary, but not sufficient. I don't have enough data yet to be sure, but it looks like he doesn't go hunting more than once a week. He likes to lie low in between."

"A careful man."

"Apparently."

Strangeland nodded. "Well, the psychos can be

careful, too. Unfortunate combination, though. But you'll get him, Livia. If anyone can, it's you."

Coming from someone else, it would have been flattery. From the lieutenant, it meant something.

"Thanks, LT."

"On this other thing, I'll let you know what I learn."

Livia got up to go.

"Oh," Strangeland said. "If you have any contacts of your own, you might want to reach out. These people aren't confining themselves to proper channels. I don't see why we need to, either."

Livia nodded, uneasy. Did Strangeland know she'd already reached out to Little, or recognize that she would? Was this her oblique way of telling Livia she'd better not keep things to herself?

As always, the lieutenant's nearly psychic intuition both impressed Livia . . . and concerned her. The trail of rapists Livia had killed was geographically disparate, her preparations were always methodical, and her methods were informed by her knowledge of forensics and detective work. But still, she knew that a lot of what protected her was what people like Trahan called "security through obscurity"—security that was the result of nobody looking.

If that changed—if someone ever noticed a

commonality among those dead rapists—it would be bad. And if the person who noticed had the kind of cop intuition of Lieutenant Strangeland, it could be catastrophic.

Not for the first time, she wondered whether she should try to find a way to tame the dragon inside her. To accept that some rapists would always plead down, or draw an incompetent prosecutor, or otherwise get lucky and avoid justice for what they had done.

And not for the first time, she didn't think she could.

CHAPTER NINE
LIVIA

Livia spent the rest of the day at her cubicle, querying databases, making phone calls—and finding no new leads on the park rapist.

She wanted to keep going, but she had a nine o'clock class to teach at a martial-arts academy in Ravenna-Bryant in northeast Seattle. All the local schools wanted her—high-school state wrestling champion, jiu-jitsu black belt, Olympic judo alternate, and Seattle cop trained in street tactics made for an attractive résumé. But four nights a week was the most she could manage with a detective's on-call schedule. And while it would have been satisfying to teach the same group of students at a single place, she worked with three different schools so she could reach as many women as possible. The most important skills for anyone were more mental than physical—awareness, avoidance, confidence in your own ferocity—and she focused her teaching accordingly, using physical training as a route to developing the right attitude rather than as an end in itself.

She was in luck—traffic was light, and she got to the school early enough to get in a little mat work. She changed into a gi in the locker room, placed her duty Glock in her backpack, then started warming up in a corner, the backpack against the wall where she could see it. It wasn't a big room—Seattle real-estate prices wouldn't allow for that—but at twenty-five feet square, it was enough. And it had all the pleasing qualities she associated with training: the trace scent of rubber, the smell of sweat, the reverberations of breakfalls, the grunts and laughter and curses. Jorge, a tatted-up former gangbanger who never hesitated to use muscle to try to overcome her superior skill, was rolling with another brown belt, and she caught his eye and nodded. There were two women on the mats, too, one a purple belt and the other a brown, and Livia sometimes trained with them because everyone deserved a more skilled partner as a learning aid. But it was the men she really liked to go with, the bigger and stronger the better. So she waited a few minutes until Jorge tapped his opponent, then cut in with him, tapping him twice while they rolled but otherwise just flowing with, eluding, and reversing his attacks. She loved everything about grappling, but more than anything, that feeling of control, of dominating someone who was doing all he could to do the same to you. After an hour of hard sparring, her gi was drenched and her caseload—and the Child's Play political bullshit—had receded in her mind to a manageable distance.

At close to nine, she changed into a shirt and shorts in the locker room, then came back out to the mats. A few of her students had arrived and were already warming up, some just stretching, others throwing palm heels and elbows on the training bags. Livia glanced at the clock, then called out, "Five minutes." They nodded and kept at it.

There was a new girl, sitting on the bench by the entrance in a tee shirt and sweatpants, watching. A jacket was draped over the bench next to her, but she hadn't yet taken off her shoes, and she was clutching a small leather purse on her lap as though afraid of what might happen if she were to let it go. She was pretty, with brown hair shaved close to stubble and a trash polka tattoo on one of her forearms—a snarling black wolf with a smear of red across its fangs.

Livia shouldered her backpack and walked over. "Hi," she said, pushing a stray strand of wet hair back from her face. "Did you want to train tonight? You just need to fill out a release, and you're welcome to give it a try."

The woman gave Livia a quick, uncertain smile. "I was going to," she said. "I should have done something like this a long time ago. I wish I had. But it just, I don't know, it seems like a lot."

Trauma, Livia thought. *Probably sexual assault. One she didn't report. And hasn't come to grips with.*

It was just a hunch, of course. But there were a number of signs—telling, taken together. The interest in women's self-defense, obviously. The nervousness. The ambivalence. The wolf tattoo, which was sharp and vibrant and obviously recent. A symbolic representation of what this woman was newly resolved to be? And the shaved head—had she been grabbed by the hair, and decided afterward to close down that vulnerability? Was she trying to make herself unattractive? Or was the hair part of a break with her past, and a determination to become someone, something, new? Livia had seen all these reactions to sexual trauma, and more. Many of her students exhibited them. She had lived several herself.

"I mean, I was going to try it out," the woman said off Livia's silence. "But maybe I'll just watch tonight. Is that okay?" She shook her head and looked away. "I feel like I'm being chicken. But . . . I don't know."

Behind Livia, someone started working one of the speed bags, the *wap wap wap wap wap wap* of the bag a confident contrast to the woman's diffident words. "You're not being chicken," Livia said, raising her voice to make sure the woman could hear her. "You're just going at your own pace. Some people want to dive in. Others like to dip a toe first. You decide what's best for you. Right?"

The woman looked at her for a moment as though trying to decide whether such a thing could be possible. Then she nodded. "Right."

"Stay for a while. See what you think. If you feel like it, come join us. If not, just watch. Fair enough?"

The woman smiled, a little more confidently than before. "Fair enough."

Livia held out a hand. "I'm Livia."

"Kyla," the woman said, and they shook.

"It's good to meet you, Kyla. I need to go teach, but we can talk more later, okay?"

She walked back to the mat. Twenty women tonight. There were never fewer than fifteen, and sometimes she had as many as thirty. She really needed an assistant or something. "Okay, let's do it," she called out. "Counterattack to the front strangle, building off last week."

Three men from the previous class had stuck around and were donning light protective gear—forearm pads, throat guards, face masks. Livia had prepped all of them for their roles, and they played them well. It was good for the women to train against each other, too, of course, but the more closely you could model the real threat, the more useful the training.

The women formed three lines. The ones at the front moved out and positioned themselves with their backs to the padded wall. On their own initiatives—no *Ready, set, go!* in class because

72

there wouldn't be one in the real world—the men moved in aggressively, shouting misogynist epithets, getting in the women's faces, doing all they could to intimidate without yet attacking. It was common for new students to initially object to a trainer calling them *bitch* and *cunt* and *whore,* and Livia always responded that she was happy to tailor the training in line with the student's sensitivities—but if certain words were unduly troubling in training, how would the woman react to them in combat? *Men use these words to frighten us,* Livia would tell them. *To intimidate and paralyze. We need to habituate to what upsets us so we can fight through it. Deny our attackers the weapon of their words.*

And what was true for the verbal was true, too, for the physical. Many women were at a disadvantage when faced with even mild violence because when it happened, the feeling was entirely unaccustomed. To be thrown against a wall or the floor, to be punched or slapped or choked—the first time was so overwhelming it often produced a state of shock. And for women who had been abused, sudden violence could tap into trauma and shut them down. Which was why, in addition to getting them habituated to foul words, Livia made her students work up to being pushed and shoved and grabbed, with increasing force the more accustomed they became to the drills. The goal was to replace a freeze in the face of violence with a conditioned, tactical response.

So when the verbal abuse failed to rattle the students, the men began shoving them against the wall, trying to choke them. The women ignored the wall slams, broke the chokes with various gross-motor-skills counters, and attacked back with thumbs to the eyes and elbows to the temples. The room echoed with their furious roars and an accompanying chorus of encouraging shouts from the onlookers. For Livia, moving among them and herself shouting both praise and technique corrections, it was a kind of music, and she would never be able to get enough of it.

They wrapped up with a speed round of stun-and-run drills. Livia glanced at the clock, saw it was ten, and started clapping. "Okay," she shouted, "great job, everyone, great job." The others all joined in. When it died down, Livia continued. "See you next week. Remember to practice in the meantime—visualization, verbalization, mental shadowboxing. Even five minutes a day is a lot better than nothing."

She chatted with a few students one on one while the class gradually filtered out. Then she grabbed her backpack, headed into the locker room, and changed back into her street clothes— jeans, a tee shirt and fleece jacket, and a pair of Harley-Davidson Huxley Performance boots. The boots weren't her most stylish, but they were good for everything else: warm, waterproof, sturdy enough for riding, comfortable enough to walk and even run in. She would shower at home.

When she came out, Kyla was still sitting by the door. Everyone else had gone. It was obvious the woman was hoping to talk.

Livia walked over. "Well? What did you think?"

Kyla gave her the hesitant smile. "I think I want to try. I wish I had earlier. I mean . . . shit. A month ago, I had a bad experience. A really bad experience. I went out with a guy from work. And . . . God, why am I still afraid to say it. He raped me. He raped me."

Livia felt the familiar surge of rage. She made a mental note to learn more about the man who did it. Maybe she'd approach him. Get to know him. Go out on a date.

But no. The nexus would be too obvious. She had to be more careful than that. It was how she'd managed to avoid trouble for so long.

"I'm sorry," she said. A place keeper, allowing Kyla to go on if she wanted to.

"I always thought he was nice," Kyla continued. "And cute. I mean, I shouldn't have gone out with him because he reports to me, which makes the whole thing even more messed up. But we would flirt at work, and one night we had a drink with some coworkers, and he walked me back to my apartment, and I was buzzed and I invited him up, and we kissed but then I told him no, it wasn't a good idea because of work, but he wouldn't stop, he was . . . touching me, grabbing me everywhere, and I tried to push him away, and I guess I pushed him too hard because he got angry and he shoved me back against the wall and my head hit and I just got so scared I froze, and then he just . . . he dragged me to the couch and pushed me down and I was scared he would hurt me worse so I just . . . oh fuck, I just let him, oh fuck."

Kyla pressed the back of her hand to her mouth and looked away. For a moment, Livia's sympathy, and her rage, were so great that she almost didn't notice that something was bothering her.

Almost.

The woman's affect was off, that was it. Victims who had processed their trauma would often unconsciously mime their memories while recounting the experience. Someone might sway for a moment, for example, while describing dizziness. Or flinch when depicting a blow. Victims who hadn't processed their trauma might recount it with no affect and no physicality at all. But this woman was somewhere between: expressions and voice inflected with emotion, but none of the unconscious miming.

One of the things Livia pounded home with her students was the dictum *Trust your gut.* When you felt something was off, you had to *believe* that feeling, even if you couldn't articulate the basis. Gavin de Becker had written a great book on the topic—*The Gift of Fear*. And here, it wasn't just a feeling—Livia could also recognize the basis. Her natural reflex empathy for a victim was getting in the way, but still she'd managed to spot the incongruity.

For anyone who knows anything about you, what better distraction than to engage that empathy response?

Even with all the rapists she had put behind bars, the enemies she had made, the thought felt a trifle paranoid. But that was the point, of course. Not to talk yourself out of a gut feeling by dismissing it as "paranoid" or anything else illegitimate.

And while you've been listening to her story, the last of your students has driven away. This neighborhood is quiet at night. The parking lot will be empty.

She was glad the Glock was inches from her hand in its bellyband holster. A lot of detectives carried more for comfort than accessibility. Livia wasn't one of them.

"Do you have a card?" Livia said. "I'd really like to talk more. But I need to be somewhere, and I'm running late already."

"I'm sorry, I didn't think to bring one. Maybe I could have one of yours?"

That didn't sound quite right. Not impossible,

of course, but the woman had described her rapist as reporting to her, which suggested a certain degree of seniority in a company. And senior people usually had business cards with them. Livia would have expected her to at least check her purse for a loose card before expressing certainty that she had none at all.

"Sure," Livia said, and pulled one from a pocket in the backpack. Kyla glanced at it but said nothing. Not even a question about what the SPD sex-crimes detective she was talking to thought she should do about having been raped by a coworker.

Livia returned the backpack to her left shoulder, where it could slide easily away if she needed to draw the Glock with her right hand. "Should we head out?"

Kyla nodded and came quickly to her feet. The movement was athletic—no hands on knees, her thighs alone doing the work. "Of course. Sorry, I didn't mean to keep you."

Livia gestured to the exit, wanting to keep the woman in front of her now. "No problem at all." She glanced through the glass as they moved, seeing nothing in the ambit of the streetlight outside.

As they reached the door, Livia said, "Oh shit, I forgot to shut down the hot water. The owner asked me. They're doing some kind of maintenance in the morning and it needs to go off tonight."

Kyla turned. "I can wait."

Another internal alarm bell went off. "No, I don't know how long I'll be. You go, and come back Thursday, when I'm teaching again. Or call me. We'll talk more."

She was glad the woman didn't offer her hand—she didn't want to take a chance on getting entangled with her, especially so close to the glass door.

"Okay," the woman said. "Thanks . . . for listening."

Livia let the woman out, doing another quick visual sweep of the street as she locked the door behind her. Then she turned and headed toward the back of the academy. As soon as she was out of sight of the front door, she drew the Glock and moved more quickly. If someone were trying to ambush her, they'd be expecting her to emerge unarmed and clueless through the front entrance. On all three counts, they were about to be wrong.

The back door was heavy steel—cover and concealment. She opened it a crack and peeked through, her left hand low on the edge, her right holding the Glock just below her chin. To her left, the parking lot was empty. Straight ahead was a dumpster, a fence behind it. Clear. She squatted, her heart pounding, and darted her head out past the door and back. Clear on the right as well.

She took a deep breath and eased through the doorway. The door had spring-loaded hinges, and she slowed it down with her free hand to make sure it closed quietly. Then she moved left, keeping her back to the brick building, the Glock in a two-handed grip now, tracking left and right in sync with her gaze. She paused and *listened*. She heard the hum of an electrical transformer, the drip of water from a leaking gutter. Nothing else. She moved left again, logging a puddle in her peripheral vision and stepping over it. A duct ahead of her was spewing steam. She moved forward to get an angle past it, and—

A man slipped around the corner less than six feet from her, a pistol in his right hand alongside his thigh. Holding the gun for concealment, not in the expectation of immediate engagement. He saw her and froze, his eyes widening.

Livia thrust her arms forward, putting her sights directly on his sternum, and shouted, "Drop the weapon!"

But even before the command had finished leaving her mouth, the man's expression was hardening, his gun coming up, his left hand sweeping in to steady his grip—

Livia shot him twice in the chest, stepping offline to increase the distance he would need to bring the gun around to acquire her. The man staggered but managed to turn toward her. She tracked up and put two more rounds in his face. The gun clattered to the pavement and he collapsed onto his back.

Livia stepped in and kicked the gun away from him. She glanced back to check her six. A streetlight was shining onto the steam, rendering it practically opaque. Which way to go? There was no cover behind her. And no way to know what might be heading toward her from behind the steam.

Keep moving. Just keep moving.

She eased forward, the Glock tucked close to her chest.

At the corner of the building, she paused and listened. But she couldn't trust her hearing because of the gunshots. She glanced back and still couldn't see anything through the damned steam.

She turned her head forward again—and a stinging wetness hit her in the eyes and face. She recognized the smell and the sensation instantly from police-academy training: pepper spray. Someone crouching low and getting the nozzle of a canister around the corner of the building before Livia could react. She gagged and staggered back to gain distance just as Kyla burst from around the corner, slamming a palm up into the Glock, blasting it back into Livia's face. Livia saw stars. Her throat was closing up and she couldn't see. She felt the woman grab the barrel of the Glock and twist it, trying to snatch the gun away and break Livia's trigger finger in the process. Livia kept her left palm tight against the butt, her free fingers wrapped around her gun hand, denying the woman leverage, forcing the muzzle down and toward the woman's face. The woman stomped Livia's instep, a hard blow that might have broken bone if Livia hadn't been wearing the Huxleys. Livia grunted from the pain and hung on to the gun. She felt the woman raise her foot for another instep stomp and jerked her foot back to avoid it.

Offense, Livia, you need to be on OFFENSE

Livia twisted the Glock hard clockwise. As the woman shifted her footing in the same direction to compensate, Livia slipped her right foot across them, pivoted, and popped in her hips in modified *ogoshi*, a classic judo hip throw. Deploying the throw without some sort of gi grip or underhook would ordinarily be useless, of course, but in this case the woman was effectively glued to the Glock and would either have to release it or go for the full midair ride.

The woman chose the second of her two bad options. As her body arced past Livia's extended hip, Livia ripped the Glock in the opposite direction, breaking the woman's grip. The woman slammed into the ground. Livia took a long step back, pointed the muzzle at the woman's torso, and, blinking furiously against the fire in her eyes, rasped, "Do not move!"

The woman rolled to her stomach. Livia's eyes were burning horribly now and she couldn't see the woman's hands. In desperation and counter to her training, she jammed a palm against her temple and shoved the skin high to get an eye open. The burning intensified. She tried to get out another command and managed no more than a choking gag. Through a blur of fiery tears she saw the woman bring her knees in, and remembered the athletic ease with which she'd stood from the bench.

She pressed the trigger of the Glock six times, aiming for center mass, not able to see details beyond that. The woman screamed and fell to her side. Livia circled left, toward the woman's feet. She jammed a palm against the ridge over her eye again and for an instant could see that the woman wasn't moving. Then her vision filmed over in another flare of agonizing heat.

Coughing and gagging and barely able to see, she retraced her steps to the back door. She remembered her academy training: *Pepper spray hurts like shit, but it won't harm you. Don't wipe it—wiping only opens the capillaries and makes it hurt worse.* Still, the urge to try to clear her eyes was almost overwhelming. Because of the pain, of course, but also because there might be other attackers and not being able to see was terrifying. She kept her gun hand pinned to her chest at modified low-ready, her free hand forward, fingers splayed, protecting the Glock and ready to come to grips with anyone who rushed her. Of course, if there was another gun in play, they wouldn't risk getting that close.

You're okay. The woman was intended as just a setup, at least initially. Otherwise, she wouldn't have been using pepper spray. She wouldn't have rushed you. She, or a third attacker, would have had a gun. And you'd be dead already.

The thought wasn't as comforting as she would have liked. But it was something.

She managed to get her keys in the lock, made it inside, and closed the door behind her. She heard sirens—someone must have called in the gunshots. Good timing. She didn't want to be staggering around with a gun in her hand, gagging and coughing and unable to speak, when the responding officers showed up to a call-in of shots fired.

She squatted, put the backpack on the floor, unzipped it, and felt around inside. There, the first-aid kit. Patrol cops carried them routinely. Detectives often fell out of the habit, but if Livia ever died in a gunfight, it wasn't going to be because she thought hemostatic bandages and a tourniquet were too heavy to bother with.

She unzipped the kit and groped around until she felt what she needed—Sudecon, a commercial pepper-spray antidote. She tore the package open with her teeth and blotted her burning eyes. Almost immediately, the pain became more tolerable. She did her nose and mouth and tongue, too, careful only to blot, resisting the urge to wipe, which would rub the capsicum irritant more deeply into her skin and capillaries.

She got out her cellphone and speed-dialed SPD to call in the officer-involved shooting. She gave her name and badge number, the address, and a description of what had happened. She was pretty sure there were no more bad guys in the area, she told them. But obviously the responding officers should be alert regardless.

The call made, the sounds of sirens close now, she realized she was safe. And simultaneously realized she had just come within about an inch of dying. Immediately she got the shakes. It wasn't her first time, of course. But those other times, she hadn't been in cop mode. She'd been hunting. It was different.

If something about the woman hadn't made you suspicious.

If he'd had his gun up, rather than along his leg.

If you hadn't been wearing the Huxleys.

If there had been one more person in the team.

No. You did everything right. You spotted it. You listened to your gut. You were tactical. You won. You WON. They're dead. You're not. You made it, girl. You made it. How many times have you told your victims to celebrate that? Are you full of shit, or is that advice for real?

85

That made her feel better. The shakes sub-sided—a little.

Okay, so what the fuck was that? Who were they?

A thought immediately blossomed in her mind: *Child's Play.*

It seemed crazy. But she knew to trust those cop hunches. First answer, right answer, more often than not.

Come on. The op got shut down this morning. This thing was in the works from long before that.

The op just got shut down. The decision to shut it down happened . . . you don't know when. The plan to take you out could have been formulated beforehand.

It felt paranoid. But there it was again—that gut feeling and the urge to dismiss it, the thing she was constantly warning her students about.

She decided she ought to at least warn Trahan. He was in the air now, from what Agent Smith had said, but she'd call him as soon as he landed.

The main thing was, the immediate threat was dead now. Or at least gone. That much was reasonably certain.

What she needed to know now was who was behind them. And why.

CHAPTER TEN
LIVIA

An hour after Livia had put the call in, the scene was crawling with members of the department's Force Investigation Team. The watch commander. The night-duty captain. A homicide detective. Internal Affairs. CSI. The county prosecutor. A representative from the Department of Justice monitoring team. And an SPD Guild lawyer. An officer-involved shooting was a shit show under any circumstances, but SPD was still operating under a settlement agreement following a DOJ finding of a pattern of excessive force, and the department had learned to be exceptionally careful about both the substance and the appearance of a thorough, impartial investigation. Which was a good thing, obviously, but that didn't mean any individual cop welcomed being subjected to it.

She answered a set of routine public-safety questions from a patrol sergeant while responding officers worked to secure the scene. *Was this your duty weapon? Were you qualified with this weapon? Do you know how many rounds you fired? How many hits? What was your backstop? Did anyone else fire a weapon?* The questions from the homicide investigator and IA were more pointed. *Did you know the deceased? Had you ever met or seen them before? At what point did you come to believe your life was in danger? Why did you believe you needed to fire ten times—four to the man, six to the woman?*

A lot of the questions felt like second-guessing, but Livia knew the media would be asking plenty more regardless, so as unpleasant as it all was, it was better to have everything pressure checked and by the book now. At least the SPD Guild lawyer was there to help her, though most of his advice—*You weren't trying to kill them, you were trying to stop them; make sure your subjective impressions of danger are reasonable and objectively articulable*—she didn't need. The FIT team took possession of her duty weapon. She knew it was routine, but still, having to surrender the Glock left her feeling both violated and vulnerable.

She had gone inside to take a break from it all and was sitting at the edge of the mats when a woman in jeans and a windbreaker walked in. It took Livia a second to recognize her—Lieutenant Strangeland, who Livia had almost never seen out of uniform.

Livia stood, feeling weirdly awkward. "LT. What are you doing here?"

Strangeland paused and looked at her. "You gotta be kidding me, Livia. Are you all right?"

Livia nodded, half-amused at the incongruity of the tough Brooklyn accent and the tender tone, half-embarrassed by the obvious concern. "I'm fine."

Strangeland shook her head, not buying it. "Jesus God almighty," she said, walking over. "Come here." She put her arms around Livia and pulled her close. Strangeland was known for being standoffish, and Livia had never seen her give anyone more than a handshake or maybe a pat on the back. And everyone knew Livia didn't like to be touched off the mat. For an instant, Livia stiffened. Then she felt emotion welling up inside her.

"Come on, LT," she said, her voice cracking. "I told you, I'm fine." To explain the quaver, she added, "Maybe just a little shaken up."

Strangeland released her and took a step back, but held on to Livia's shoulders for a moment, looking at her. The naked concern in Strangeland's eyes was too much, and Livia had to glance away. It had been like this ever since the men had taken her and Nason. She had hardened herself so well to cruelty. But for whatever reason, even all these years later, kindness could undo her. And especially now, it seemed, when the sole friend she'd had on the scene was the SPD Guild guy who was only there to do his job.

"They take your gun?"

Livia nodded.

Strangeland reached into her bag and retrieved a Glock. "The 26, right?" She extended it butt forward.

Livia tried to say something, but couldn't. Goddamn it, she wasn't going to cry in front of the lieutenant. She wasn't. She looked away.

Strangeland said, "Pepper spray's a bitch. You used the Sudecon?"

Naturally, the lieutenant's compassion made it worse. But it was so obvious a ploy that it was also funny. Livia wiped the tears quickly with the back of a hand and nodded.

"It's okay. You know the drill. An officer-involved shooting, the duty weapon becomes part of an investigation. But that doesn't mean the cop goes unarmed. Take it, girl. A lot of people are going to be watching this thing closely. And every one of us has got your back."

Livia nodded again and blew out a long breath. She took the gun, checked the load, and slid it into the bellyband holster. Instantly she felt more in control.

She cleared her throat. "Thanks, LT. I guess I needed that."

"Understandable. And anything else you need, you damn well better tell me. You got it?"

Livia nodded.

"No. I want to hear you say it."

"If I need anything, I'll tell you."

"Good. I don't want to see any of your

lone-wolf routine on this, okay? Surviving a shooting is harder than you think. I'm not just talking about the investigation. Or the media. I'm talking about your feelings. Which, yeah, I know you pretend not to have any, but that's as much bullshit when you do it as it is when I do."

Livia gave her a small smile.

"What?"

"I promise not to tell anyone you have feelings."

Strangeland laughed. "Yeah, you better not. They wouldn't believe you anyway."

"You know, LT, I think this is the most I've ever heard you talk."

Strangeland laughed again. "I talk when I worry. And I worry about you, Livia. Don't underestimate this. The aftermath. You're going to be on administrative leave—"

"Administrative leave? I can't, I've got the park rapist, I've got—"

"Forget it. The leave is mandatory, it's not in any way my call. And you'll be required to meet with a psychologist, too. Just procedure, it's nothing about you. I'm not even going to waste my breath advising you to be open with the shrink. I just want you to be open with me. If you need to be. If it helps."

The thought of going after the park rapist with one arm tied behind her back—and right after the Child's Play op shutdown, too—made Livia want to scream. If she couldn't stop him, if someone else were attacked . . .

She knew it was all bound up in her inability to protect Nason. In her lingering sense that what had happened to Nason had been Livia's fault. But knowing it, and knowing the belief was neither reasonable nor logical, didn't seem to help much. The feeling itself just . . . persisted. Every day, one way or the other.

Fuck it. She'd figure something out. A way to keep working the park rapist. To stop him.

Right. That's right. Be smart. Stay calm.

She nodded and said, "Okay."

"Well, that's not exactly a promise, but I guess it's as close as we're likely to get."

The FIT homicide detective walked in—a stocky white guy, about forty, brown hair swept back, and a porn 'stache circa 1970. What was his name again? Phelps, that was it. The FIT people were decentralized, operating at the Airport Way Center, separate from headquarters, and Livia hadn't met him before tonight, though she knew the name. "Detective Lone," he said. "I was looking for you. Some follow-up questions."

"Hiya, Phil," Strangeland said. "Give us ladies a few minutes, okay?"

"Hey, Donna. Look, you know the more efficiently I take care of business, the better it'll be for everyone. IA, county prosecutor, DOJ . . . gonna be a lot of eyes on this."

"I get that. Just a few minutes, okay?"

Phelps nodded and headed back out. Livia was surprised—he was with FIT, so it was his crime scene. "That was good of him," she said.

"Yeah, he's not a dick. And he's right about the efficiency. But a few minutes won't make a difference. Now tell me what the fuck happened here tonight."

They sat at the edge of the mats and Livia filled her in. If she'd been a civilian witness, Strangeland would have had to steer the interview to ensure she was getting productive details. But Livia kept it relevant.

When she was done, Strangeland said, "Sounds like about as righteous a shoot as I can imagine. And you're articulating it exactly right. This was clearly a team; they attacked you; they refused clear verbal commands; you were blinded and choking and fighting to retain your weapon. The media's going to be asking why you fired so many rounds, and why you didn't just use your jiu-jitsu or shoot them in the hands and feet and all that shit, but that's just theater, none of it will stick. They'll make a little more hay out of the excessive-force complaints in your record, but they're all from long ago and none of them has ever been substantiated, and coming from the scumbags in question, the allegations aren't exactly credible."

Livia wondered whether Strangeland thought

the allegations were true. If so, the lieutenant knew better than to ask.

"There's a video camera over the back door," Strangeland went on. "If it didn't pick up any of the action, nothing lost. If it did, I assume it will corroborate your story. So the one thing I'm not particularly worried about here is FIT concluding anything other than that this was righteous self-defense. That's what matters. The media bullshit is just a sideshow."

The way she phrased it raised more questions than it answered. "What are you worried about, LT?"

"Number one, what we already talked about. The aftermath."

"I'll be fine."

"Yeah, you always make me nervous when you say that. But I suppose so far it's been true."

"What's number two?"

"Number two is, Who are the people who tried to have you killed tonight? And are they going to try again?"

"Yeah."

"No, I'm asking you, Livia. Who are they?"

"I don't know, LT."

"I know you have enemies. Every rapist and child molester scumbag you've ever put away who pleads down or gets early release or whatever. But from what you've described, from what I can see, this attempt on you was more professional than that."

"I had the same thought. Though some of those scumbags were gang members. Or rich enough to buy professionalism."

"So you like, what, Hammerhead for tonight?"

Hammerhead was a white-supremacist gang Livia had been investigating—more deeply than the lieutenant knew—a year before. This didn't feel like their work. And Strangeland's question felt like a feint to her. If Livia bit, Strangeland would think she was bullshitting. And therefore hiding something.

The problem was, she *was* hiding something. This might not have been Hammerhead, but Hammerhead led to Senator Lone, and Rithisak Sorm, the child-trafficking kingpin. She'd killed both of them in Bangkok, along with a string of their accomplices. Payback for that? Okay, but by whom? And whatever theories she might develop, she couldn't share them with the lieutenant.

"Not really," Livia said. "I mean, I wouldn't rule it out at this point. But . . . no."

"Then who?"

She thought of Child's Play again. It still felt crazy. But the thought was persistent. Which usually indicated something real was behind it. And anyway, it was something to give the lieutenant that wasn't connected to Bangkok.

"The Child's Play task force," she said.

"What about it?"

"Just . . . the timing. I mean, Agent Smith

shows up this morning and pulls the plug just like that. And however the decision got made, like you said, they never informed anyone, never explained . . . I don't know. Maybe it's all just a coincidence, but it feels weird."

"You think the Child's Play op got too close to a child-porn ring in the Secret Service, and someone decided to whack you to shut you up?"

"Well, it sounds far-fetched when you say it like that."

"But you're not saying no."

"You asked me what I think. I think it's a weird coincidence. Maybe it's nothing, but I'm still going to warn Terry Trahan. The contract hacker they paired me with. I mean, not to jump to crazy conspiracy theories, but if someone wanted to tie off loose ends, he's at least as much one as I am. He developed the encryption app those Child's Play members were using. And someone at the Bureau shut the whole thing down right after Trahan alerted his supervisor."

"They're on a plane now, you said."

"Red-eye to DC, yes."

"Yeah, it all sounds crazy, and maybe we'll come up with something more likely. But . . . I'll find out what flight. Make sure you call your boy Trahan when he lands. And I want to talk to this Agent Smith. The captain wants to go through channels, but it was bullshit, her telling one of my officers what she can or can't work on without it going through me."

Phelps walked back in, clearing his throat ostentatiously to announce his presence. Strangeland looked up. "What do you got, Phil?"

"More questions."

"No, I mean what have you found?"

"Come on, Donna, you know—"

"Listen, either Livia gunned down two innocent people here tonight, or this was a righteous shoot. Your offering her a touch of professional courtesy won't change what happened. Or the result. But it might help an officer subject to a FIT investigation sleep a little better while this thing plays out. The video show anything?"

Phelps looked at Strangeland for a moment, maybe caught between some innate stubbornness and the desire to offer a little comfort to a fellow cop. Then he sighed and looked at Livia. "The video looks good for you."

Livia felt a surge of relief. Not that a video would have contradicted her account. But with that steam vent, it might have shown nothing at all.

"We've got officers searching for other cameras in the neighborhood," he went on. "It's mostly residential, so let's not get our hopes up. On the other hand, more and more homeowners are installing video doorbells and other video security, and half the time they've got the units pointed straight at the street. Which is technically illegal, but it helps with police work, so we tend not to complain. Maybe we'll get lucky there."

Strangeland reached out and squeezed Livia's shoulder. "Anything else?"

Phelps shrugged. "The woman had a tattoo on her arm."

Livia nodded. "I saw it when we were talking. Trash polka style. A wolf."

Phelps nodded. "Here's the thing. It's a fake. Temporary."

Strangeland looked at Livia, then back to Phelps. "What do you make of that?"

"You said the woman was there for a while, Livia, is that correct?"

"The whole hour I was teaching. And we were the last two to leave."

Phelps looked at his notes. "So she was seen by, what, twenty people? Thirty?"

"At least."

"I had to guess, I'd say the tattoo was just to give all the witnesses something big and shiny and obvious to identify after you were killed. And give us something nonexistent to waste our time looking for."

Strangeland nodded. "Any way to ID the two of them?"

Livia noted that the lieutenant didn't call the man and the woman *victims,* which would have been the usual reference.

"Not yet," Phelps said. "Neither of them was carrying ID. Or anything else. Not even a car key."

"Jeez," Strangeland said. "It's almost like they went out intending to commit a murder or something."

"Certainly appears that way."

"Okay, then," Strangeland said. "So you agree this was meant to be a hit. Someone trying to take out a cop."

Phelps shrugged. "That's my working theory, yes. But not just any cop. They wanted that, they could have done another Lakewood."

The reference was to the 2009 execution of four Lakewood officers eating in a coffee shop before their morning shift. The gunman had seen their cruisers, stopped, and walked in solely to murder whatever cops he found.

"So, Livia," he went on. "It's time for you and me to talk about what enemies you have."

Livia glanced at Strangeland. "That's going to be a long talk."

"Well, we should be getting to the FIT office anyway. There's plenty of coffee there. At this point, I'll tell you my personal priority is to wrap up the officer-involved aspect of this investigation and focus on the likelihood that two people just tried to assassinate an off-duty Seattle cop. And might have gotten away with it, too, if the cop in question hadn't been so tough and resourceful."

Livia was surprised and a little touched. "Thanks for that, Detective Phelps."

"Call me Phil. Now let's figure out who's out there with reason to want you dead."

As Livia predicted, the conversation about her possible enemies took a long time. She and Phelps started with felons she'd had convicted who had since been freed from prison. Then convicted gang members still incarcerated, because even from prison, gang members could direct crimes outside. And finally, arrests that didn't lead to convictions but had caused social embarrassment or other difficulties for the individuals in question. By the time they were done with just the preliminary review, it was four in the morning. If they'd been at headquarters, the morning shift would already have started.

"This Child's Play thing," Phelps said. "Tell me more about that."

Livia rubbed the back of her neck. She was tired now but still amped from the attack, which in this windowless, fluorescent-lit room was beginning to feel surreal. She'd interrogated plenty of suspects in rooms like this one, asking them the same questions different ways, gradually teasing out the lies. She didn't know Phelps. Maybe what he'd told her about believing she'd defended herself against an assassination attempt was the truth. Or maybe it had been intended to lull her.

After all, whatever semantics the PR people came up with, in the end Phelps was in charge of investigating Livia for a possible homicide. That would be bad enough under any circumstances. For Livia, though, the scrutiny felt worse than uncomfortable. It felt dangerous. She kept her activities compartmentalized—sealed off and far from her everyday life. But she'd read an article somewhere, something about how undersea mountains and trenches exert a gravitational force on the water thousands of feet above them, a detectable force that enabled scientists to map the contours of the deepest seabeds by measuring their effects on the surface. She'd always assumed that what she kept buried down deep was imperceptible to the people around her. But she hadn't ever pressure checked the notion the way it might be pressure checked now.

She reminded herself that it was natural, unavoidable, for a cop in her position to be anxious. It wouldn't come across as anomalous or incriminating or anything else.

Okay. She leaned back in the plastic desk chair and looked at Phelps. "You ever get tired?"

"Not when I think someone just tried to assassinate a cop. How about you?"

She had to give him a grudging smile for that. She actually wanted to believe he was sincere. Which of course was exactly what a good interrogator tries to get a suspect to feel.

"Look," she said. "I want to be clear. I'm not saying the Child's Play op shutdown had anything to do with tonight, all right? I know there's a mandatory psych eval after an officer-involved. I'd rather not go into that with people thinking I wear a tinfoil hat."

Phelps laughed. "I get it. Probably just a coincidence."

"Exactly." She was aware that he had fed her the very word she'd used when briefing him earlier. It was that same interrogator's technique—a way of establishing rapport and eliciting more information. No wonder so many cop marriages failed. Probably every little thing started to feel like a manipulation.

"Still," Phelps said, "the notion is that, what, there's a child-porn ring inside the Secret Service, and the FBI contract hacker you were working with"—he consulted his notes—"Trahan, right. And Trahan spotted it because they were using his custom-developed encryption software. And then the Secret Service tried to have you killed as part of a cover-up. Is that it?"

"Those are your words," Livia said. "All I said was that the timing is odd."

Phelps nodded. "I think it'll be more productive to stay focused on rapists you've sent away. Scumbags with a grudge."

Livia tended to agree, but saw nothing to be gained by saying so. "It's your investigation."

Phelps's cellphone buzzed. He glanced at the screen. "It's the lieutenant."

"Strangeland?"

He smiled. "Probably checking in to make sure I'm not sweating you too much. Don't worry, she's calling me because she knows she shouldn't be calling you, and this is her way around it. I've known Donna a long time. She'd deny it, but she can be quite the mother hen."

He clicked the "Answer" key and raised the phone to his ear. "Hey, Donna. We're still at it." A pause, then, "Look, I broke protocol earlier as a courtesy, but for the rest of the interview, you know I'm supposed to keep the subject sequest—"

Another pause, longer this time. Phelps frowned. "Hey, now, there's no need for that kind of language. We're on the same team, even if we have to play different positions. But fine, you win. Hold on."

He put the phone on the table and pressed the speakerphone key. "Can you hear us? It's Phil and Livia."

Livia said, "Hey, LT."

"Turn on the news," Strangeland said. "That flight Trahan and Special Agent Smith were on. The red-eye to DC. It went down in Lake Michigan."

CHAPTER ELEVEN
RAIN

I met Larison in the arrivals lounge at Dulles Airport in Virginia. He was coming in from Costa Rica. Narita would have been the most convenient departure point for me, but given my mystery caller's mention of nearby Tokyo, I decided that Nagoya, though less convenient, would be a more comfortable way to begin my trip.

Security was heavy—a plane had gone down that morning in Lake Michigan, and the chatter on cable news was all about ISIS. The politicians were outdoing themselves to pro-pose retaliation—with Senator Walter Barkley, the front-runner in the presidential election, appar-ently increasing his lead in spot polls by promising to kill the families, including children, of ISIS members, and blaming the incumbent for the downed plane because "he was soft on ISIS." And the head of America's biggest private military contractor, Oliver Graham, was using the incident to argue for the abolition of the Transportation Security Administration and the handover of its responsibilities to Graham's company, Oliver Graham Enterprises. It was all such an obvious racket—Graham wanted the Pentagon to turn over the entire fight against ISIS, and all the Middle Eastern wars as well—I was amazed anyone took it seriously. But apparently, people did.

Despite the hysteria, though, I cleared customs easily enough. Taro Watanabe hadn't visited the United States in several years, but his passport was current, and all his affairs were in order. Besides which, meek-looking, middle-aged Japanese salaryman types hardly fit the profile that occupies the mind of your average ICE or other federal agent.

Larison stood when he saw me and gave me the familiar shark's smile, albeit one with some incongruous warmth in it. He hadn't changed much—the same brown hair, olive skin, and weightlifter's physique. And the same undeniable aura of danger. Having lived uneventfully for several years in the quiet of Kamakura, I had learned to relax a little about watching my back. But one look at Larison had me checking my perimeter, even in the middle of a crowded airport.

He walked over and we shook. Larison had large hands and an overly aggressive grip, but back in the day I'd trained to the point where I could crush an apple one-handed. Grip strength was a huge advantage in judo *randori*, and not a bad asset if you found yourself fighting for your life at close quarters, as well. If Larison thought of a handshake as some sort of contest, he was lucky I was past the age where those sorts of games interested me. Otherwise, he might have found himself with a fractured metacarpal.

"Checking your six?" he said, still smiling. "I thought you wanted an airport because they're safe. What is it about me that scares people so much?"

I couldn't help returning the smile—I didn't have many acquaintances, and it had been years since I'd gotten together with one. "Don't pretend you don't love it," I said.

He laughed. "Yeah, I suppose it has its advantages. But sometimes I wouldn't mind being able to do it your way. Nobody ever notices you, unless you want them to. I almost overlooked you coming out of customs just now."

"It's not like I haven't tried to teach you."

"Yeah, and Dox, too, that goofball sidekick of yours. Biggest guy I've ever seen who could ghost like that." He glanced around. "Hey, he's not here with you now, is he?"

I wasn't sure if he was serious or not. "No, he's not. And don't call him my sidekick. I'll never hear the end of it."

"You know what I mean. I told you, he's as protective of you as a goddamned dog."

"Yeah. A rottweiler."

He laughed. "I have to admit. By the end of

the whole thing? He'd really grown on me. I don't meet that many people I don't spook. Hell, once or twice, he actually spooked me. It was refreshing."

We rented a car. Larison knew Horton's address, naturally, though it wouldn't have been difficult to find the place regardless, considering the detailed description Horton had given me. I offered to drive first, knowing Larison would understand that by *first* I meant *the entire way*. One of the things he'd picked up on when we worked together was that I had a hard time not being in control. Always anticipating an ambush can lead to an abhorrence of passenger seats, literal and metaphorical. Not that Larison was any different, of course, so his willingness to ride shotgun showed more than just courtesy—it showed trust, too.

During the four-hour drive to Horton's place in Coleman Falls, we caught up. We started by reminiscing about the hairier aspects of working with Horton to thwart that coup—ambushes by gunmen in hotel corridors; a nonstop cross-country ride in the back of a sweltering U-Haul truck while half the government's antiterror apparatus tried to hunt us down; kidnapping Horton's daughter, a sweet college kid named Mimi Kei, to make him back off when he was trying to fuck us.

"You want to know why I've got a soft spot for

your buddy, that's the biggest reason," Larison said. "I was in a bad place at the time. A really bad place. Hort's people had threatened to have Nico's nieces and nephews raped and his parents and sisters and brothers-in-law mutilated and maimed. Then they were going to tell Nico how it had been my fault, because I crossed them. Turn the one person in the world I . . . care about against me. And I was going to do Hort's daughter in revenge. Send him her fucking head in a UPS box. I didn't just grab her to get leverage. I wanted to punish him. But that Dox with his chivalry or whatever wouldn't let me. If he hadn't stopped me . . . I've done some dark things, I think you know that, but that would have been too much. It would have ruined me. It would have ruined . . . what I have with Nico."

It was strange, how time and distance could make people closer. When we were part of the detachment, Larison was barely keeping it together, radiating so much danger and pent-up violence that we were all heading toward an outcome where either he killed us or we killed him. But somehow we'd gotten past it. Not that he wasn't still a formidable piece of real estate, but for him to talk like this about potential regrets, and about the man he loved, who represented probably his only vulnerability . . . it was a remarkable change.

Beyond Lynchburg, the road narrowed to two

winding gray lanes; the foliage grew thicker and older, sometimes forming a canopy overhead in the reds and yellows of autumn, and the houses became increasingly sparse and secluded. For a while it rained, but then the sun broke through, casting misty streaks through the tree branches. I could see why Horton liked it out here. It felt a million miles from DC.

"I'm going to give him a call," I said. "Let him know to expect us."

"I had a feeling you were going to say that. Come on. Don't you want to see him crap himself when we show up?"

"He's not going to crap himself. But he might just grab a shotgun. We're here for a talk, not a shootout."

Larison reached down to the soft carry-on between his feet. When he leaned back a moment later, he was holding a Glock with an exceptionally long magazine. "I could use another shotgun," he said. "Make a good souvenir."

It hadn't been so long before that Larison wouldn't have been able to surprise me with a weapon—because I would have searched him before getting in a car with him. As it was, I was more surprised than disconcerted.

"Is that the 18?" I said.

"Machine pistol, yeah. Thirty-round mag, twelve hundred rounds a minute. Like the commercial says, don't leave home without it."

"How the hell did you get that through customs?"

He laughed. "I came through customs with nothing more suspicious than my underwear. I keep stashes all over the DC area. I got in ahead of you and stopped by one of them."

It was the kind of thing I would have done, and I realized I should have anticipated it. I wondered if my oversight was because I trusted Larison, or because I was getting old.

Or maybe those were the same thing.

"Well, it's good you have it. But let's try to do things so that you don't have to use it."

"Yeah, yeah. Like I said, I knew you'd want to warn him. Go ahead."

I fished the burner I was carrying out of a pocket.

"I've got a sat phone," Larison said. "Harder to track. Why don't I power it up?"

"No, use the burner. It's not associated with Horton or anything else."

"Okay by me."

I handed it to him. "You mind dialing?"

He laughed.

"What?"

"Just the juxtaposition. Your high-risk lifestyle, and your care about not using a cellphone while driving. It's endearing."

I didn't mind being made fun of. I'd known plenty of people along the way who adopted an attitude of *If I can survive the Valley of Death, why the hell should I worry about something like a seat belt?* I understood the bravado. But most of the people I'd known who lived it also died from it.

He powered up the phone and input the number. I heard a ring—he'd put it on speakerphone.

A moment later, that unmistakable Delta baritone. "Hello."

"It's me," I said.

"I had a feeling you might be calling."

I hoped he was just saying that. "I thought I might take you up on that whisky," I said.

"That would be lovely. When can I expect you?"

"In about twenty minutes. Is that all right?"

"More than all right. Do we need two glasses, or more?"

No doubt, he had good instincts. "Three. I'm with a friend of yours. The one you contacted to reach out to me."

There was a slight pause. I wasn't surprised. I hadn't expected him to take a visit by Larison lightly. No one would, and especially not Horton.

"That'd be fine. I'll be out on the porch expecting you."

CHAPTER TWELVE
RAIN

By the time we arrived, the sun had dipped below the tree line, casting long shadows across the winding driveway that led through a thicket of woods to Horton's house.

I stopped the car about thirty feet out. Horton was standing by a post, no doubt having heard the car's tires crunching on the gravel from a long way off. And probably having been alerted by various electronic countermeasures as well.

We got out slowly, giving Horton plenty of time to see our hands, as he was being careful to let us see his. Of course, he might have had something concealed in a holster behind him. The heavy post he was standing alongside could also conceal a weapon, while providing some cover if things became unpleasant. If it went that way, though, he'd have two moving targets to contend with. One of whom had a machine pistol in the bag slung over his shoulder.

But the tactical analysis was mostly reflex. The only reason Horton might have had to kill us was fear that we would first try to do the same to him. If Larison had shown up alone and unannounced, one or both of them would have wound up dead.

With me there, though, and with the call we'd made first, I expected everyone to behave.

Horton didn't come down the stairs to greet us, preferring to maintain the high ground. I took in his appearance as we approached. A shaved head had been his trademark when he was active-duty, but he'd grown his hair out now. Despite a fair amount of gray, hair made him look younger. And despite the sweater he was wearing against the chill of the approaching evening, I saw a bit of new girth around his middle. Still, he remained a powerful-looking, barrel-chested man, with the erect bearing of someone who took pride not only in his own distinguished army career, but in being able to trace his military ancestry all the way back to the Fourth United States Colored Infantry, which fought with Major General Edward Ord's Union Army of the James at the decisive Battle of Appomattox Court House.

We reached the top of the stairs and he shook my hand. "Good to see you, John."

"Likewise," I said. "Thanks for having us." Maybe that wasn't an entirely accurate description of my showing up alongside a virtual killing machine with an enduring hard-on for Horton, and with only twenty minutes' notice on top of it. But with age, it seemed, came something of a diplomatic touch that had eluded me during my youth, when all my solutions seemed to involve posturing and violence.

Horton turned and extended his hand to Larison. "Daniel, it's fine to see you, too."

Larison looked at the hand for a moment but made no move to take it. I felt an electric tension building and thought, *Come on, do we not have enough people constantly trying to kill us without doing it ourselves?*

Then Larison nodded and accepted the handshake. "Been a long time, Hort."

Horton gave him a half smile, half grimace. "I'm glad you came. I've been meaning to tell you something for a long time. I wanted to wait until we were face-to-face, though maybe that wasn't wise, because in other circumstances I might not even have seen you coming."

Larison said nothing, and Horton went on. "I'm sorry for what I did to you. And for what I threatened to do. It wasn't right. It isn't who I am, or at least not who I want to be."

Larison maintained his silence, and again I felt that electric tension building.

"Easy to say now," Larison said after a long moment, the gravelly whisper sounding like the shake of a rattlesnake's tail. "When you're out of power. When it doesn't matter anymore."

I thought, *Shit, here we go . . .*

Horton nodded. "That's fair."

Larison glanced at me as though reading my thoughts, then shrugged. "On the other hand, I put you in a tough spot with those torture tapes."

Larison had made off with a number of CIA war-on-terror torture videos—many of whose subjects the government had subsequently disappeared. He'd demanded a hundred million in exchange for the return of the tapes, and claimed to have set up a dead-man switch that would propagate video highlights to every major media outlet if anything happened to him. Horton had been brought in to solve the problem. In the end, it had turned into a very ugly standoff.

Horton's silence was acknowledgment of the truth of Larison's point. So Larison didn't really need to add anything, but he did. "I'm sorry for snatching your daughter. I hope she's doing fine."

Horton said nothing for a moment. Then he nodded. "Thank you." For the thought, or for not having harmed her, I wasn't sure.

I blew out a long, silent breath, glad it looked like no one was going to kill anyone else. For the moment, anyway.

"I expect you gentlemen have come a long way," Horton said. "I have an exceptional Glenlivet I believe I mentioned to John here. Maybe we can open it and talk."

CHAPTER THIRTEEN
RAIN

Horton handed us each a cut-glass tumbler, retrieved the whisky from a cabinet, and led us back out to the porch, where we sat on some wicker furniture in the corner. In the cool air, moist from the recent rain, I could smell the whisky as soon as Horton uncorked the bottle. He poured three healthy quantities, and we touched glasses and drank.

I raised my glass in appreciation. "If word gets out, this could put Macallan out of business."

He smiled. "It should. Better than the twenty-five, and a fraction of the price."

Larison glanced around. "I can see why you spend a lot of time out here."

That was about as much small talk as I imagined Larison would ever make. And even that much was probably at least half intended to be cover for his tactical scan of the property.

"I don't get many visitors," Horton said. "Once I'd done my bit for king and country and eschewed the board memberships and talking-head positions I was being offered, people realized I was no longer of particular use."

He said it with an amused smile, and without

any noticeable bitterness. If anything, he sounded relieved.

"If you like the quiet so much," I said, "why did you reach out to me?"

"That was a favor for a friend," he said, glancing at Larison. "Someone else I wronged and wanted to make things right with."

"The contact?" I said.

He shook his head. "A contact of the contact."

Larison, approaching whisky as he did life, drained his glass and got right to the point. "I think this might be easier if you used a few actual names."

Horton sighed. "I imagined it might come to this. I have to ask you, what would you do with any names I might give you?"

"I told your contact the answer was no," I said. "But he revealed a little more than I think he would have if he'd known I was going to walk. Is that likely to be a problem for me?"

I was hoping the prospect of learning more about what his contact was up to might, along with the whisky, loosen Horton's tongue.

Horton shrugged. "I suppose that depends on what he told you."

"Then there's a possibility he could be a problem for me."

"I doubt he would have told you that much."

"Why don't you just tell me who he is, so I can decide for myself?"

117

A minute went by after that, no one saying anything, Horton and I sipping our whiskies, Larison scanning the grounds, each of us waiting for the silence to affect someone else first.

Finally, Horton cracked. "My contact isn't a man you want to cross," he said. "My reticence is more about protecting you than protecting him."

"He told me something similar," I said. "And I told him I'd rather have the information so I can make up my own mind."

Horton nodded. "I understand. But as I said, there's another player in the mix. And regardless, I don't want another stupid war that could hurt people I care about. I've been through that once before, remember. I don't care to repeat the experience."

"You started this when you reached out to me," Larison said. "Now you want to just unring that bell? I don't think so."

Horton shook his head. "I should have known. No good deed goes unpunished."

"Can we just cut the shit?" Larison said. "Let's stop pretending this is about protecting someone else. It's about protecting you."

Horton looked at Larison, a bit of irritation creeping into his expression. "The one doesn't preclude the other, Daniel. The point is, in my considered opinion, the information you want is only likely to create danger where most likely none currently exists. John, you declined my contact's offer. As far as I'm concerned, then, there's nothing more to discuss. I won't tell you his name, and I won't tell him you want to know it. And we can all get back to—"

He frowned, pulled a smartphone from his front pocket, and looked at the screen. He glanced at Larison, then at me. "If you gentlemen didn't come here alone, now would be the time to tell me."

Larison did another quick scan of the property, his hand instantly inside the shoulder bag. I looked at Horton. "What is it?"

"Someone just turned into the driveway. We'll hear them in a few seconds. By then it'll be too late. We'll be flanked by the other two approaching through the woods. I'd recommend you both follow my lead."

He stood and strode toward the front door. Larison pulled the machine pistol and started to raise it in Horton's direction. I put a restraining hand over his and said, "No."

"How do we even know—"

"We don't," I said. "But we'll find out."

We followed Horton into the house, Larison shutting the door behind us. Horton opened an interior door under a stairwell, something that looked as though it would lead to a cellar. He started down without a backward glance.

Larison looked down the stairs, then back to the front door. "I do not fucking like this. You gave him twenty minutes to get ready. That's like a week for a guy like Hort. We don't know what—or who—is down there."

I hated to admit it, but he had a point. "You're right," I said. "One of us should go down. The other should stay. My call on warning him, so you choose."

"You go. You trust him, I don't. Shout if there's a problem. I'll do what I can."

I glanced at the Glock. "You can start by keeping that thing on semi-auto if you have to come to my rescue, thanks."

He gave me the shark's smile. "Go. I told you, I've got you covered."

I headed down a long riser of carpeted stairs that led to a bare unfinished basement—concrete floor, unpainted sheetrock walls, and one enormous, built-in gun safe, the combination for which Horton was already dialing. He threw the wheel and glanced back at me. "Where's Daniel?"

"He stayed upstairs."

"He thinks I'm trying to set you up? Or wants to play cowboy?"

"You know Larison. Probably a bit of both."

He pulled open the door to the safe. Inside was a walk-in space about a hundred feet square and containing an arsenal that would do a small nation-state proud. Pistols. Shotguns. Submachine guns. A Barrett M107CQ—a fearsome .50-caliber rifle that could stop almost anything short of a tank. Stacks of ammunition, the individual shelves labeled by caliber and load, with designations like *tracer, armor-piercing,* and *incendiary.* Night-vision equipment. Body armor. A steel trapdoor, which I assumed led to some sort of safe room below. And a wall of flat-panel monitors receiving a high-definition video feed from all around the property and surrounding woods. On one of the monitors, I saw a black Suburban coming up the driveway, the crunch of its tires playing through a speaker built into the wall. On another, two men moving stealthily through the woods in camouflaged full-body armor and carrying what looked like suppressed HK MP7A2 submachine guns. On a third, Larison sprinting across the front lawn and into the woods.

"What's he doing?" I said.

Horton looked at the monitors as he pulled a body-armor vest from the wall and handed it to me. "Knowing Daniel, I'd say taking the fight to the enemy."

Larison made it to the woods. A different monitor picked him up and zoomed in tight. Whatever security system Horton had, it obviously involved motion detection and some form of AI.

"Doesn't he get it?" I said. "Whoever they are—and if we come through this, you're damn well going to tell me—they knew we were here. Whether it's satellite, or drone, or low-flying aircraft, they had eyes on you, and we walked right into it. And if they're still watching, they're relaying intel on our movements to the team on the ground. Yeah—there, look."

The Suburban stopped, still in the driveway, about fifty yards from the house. The two in the woods broke left and began moving clockwise, around the house and toward Larison's position.

"You could call him," Horton said. "But I doubt he'll answer. When Daniel gets focused on killing, he doesn't care to be bothered."

"He's carrying a satellite phone, but it's powered off. What about all your cameras? Do they have speakers?"

"Microphones, not speakers. We can hear what's out there, but they can't hear us."

I pulled on the vest and affixed the Velcro straps. It was heavy, with integral plates, shoulder pads, and throat protection. "He thinks they can't see him now because he's in the woods," I said. "But if they've got a drone or low-flying aircraft, they could have infrared. They'll map his heat signature and direct those two guys right to him."

Horton pulled on his own vest and began adjusting it. "I imagine he's counting on that."

Larison stopped for a moment, his head tilted up like that of an animal sniffing the wind for some trace of its prey. He looked left, then right.

Then he started moving again, deeper into the woods. I could hear wet leaves squashing softly under his shoes.

"You need to remember," Horton said, taking an M4 from the wall and slinging it over his neck, "I know this man. I trained him. He moves like a cat, hears like a dog, and hides like a rabbit. And strikes like a damn rattlesnake. They're not going to see him until they've practically stepped on him."

Larison reached a long rotting log. He stared at it for a moment, glanced around, then looked at the log again. He dropped to his knees and wiped his hands back and forth along the wet ground, then smeared mud onto his face and neck, creating some camouflage. He scored his fingers along the leaves at the base of the log, disturbing their natural pattern. Then he moved off a short distance to a depression in the ground that looked like a channel cut by the rain, thick with fallen leaves and branches. He dropped to his belly and began burrowing in. Within seconds, the camera had lost him.

The two men crept closer, heading right toward his position.

"You were right about the thermal," Horton said, loading spare magazines into pouches on the armor. "They know where he is. Or almost know. Just like he was hoping."

The two men crept closer, moving slowly and

carefully. But they were in the woods. And no matter how much you try to ninja your way in the woods, dead leaves, even wet ones, are a bitch.

"From where he's dug in, he might not even be able to see them," Horton said. "But I guarantee you, he can hear them. That's one more sense in play than they've got."

The two men stopped, the HKs at the ready, their torsos swiveling. I could imagine their thinking: *Where the hell is he? The spotter said he's right here. Is the intel wrong? Did we overshoot?*

Then they saw the disturbed leaves under the rotting branch. One of them pointed. The other nodded. They brought up the HKs and angled their heads, aiming through their sights—

There was a loud burst of machine-pistol fire. The men cried out and jerked and twitched as rounds ripped into their thighs, below the protection of the armor. They went down, one of them getting off a long suppressed burst from the HK en route. It looked to me like the shots went wide of Larison's position, but I wasn't sure.

On the ground now, the men rolled to their backs and started to bring up their weapons. There were two more loud bursts from Larison's Glock. The men screamed and rolled in opposite directions. From their backs again, they tried to sight on Larison. But the barrels were weaving and shaking. I looked and saw why—the last two bursts had shredded their hands. One of the men lost his weapon and groped for it on the ground next to him. The other switched to a left-handed grip and pointed toward where Larison's fire had been coming from. There was another burst from the Glock. The man screamed and the HK spun to the ground. Larison sprang from his hide in a shower of leaves, a grim smile visible on his mud-smeared face. The man tried to pick up his gun with his bleeding hands, but in the time he struggled to do so Larison had reached his position. Without a word or an instant's hesitation, he sighted down the barrel of the Glock and put two rounds into the man's throat just above the ballistic neck protection. The other man rolled away. Instantly Larison pivoted and put two rounds into the back of his neck, precision shots again taking advantage of gaps in the armor.

Larison dropped into a half squat and scanned. Apparently satisfied, he ejected the Glock's magazine, popped in a fresh one, and slipped the gun back in his shoulder bag. Then he picked up one of the HKs, checked the load, and started moving toward the driveway, where the Suburban was still parked.

"Damn it, that thing's probably armored," I said. "Give me the Barrett!"

Horton hefted the Barrett and started to hand it to me, but then paused, looking at the monitor.

"It's a safe bet if they were wearing armor, they're using armor-piercing rounds," he said. "And Daniel just checked, I imagine to confirm that very thing. Besides, it's too late. By the time we get there, it'll already be over."

I looked and saw that he was right. Larison was at the edge of the woods. He burst onto the lawn in a sprint. The Suburban revved its engine.

Horton placed the Barrett back on its wall mount. "Never got around to properly leveling that lawn," he said. "Moles and gophers out there, too. Daniel would have noted all that on his way to the woods."

The driver threw it into gear, and the Suburban barreled toward Larison. A man leaned out the passenger-side window and took aim with the same model HK Larison was now carrying. But Horton was right—the vehicle was bouncing, and as it picked up speed, the bouncing got worse.

Larison stopped as suddenly as he had appeared, the HK at eye level, his stance balanced and aggressive, his demeanor as calm and focused as though he were on a gun range, not facing down a charging Suburban with someone inside taking aim at him. The gunman leaning out the window must have recognized that Larison, stationary and still, had the targeting advantage, and let off a long automatic burst that tore up the grass five feet to Larison's left. For all its effect on Larison, it might as well have been soft music.

The Suburban hit another bump and bounced high. The instant it set down, Larison let off a three-round burst. The guy in the window jerked back and let loose a long *burrrrrp* of suppressed fire, all of which went high. The Suburban was thirty feet away now and still accelerating. Larison adjusted his aim and fired a long burst. The windshield exploded, and Larison dove left just as the Suburban overtook his position. He rolled to his feet and brought up the HK, but the Suburban was past him now, barreling toward the woods. It crashed into a cluster of trees and stopped. Larison raced up behind it, the HK up, stopped ten feet out from the rear and slightly to its right, and stitched a long burst across the passenger side, the AP rounds punching through the metal like it was cheese.

I stared for a moment, impressed as always by his coolness and precision. "Don't think that's going to buff out," I said.

Larison circled around to the driver side, hosing it down with a one-second burst that put probably ten more AP rounds inside the vehicle. He dropped the HK, pulled out the Glock, sidled up close, and glanced inside. Then he yanked open the door with one hand, the other keeping the Glock up and ready. Whatever he saw inside, it merited a pair of two-round bursts. Then he scanned the area and headed back to the house, brushing a few pine needles from his shirt as he moved.

I looked wordlessly at Horton. He smiled and said, "Did I mention I trained him?"

A moment later, Larison called out from the top of the stairs. "Everyone cool? I'm coming down."

"We're good," I called back. "You didn't even give us a chance to get our cleats on."

He snuck a peek from behind the bannister and, seeing that it was just Horton and me, proceeded down the stairs. He stood looking at us for a moment.

"What is this, cosplay?" he said. "You guys are dressed as, what, soldiers?"

Jesus, I thought. *This is worse than having to put up with Dox.*

He flashed the shark's smile. "Just giving you a hard time. I actually needed the workout." He looked at Horton. "I haven't had that much fun since you tried to kill me in Costa Rica."

Horton nodded. "A mistake I'm not likely to repeat."

"We need to get the hell out of here," I said. I looked at Horton. "Tell us who's your contact. Because you and I know he's the one who sent those men."

There was a pause. Larison tilted his head for a moment as though listening to something.

"Oh, shit," he said. "Helicopter."

CHAPTER FOURTEEN
LIVIA

Livia and Phelps headed into the snack room and turned on CNN. The network was playing stock footage of Boeing 737s—the model that had crashed. So it seemed no one had managed to film anything with a cellphone camera. Not surprising, since the plane had gone down over the middle of a lake at roughly four thirty in the morning.

But a husband and wife had been on the lake fishing, and a network talking head was interviewing them live on their boat. "I saw a huge ball of fire," the husband said. "Way out over the lake. I said, 'Honey, look, what the hell is that?' And then we heard a boom, and we watched this thing fall out of the sky. I hadn't even had my coffee yet, I didn't know what to think. A UFO? A comet?"

The wife added, "Now you're telling us it was an airplane. My God, those poor people."

Rescue efforts were underway, with helicopters over the crash site and divers in the water. So far, there were no survivors. Just some floating wreckage. The FAA was working to recover the black box, but apparently the lake was nearly a thousand feet deep at the crash site, so expectations of a speedy resolution were low.

Livia's mind was telling her, *Come on, just a coincidence.* But her gut was saying, *This is extremely bad.*

After a few minutes, the talking heads started repeating themselves. Phelps, still watching the screen, said, "What the hell do you make of that?" It wasn't clear whether he was talking to Livia or to himself.

"It's your investigation," Livia said. "You tell me."

Phelps nodded. "It's . . . Jesus. It's a hell of a coincidence, I'll say that."

Phelps's cellphone buzzed. "Strangeland," he said. He put the phone on the table and pressed the speakerphone button. "Hey, Donna. We're watching CNN."

"Livia, are you there?"

"Right here, LT."

"If Detective Phelps is done with you for the night and you no longer need to be sequestered, I'm coming to pick you up myself and make sure you're safe."

"I don't think—"

"I don't want to hear it, Livia. I do not want to hear it. I'd rather have people laugh at us for being conspiracy theorists than take a chance with your safety. Phil, are we on the same sheet here?"

"I'm . . . still processing."

"You think this is a coincidence?"

"I don't know what the hell to think."

"Well, you figure it out. You clear this case and prove what happened to Livia tonight had nothing to do with that plane crash, no one's going to be happier than me. But until then, if you're done with Livia, like I said, I'm coming to pick her up. I don't want her walking out of that building by herself."

Phelps looked at Livia. "I'm done with her. And yeah, we'll wait for you together."

"Do that. Thank you."

Twenty minutes later, Livia was getting into the passenger seat of Strangeland's Crosstrek. The parking lot of the Airport Way Center facility was empty.

Strangeland nodded to Phelps, who held the door for Livia. "Thank you again, Phil. You learn anything, I want to know."

Phelps nodded. "I get it." He closed the door and Strangeland drove off.

Livia didn't bother with her seat belt. At the moment, she was more concerned about being able to react to another attack than she was about a car wreck. "My place is in Georgetown."

"I know where you live. You're not going home tonight. Or this morning, rather. You're staying with me."

"LT, you really don't have to—"

"Don't you tell me what I have to or don't have to do," Strangeland said, giving the Crosstrek an angry burst of gas and cutting the wheel hard as they turned out of the parking lot. "I don't believe in coincidences and neither do you. This whole thing stinks, and until we know more, we're not taking chances. Now. You tell me what you didn't tell Phelps."

"What do you mean?"

Strangeland glanced at her, then back to the road. "I've always respected your mysteries, Livia. You know that. I know some things about your past, the rest I can guess, and I have some ideas about how it all affects your present. I've never pressed you on any of it. You're a good cop. You're a good human being. The world would be better off with more people like you, not with one less. Now tell me what you know about this thing that you didn't tell Phelps. If you don't, there's no way I can help you. And don't you fucking dare put me in that position."

Livia didn't know how to respond. She really had told Phelps everything about the Child's Play op. Other than the part about reaching out to Little. Little knew too much about her, about Bangkok, and she didn't want to emphasize that connection.

On the other hand, Strangeland was already acquainted with Little. He'd gone through

132

department channels, seeking out Livia to work on the anti-trafficking task force that had taken her to Thailand. Livia had used the opportunity, and the access to federal intelligence that came with it, to return to Bangkok and track down and kill the remnants of the gang that had trafficked and raped her and Nason. She didn't want Strangeland to know she was still in touch with Little. Didn't want to close that circuit. But if she didn't, and Strangeland found out some other way . . . it wouldn't look good.

Shit. She'd always been so careful. She'd worked so hard to keep things separate. The cop and the other thing. The dragon. But this . . . for all she knew, the two people who had tried to kill her tonight were connected to the traffickers she had taken out in Bangkok. Or to the senator. The FBI had investigated his demise in Bangkok, she knew that. The powers that be had decided to cover up the actual manner of death with a story about a heart attack. Better that than revelations about how this pillar of the Washington establishment had spent the entirety of his illustrious career raping children right under the noses of everyone around him, and maybe even with their complicity.

But a cover-up in public didn't mean someone wasn't intent on payback in private. In fact, the cover-up might have been specifically chosen with payback in mind.

Obviously, she couldn't tell Strangeland anything like that. But she had to tell her something.

"I reached out to Little," she said, telling herself she wasn't revealing anything the lieutenant wouldn't figure out for herself. Of course she would reach out to whatever federal contacts she had. Who wouldn't? Besides, Strangeland had even encouraged her earlier to do so.

"Why didn't you tell me sooner?"

Livia was ready for the question. "I know you don't trust him."

"Do you?"

"Not really. But he's the only high-level federal law-enforcement contact I've got. Anyway, he told me he'd work his Bureau Rolodex and see what he could find. So there was really nothing to tell you yet."

"Why do you play it so close to the vest with me, Livia?"

She was ready for that one, too. Or at least some version of it. "You said you know about my past."

"Enough of it, I imagine. Yeah."

"Maybe you don't know this. My own parents sold me. And my little sister. I was thirteen. She was eleven. The rest is probably what you imagine."

She hated saying even that much. Hated that it could still make her feel . . . ashamed. And tainted, because of everything it was connected to. And she especially hated using Nason as . . . fuck, as some kind of cover. But she had to give Strangeland answers the lieutenant would find emotionally satisfying. Or she'd keep pressing.

Strangeland nodded slowly. She didn't take her eyes off the road, and Livia sensed that in not looking over at that moment, the lieutenant was showing her a kind of compassion. Respect for her privacy, an acknowledgment of the intimacy of what Livia had just related.

A moment passed. Strangeland cleared her throat. "I am more sorry than I will ever know how to say."

Livia didn't respond. She'd spoken about it only once before. With Dox, who she called by his real name, Carl. When their lives had depended on it. To get through that conversation, she'd shut down her emotions, thrown the circuit breakers on every feeling connected to the past, to those memories, to everything. It had been exhausting. And afterward, what she'd managed to wall off for long enough to tell Carl what he needed to know had burst out of confinement, scalding and searing and fresh. She wasn't going to say more. She couldn't go through that again.

"I'm sorry for pressing," Strangeland added. "Like I said, I've always known not to."

Livia shook her head, not thinking, not feeling, just disconnecting.

When she'd gotten it tamped down the way she needed to, she said, "I'm only telling you because it's not easy for me to rely on people. If you want to know where my lone-wolf routine comes from, start there."

"I think I get it."

"I don't know if you do. I don't know if *I* do. But . . . that's the way I deal with personal shit."

"Well, on this thing, you're going to have to rely on someone. If this is all a coincidence, then fine. But we're going to need resources to make that determination. Someone who can reach out high-level to the Feds."

"LT, if this wasn't a coincidence, we're talking about people who brought down *an airplane*. What do you think, we're looking for some King County Council member?"

Strangeland grimaced. "You're saying this *was* the Feds."

"If it's not a coincidence, that's my working theory. I just don't know which ones. Or why."

"Maybe Homeland Security. Maybe the Bureau. Jesus, I feel insane just talking about this. The one thing I'm sure of is that we need to make a public stink."

"How do you mean?"

"Okay, if we're really going to put on our tinfoil hats here, someone just brought down a plane, and tried to have you killed, to stifle what you might know about Secret Service agents being part of a child-pornography ring. We get the chief involved, the mayor, hell, maybe the governor. A lot of people asking a lot of questions in a lot of places. Make the conspirators understand they missed their chance. The cat's out of the bag. Worse, in fact. Because if something happens to you, it's further proof of the conspiracy and they'd just be bringing more heat on themselves. Hell, I'd call a goddamn press conference, but we're probably going to sound crazy enough just running this up through chain of command."

Livia said nothing. What Strangeland was saying made sense. And even if it didn't, she doubted she'd be able to talk the lieutenant out of it. But she still didn't like it. She didn't want all this attention. She was afraid of where it could lead. She wished there were some way she could just handle the whole thing her own way, before any of it could lead back to Bangkok or anything else.

And then she realized. Maybe there was.

CHAPTER FIFTEEN
RAIN

A moment later, I heard it, too—the distinctive rhythmic buzz of approaching rotors.

Horton dipped his head toward the stairs. "That's an MH-6," he said. He stepped into the gun room and flipped a wall switch. The steel trapdoor swung open with a mechanical whine and a light came on from below. "Could have a chain gun or minigun. Could even be loaded up with rockets. Come on, we don't have much time."

We followed him into the gun room and he secured the door behind us. A second later, there was a concussive *boom* and everything shook. Then a second. I hadn't been mortared in decades, but the teeth-rattling, jarring terror was instant total recall.

"Rockets," he said. "Goddamn it, you know how long it took me to build this place? I told you, no good deed."

Under the trapdoor was a steep riser of stairs. We headed down, Horton in front, Larison bringing up the rear. At the bottom of the stairs was a wall switch. Horton flipped it and the trapdoor closed above us.

It was a safe room, as I had suspected, about the same dimensions as the gun room above. With the three of us, it felt cramped because the walls were crammed with supplies: Food rations. Water. Medical equipment. Rebreathers. More weaponry, including a Stinger portable antiaircraft missile launcher I recognized from a lifetime earlier in Afghanistan. One wall featured another steel door secured with four heavy bolts. Horton pulled the slides as two more explosions shook the room, then tugged hard on the handle. The door slowly opened. Beyond it was a dirt-walled tunnel, reinforced by periodic steel beams, narrow but tall enough to walk in upright and leading about fifty yards in the direction of the road. Along the ceiling were fluorescent overheads and a series of pipes that I assumed, based on the notably nonmusty air, provided ventilation.

Another explosion rattled the room. "Oh, you motherfuckers!" Horton said. He pulled the Stinger from the wall, secured it around his neck and shoulder with the attached canvas strap, and started jogging down the tunnel.

Larison and I glanced at each other. He shrugged and followed Horton. I started after him, then paused. There was a scoped GM6 Lynx portable .50-caliber rifle on the wall. I'd read about the weapon but never used one—the firepower of the Barrett, but relatively lightweight and with a specially designed barrel that supposedly absorbed enough recoil to make it possible to fire accurately from the shoulder.

Better to have it and not need it.

I grabbed the weapon, checked the load, and saw red- and silver-tipped rounds—incendiary and armor-piercing.

But shit, I really hope I don't *need it.*

I stuffed a spare magazine into my pants and headed off behind Horton and Larison. There was the sound of another explosion, less concussive now because we were no longer under the house. I wondered why they hadn't just started off with the helicopter, and realized they thought gunmen would be more certain, and certainly lower profile. Using the helicopter for more than spotting and surveillance was a plan B.

At its end, the tunnel split off into two more corridors, forming a Y. We followed Horton down the left side, which dead-ended about fifty yards on. A steel ladder led up about ten yards to another trapdoor, presumably camouflaged on the other side. I estimated we were about eighty yards from the house, just inside the tree line, and maybe a quarter mile from the road.

Horton and I climbed the ladder, again with Horton in the lead. Larison waited at the bottom to engage anyone who might find a way to follow us. The explosions had stopped, but this close to the surface I could hear the helicopter overhead again. "Wait," Horton said. "It's too close. Give it a moment—the pilot will circle to assess the damage and see if anyone comes out." He unslung the Stinger, opened the sighting mechanism, and popped in the battery cooling unit.

"How did you . . ." I said, and trailed off.

He pulled two heavy bolts back from the underside of the trapdoor. "Build this?"

"Yeah."

"I hired the same guy who advised the Sinaloa Cartel on the tunnel they built to bust El Chapo Guzmán out of a Mexican maximum-security prison. That one was a mile long. This was easy by comparison."

"What about the hardware?"

Horton glanced at the Stinger and smiled like a parent proud of a newborn. "Oh, this? You might have heard of Operation MIAS—Missing in Action Stingers. The buyback program for missiles we gave the mujahideen fighting the Soviets in Afghanistan, and then lost track of. I was in charge of it."

The sound of the helicopter grew distant—it was circling the house, as Horton had predicted. "Now," Horton said. He pushed up the trapdoor and climbed through. I followed him. We were at the edge of the woods, about where I had thought. There was smoke everywhere, thick and acrid. I heard the roar of flames. I turned and saw

Horton's house. Half of it was gone, and the rest was on fire.

For a moment, Horton stood staring at the ruin. Then he placed the Stinger on his shoulder and opened the sighting mechanism. I stepped to the side to be sure I was well out of range of the backblast. The helicopter emerged from behind the smoke of the burning house, buzzing and dark green, looking like some weird half egg, half deadly insect.

Horton took aim and fired. The missile left the firing chamber with a pop like a gunshot and hung in the air for a moment. Then its internal fuel kicked in and it took off with a sound like a jet clearing a runway, accelerating ahead of a long trail of smoke directly toward the helicopter. The sight of the tail fire and smell of the smoke were surreal—dissolving decades of urban living, and making me feel I'd awakened in one of the combat zones of my past.

The helicopter banked hard, the space behind it suddenly occupied by a half dozen countermeasure flares. The missile locked onto one of them and exploded in a ball of fire. The helicopter spiraled madly, and I thought it was going down. But the pilot must have been good, because after a moment he stabilized and began circling back to our position. The chopper's nose was down to increase its acceleration, but in a second its guns would come up, and rockets, too, if the pilot had any left after what he'd done to the house.

I brought up the Lynx and leaned in hard. A .50-cal fired from the shoulder is like getting kicked by a horse, and my now reengaged muscle memory had no confidence in whatever I'd read about specially designed recoil. I sighted through the scope, my heart hammering, let out a deep breath, and pulled the trigger.

There was a *BOOM!* as loud as an exploding mortar round. And as tightly as I was squeezing the pistol grip, the recoil was still harder than I was ready for. The first round went high. The helicopter slowed and began to straighten, its guns coming up. I fired again—*BOOM-KICK!*— but this time I'd overcompensated and the shot went low. The pilot, maybe spooked by the near-misses—or rather, near-hits—began to fire his guns even though his nose was still low, twin geysers of flame and smoke roaring out from alongside the craft's belly. In my adrenalized slow-motion vision, I saw the earth ten yards in front of us begin to erupt as though bombs were going off in it, clods of dirt and grass and rock exploding in all directions, the shriek of thousands of rounds a minute invading my ears and my mind. I'd never expected to hear that sound again, and its sudden reemergence in the here and now was beyond terrifying—it was disorienting, leaving me in some kind of limbo between the man I thought I was and the soldier I'd thought was gone.

The nose kept coming up, the sound of the guns obliterating everything, the erupting earth coming closer, closer—

And then a weird calm possessed me—combat reflexes, ancient but not atrophied, kicking in. I sighted, breathed, and eased back the trigger—*BOOM-KICK!* And this time, the shot punched through the forward glass and there was an explosion of fire in the cockpit. The helicopter corkscrewed, and for an instant I could see the pilot, fighting to regain control. I fired twice more and missed both times. I thought he was done anyway, but once again he managed to stabilize, a giant metallic insect shuddering in the air with its side to me.

Fuck. The calm I'd felt a moment before was slipping. I dropped the magazine and slammed in the spare. I sighted on the fuel tank and eased back the trigger—*BOOM-KICK!* High again. I fired again—*BOOM-KICK!* Low.

"Take him the fuck out!" Horton yelled behind me.

"What do you think I'm trying to do?" I yelled back. I sighted again and squeezed off my last three rounds—*BOOM-KICK! BOOM-KICK! BOOM-KICK!*—

The helicopter erupted in a ball of flame. An instant later we were concussed by a giant

KABAM! The helicopter, spinning and nearly invisible inside the fire, began to plummet, its rotors still turning incongruously, burning debris falling all around it.

"Daniel!" Horton shouted into the hole. "Get up here, we need to haul ass before that thing's ordnance starts cooking off!" He clapped me on the shoulder. "Damn fine shooting with that beast of a rifle. Your sniper buddy would be proud."

Larison practically levitated out of the tunnel. The second he was out, Horton threw the trapdoor closed. The edges were crenelated and covered with leaves, and the moment it was shut it was all but invisible.

I dropped the Lynx and we ran to the car. Larison glanced back at the burning house and said, "Got a feeling they're going to miss you at the volunteer fire department today."

I got in and fired up the engine. Larison, distrustful of Horton, ducked in back. With no time to argue, Horton accepted the fait accompli and jumped in the passenger seat. The instant he had the door closed I threw it in reverse and stomped the gas, pulling the parking brake two seconds later and cutting the wheel right. The car spun violently, the wheels spitting gravel, Horton and Larison grabbing on to what they could to avoid getting thrown against the doors. Just short of 180 I released the brake and punched it, catapulting the car toward the road, the two of them scanning as I drove, their guns at the ready.

"Go left," Horton said as we hit the road. "Opposite direction of the police department and yes, the volunteer fire department, too."

"Where are we heading?" I said.

"For now? Just away. These switchbacks will take us through the eastern part of the George Washington and Jefferson National Forests. Which, by the way, is likely where those wayward .50-cal rounds of yours made landfall, in case you were worrying. I'm glad it's been raining."

The truth was, in the terror of the moment I hadn't even thought of it. But it was good to know the rounds had a national forest to land in. A .50-cal round can travel for miles and do tremendous damage. Particularly rounds like the ones I was firing—armor-piercing and incendiary.

I didn't expect to see much traffic, but I didn't want to take chances, either, so I slowed to a normal speed. "And then?"

"I have no idea. I just want to make sure we have time to talk. Back at the house, it's going to be local police and fire department, and Feds shortly thereafter. At some point, I'm going to have some explaining to do. We need to figure out a way to keep you gentlemen out of it."

"It was a nice place," I said. "I'm sorry."

"Forget it. It was my own damn fault, for not seeing it coming. Anyway, it's just a house.

The one good thing that came out of the late unpleasantness regarding my daughter is it reminded me of what matters and what doesn't. And what matters right now is Oliver 'O. G.' Graham."

Graham again—the guy I'd just seen on television, trying to get the public behind his notion of turning over all of America's wars to Oliver Graham Enterprises.

If Graham was behind any of this, it wasn't good news. A former Navy SEAL, and founder and CEO of OGE, he did billions in contract work for the Pentagon, the CIA—and, if the rumors were true, for the intelligence and security apparatus of plenty of other countries, as well. The joke among his detractors was that you couldn't spell *rogue* without O-G-E. In and out of congressional hearings that seemed never to be able to pin him down, he was obviously protected from very high up. Which I supposed came with the territory, when you were the head of effectively the world's biggest mercenary army, and willing to do things even the blackest of government black operators were hesitant to touch.

I glanced at him. "Graham is your contact?"

"My contact. And the man who just tried to punch all three of our tickets. And whose ticket we are now going to punch in return."

PART 2

CHAPTER SIXTEEN
DOX

Dox was kicking back in one of the teak lounge chairs on the second-floor deck of his villa in Ubud. It was one of his favorite times of day in Bali—the humid air was finally cooling, the indigo above him had deepened to black, and the moonless sky was studded with so many stars it was as though someone had tossed a bucket of powdered sugar across a vast, dark canvas. He could hear insects buzzing in the rice fields around him and in the trees beyond that, but the Cohiba he was smoking kept them at bay. He had to admit, Cubans had tasted a touch better when they were contraband in the States, but a fine cigar was still a fine cigar, no matter how much the politicians tried to make them their playthings.

He took a puff, held it in his mouth for a moment, then blew it skyward, watching in the glow from the living room behind him as the smoke wafted away. It was strange. It wasn't so long ago that on nights like this he would have jumped on his Honda Rebel and ridden into town for a little fun. Maybe catch some blues at the Laughing Buddha, or play a few rounds of pool at the Melting Pot, or maybe No Más for a Bintang and a chat with Ria the bartender, who he always called Lovely Ria, riffing on the Beatles song, and whose bed he sometimes shared when it was a quiet night and she got off early.

But lately, he seemed to enjoy solitude more and more. He'd always been happy with his own company—he wouldn't have made much of a sniper if he'd found solitary work objectionable—but it was also true that back in the Corps, when he wasn't behind the scope he could be something of a party animal. It wasn't that he wanted to be alone now, exactly. He just preferred it to what appeared to be the available options. He'd always imagined settling down at some point, finding the right woman and raising a couple of ankle biters, or maybe even a few, teaching them to fish and shoot and take care of themselves and, most of all, to follow their passions, wherever that might lead in this crazy ride of life. And he'd been tempted a few times, but something had always held him back.

On nights like this one, though, he often found himself thinking about Labee. More than he should have, he knew. Labee, who everyone else knew as Livia and who he'd met and then partnered with to deliver some righteous killing to that human trafficker Sorm in Thailand . . . well, he'd never known anyone like her, and he'd half fallen in love, he knew it—maybe a little more than half, if he was being honest with himself. And what had happened between them had been good, really good, albeit also a little outside his wheelhouse. He'd just felt such a bond with her. A respect and a fascination and a protectiveness. Not to mention the attraction itself. He hadn't pushed or anything, maybe just a subtle hint or two as they said goodbye, but he could tell she knew he'd have been willing to give it a try. But she didn't want to, he could tell that, too. She'd shared things with him he thought she might not have ever shared with anyone; the name she'd been given at birth was the least of it, though he did love the way it felt in his mouth when he said it. *Labee.* He hoped she enjoyed the feel of *Carl* as much, because he'd told her to call him that even though no one but his parents did. But as special as it was, as much as he felt that bond even now, and as wistful as he was getting ruminating about it, he had to accept it just wasn't meant to be.

"Shit," he said aloud. "Maybe you should go into town. Beats turning into some kind of solitary sad sack."

He heard the phone ring in the living room behind him. Not the cellphone he used for local matters—the satellite phone, the number for which only a few people knew. Kanezaki, his contact at CIA. Larison, the damn angel of death himself. And John, of course. And John's lady, Delilah. Or erstwhile lady, he supposed, which he

153

personally found pointless and sad. He'd tried to get John to talk about it, but the man was hurting so much he just wouldn't.

And Labee. But no, why would she be calling him now, after a whole year had gone by? Probably it was just old Kanezaki, who was always trying to get him mixed up in some kind of off-the-books skulduggery, and usually succeeding, too. Well, his timing wasn't half-bad. Dox thought doing something operational right now might be just the thing to make him feel less morose. Though at some point, he'd have to consider treating the underlying elements of this midlife crisis or whatever it was that seemed to be ailing him, and not just the symptoms.

He set down the cigar in the ashtray, got up, and went through one of the sliding screen doors. He picked up the phone and didn't recognize the number. Well, that was no surprise, the people he associated with tended not to use the same phone for very long. He pressed the answer key and held the phone to his ear. "Hello."

"Carl?"

He felt a rush of joy so big it almost stunned him. But he was too glad to hear her voice to be embarrassed. "Labee? Is that really you?"

"Yes. How are you?"

"I'm fine, is everything all right?"

"I'm okay. But something weird happened, and . . . I don't know who else to ask."

He felt a flush of concern wash through him. She wasn't the type to make a big deal out of nothing. The opposite, in fact.

"I'm glad you called," he said. "Tell me what's going on."

Damn. What was going on was, two people had tried to kill her. In what, in his not-inexpert opinion, sounded like a reasonably competent operation—though given that the op had failed, maybe not quite the level of professionalism he and John were justifiably known for. He listened to her theories about why, of which there seemed to be two main ones: First, it was about her discovery of a possible child-pornography ring within the Secret Service. And second, that it might be related to what they'd done together in Thailand, and what she'd done there herself before that.

"Which makes me realize," she said. "And I should have spotted it before. If this is about Thailand, they could be after you, too."

"Don't you worry about me. I've had people trying to kill me since I was a teenager, and no one's managed it yet. Besides, with that plane going down with your hacker partner on it, I think your first theory is the more likely."

"I agree."

"Now, you need to take this seriously."

"Why do you think I'm calling you?"

He smiled, loving the way she refused to ever

take shit, and also gratified that she knew she could rely on him.

"Well," he said, "I was initially hoping you just missed me, but okay, fair point. And at the risk of you getting irate because you think I'm talking down to you, I'm going to tell you now you need to change your habits for a while. Ditch your cellphone, or at least keep it powered off in a Faraday case except when you really need it—"

"My usual phone is already turned off. Anyway, how was I able to reach *you* just now?"

Her habit of counterpunching could be as exasperating as it was endearing. "This is an encrypted satellite phone. Unless someone's flying an AWACS plane, the signal can't be triangulated the way cellphones can. Plus, oh, it occurs to me, I didn't just have two people try to kill me, unlike someone else I could name."

She laughed a little. Damn, he did like making her laugh. It was never easy and always felt like a tiny miracle.

"I see your point," she said.

"And you have to watch yourself extra carefully at choke points. Places you're known to frequent, like that dojo where you were teaching when this happened. Primarily we're talking about work and home."

"Well, I'm on administrative leave until this officer-involved investigation is completed, so work isn't the problem it ordinarily would be.

And my lieutenant is thinking the same way you are. She's having me stay with her."

"Well, that's not bad, other than, one, she's your lieutenant and people might figure it out, and two, you just said it to me over the phone."

There was a pause. "Shit," she said, for once lacking a stinging rhetorical comeback.

"I didn't recognize the number, though. Burner?"

"Just a new phone."

"Okay, good. But it wouldn't hurt you to pick up a burner. Ideally, the way we did at the night market to make it really untraceable. That should hold us until we can get something more secure in place."

At the night market in Bangkok, he had bought a couple of cellphones on the spot from some teenagers. No new purchases, no phones newly activated, nothing for the all-seeing national security state to glom on to.

"Are you going to tell me not to use credit cards, too?"

"Well, I was, because I'd rather have you irritated at me than leave something to chance. But I'm glad there's no need."

He thought he might have made her smile with that. That was good. But overall, he was worried. He'd seen her in action and he knew she was competent as hell. But still, if her theory was right, she was up against someone capable of dropping a fucking airplane without leaving fingerprints.

"Actually," he said, "one more thing. Keep your passport with you. And a lot of extra cash. You don't want to be reliant on ATMs, and you never know when you might have to get out of town suddenly."

"Anything else?"

"Hell, yes, anything else. I know low people in high places. And some of them know even lower ones in even higher places. We'll figure out what's going on here. And we'll take care of it."

"You're talking about K.?" she said. It was how he'd initially referred to Kanezaki. She'd since learned his actual name, but for whatever reason they'd stuck with the abbreviation.

"Yeah, K. That boy is consistently an intel gold mine. But someone else, too."

"Who?"

"A friend. Who against formidable odds once rescued me from a jam with some maximally unpleasant people. And who knows more about killing and surviving than anyone I've ever known."

"More than you?"

"Let's just say, a lot of what I know I've learned from working with him. Though don't quote me on that, because he can be insufferable about his talents, and I don't want to feed his Yoda complex."

There was a pause. Then she said, "Thank you, Carl."

"It's nothing. I'll reach out to him as soon as we're off the phone."

"No. I mean . . . thank you for you."

He wanted to tell her he'd missed her. Really missed her. That he hadn't fully realized how much until he'd heard her voice right now. And how worried it made him to know she was in trouble.

But shit, he was being stupid. "Nothing to thank me for," he said. "If you hadn't dropped those goons in Sorm's nightclub, I wouldn't even be around for you to enjoy my conversation."

"If that was a debt, you already repaid it."

"All right, then. I'm going to help you just because I care. And that's never going to change. Can you handle it?"

There was another pause. She said, "Yes."

He felt himself getting stupid again and pushed it away. "All right," he said. "Let me get in touch with K. and the other friend I mentioned. And depending on what we learn, I might just pay you a visit. Sounds like you could use a bodyguard right now."

"I don't need a bodyguard," she said, and he realized he should have known a comment like that would make her prickly.

"My God," he said. "Will you really deny me every last dignity, and force me to confess that

159

the bodyguard thing was just a ruse to conceal my longing to see you again?"

She gave him one of those soft laughs, probably knowing he wasn't being completely facetious. "I don't know what to do with you," she said.

"Pardon me, but the drop-down menu of my mind just offered up so many enticing possibilities that for a moment my brain froze."

She laughed again.

"You might not need it," he said. "And I know you don't want it. But will you stop being so selfish? You called me, and now I'm concerned. If you won't let me get involved, I'm just going to lie awake at night."

He imagined her smiling. After a moment, she said, "You win."

He nodded, glad that he was going to get to see her, and relieved that she was being sensible. "Get a new phone. And call me in a few hours. I ought to have a better idea by then of what's going on."

He clicked off.

He considered for a moment. He knew she was too proud to admit how scared she must be. He hoped knowing she could count on him was at least something of a comfort.

But she wasn't the only one who wasn't admitting to being scared. Anyone who would bring down a damn plane to silence an enemy wasn't just capable. They were committed. And god-awful ruthless on top of it.

Well, they better be. Because as far as he was concerned, anyone intent on harming Labee was about to get a lesson in what ruthless really meant.

CHAPTER SEVENTEEN
RAIN

For the next half hour, I followed Horton's directions and kept to back roads. Horton and I had ditched our phones, and Larison's sat phone was still off, though probably untrackable regardless, so that was covered. And the car didn't have a GPS navigation system, so no vulnerability there. Still, a near-hit like the one we'd just been through shakes you up. Because if you hadn't spotted the danger before, how could you be sure you were past it now?

Eventually, we came to an empty campsite. We parked under a stand of trees, with a granite cliff to our backs. It was inherently comforting to have some cover and concealment, though if we had to face another minigun-and-rocket-equipped helicopter, a little rock and some tree branches were going to be about as useful as tissue paper.

We got out of the body armor and put it in the trunk. I felt strangely naked without it, given what we'd just been through, but at this point there was likely more risk of a park ranger calling in some suspicious militia types than there was of another attack.

I hoped.

At any rate, we seemed to have the area to ourselves, perhaps a consequence of the recent rains and the relative lateness of the hour. We sat at a picnic table, the tips of the Blue Ridge Mountains in the distance incongruously placid in the gray light of the setting sun.

Horton said, "You know the worst part?"

Larison and I didn't answer, and after a moment he continued. "That Glenlivet. I wish I could have brought it with us. Could use a drink right about now."

"Well," I said, "at least we got to taste it."

Horton gave me a rueful smile. "There's that."

"Graham," Larison said. "He was watching you—maybe with that helicopter, probably with something subtler and more persistent."

Horton looked at me. "Apparently so. However your conversation with him went, he must have been concerned that you and I were going to close the loop in a way he would find unfavorable."

"Tell me what you know," I said.

He shrugged. "As I said earlier, not that much. He told me he had a job. Very sensitive. Something that needed to look natural. He asked if I could broker an introduction."

"How did he even know you and I were acquainted?"

"Because Ben Treven told him so."

Treven. Another black-ops soldier who had once reported to Horton, and with whom I

163

worked as part of the detachment Horton had assembled to stop a domestic coup.

"Why?" I said. "What's his angle?"

Horton glanced at Larison, then back to me. "Ben has moved on from employment with the US government—in part, I regret to say, because my own manipulations made it untenable for him to stay. He's with OGE now, and not particularly happy in the private sector. Graham was asking about you, having heard stories he thought might be myths. Ben made the mistake of acknowledging he knew you, at which point Graham dangled all sorts of career advancement if Ben could make it work out. Ben's been chafing at no longer being on the inside, and he rightly blames me."

I didn't detect any incongruities. At least so far. "He called and said you owed him."

"That's right," Horton said. "He didn't have contact information for either of you, otherwise doubtless he wouldn't have used me as a middleman. I spoke with Graham, then reached out to Daniel here. You both know the rest."

Larison said, "You trust Treven?"

Horton shrugged. "If he weren't trustworthy, he would have been one of the men you killed in the woods around my house just now. Or he would have killed you."

Larison shook his head. "You had it right the first time."

I couldn't disagree. Treven was exceptional. But Larison was supernatural.

"Regardless," Horton said, "the fact that Graham didn't find him suitable for this particular mission ought to tell you everything you need to know."

"It tells me some things," Larison said. "Not everything. You didn't just train him, Hort. You were some kind of father figure. You're not objective about Treven. You never have been. And if you can't realize that, it's a bad fucking sign."

Again, I didn't disagree with Larison, but I didn't see a benefit to his getting in Horton's face more than he already had—especially because of the way Horton was now looking at him.

"Killing you himself is one thing," I said, looking at Horton, trying to interrupt any ugliness. "But how's Treven going to react if he learns Graham tried to do it?"

"If you're wondering whether we have a man inside," Horton said, still staring at Larison, "right now, I wouldn't want to bet either way."

"Graham told me the job was three people in law enforcement," I said, doing the conversational equivalent of getting between two people who are heading toward blows. "A Fed, a local, and a consultant. Does that mean anything to you?"

Horton broke the stare with Larison and looked at me. "No. Was there anything else?"

"The work had to look natural," I said, relieved that we seemed to be back on track. "Which makes sense, since he was intent on involving me. The time frame was tight—maybe three days. He claimed the job would be easy because they had extensive intel and could help control the environment. And the local law enforcement was a woman—a Seattle cop."

Horton shook his head. "Still doesn't mean anything to me."

"Try this," I said. "The price was a million US."

"A million?" he said, raising his eyebrows. "That's a hell of a premium, even for three. I'd be surprised you didn't want the work, if I didn't know about your reticence regarding women."

"And the diamonds we took from you," Larison said, giving him the shark's smile.

Fortunately, Horton ignored the taunt. "So three jobs, a million US, and it was critical it all looked natural because Graham went to a lot of trouble to ferret you out. Now, why natural?"

"Blowback, obviously," Larison said. "The targets are high-profile. And connected in some way, such that if all three were seen to be assassinated, it would reveal something the people behind it wanted to keep obscured."

"Agreed on all that," I said. I looked at Horton. "And the fact that Graham was devoting significant resources to watching

166

you, presumably to ensure that you didn't get a visit from me, also suggests this whole thing is intended to conceal something big. Not to mention the fact that he was willing to send in a helicopter gunship to sleepy Coleman Falls to make sure our conversation didn't get past a single tumbler of Scotch."

"I had to guess?" Larison said. "I'd guess a joint federal–Seattle law enforcement operation that threatened some aspect of Graham's empire."

Horton nodded. "Could be that. Or a law-enforcement operation that threatens some government program. The Pentagon or CIA wouldn't want to be directly involved in the assassination of multiple law-enforcement agents. Sure, the plan was for things to look natural, but why take a chance on leaving fingerprints when you can bring in a reliable contractor as a cutout?"

I nodded. "And if the risk is big enough, the contractor doesn't want to take it, either. He brings in a subcontractor."

"That's right," Horton said. "And whatever the pay was for OGE, or whatever the stakes, by contrast Graham was treating a million dollars like walking-around money."

Larison did one of his periodic scans. "Great, so this thing is obviously big. But we still don't know shit about the specifics. Without which, you might want to go to the car and get back into that body armor. We're going to need it for a while."

"Treven," I said. "How much do you think he knows?"

Horton rubbed his chin for a moment. "When I spoke to him, he claimed not to know anything, other than that Graham wanted you for your 'natural causes' expertise."

"Probably telling the truth," Larison said. "If this is as big as we think, why would Graham share it with the hired help?"

"Agreed," I said. "Still, Treven might have pieces. The relevance of which he'll be able to see only if we put our heads together."

Larison cracked his neck. "Which brings us back to the question of whether we can trust him. I'd say the answer is no."

"I can call my CIA guy," I said, meaning Kanezaki. "His intel is typically gold. Albeit usually with a price to match."

"Why don't I reach out to Ben first," Horton said. "He's the most directly involved. Even if it turns out he's untrustworthy, what could he tell Graham that Graham doesn't already know? With all the bodies back at what's left of my house, he knows we survived. And he knows we'll know he was behind it. We might not learn much from Ben, but we wouldn't be risking anything asking."

I considered. "If Graham is monitoring other

potential vulnerabilities the way he was monitoring you, you might create danger for Treven the way we created it for you."

Horton shook his head. "Graham already knows about that connection. He exploited it in getting Ben to reach out to me in the first place. He's probably expecting me to be in touch at this point. If there's danger to Ben, it exists either way."

We were all quiet for a moment. Larison reached into his bag, pulled out the satellite phone, and powered it up.

"Hold on a second," he said. "There's a text. Your buddy, Dox. He wants me to call him."

I shook my head, wondering if maybe I'd misheard. "Why is Dox texting you?"

"I told you. He wants me to call."

"What I mean is, I didn't know you were in touch."

"Not often. But yeah, he sometimes calls to shoot the shit. Guy likes to talk. It annoyed me at first. But . . . like I said, he grows on you."

"Well, call him," I said. "If we're up against all of OGE, we could use the help."

Larison input the number, waited a moment with the phone to his ear, then said, "Hey. Just got your message."

A pause. He looked at me. "Have I got a way of getting in touch with him? I guess so. He's sitting right next to me."

What the hell?

Another pause. "You're the joker, not me. Here, I'll put him on."

He handed me the phone.

"Yeah?" I said, feeling distinctly uneasy.

"Sir, it's come to our attention that you are part of a core demographic in need of our miracle new penis-enlargement supplement. For a limited time only, we are offering double doses for the low introductory price of just nine ninety-nine a month. And sir, given the demographic you are unfortunately a part of, I feel confident in assuring you our supplement would be a bargain at twice the price."

The Texas twang was unmistakable. So was the salutation. I sighed. "Are you going to tell me next you're not just the president of the company, but a customer, too?"

He laughed. "That's pretty good, partner. I think retirement must suit you. I don't know if you've grown anything else, but it sounds like you've grown a sense of humor. Now where the hell have you been? I sent you a message on the secure site last night."

"I've been traveling. Why are you . . . how did you know who I'm with?"

"I didn't. I just didn't know how else to get in touch with you because you won't even leave a damn sat phone turned on, and you weren't responding on the secure site. From the sound of things, I got lucky. Why didn't you call me if you were going to get the band back together?"

"I was planning on it. Things have been developing a little faster than I'd like. Is everything okay?"

"Things are fine with me. But I've got a friend who needs some help, pronto. That's why I've been trying to reach you. And you're traveling, you say? That's my bad luck. I've got a little layover at a major airport in your neck of the woods. Would have been nice to see you. Well, maybe we'll still get the chance."

I was still struggling to connect all the dots. He knew I was in the Tokyo area, so the airport would have been Narita. But where was he going? And why the sudden urgency trying to reach me?

"I've got a bit of a situation here myself," I said. "Which is why I was going to call you. Who's your friend?"

"A nice lady I met and partnered with while doing some contract and related work recently in your overall Southeast Asia region."

Dox was a dictionary of euphemisms, but I'd never known him to use "partner" for other than something both professional and serious. "Nice lady," on the other hand, could mean anything from someone he admired from a distance to a girl he was shacking up with. And as hardheaded as he was in almost every other way, I knew Dox could be a sucker for a damsel in distress.

171

"Partnered with?" I said. "I'm sorry, I just survived a helicopter attack and I'm a little rattled."

"Helicopter attack? Who'd you piss off this time?"

"It's a long story and I'll fill you in later. Who's your friend? What kind of trouble?"

"A police detective who seems to have stumbled onto something so nefarious the powers that be are now intent on killing her to cover it up. I mean, they even—"

"Wait a minute, a Seattle police detective?"

"Yeah, how'd you know?"

"The guy behind the helicopter attack I just mentioned. Less than a week ago, he tried to hire me to kill a Seattle cop. And a federal agent, and a consultant. I told him no, but—"

"Well, fuck me running. That's my gal. The agent and the consultant were part of the same law-enforcement operation she was working on. And that plane that got blown up, or whatever happened, the agent and the consultant were on it."

"Hold on. You're telling me that—"

"Yeah, I'm telling you that. Sounds like you were a damn plan A—kill all three of them and make it look natural. But you said no, so they went to plan B. Kill two of them in a plane crash and blame it on ISIS or whoever. Conceal a murder in a massacre. And kill my gal the old-fashioned way, with bullets, but she's got a ton of enemies due to her years of dedicated police work and her murder gets attributed to that. No one makes the connection—that all three of them were killed because they uncovered a child-pornography ring right in the middle of the damn Secret Service."

"That's what this is about?"

"Sure sounds like it. The FBI pulled the plug on the operation the very morning of the night two shooters showed up and tried to kill my gal. But she's so fine, she killed them dead instead. Now tell me who's behind this whole thing, 'cause they tried to kill my gal and brought down an entire plane full of innocent people just to cover their own asses, and I'm not going to stop until they've been delivered some righteous fucking justice."

"Oliver Graham."

"Well, shit. Why am I not surprised? Like they say, you can't spell *rogue* without O-G-E. But what's his angle? Just a cutout for the Secret Service?"

"Seems a reasonable inference. But we need more intel on who's ultimately behind this."

"And how we get to them."

"Exactly. We're working a couple contacts now. One is Treven—"

"Ben Treven? How's that boy mixed up in this?"

"I don't know that he is. But he brokered the introduction to Graham. And he's currently employed by OGE."

"Well, that sounds promising. And when I'm off the phone with you, I'm fixing to call our mutual friend at Christians In Action. Would have pinged him sooner, but I nearly missed my flight as it was and besides, I wanted to get with you first."

"I was going to do the same myself. He's still stationed at Langley, is that right?"

"Yeah, he's more management than field now. But his intel is better than ever. He was a big help to me and my gal during that recent Southeast Asian imbroglio."

Something occurred to me. "You keep calling her your gal. Are the two of you . . ."

"Nah, it ain't like that. Not that she's not in love with me, you know my effect on women, but no."

For whatever reason, it sounded a touch defensive. Which of course engaged my latent urge to give him some shit—payback for the far more generous portions he typically ladled out to me.

"Okay," I said. "It was just the 'my gal' that was throwing me."

"Look, would you prefer 'my friend'? I'm happy to refer to her that way instead."

"Whatever you like. I mean, I'm your friend, right?"

"Generally yes, though at moments like this you give me cause to wonder."

"Well, you don't refer to me as your 'guy,' do you?"

"I can see where you're going with this, partner, and I can see where it ends up, too, with you reminding me for the umpteenth time about how I was all set to go off with Tiara the lady boy but for your untimely intervention. And that's fine, I'll own all of it if it makes you happy. But right now, I want us to get it in gear, because as capable as my friend is, with OGE in the mix it's even more clear to me than before that she needs our help. *Comprendez*?"

Coming from Dox, "*Comprendez*?" wasn't a question. It was your last warning. All at once, it was obvious: whatever was between him and this Seattle cop, it was serious. And because Dox being serious about a woman was new to me, I'd been slow to process it.

"You're right," I said. "I'm sorry."

"Ah, shit, forget it, I'm just tense. And it's not like I've never given you a hard time, either, and I certainly will again. But yeah, you contact Treven, I'll get in touch with our mutual acquaintance, and hopefully at that point, between the two of us, we'll have enough pieces to figure out how to shut this shit down like it ought to be. Larison's on board?"

I glanced at Larison. "Yeah. He's on board."

"Good. Sounds like we might be spending some time in dark alleys, and I don't mind the idea of the angel of death being there with us."

"So you guys have been in touch."

"Yeah, you know, from time to time. He's a better conversationalist than some people I might mention."

Well, it didn't take him long to deliver on his promise to give me a hard time again. But I let it go. "Horton's here, too."

"You trust that hombre? Larison sure doesn't."

"I think some of that's changed." I glanced at Horton. "But right now? Yeah. I trust him."

"Well, he's a capable sumbitch, I'll give him that, albeit a bit devious for my tastes. Or at least he was back in the day—I'll accept maybe that's changed if you say so. Plus he knows where a lot of the bodies are buried. And given what it seems we're up against, we're going to need all the intel we can get. Where are you, anyway?"

"Near DC. Between our CIA friend being close by, and OGE being headquartered in Virginia, and the attack that just went down here, I'm hoping you're heading this way."

"Negative on that. I'm not going to leave my friend alone while the head of the world's biggest mercenary army has her in his sights."

"Could she come out here? Sounds like she should get out of town and be on the move regardless."

"Yeah, I advised her on some of your basic best practices for fugitives. And she's already pretty damn tactical on her own. But . . . that's an interesting idea. Tell you what, I'll get in touch with our deskbound friend and see what he knows, and let's you and I revisit once I'm stateside. Hey, put old Larison back on for a minute, would you?"

I handed the phone back to Larison. He listened, then said, "Yeah. Yeah, don't worry, we'll leave it on. Talk to you soon. And watch your back."

He clicked off.

"What was that?" I said.

"He said he admires your paranoia, but he wants to be able to reach us and we should leave the satellite phone on."

I could see this was a battle I wasn't going to win. I briefed the two of them on what I'd just learned from Dox.

"Well," Horton said when I was done. "Now we know what was big enough to risk all the attention a helicopter rocket attack on my house is going to cause."

I nodded. "And why the initial hits they wanted me for were supposed to look natural. And worth a million dollars."

Larison laughed.

I looked at him. "What?"

"It's nothing. I mean, it's not really funny. It's just a good thing you didn't take that contract.

Not saying you couldn't have brought it off the way they wanted. I'm sure you would have. But that Seattle cop Dox is calling 'my gal' . . . well, let's just say I wouldn't want to be the one to punch her ticket. From what you've told us, I'd say whoever did it would have to kill Dox, too."

I didn't respond. I hadn't even thought of that, but now that Larison had pointed it out, the prospect actually made me feel mildly ill.

It's okay. It didn't happen. And it wasn't going to happen. You don't do women. Or children. And you're not going to. Ever.

Or at least . . . not ever again.

"Let's call Treven," I said, shaking it off.

"I've got a better idea," Horton said. "I know where he lives. Why don't we pay him a visit?"

CHAPTER EIGHTEEN
RAIN

Treven's place was in a town called White Sulphur Springs, West Virginia—on the other side of the national forest, about an hour's drive for us. And about ninety minutes from Roanoke, where OGE was headquartered. "It's a small town," Horton told us as we drove, "though notable for the presence of a resort called the Greenbrier, which itself is notable because it served during the Cold War as the secret location of Project Greek Island—the emergency bunker where Congress was supposed to be relocated in the event of a nuclear war with the Soviets."

"Who would want to save Congress?" Larison asked.

Horton chuckled. "Well, since it was Congress appropriating the money for the plan, there's your answer. Anyway, when he's not doing whatever he does for OGE, I know the quiet suits Ben. For a variety of reasons, he's feeling estranged from Washington."

I thought of my *minka* in Kamakura. Far enough from Tokyo to support the notion that I was done with the city. Close enough to suggest something else.

Showing up to Treven's place in person, as opposed to picking up the phone, had its advantages and disadvantages. On the one hand, in person wouldn't leave an electronic trail anyone could follow. It would also give us the best chance of assessing him, and maybe of persuading him.

On the other hand, if Horton were wrong about Treven's relative trustworthiness, things could become unpleasant. And though we judged the chances of physical surveillance low—OGE had been devoting a lot of resources to watching Horton and had just lost them—we might be wrong.

Treven lived in a white one-story clapboard house on the corner of a quiet street dotted with similarly nondescript homes. The only indications that the occupant might be security conscious were subtle: a surrounding chain-link fence; well-lit grounds; the absence of any shrubbery on the perimeter, denying concealment to anyone hoping to break in to the house or set up a close ambush. The curtains were drawn, but there was nothing out of the ordinary about that. Of course, there would be additional security layers, not all of them defensive, that wouldn't reveal themselves to a casual inspection.

We circled the block and didn't see anything that concerned us. The parked cars we passed were empty. The likely surveillance and ambush spots were clear. Still, there was no moon and few streetlights, and it was hard to be sure. I wished we'd brought along some of Horton's night-vision gear. In fairness, though, we'd left in a bit of a hurry.

In the end, we decided on a direct approach. Horton, leaving his M4 in the car, opened the gate, walked up a short flight of stairs to the front door, and rang the bell, keeping his hands in plain view. It was a safe bet Treven would see him, and the car waiting in the street, via a hidden camera. At which point Treven would have the advantage. The question was what he would want to do with it.

We waited. The windows were open; I was behind the wheel, the engine running; and we were parked at an angle to the door that would force Treven from behind cover if he wanted to shoot at us, if things got ugly. All sound tactics. But Larison was still tense, the Glock at the ready—a measure of his respect for Treven's skill, I thought, despite his earlier prediction about how it would have ended had Treven been one of the men in the woods.

Another moment passed. Then a light came on inside. The door opened—Treven. It was hard to tell at this distance and at night, but he didn't seem to have changed—the same blond, all-American football-hero type. In fact, he'd played college ball, Larison had once told me—linebacker at Stanford, where he'd been benched for unnecessary roughness as often as he'd taken the field, before dropping out of college entirely.

"Hands are empty," I said.

"Yeah? If he doesn't have a pistol in the back of his jeans, you can have my share of Hort's diamonds."

That wasn't a bet I was willing to take. Treven glanced at the car, then spoke for a minute with Horton. The two of them came down the stairs toward the car. Larison started to get out.

I put a hand on his shoulder. "Not with the Glock."

"Are you fucking serious?"

"What would you do if you saw you coming out of a car on a moonless night holding a gun?"

"I'd run the fuck away."

"Or you'd shoot first and run later."

"He's carrying. And I'm not getting out of this car with nothing to offer but a handshake."

I thought for a second. "Okay. You stay put. I'll get out."

"What are you now, some kind of diplomat?"

"Somebody's got to be, if we're not going to all just shoot each other."

He shook his head disgustedly. "Well, better you than me. Okay, go make some peace, if you can. I've got your back."

I stepped slowly out of the car, giving Treven

a little two-handed wave to let him see as well as possible in the dim light that I wasn't holding anything.

He regarded me, his hands on his hips. But the thumbs were forward, not hooked behind—faster access to a pistol in a waistband.

"Rain," he said. "Can't say I was expecting to see you."

I nodded. "Sorry for the surprise. How've you been?"

"No complaints." He glanced at the car. "Larison getting out?"

"He's got a pistol. Like you. I asked him to stay put because everyone's a little nervous, and I'm looking for a way to make sure this stays convivial. But I'm sure he'd like to say hello, if you're okay with that."

Larison looked out the window. "Treven, you dumb shit, if I were here to kill you, would I be sitting in a car in front of your fucking house?"

Diplomacy, I thought. *Larison style.*

Treven did a quick perimeter scan. "Probably not."

"Right. Are you going to try to kill me?"

"Probably not."

"Good. Then I'm going to get out."

Treven took a half step offline, positioning Horton in the potential line of fire. Larison slowly exited the vehicle. He closed the door, which I know must have been hard for him, because the door would have provided some cover, and then eased the Glock into the back of his pants, which I imagined must have been harder still. Then he walked forward and held out his hand. "It's actually good seeing you, you prick."

Treven smiled. "Yeah, I was thinking the same about you."

They shook, and a little of the tension went out of the air.

"I was briefing Ben about the little problem we just had," Horton said. "Obviously, there's more to discuss."

Treven gestured to his house. "You're welcome to come in. I don't get a lot of visitors, but there's some beer in the fridge."

"I would enjoy that," Horton said. "And under any other circumstances, I'd gladly accept your hospitality. But right now, I don't think you want to be seen with us. Which is why we decided not to call and leave any kind of electronic trail. Maybe we could just go for a ride."

"Rain and Hort can sit in front," Larison said, anticipating the objection. "You and I can stare at each other suspiciously in back."

Treven didn't respond.

Horton said, "Son? I truly do not believe you had anything to do with what happened a short while ago at my house. And I have no desire to put you in an uncomfortable position. But the fact is, your employer seems intent on making me dead.

If you have any notions on how I might prevent that, I'd be grateful if you could share them."

Treven's eyes shifted from Horton to Larison and then to me. After a moment, he nodded. We got in the car, Treven and Larison waiting until Horton and I were seated and easing in simultaneously just after.

"There's a little Baptist church a few minutes outside of town," Treven said. "Set off the road, parking lot in back, no cameras. It'll be empty. We can talk there."

I followed his directions, and five minutes later we were sitting at a picnic table behind the church in question, the night quiet but for the crickets in the surrounding woods, the only illumination a single light casting long shadows from the back entrance of the church fifty feet away. The night air was moist and had grown cool enough to turn our breath to vapor.

We took turns finishing briefing Treven on what had happened, and on our theories about why. Something about his body language, along with the fact that he offered no questions, gave me the sense that even if he had nothing to do with the attack at Horton's house, he wasn't inclined to help us.

The briefing was followed by a tense silence, and for a long moment the only sound was of the crickets around us. Treven said, "All right. What does any of this have to do with me?"

Yeah, I thought. *I hate to be right.*

Horton looked at him. "You reached out to me. Asked me to do you a solid—put your boss in touch with Rain here."

Treven shook his head. "Not a solid. You owed me."

"Call it what you want," Horton said. "I did what you asked. And earlier this evening, it got my house rocketed and nearly got me and these two men killed."

"Again," Treven said, "what does any of that have to do with me?"

Larison was looking at Treven intently. *Do not go for that gun,* I thought. *Do not.*

But there was no way I could stop him if he did.

"Maybe it has nothing to do with you," I said, wanting to get some words out to puncture the ominous silence. "At least not directly. But what are the stakes here? What's really going on? Not king and country. Not geopolitics or national security or anything like that. It's about a child-pornography ring at the Secret Service. And covering that up."

Treven shrugged. "You don't know that. It's speculation."

"If you have a more compelling theory," I said, "I'd like to hear it."

He shook his head. "I might, if this had anything to do with me."

"What about the plane?" Larison said.

Treven looked at him. "First of all, the word is, that was ISIS."

Larison shook his head disgustedly. "Come on, even you're not stupid enough to believe that line of bullshit."

Treven laughed. "You think it's stupid to believe ISIS wants to blow up US planes?"

Larison frowned. "I think it's stupid to have unquestioning faith in evidence-free governmental claims. Especially when politicians make hay out of them. Have you been listening to that candidate for Bullshitter in Chief, Senator Barkley? He's humping the ISIS angle to death, and he's up five points in the polls as a result."

"Just because a politician is benefiting," Treven said, "doesn't mean—"

Larison cut him off. "Oh, for Christ's sake, Treven, you've dealt with these people. You *know* they do false-flags—you were on the wrong end of one, just like I was. But now all of a sudden they say something and you automatically believe it's true? Why? No, I mean it, you know better, so why? Who are you trying to protect?"

Even in the dim light, I could see Treven's face darken. "Myself," he said. "Don't act like that's an alien concept for you. And don't pretend you've ever been motivated by anything else yourself."

Larison shook his head in disgust again. "Jesus,

187

when did you turn into such a fucking ostrich?"

Treven leaned toward Larison. "Same time you turned into such a Boy Scout. And you call *me* a dumb shit. That's fucking hilarious."

Larison's eyes narrowed. I thought of how Dox had miraculously defused the tension the last time we'd all worked together, with a crazy Cleavon Little impersonation. But I didn't have anything like his over-the-top sense of humor.

"I don't know about either of you," I said, this time not trying to puncture a silence but instead to interrupt a pattern, "but speaking just for myself, yeah, saving that school . . . that meant something to me. Treven. Tell me you don't ever feel bothered by the cost of it. Or wish there were some way you could atone."

Treven scanned the woods. "Maybe I do, but at least I don't whine about it."

I shook my head, tamping down my urge to hit back. "You sure do make it hard for anyone to help you."

He laughed. "Oh, that's what this is about?"

"No," I said. "That's incidental. But also unavoidable. Because if you're in denial about working for an outfit that blows up civilian planes to protect child predators, it's going to eat at you."

"Let me explain something to you," Treven said. "I like my gig with OGE. I like the work, I like the benefits, I like what the future holds.

And no offense, but I'm not going to jeopardize all that because a couple of burnouts I happened to work with a long time ago think it would be good for my soul."

He looked at Horton. "Hort, you owed me. A lot. And all I asked in repayment was that you make a couple of phone calls. Which you did. So great, we're square. Whatever might have gone wrong in your transaction wasn't my doing and isn't my problem. So thanks for the visit, but I'm getting cold."

Larison was watching Treven. The irritation was gone from Larison's expression, replaced by an odd flatness. I could imagine his calculus: *If you're not with us, you're against us.* And I could imagine the destination to which that logic must have already led him.

As formidable as he was, that was Larison's one weakness: you could read the danger he radiated. If I had decided to kill Treven, there would have been no changes in affect. I would have kept trying to cajole him right up until it was done. But when Larison made a decision, if he wasn't ghosting up on you from your flanks, you'd have a chance to know his intent before he acted on it. For most people that wouldn't be enough to make a difference. For Treven, though, it might.

Which meant things at our church meeting were on the verge of getting ugly.

Horton must have recognized it, too. He said,

"John's right, son. And with due respect to Daniel, you're not dumb. But you are the youngest in this group. It makes me sad to see you intent on repeating the mistakes of people like me, who really were dumb and now know better."

He stood and added, "I know you want to believe this thing doesn't have anything to do with you. A few hours ago, I was telling myself the same. Then a helicopter turned up and rocketed my house to ruins. So if whatever this thing is turns around and bites you on the ass, like it seems to do for anyone who touches it? I'll still have your back. Even if tonight, you didn't have mine."

The rest of us stood—slowly and with hands out front, I was relieved to see, everyone apparently still intent on good, reassuring manners, despite all the harsh exchanges.

Horton, Larison, and I started moving toward the car. "You coming?" I said to Treven.

"I'll walk back," Treven said. "Fewer chances of us being spotted together."

It was a reasonable concern. But I thought it was secondary to what he must have made of that flat expression I'd seen on Larison's face.

The three of us spread out as we headed to the car. We had to move a little oddly, not wanting to turn our backs on Treven.

We got in, Treven eyeing us closely the whole way, just as we were eyeing him.

"Hey," he called out as I started the engine.

I looked at him.

"If any of you shows up in my life again, I'm going to assume it's not for another talk. Because we have nothing more to talk about."

Larison started to say something, probably not something diplomatic. But Horton got there first. "Remember what I said, son. If you need me, don't be too proud to reach out."

CHAPTER NINETEEN
LIVIA

The morning after the attack, Livia and Lieutenant Strangeland headed from Strangeland's place to meet Charmaine Best, the chief of police.

Livia was nervous. She'd barely slept, which wasn't a huge surprise. But it wasn't just the aftermath of the attack. Staying with the lieutenant, which would have been weird under any circumstances, was dialed all the way to surreal given that the reason behind it was the possibility of another attempt if Livia tried to go home.

She'd met Strangeland's partner—Mia, a trauma surgeon with the University of Washington medical system. It was interesting to get a glimpse of Strangeland's personal life, and Mia had been welcoming enough, but the woman was on her way to work when Strangeland and Livia had arrived, and the meeting had been rushed and awkward. Their house was nice—a single-family place in Crown Hill, lots of books and LP records and a homey vibe Livia wouldn't have associated with the lieutenant. Of course, how much did she know about Strangeland really? Maybe as little as the lieutenant knew about her.

So she'd lain on the guest-room bed for a few hours, the attack playing over and over in her mind, trying to beat back her fears about what would happen if the investigation went wrong, or what might be discovered about her even if it went right, and who the hell could be after her, and if they actually blew up an airplane as part of a cover-up, and what she was going to do, and on and on and on. Until she'd finally broken down and done what she'd realized earlier she should do, which was to ask Carl for help. And it was the strangest thing—as soon as they were done talking, she felt so much better, and immediately fell asleep.

And twenty minutes later, Strangeland had knocked, because they had an appointment to see the chief and needed to get moving.

Livia had never met the chief, but of course she knew of her—SPD's first black police chief, a twenty-six-year veteran of the force, respected by the rank and file. A reputation for standing up for her officers, even with the scrutiny of the DOJ settlement monitoring and in the face of media distortions and second-guessing. Which was somewhat comforting under the circumstances. Still, all that was just reputation. There were no guarantees.

She'd asked Strangeland what to expect. And Strangeland was uncharacteristically enigmatic. "You'll like her," she said. "But don't let her lull you. Remember that old saying, *Don't trust anyone over thirty?*"

Livia nodded.

"Well," Strangeland went on, "let's just say the brass is all over thirty."

Best immediately rose from behind her desk when her assistant ushered in Livia and Strangeland. Livia was impressed by that—none of the *I don't have to get up for you* power games rampant within most bureaucracies. In fact, Best came over and gave Strangeland a hug, saying, "Donna, good to see you, thanks for coming," as though this meeting might have happened somewhere other than in the chief's own office.

Then she turned and extended her hand to Livia. "Detective Lone, it's an honor to meet you. I've heard nothing but outstanding things."

"Thank you, Chief Best," Livia said, feeling out of her element in the midst of all the wall photographs of Best shoulder to shoulder with the mayor, the governor, and various other VIPs, and the views of the city and Elliott Bay beyond.

"Please, call me Charmaine." She gestured to a couch and chairs in the corner of the room. "Why don't we sit over here? And can I get you anything? Coffee?"

Strangeland, who as far as Livia knew had never refused a coffee in her life, said, "Coffee would be great, Chief. Appreciate it."

"Just a water for me," Livia said, thinking it

was better to accept some form of hospitality, but feeling wired enough as it was. "Thanks."

Best called out, "Lloyd, could you bring us a pot of coffee and a pitcher of water? Thank you." Then she turned to Livia. "How are you feeling?"

The woman's concern and compassion were reminiscent of Strangeland's. The difference was, Livia knew that with Strangeland, it was genuine. With the chief, who had to be some kind of politician to get where she was, anything was possible.

"I'm okay. Thanks."

"No, Livia. How are you feeling?"

The woman really knew how to project empathy. She must have been a great interrogator. Which, at the moment, wasn't exactly a comfort.

"I'm still . . . processing," Livia said.

Best nodded. "Of course you are. That's going to take a while. You know, I had my own officer-involved almost twenty years ago. Clean shoot, returning fire after one of those 'routine' traffic stops. A man named Elbert Tidbury, who it turned out had an outstanding warrant. But still, it was a real nail biter before I was cleared. And that was all long before the DOJ settlement. But Detective Phelps is one of the best: methodical, dispassionate, and smart as hell. Exactly the kind of cop you want to clear the case—and clear the air."

Livia nodded. If the chief had heard anything

preliminary from Phelps, she was keeping her cards close.

Lloyd brought in a tray with the beverages, set it down, and left, closing the door behind him. Best gestured to the couch. "Please."

They sat. Best poured coffee for Strangeland. She didn't ask about cream or sugar—obviously, she knew the lieutenant well. Which only increased Livia's discomfort about the unfamiliar terrain. The brass knew each other, had a history together, while Livia was bumping up against all that for the first time. And while Best's hominess didn't seem like an act, exactly, there had to be some level of calculation behind it. In a social setting, putting people at ease was gracious. When you did it in an interrogation room, it was intended to encourage the suspect to open up.

"Now," Best said, filling the two water glasses, "tell me more about what happened with the Child's Play operation. And what Agent Smith said to you before getting on that doomed flight."

Livia filled her in. When she was done, Best was silent.

Strangeland said, "Something's rotten here, Charmaine."

Best nodded. "I agree."

Strangeland set down her coffee. "I mean, the Bureau shutting down a joint op—conducted right here in Seattle, with an SPD officer attached—without a word to you first? And that would be bullshit enough. But two shooters coming at Livia and that plane going down a few hours later? Something is way fucking wrong about this, if you'll pardon my language."

"Agreed again."

"Good. Thank you. Now, what are we going to do about it?"

Livia glanced at Strangeland. The lieutenant was pushing it a little hard, and maybe, in her concern for Livia, forgetting that she was talking to the chief, not to one of her officers.

But Best seemed not to be put off by it. "I already have a call in to J. J. Arrington, the head of the Bureau's Criminal Investigative Division. As head of the VCAC, Agent Smith reported to him."

Strangeland nodded. "What about the head of the VCAC International Task Force? They would have been working with Smith to liaise with overseas counterparts. The Child's Play operation involved multiple foreign jurisdictions. Smith wasn't the only VCAC person who might shed some light."

Best pursed her lips in the first sign of what Livia thought might be irritation. "I understand how you feel. But the way to get cooperation from the Bureau isn't to go around the person in charge. Which is why I've started with Arrington."

"Okay, good, but in the meantime, Livia's in danger."

Best nodded. "And that's why I'm going to have two SWAT officers assigned for close protection twenty-four-seven until we've ascertained who, if anyone, the attackers were affiliated with."

For an instant, Livia thought she saw something ripple across Strangeland's expression—discomfort? Suspicion?—and then it was gone. But maybe it was just Livia's own projection, because although she was relieved to hear Best describe the two as "attackers," the thought of being shadowed by SWAT officers . . . she hated it. She didn't want to be watched. She didn't want to be seen.

Strangeland glanced at Livia as though reading her mind. "Don't even think about trying to say no to that, Livia."

Best raised her eyebrows. "Is that even a possibility?"

Strangeland shook her head. "No. It's not. Detective Lone sometimes has a hard time accepting help from people who care about her. But we've been making progress on that."

Livia said nothing, knowing it wasn't a battle she could win. And that fighting it would have looked strange. What cop in her position wouldn't want some kind of protection, at least until more was known?

But she had a feeling the real route to solving this thing, whatever it was, went through Little, and Carl and the friend he'd mentioned, and

Kanezaki, and whatever contacts they had. Having a couple of SWAT guys on her back wasn't going to make those channels any easier.

"What else can I do?" Best asked, and Livia had to admit, the woman's reputation for standing by her officers seemed well deserved.

"I've been thinking about that," Strangeland said. "And what we can infer about why Livia was attacked. It seems the most likely explanation is that someone is intent on preventing a front-page scandal about a child-pornography ring operating out of the Secret Service. I think the right way to defuse that motive is to make a very public stink."

Best's expression was neutral. "I don't follow."

"Well, I think maybe you, or even the mayor, could give a press conference, announcing what Livia was working on and what she uncovered, and that the two Bureau employees she was liaising with were on that plane. And that we believe it's all connected. We'd make it harder for them to move against Livia again. Because if anything happened to her, it would be proof of the allegations. It would bring a ton of heat. They'd see they'd missed their opportunity, and back off."

Best nodded for a long moment as though considering the idea, but Livia sensed that what she was really considering was how to phrase her refusal.

"It's an interesting idea," she said after a

moment. "But can you imagine the reaction if we were to publicly accuse the Secret Service—the Department of Homeland Security, for God's sake—not just of trying to murder a Seattle cop, but of blowing up a US airplane, all to conceal a child-pornography ring that we suspect but are nowhere near being able to prove the Secret Service might somehow be involved with?"

"Of course I can imagine," Strangeland said. "But—"

"And that's just the guaranteed cost. Let's set that aside for a moment and consider the potential benefit. We have no way of knowing that publicity would make these people back off. Even if this isn't all a coincidence—and we don't know that—upping the stakes might make them want to silence Livia even more. Maybe right now, they're thinking that with the contract hacker gone—who, from what you've explained to me, was ideally positioned to connect Child's Play with the Secret Service in the first place—and no one asking too many questions, maybe it's not worth another attack on Livia."

Strangeland nodded her head quickly. "Yeah, but they don't know—"

"This is exactly my point. They don't know how much the contractor told Livia. How much of a threat she is. If she becomes a focal point for scrutiny, they might reassess. And we would have caused that."

Livia didn't necessarily agree. But anything that kept her out of the news was fine with her.

Strangeland said nothing. Livia sensed she knew she'd lost and was struggling with the urge to go on fighting regardless.

Best reached out and touched Strangeland's hand. "Donna. I have the utmost gratitude and respect for your devotion to your officers. For your desire to find some way to protect your detective. But a press conference isn't the way to do it. And neither would an anonymous call to a sympathetic reporter, most of whom, believe me, I know personally. No news organization anywhere would run a story as thinly sourced as what we have, and no one would pay any attention even if they did."

That was a not-so-subtle warning: *If you're thinking about trying to end-run me on this? Don't. I'll know it was you.*

Strangeland nodded. Livia saw that her coffee was only half-finished. It was about as glaring a sign as Livia could reasonably imagine of the depth of her distress over the situation.

"I know it's not what you wanted," Best continued. "But Detective Phelps's investigation, my inquiries with the Bureau—which I will escalate if necessary—and, most of all, SWAT protection, are, in my opinion, the right way to proceed."

Livia knew it was over. And in case Strangeland

didn't, she quickly said, "Thank you, Chief. Charmaine. I really appreciate all you're doing."

Best stood and Livia followed suit. Livia felt the hug coming, and forced herself not to recoil. There were other huggers on the force, and as uncomfortable as the contact made her, she had some practice concealing it.

But maybe Best had some notion, because the hug was notably brief. Strangeland stood and received one in return. Somehow it seemed devoid of the warmth that characterized the one Best had delivered at the outset.

Best walked them to the door of the outer office. But like the hugs, the homey courtesy felt different to Livia now. Less natural. More performative.

"If there's anything else you need, Donna," she said as they reached the doorway, "I want you to let me know. Livia, that goes for you, too. Whether it's through your lieutenant or directly. You know how to reach me."

They both thanked her and headed to the elevator. Once they were alone, Livia said, "Thanks, LT. You tried."

Strangeland shook her head. "I don't like this."

"She had a point," Livia said. "The chief, the mayor . . . they're all politicians. They're not going to publicly accuse the Secret Service of covering up a child-pornography ring. Not without a lot more proof than we have."

They got on the elevator. Strangeland pressed the "Close" button but didn't choose a floor. She obviously wanted them to have a moment alone.

The doors closed. It was just the two of them.

Strangeland looked at her. "What are the chances of you being able to get that proof?"

Livia wasn't sure where she was going with that. "You mean . . . Little?"

"Yeah, Little. Have you heard anything?"

"Not yet."

"Ah. I wondered if he was the one you were talking to this morning. In the guest room."

Shit. That had been Carl. Had the lieutenant overheard? Livia had noted that the house doors were all hollow-core, and she had been careful to keep her voice down.

"I couldn't hear what you were saying," Strangeland went on. "And I wasn't eavesdropping. The walls of our house are so thin Mia and I use headphones if one of us is watching TV in the living room and the other is trying to sleep. But I heard you talking, and there was something about the tone. Was it someone who could help? I'm not asking you more than that."

Livia hesitated, then said, "I think it's someone who could help, yes. He's at least going to try."

"Good. Now tell me how *I* can help."

Livia wasn't sure what she meant. "You already have."

"I didn't like the way that went down with the chief. Yeah, her reasons for keeping this quiet were defensible. But put it all together, and what it really adds up to is her protecting her own ass. Going through Bureau channels. Publicizing nothing, not even through an anonymous leak—which she could easily do, given her contacts. And those SWAT guys could be minders as much as bodyguards. If you need room to maneuver, are you going to have it with those guys watching you all the time?"

"I thought you wanted them to. You just said—"

"I said what needed to be said to make the chief feel like she'd won. If I'd backed down too easily, it would have made her suspicious. So no, I don't want you being shadowed by a couple of informers who report to the chief. What I want is for you to be safe. If you need to disappear for a while—like you did in Bangkok last year—to make that happen, then I want you to do it. You're on administrative leave. Phelps looks set to wrap up his investigation quickly, but if need be I could get him to slow-walk it. Buy you a little time."

Livia shook her head, feeling completely bewildered. Bangkok? How much did the lieutenant know? Or suspect?

"LT . . . I'm not sure what you're telling me."

Strangeland pressed the button for their floor, and the elevator started moving. "Jesus, Livia, are you really going to make me spell this out? I don't think you're safe here. I think there's a target on your back, and a couple of SWAT guys might make it harder to get to you but they're not going to stop it, either. At least not forever. I think you should get out of town. I'd say lay low, but that's not your style, and it's not going to solve the problem. What I want, what I think you need, is for you to work this case. And blow it wide fucking open."

CHAPTER TWENTY
BEN

Ben waited until the car's taillights were no longer visible, then cut through the woods, parallel to the road. He didn't think Hort or Rain would back out on him, but that fucking Larison was capable of anything.

A quarter mile along, he cut across the silent street and into the woods on the other side. It was hard not to imagine Larison making his case to Hort and Rain, persuading them. Larison gets out of the car, hunkers down in the drainage ditch along the road . . .

He moved easily through the tree branches, deeper into the woods, going slowly and stopping frequently to look and listen. Jungle warfare was mostly training for him; his actual experience was almost entirely urban. But the training was no-shit, and the darkness of the night forest was a comfort.

What if they have night-vision?

And suddenly his comfort was gone.

They don't have night-vision. From what they told you, they left Hort's in a hurry, in Rain and Larison's rented car. They didn't have time to gear up, and they weren't planning to kill you. You're fine.

Yeah. He was fine. It was just Larison. That guy always put him on edge.

After close to two hours, he reached an overlook at the edge of town, from which he could make out his house. He sat with his back to an embankment and watched. It was probably unnecessary, but he wanted the opportunity to assess a little further just in case they had decided to hit him not along the road, but where they knew he was heading.

The demands of moving tactically now behind him, he realized how pissed he was that these jokers actually thought he was going to help them. And how much of a problem they had potentially created just by asking him.

The truth was, he hated the gig with OGE. But following the "misunderstanding" about those false-flag attacks across the country a few years earlier, what was he going to do? Yeah, it had all been cleared up after the fact, so at least no one was still trying to kill him or put him in prison over it, but the initial stink and uncertainty had lingered enough so that he was no longer exactly top-secret-clearance material. He was done with the military's Intelligence Support Activity, or rather, they were done with him. It grieved him— literally, grieved him—but he had to accept it. He wasn't elite anymore, wasn't an insider, and that was never going to change.

But what were his alternatives? His personal

life was shit. An ex-wife who wanted nothing to do with him—who'd actually told their daughter that the new man in their house was Ami's father. A brother, Alex, and okay, they didn't hate each other anymore, but it wasn't like they had anything in common, either, and the few times they'd tried to be in touch since Ben had helped him out, it had just been awkward. Their parents were long gone, and their sister, Katie, who had held it all together, had been gone even longer.

All he'd ever been good at was running and gunning. And if he couldn't do it with ISA, then he might as well do it with one of the private-sector operations. Of which OGE was the best.

At least OGE valued him. They had employees from CIA, Delta, DEVGRU . . . but he was the only former ISA, so even within some pretty specialized company, he still had a certain degree of swagger. Though he wondered if the others suspected he was tainted. He told people he'd left for the private sector's better per diem, but who would ever leave ISA just for a few dollars more? Not him, that was for sure.

And then Graham had asked him what he knew about this guy John Rain, who the scuttlebutt said had worked with Ben countering those false-flag operations. *Is this "natural causes" stuff real? Graham had asked. Or is all that just legend?*

Ben had acknowledged they'd worked together. And that, yeah, the natural-causes stuff was legit. Graham was pleased. He told Ben he had something important for Rain, and it would mean a lot if Ben could put them in touch. *This is the kind of thing the future of this company is all about,* Graham had said. *And I want you to be part of that future.*

But hell, now that he was thinking about it, Graham's assurances about Ben's place in the future of the company felt a little slick. Maybe he'd been a sucker for that line of bullshit because he so badly wanted to believe it. Because damn it, what other kind of future did he have?

So what was he supposed to do now? Tell Graham these idiots had paid him a visit? Tell him about their accusations? If he didn't, and Graham found out anyway, Ben would look disloyal.

But if the accusations were true, could acknowledging that Ben knew anything put him at some kind of risk?

It was hard to know what to make of it. There were a hundred reasons Graham or whoever might have made a run at Hort and Larison and Rain. It didn't have to involve downed planes and child-porn rings.

He thought again about Graham's *You're the future of this company* line. If Ben had believed that because he'd wanted to, could he be running the same kind of deception op on himself about the plane and the rest?

What if you are? Like you said earlier, what does any of this have to do with you?

He decided he should just come clean with Graham. Tell him everything, and not take any chances about getting caught concealing something later. *Yeah, they showed up at my house. They told me blah, blah, blah. I listened politely and then told them to fuck off.*

It was the safer way to play it. The smart way.

So why was it making him feel so crappy?

CHAPTER TWENTY-ONE
DOX

Dox cleared customs at Sea-Tac with nothing more than a backpack and a disarming smile. Just twenty-four hours earlier, he'd gotten the call from Labee. Immediately following which he'd gone online, booked a flight he knew he might not make, jammed some gear in the pack, jumped on the Rebel, and hauled ass out to Denpasar with his hair on fire. He'd been so on autopilot he barely even remembered what he'd thrown in the damn bag. Well, skivvies, naturally, that's right. A pair of jeans, and some tee shirts. A fleece, thank God, because living in Bali, it was a little hard to imagine how chilly it could get in Seattle. And of course the essential don't-leave-home-without-it items—in this case, his trusty Emerson Commander folder and the nasty little Fred Perrin La Griffe he wore on a lanyard as backup. As soon as he was done with the ICE people and out in the arrivals area, he ducked into a restroom stall, where he clipped the Commander to the front pocket of his cargo pants and hung the La Griffe around his neck. It would have been nice to have a proper firearm on his person, too, but that was way too much time,

211

paperwork, and scrutiny for international travel, so for the moment a couple of sharp pointy things would have to do.

Luckily, they wouldn't have to do for long. After talking to John and Larison from Narita, he'd reached Kanezaki and gotten right to it. "Tom," he'd said, short for Kanezaki's *nisei* given name of Tomohisa, "forgive my uncharacteristic lack of small talk, but I don't have a lot of time. I'll be arriving in Seattle in about sixteen hours, and I need a package waiting for me. Ideally a scoped Rangemaster .308 or SR-25, but you know me, I can be flexible. The main thing is, I'd prefer magazine-fed to bolt-action, and don't need anything particularly heavy caliber because this is all just antipersonnel and I don't expect to be operating at significant range."

There was a pause. Kanezaki said, "Is that all?"

"Amigo, you know I respect your inveterate urge to act like something's a bigger deal than it really is so as to extract greater concessions in return. It's even something I've learned from. But I'm telling you, now is not the time. This is a personal matter, and I'm asking you as a friend to help me out without the usual negotiating bullshit. Now, can you get me what I need?"

Another pause. "I hear you. And I'm telling you straight up that I can't move that kind of hardware that fast. Not domestically, anyway, and certainly not in sixteen hours. Is there some other way I can help?"

Dox smiled. He'd meant it when he said he'd learned from Kanezaki's negotiating style, and one of the things he'd picked up on over the years was that if you started with a huge request, you were much more likely to wind up with whatever it was you were really hoping for. Not that Dox would have objected to a proper rifle—in his experience, gunfights were always more pleasant conducted from far away—but the way he was picturing things, he thought something smaller would probably do nicely.

"All right," he said. "Thanks for your candor, and I'm sorry for putting you on the spot. I suppose I could make do with a pistol."

"Look, even a pistol—"

"Ah, that's what I'm talking about, you're doing it, but I don't blame you, I know it's just a reflex, an unconscious habit I'm here to help you overcome."

"It's not a habit, I'm telling you the—"

"Tom, just stop. Stop now and listen to me. I told you, I'm asking you as a friend. That's not something I do lightly, and I wouldn't expect you to do it lightly, either. Because if you ever need something from me as a friend, I promise, you will never have a better one. And whoever you're having a problem with will never have a worse enemy. Now, I've told you I'm in a jam and you

213

said you can't get me a rifle and I said fine, all I need is a pistol. But if you tell me you can't do that, and give me some line of bullshit about oh you want to help and maybe you can get me a slingshot or a spitball straw or whatever, you might as well just tell me I was wrong in thinking we were friends. *Comprendez*?"

Another pause. Kanezaki said, "Same model as last time okay?"

Last time was a Wilson Combat Tactical Supergrade, Dox's preferred carry. "Same as last time would be more than fine. Plus extra mags and ammo and a bellyband holster. Thank you, Tom. I don't have time to discuss terms right now, so for now let's just say I owe you."

"You don't owe me. We're friends."

Dox laughed, a little surprised by that. "Well, now I feel like shit."

"Don't. I never know what's going on until I've pushed a little. If you really need this, it's done. But I was serious about the rifle. I just can't, not in such a short time frame."

"Don't worry about it. I believe you."

"Is there anything else I can do to help?"

"I hope so. I'll tell you what I know about the situation, which, given your lust for knowledge about the skulduggery of your colleagues in the so-called intelligence community, ought to have its own value to you. But if you have any insights, yeah, it could be a big help to me."

Unfortunately, Kanezaki had been uncharacteristically bereft of insights. He knew the players—everyone knew Graham and OGE, and in fact it would have been a surprise if Kanezaki himself didn't resort to their services from time to time—but the Secret Service angle was a black box. Still, when Dox told him about what might really have happened to that airplane, he'd been aghast, and Dox knew from experience that the reaction was genuine. He'd told Dox he'd find out what he could. And that was a lot, because when old Kanezaki put his nose to the dirt, more often than not he would uncover a tasty truffle.

Dox strolled through the terminal until he found a payphone. Still available in most of your major airports, but definitely an endangered species in the age of cellphones everywhere. Well, smoke 'em if you got 'em, as the saying went. He and Labee would come up with something more secure once they'd had a chance to talk in person.

The thought gave his heart a little giddyup.

Hey, you're out here for the right reasons, aren't you?

He paused for a moment, looking around the terminal. All the normal people with their normal problems, hurrying along with their bags to who knew what or where.

Why *was* he here?

He knew he wanted to see her. Under any circumstances, he knew that.

But even more, he wanted to protect her. Wanted to kill whoever was after her. Wanted her to be safe. Hell, more than safe. As happy and fulfilled and at peace as she could be.

And if he could help with that, then even if he never saw her again, he'd be okay with it.

He smiled, knowing it was all true. But he did still just want to see her. The truth of one didn't nullify the truth of the other.

He fished some quarters from a pocket and put through the call. Two rings, then: "Hello?"

"Labee, darlin'. I do believe I'll never tire of hearing your lovely voice."

"Carl?"

"Who else?"

"Are you . . . this is a 206 area code."

"Well, I told you I was coming out."

"I know, but—"

"And I was afraid if we talked about it again, you'd just try to shoo me away."

"Yeah, I might have." But he sensed she was smiling.

"Which is exactly why I came pronto. Have you been living like a fugitive, like we discussed?"

"Yes."

"Good. But I happen to know that's more difficult and tiring than the average person realizes—even more than the average badass cop realizes. So I was thinking I could help out."

"Did you talk to your friend?"

"I did. He thinks you should get out of town. I agree."

There was a pause, and he thought she was going to protest. But she said, "So do I."

"You do? Well, that's great."

"You sound surprised."

"Why would I be surprised? It's not like you've ever pushed back when I've suggested something."

She laughed. Only a little, but with Labee a little was always a lot. "The timing sucks, because I've got a big case. Not Child's Play, something else. And I just hate . . . I hate to drop it. But even my lieutenant thinks I should go. And I'm on administrative leave, so I guess I can."

"I'm at the airport now. Why don't you come meet me and we'll git?" He wasn't looking forward to the conversation with Kanezaki: *Sorry I didn't show in Seattle for the gun you worked so hard to get me, can you deliver it to the East Coast instead?* But he'd deal with that later.

"I need to go home first. Get a few things."

"Negative, home is the last place you should be going."

"I know, but there are some things I'm not going to feel comfortable traveling without."

He imagined she was talking about weapons. He was about to argue and tell her they'd take care of all that on the road. But it wouldn't be a bad idea for her to have a passport. And besides . . .

"I'll tell you what," he said. "Why don't I just reconnoiter first? If the coast's clear, you show up, grab your gear, and off we go."

"And if it's not?"

"Then I make it clear. And you show up, grab your gear, and off we go."

"Who would you even be looking for?"

"Someone a lot like me, actually, though not as handsome and probably not as competent, either. The main thing is, they don't know me, and they'll be looking for you. That's an easy thing to spot, even for an antediluvian knuckle dragger such as myself."

"I figured out a while ago that you're not half as antediluvian as you like people to think."

He loved that she knew the word. Mostly he liked the dictionary lingo just to mess with people. Tell them their office was noisome, then laugh when they turned down the music or whatever. He'd yet to come up with one that could stump John, but he wasn't going to give up, either.

Smiling, he said, "Ah, that's just because you're a cop. Your average person would never know. But hey, at least you get that I'm a knuckle dragger, antediluvian or not."

She was quiet then and he knew she was weighing his proposal about scouting out her house. The idea was solid, so her hesitation must have been just the result of her innate stubbornness and general unwillingness to accept help, no matter how sensible or well intended.

So he was pleasantly surprised when she simply said, "Okay. You reconnoiter first."

Knowing she wouldn't have accepted the help from just about anyone else made him feel a rush of gratitude and tenderness. He pushed the feeling aside. He needed to focus.

"Good," he said. "How far is your place from the airport?"

"Maybe a half hour."

"In Seattle?"

"Yes. Georgetown. South of downtown, north of the airport."

"All right, then. You give me the address and a thorough description of the overall terrain. I need to pick up a present K. got me, and then I'll head over straightaway and call you as soon as I'm sure everything is copacetic. You just stay close—but not too close—and be ready to get in and out for your gear when I say so."

CHAPTER TWENTY-TWO
BEN

"Ben," Oliver Graham called out as he rounded the big office desk in a starched shirt and cowboy boots. "Come on in. And Curtis, you mind bringing us a fresh pot of coffee? Not even nine and I've finished the first one."

"Yes, sir," Curtis said, the crisp response conditioned, or at any rate comfortable, for a guy Ben knew was a former Marine.

Ben walked into the office. It was done up like some kind of drawing room—plush carpet, overstuffed leather chairs, mahogany everywhere, and a view through one of the giant picture windows of the green ridges of Catawba Mountain to the north. There were a lot of expensive antiques, mostly of Civil War vintage, including a beautifully maintained Thomas Griswold Confederate cavalry officer's saber, and an 1860 Henry lever-action rifle. The only suggestion that the place was corporate and not a club was the ego wall visitors had to pass on the way to the sitting area, where they couldn't fail to miss the dozens of framed photos of Graham shoulder to shoulder with grateful-looking princes and potentates.

In fact, it wasn't just Graham's office that had the private-men's-club touch—it was the whole facility. The place was previously a horse farm, and Graham had done nothing to change the vibe since buying it and turning it into OGE's headquarters. It even still had horses in the stables, one of which, a black Arabian stallion called Charon, Graham rode several mornings a week as part of an eclectic workout routine. The man had grown up riding in Texas and had kept the habit, along with the boots. Those concessions aside, though, everything about him and his surroundings was eastern gentry on steroids. None of it was to Ben's taste—in fact, he didn't feel like he had any particular taste—but he supposed that if you were from out of town and wanted to ingratiate yourself, you had to do as the Romans do, and maybe even better.

"Come on now," Graham said, clapping Ben on the shoulder. "*Mi casa tu casa.* What's on your mind? That was a cryptic call this morning."

"I didn't want to say too much over the phone."

"I figured as much. Well, this is as good a place as any for a private conversation. Swept twice a day for bugs by three different teams. What happens at OGE stays at OGE. Other than the good outcomes we leave behind us, anyway. Come on, let's sit."

By the time they reached the sitting area, Curtis had overtaken them. He placed a carafe on the coffee table, turned smartly, and headed out. Cups, saucers, and cream and sugar were already waiting.

Graham took the chair facing the room, so Ben settled onto the couch with the stunning views. The sun was over the peaks now, and in the mist from the recent rains, the Blue Ridge Mountains were justifying their name.

"Help yourself," Graham said. "I'll try to hold off for a few minutes. It feels a little early yet to start on my second pot."

Ben poured himself a cup and took a sip. Yeah, Graham was only a little older than Ben, but he'd already made a fortune. And yeah, back in the day he'd been a SEAL, which was something, but his only combat deployments—Haiti and the Balkans—weren't all that. Besides, Graham had left after only three years, when his father died and Graham took over the old man's machine-tool company, using his military contacts and some good timing to morph it into what became OGE. But still, Graham was the boss, and Ben needed the gig, so though he didn't particularly give a shit about the coffee, he remembered to nod appreciatively.

"I got a weird visit last night," he said. "I thought you should know about it."

For the next twenty minutes, he briefed Graham on everything that had happened. He knew that at least some of what Hort and company had told him was true—he'd driven past Hort's place at first light, and it was cordoned off by state troopers. He'd asked what was going on, and one of them told him it had been a fire. Local media was reporting the same—a big fire at local legend Colonel Scott "Hort" Horton's place, the blaze so severe the volunteer fire department wasn't allowed to get near it, and the colonel missing and feared dead. But Ben knew what he was smelling—wood smoke, sure, but if it was true there was nothing like the smell of napalm in the morning, there was nothing like the aftermath of a rocket attack, either. On top of which, Ben had stopped by a Coleman Falls diner, where the talk was all about helicopters and explosions, and how the colonel must have fallen afoul of the Russians.

When Ben was done, Graham leaned back and crossed his cowboy boots on an ottoman. He shook his head slowly, as though saddened by the whole thing.

"Well," he said after a moment, "I'm glad you came to me, Ben. It was the right thing to do. More coffee?"

The man seemed so calm, Ben had no idea what he was thinking. But after a tale like that, and allegations like that, the calm itself felt artificial. Ben hoped he hadn't said too much. He reminded himself that there were risks in saying too little, too.

"No, thanks," he said. "I'm good. Anyway, none of this is any of my business unless you want it to be. I just thought you—"

"Let me ask you, Ben, you believe what those three were telling you? I mean, we're blowing up planes now? And involving ourselves in child-pornography cover-ups?"

The question felt dangerous. "Honestly, sir, that sort of thing feels above my pay grade. And like I said, it's none of my business."

Graham nodded. "That is indeed an honest answer. But I hope 'above my pay grade' won't be the case for too much longer. I really do. I've told you before, I look at you, and a few others like you, and I see the future of this company."

Ben nodded. He wanted to believe it was true. But where was Graham going with it?

Graham swung his feet back to the floor, leaned forward, and picked up the carafe. "You sure about that coffee?"

"Maybe just half a cup."

Graham smiled and filled it all the way, then said, "What the hell" and did the same for his own. He took a sip and made an *mmmmm* sound. "That's a Peruvian varietal, from Ritual Coffee Roasters in San Francisco. I can't get enough of their coffee. I have twenty pounds flown in every month, and it's barely enough for my habit. Say, you're from California, aren't you?"

It was weird to hear him mention Ritual.

Ben associated it with Sarah, another busted relationship he preferred not to think about.

He nodded. "Yeah."

"Good place. I trained at Coronado. Say what you will, the hippies roast good coffee."

Ben waited, sensing the guy was trying to draw him out with the silence, and determined not to fall for it. He'd relayed the facts. Anything else could only create more problems.

"Anyway," Graham continued, "here's the thing. Yeah, Hort and I have had our differences over the years. And Rain and I talked, and I wouldn't say it went well. I would have preferred for everyone to just leave it at that. But if the two of them, and now their buddy Larison, are forming some kind of cabal, well, that's a different story. And if they're approaching you now—one of my people—I'd have to call it confirmation that I have a real problem."

Based on what he'd learned from Hort, Larison, and Rain, Ben didn't think Graham was lying, exactly. But he wasn't acknowledging that he'd already tried to have the three of them killed, either.

"Because what am I supposed to do," Graham went on, "knowing three trained killers are out there gunning for me? Am I supposed to just live with that? I mean, would they? Would you?"

Ben sensed the last question wasn't rhetorical. "No," he said.

"Of course you wouldn't. It would be foolish. It would be suicidal. Because of their own paranoid delusions and projections, they've put me in a position I'd rather not be in. But denial . . . well, you know what they say about denial."

Ben nodded, seeing where this was going now, not wanting to show what he really thought of it. "It has no survival value."

"Exactly. And when survival becomes a zero-sum game . . . well, what choice have they really left me?"

Ben sipped his coffee. He wasn't going to offer. Graham would have to ask.

After a moment, Graham said, "What do you think about Paris?"

That wasn't the question he was expecting. At least, he didn't think it was. "Paris?"

"The operational environment."

Ben shrugged, not sure why they were suddenly talking about this. "Depends on the details. But the RG and the other intelligence and security forces are good. And with more latitude than ever after the November 2015 attacks."

"I'm not thinking about their security forces."

"What, then?"

"Rain, of course. And Larison. And Hort."

"I'm sorry, I'm not following. What do they have to do with Paris?"

"Next week, I'll be there for business development. Meetings, a lot of wining and dining. The French aren't stupid. They close more armaments deals with Michelin three-star meals and Domaine Leroy Musigny Grand Cru than the Russians do with the world's most coveted courtesans. Now, I have a great team that travels with me for close protection. All former DSS and, ironically, under the circumstances, Secret Service. They focus on every known pattern. But right now, I want someone who knows to look for more than patterns. I want someone who's looking for something very specific."

"Rain and company."

"That's right."

"You think they're going to come at you in Paris?"

"I'm sure of it. Because you're going to tell them you're in charge of my close protection there."

Ben didn't respond. He was torn between admiring the cleverness of what Graham seemed to be proposing, and not wanting to be mixed up in this shit at all.

"You catching my drift?" Graham said.

"I think so. You want me to tell these guys I've changed my mind. I want to help them. I give them key intel and an inside man. I'll know what they're planning, I'll tell you, you'll preempt."

"That's the idea. Now, assess. Strengths? Weaknesses? Opportunities? Threats?"

Ben looked out at the mountains for a moment

and sipped his coffee, trying to ignore the way his stomach seemed to be doing a slow roll.

"It all comes down to whether they buy it. If they smell a setup, they won't show. Or they'll factor the setup into their own tactics. If not, though, they'll walk right into it and never see it coming."

"Agreed. So what I need, then, is someone who can sell it to them. What's that old George Burns line? 'Sincerity—if you can fake that, you've got it made.' Can you do that, Ben? Fake it enough to sell it?"

Ben's stomach continued on its unpleasant trajectory. "They'll want to know why. Why the change."

"And what will you tell them?"

He saw it. He didn't like it, but he saw it. "That I thought about what they told me. The weight of it. The mistake I'm making."

"Will that be enough?"

Ben hesitated, then said, "No."

"Then what else will you tell them?"

He wasn't sure whether he should say more. Didn't trust his own reasons.

Fuck it.

"I'll tell them I realized you're full of it. That you're just stringing me along with a slick line of 'You're the future of this company' bullshit."

"Do you really think that?"

"I'm not sure."

"Honest again. And I'll be honest in return. It doesn't even matter. You know what does matter?"

"No."

"Loyalty. People who demonstrate their loyalty to me are rewarded. People who don't are treated differently."

"That seems reasonable."

"How did Sonny Barger put it? 'Treat me well, and I'll treat you better. Treat me badly, and I'll treat you worse.' "

Ben was getting tired of Graham's secondhand aphorisms. He said nothing.

"You're at a crossroads, Ben. I know how that feels. I've been there myself. But a crossroads is also an opportunity. Do you know why?"

"I guess because you can go in a different direction without getting your boots muddy."

Graham laughed. "Something like that. A wise person once told me, 'If you want something you've never had before, you have to do something you've never done before.' That's the crossroads I'm talking about."

Ben nodded.

Graham looked at Ben's cup. "Warm that up for you?"

"Sure."

"What did I tell you? This stuff is addictive."

Graham filled Ben's cup, then his own. They were both silent for a moment. Ben realized he wasn't going to ask. The point was that Ben had to offer.

"I'll call them," he said.

Graham sipped his coffee. "And can you sell them?"

"Yes."

"And will you sell them?"

"Yes."

"Say it."

I didn't ask for this, Ben thought. *I didn't want it. You assholes put me in this position. It's your doing, not mine.*

He looked at Graham. "I'll sell them. They'll believe me."

"And what will happen after that?"

Ben nodded, imagining. "They'll walk right into it."

CHAPTER TWENTY-THREE
DOX

Dox checked the secure site. No actionable intel from Kanezaki, but good news about the hardware: the package would be delivered at a place called All City Coffee. He checked it out online, and okay, good, it wasn't far from Labee's loft. Not for the first time, Dox had to give Kanezaki props for his tradecraft. With all the security and cameras and the like, the airport itself would have been too hot. And depending on where Dox was heading, downtown might have been needlessly far. Something more on the periphery, and characterized by lots of transient coffee lovers, sounded just right, and the online photos and descriptions he found made him sure of it. Lots of singletons sitting at a scattering of tables, absorbed by their laptops and minding their own business; nice combination of young and old, men and women, hipsters and working class. Not the kind of place where it would be easy to stand out, or to be noticed or remembered.

He texted Kanezaki from the sat phone to let him know to expect him at—he checked his watch—ten thirty. A minute later, he got the reply: *Woman in a headband with a copy of the*

Seattle Times. Ask her if the place is the only one or if it's a chain. Response is "This is the one and only."

Good to go. He went outside and oh yeah, he was glad he'd brought the fleece—the morning was cold, misting, and gray. He didn't like to admit it, but his blood might have thinned some from all the time in the tropics. And despite some extreme cold-weather training and deployments back in the day, which he'd handled just fine, thank you, he'd take sweating to shivering any day. He pulled on a wool hat he'd bought at the airport—a Seattle Seahawks beanie in the team colors, navy, green, and gray. Ordinarily, he wouldn't wear something so distinctive when he was operational, but he had a feeling that in these parts, anything Seahawks would blend in just fine.

He got in the taxi line—using Lyft or Uber, you might as well just attach a damn monitor to your ankle—and twenty minutes later, he was standing in front of a Starbucks about a quarter mile from All City. Once upon a time, he would have given the driver his actual destination, because come on, who would remember or care? But he had to admit, working with John all these years had taken his tactics, or call it his paranoia, up a notch. He went inside, used the restroom, and then walked to All City, taking the opportunity to get familiar with the terrain. The area was the definition of mixed use—light industry, small apartment buildings, modest single-family houses, and a handful of stores and restaurants, some of the buildings well kept, some fairly dilapidated, most looking at least a century old or better. It was nice seeing Labee's neighborhood, and he wasn't surprised that she preferred to live on the edge of things rather than at the center, keeping the city at a distance the same way she did people.

And there it was, world-famous All City Coffee, occupying most of the first-floor corner of an old two-story brick building, a used record store to one side and some kind of glassblowing place to the other.

He walked in, the door swinging shut behind him, and the second he smelled the coffee he realized how much he needed a cup. He'd flown first class and had slept on the way, but he was feeling the time-zone change now.

He strolled up to the counter. A twenty-something tatted-up barista sporting a high-and-tight up top and a Grizzly Adams beard below said, "What can I get you?"

Dox gave him an appreciative nod. "Coffee, black, and plenty of it."

"Large, then?"

"I'd take it in a tureen, if you had one. Barring that, though, yes, a large."

The guy laughed. "Coming up."

While the guy went about preparing the coffee, Dox turned to scan the shop. There were a dozen people inside, most of them sitting alone, and it took him a minute to spot the delivery woman because man, she wasn't at all what he'd been expecting. He'd pictured a white lady, or maybe Asian, midthirties, fit, maybe someone he could make as former military or intelligence. But there in her headband, peering at a *Seattle Times* open on the table in front of her through the reading glasses perched on her nose, was a nicely rounded black woman who looked old enough to have a couple of grandkids, and an expression so sweet and gentle he wondered if maybe she did.

He paid for his coffee and sat at the adjacent table so that his back was to hers. He took a sip—*Ooh, yes, thank you, Jesus*—then stretched and looked around as though taking in his surroundings.

"Pardon me, ma'am," he said quietly, leaning over. "I apologize for interrupting your morning paper, but can you tell me, is this place the only one, or is it a chain?"

The woman turned and looked at him over the reading glasses. "It's the one and only, sugar," she said with a sunny smile. "You enjoying that coffee?"

Good to go. "Yes ma'am, I am."

She turned to face him more fully, at the same time easing a canvas shopping bag from her lap to the floor alongside his chair. If he hadn't been ready for it, the move would have gone right by him. Damn, but this lady was smooth.

"I'm glad to hear that," she said. She raised the paper cup she was holding. "I prefer a latte myself—coffee's gotten hard on my stomach, but milk keeps it tolerable. People so often forget to appreciate the little things, isn't that right?"

"Yes ma'am, in my experience that is a common affliction, though no less unfortunate for being widespread."

"Well, I can see you're not like that. And I'll tell you, it makes me glad." She turned, folded her paper, slipped it into a canvas bag identical to the one now on the floor next to his chair, then sent the reading glasses in after it. She stood, picked up her latte, and lifted it to him as though in toast. "It's been a pleasure talking to you, young man. And much as I'd like to linger, I have to pick up my grandkids."

"I'll bet you do. And if you don't mind my saying, I think they're lucky to have you."

She smiled. "I like to think so, too. But that's sweet. You be careful out there, all right?"

"You've certainly made that easier, ma'am, and I'm grateful."

She left the café and turned onto the sidewalk, moving past the windows with slow, arthritic care.

Damn, he thought. *I hope I'm that good when I'm her age.*

Of course, it was one thing to handle a package, and another to put a round in a dime-sized target from five hundred yards in low light and other adverse conditions. One was a slightly more difficult and perishable skill than the other.

Well, he'd faced his mortality before. He'd probably have occasion again. But not today. Today was someone else's turn. Whoever was after Labee.

He'd debriefed Labee extensively about her place, at the end of the call from the airport, and imagining things from the standpoint of the opposition, he envisioned three primary possibilities. One was to position someone, or a couple of someones, near the entrance to the building. But she'd told him that other than her loft—which the owner leased to her cheap just to have a cop living over the store—the place was industrial. An auto-wrecking operation, a metal-recycling plant, and a machine shop, all of which produced a lot of daytime activity around the building's perimeter. Plus there was extensive antitheft video surveillance, especially around the entrance, all of it advertised with signs. So not an easy or desirable place for a gunman to wait. The second was to position someone inside her loft itself, which was on the third story, in a space otherwise devoted to storage. But Labee had assured him no way on that, her countermeasures were formidable. Meaning most likely possibility number three, which was a sniper.

Dox had spent a little time with some online mapping applications in the cab on the way to All City, and if he had been the sniper in question, he would have liked what he saw. The entrance to Labee's building was right on the east bank of a river called the Duwamish. The opposite side was industrial—barges, container storage, and junkyards, much of it looking overgrown and even disused. Somewhere in all that metal and fencing and weeds, there was going to be an elevated, concealed position with line of sight to the entrance to Labee's building. If OGE had a sniper on the payroll—and since they attacked Horton's house with a damn helicopter gunship, why wouldn't they—that's where he'd be.

He shouldered his pack and hit the restroom to confirm the bag contained what he expected—yes indeed, Combat Tactical Supergrade, loaded, three extra mags, also loaded, bellyband holster. Good to go. He secured the holster and slid the gun into it, pulled the fleece over it, then checked himself in the mirror, liking the low profile. The spare mags he distributed among his cargo-pants pockets. He headed out, discarding the bag in a trash can a few blocks from All City, and continued on foot, knowing from his online exploration that it was about two miles to his destination.

He crossed the river at the First Avenue South Bridge, which itself would have offered solid access to Labee's building, but was otherwise unsuitable because of its lack of concealment combined with a fair amount of car traffic. Someone sufficiently skilled and patient—someone like Dox—might have found a way to set up in the steel latticework that undergirded the bridge itself. But since according to the signs the damn thing was a drawbridge, there would be a significant suck factor involved in having your devilishly clever sniper hide suddenly hoisted into the air and rotated ninety degrees above the river a hundred feet below. So no go on the bridge. The better bet would be directly across the river, somewhere along the western bank, in a part of town called South Park. Closer shot, fewer obstructions. And fewer moving parts, literally and figuratively.

He walked, his breath fogging in the cool, moist air, over the bridge now, heading down a cracked and overgrown sidewalk, past a chain-link enclosure jammed up with steel barrels. There was a good amount of car traffic, but no pedestrians to speak of, just a few street people. The foliage under the bridge behind him was dotted with tarps and tents—homeless encampments. On another occasion, he would have helped out with a few bucks, but there was a time for humanitarianism, and a time for business.

He passed some workmen at a building site,

then came to a traffic light and saw the street he was looking for—South Holden. He made a left onto it and then another left, onto Second Avenue South. He passed the remnants of a solitary homeless encampment—a tattered mattress, a torn tarp, ashes from a cook fire—but whoever had been there was nowhere to be seen now.

The road transitioned from paved to gravel. Twenty yards ahead, on the right side of the street, he saw shipping containers, stacked two, three, and four high. If any were open, they'd be damn near perfect concealment. This was it. This was the spot.

He felt a little adrenaline surge and realized that what had begun as a *Let's rule this out* exercise had morphed into something much more concrete. He wasn't evaluating the possibilities from his own perspective any longer, but rather from his quarry's, a man he was suddenly certain had recently walked this exact path, tactically evaluating it the same way he was. And who even now was positioned somewhere not fifty yards from here, proned out and watching the entrance of Labee's building through a high-quality scope, his heart rate probably no higher than sixty beats a minute, a man who would precisely and dispassionately and almost certainly without ever even knowing why put a bullet through her brain before calmly walking away and never being found.

This time, the adrenaline wasn't a little surge. It was a full-on dump. He paused for a moment, looking out over the gray-green water. There it was, visible through a clump of stunted trees—Labee's building. He couldn't see the entrance from here, only the roof and the third story. But from on top of those containers, you would see everything.

He breathed slowly and steadily. After a moment, he felt calm again. He continued walking, glancing at the containers as he went by. He didn't see anything, but he would have been surprised if he had—the containers were closed on the side facing the road. If any were open, it would be on the side facing the river, with the view of Labee's building. In or on or between them, that's where you'd want to be.

He kept moving, trying to decide on the best approach to the containers. And then he saw another possibility. Up ahead, inside a dirt lot behind a chain-link fence, was a collection of fat metal pipes, each about fifteen feet long, maybe three feet wide, and stacked four high and four across. They were rusted red, and the dirt around them was carved into what looked like a dry moat—a depression created by rain runoff. Whatever these pipes had been intended for, they'd never been used for it, and it looked like someone had decided it would be more expensive to move them than to just let them sit.

And with one end backed up against a stand of trees and thick weeds, and the other end open to the river . . .

Where would you set up—the containers, or the pipes?

As he got closer to the lot, he decided the pipes would offer at least as good line of sight and substantially better privacy. They were surrounded by broken-down machinery—some kind of collapsed conveyor belt, the remains of a tractor, a pile of engine debris. Someone had hung a *No Trespassing* sign from the fence, but the sign itself was rusted and dangling crookedly from a single screw. And though the gates were chained shut, and the fence topped with barbed wire, here and there were holes big enough for a man to squeeze through. Overall, it looked like about as much of a no-one-gives-a-shit kind of place as you could reasonably ask for. Squirm through one of the fence holes with a sleeping bag and some provisions, and a man could wait in one of those pipes for days if he had to, the muzzle of his rifle well back from the opening, practically invisible from any passerby who might glance his way.

He could have continued along the road as it hooked left until he was behind the lot. But that would have meant walking directly in front of the pipes, which would have *A,* alerted anyone inside one of them to a potential problem, and *B,* entailed strolling directly across said person's line of fire, neither one of which was a particularly attractive possibility.

So instead, he backtracked until he came to the parking lot of a place called Bob's Automotive Repair. He followed the driveway to a parking lot around back, which he thought would likely lead to another lot, and then another. He might have to hop a few fences, but if all went well, in a matter of minutes he expected he'd be coming up from behind those pipes.

But the *if all went well* part didn't last long. Just as he reached the fence at the northern edge of the lot, he heard someone call out from inside the garage, "Can I help you?" Which in Dox's not-inconsiderable experience in such matters was the polite way of saying, "What the fuck are you up to?"

He looked over and saw a bald guy holding a steel ratchet and wearing dark coveralls with a patch declaring an eponymous *Bob* heading his way from the garage.

Dox stopped and gave a little wave. "Apologies if I startled you," he called out in a Yankee accent. "I'm embarrassed to say, my father's AWOL from the senior-care facility again, and the last three times, we found him sleeping rough around here. You haven't seen him, have you? Big guy, bigger than me, but older, obviously. Got a patchy white beard and answers to Bill, though pretty much everything else he's forgotten."

"No," Bob said. "I haven't seen anyone like that. Have you called the cops?"

"Yeah, I call them every time. And never hear back. Reckon they've got bigger fish to fry than an escaped nursing-home resident. So I've gotten in the habit of just reeling him in myself. Got a change of clothes for him in the pack, some clean dignity pants just in case. I'll tell you, it's hard watching your parents get old."

Bob looked around. "Why does he come here? He used to work around here or something?"

For a second, Dox wondered whether the guy was legit. But the coveralls, the grease stains on his hands, and just the overall vibe made him confident the thought was needlessly paranoid. Still, was the guy trying to trip him up by getting him to commit to specifics? Probably not, but no sense taking a chance, either. "No, it seems he and my mother began their courtship, such as it was, by hooking up in these parts unbeknownst to their parents. Sometimes he forgets she's long gone, and I guess in his mind he's back in better times. In some ways, I'm glad for him, because they had a happy marriage. But on the other hand, I can't just let him wander around outdoors and freeze to death. Anyway, I'm sorry again if I startled you. I'm just going to head on through these lots and see if he turns up."

He turned and hopped the fence before the guy could respond. He felt he'd been convincing, but on the other hand the guy had been suspicious enough to challenge him, meaning he might also be the type to feel it was his civic duty to inform the police of something mildly untoward.

He hustled across the next two lots and jumped the next two fences without further problems, then began moving in stealthily, keeping his trajectory perpendicular to the pipes, away from the openings. He wanted to go faster, but was mindful of the possibility of trip wires and of the problems that could ensue if one of his boots snapped a branch or crushed a stray leaf. He reached the middle of the pipes and carefully moved along, away from the water, until he was just short of the tree-side openings.

Which one? You'd want to be up high, of course. Over to the right, because the angle is slightly better. But not all the way to the right, because being on the end would feel less random and less secure.

And then he smelled something. Blood. He looked down and saw a depression in the weeds at the tree-side pipe openings. The ground underneath was wet and stained dark.

All at once, he knew what had happened to the mysterious inhabitant of the empty homeless encampment. Poor bastard must have seen someone sneaking in here, probably late at night.

Come over to investigate. Or maybe he thought it was another homeless person and was looking to share resources, or just for some simple human company. And got his throat slit for his troubles.

For some reason, even beyond how he was feeling about protecting Labee, seeing what had happened to some poor homeless guy made him mad. By instinct and experience, he pushed it away. He could indulge all the feelings in the world later, and in fact he knew he would. But he had a task at hand, and the right approach was to focus on the mechanics of what was needed to get that task done.

He carefully set down the pack. Drew the Wilson. Inhaled deeply and blew out. *Showtime.*

He ducked his head around for a quick peek inside the nearest ground-level pipe. Clear.

Then again for the nearest second-level pipe. Clear.

The one above that was too high to see into from the ground. He'd have to climb.

He moved carefully left until he was in front of the ground-level pipe he'd just checked. Squatted and peeked into the one to the left of it. He knew from the smell even before he saw the shape—the body of the homeless guy, his head tilted back and his throat wide open. The sniper must have dragged him in by the ankles from the other end.

Dox didn't think about it. He just popped his

245

head up for a peek into the opening of the pipe above the one with the dead guy. Clear.

He planted a boot carefully on top of the pipe with the dead guy, tested the footing, and slowly pushed up, his free hand on top of the second-level pipe so as not to give himself away to anyone who might be lurking in the one above it. Keeping the Wilson alongside his head, he raised his head until his eyes were just over the bottom edge of the third-level pipe, and bingo, there he was—a sniper, dressed all in black but silhouetted perfectly against the opposite opening. Classic prone position, feet turned out, a rifle on a bipod pointed forward, and the man obviously relaxed and intent behind the scope. Dox watched him for a moment, surprised and wanting a moment to examine why. He'd been expecting the guy to be in a pipe one level higher, that was it, but as much as he'd been trying to get in the guy's head, it's not like he was psychic, and you had to allow for variations.

But why not the top one? The angle would be better, and—

He heard it. Or *heard* wasn't quite the right way of putting it, it was subtler than that, his unconscious applying a template built from long experience to something otherwise imperceptible from up and to his left. What it was he wouldn't ever be able to say, because in fact it was less a sound than just . . . something out of place. Something stealthy. And unnatural. And malevolent.

He understood everything then, not in words, but the instantaneous language of survival—

shooter one level from the top, spotter on the top level and to the left of the shooter to engage any problems from an elevated position while forcing a right-handed intruder to shoot across his own body, rotating team, one man behind the rifle to engage the target, the other focused on rear security, switching off periodically to prevent fatigue, and if you'd approached the pipes from one of the open ends instead of from the side you'd be dead now

—everything all at once, with no questions, no surprise, nothing at all other than the need to react *now*.

Using his grip on the second-level pipe for stability, he dropped into a squat atop the ground-level pipe, brought the Wilson up and across his body, and got off three rounds at the face he saw emerging from the opening of the top-level pipe up and to his left. The guy fell back, but Dox knew he hadn't hit him, the angle was for shit and all he'd been trying for was an extra second. If he leaped to the ground he would have been wide open against a shooter with cover, concealment, and an elevated position. So instead he fired again, just suppressive fire to keep the guy from getting back in the game while Dox was out of position, and he kept on firing while he scrambled like a spider monkey on speed up the pipes, right past the opening of the sniper's pipe but so fast the guy didn't have time to access a pistol and acquire him. He reached the top pipe and hauled himself over it just as the spotter finally got off two shots of his own, the rounds whizzing by so close despite the tough angle that Dox could feel them practically kissing his calves as he swung his legs around.

Lord almighty, that's a no-shit shooter if ever I saw one

He jumped to his feet, dropped the near-empty magazine, slammed in a fresh one, and scanned, searching for an angle. He didn't see one.

Fuck, maybe you should have scrambled into the sniper's pipe instead of up here but too late now

Presumably, the sniper had a pistol, too—Dox sure would have—which meant that in about a second and a half Dox was going to be facing two skilled operators, accustomed to working as a team, who could come at him from either end of the pipes, separately or together.

Not good odds. But one slim chance.

He raised his leg and stomped the near side of the pipe to the left of the one the spotter was in, which was the last in the top row. The kick landed with a huge metallic *boom!* and the pipe rocked, but didn't go over.

Fuck, someone must have wedged something between the pipes to stabilize them. Okay, do or die. He took three steps back, then ran forward and leaped into the air, retracting both legs and bronco stomping the side of the end pipe as he landed. And somehow, the pipe shot off whatever had been holding it and dropped over the side. Dox landed on his ass but was up again even before he heard the falling pipe slam into the ground with a bass-note thud—just in time to see the spotter trying to acquire him again. Dox fired three rounds and the spotter ducked back into his pipe. Dox backed up as far as he could, then ran forward, and as he leaped into the air he saw the spotter again, drawing a bead on him—

His heels slammed into the near side of the spotter's pipe, and the guy's shot went wild. The pipe rolled to the edge, but didn't go over. The guy disappeared for a second, presumably having some trouble keeping his position after suddenly finding himself upside down in a rolling pipe. Dox backed up again, everything moving in slow motion now in his adrenalized vision, sure he was taking too long, that the guy was going to adjust to his tactics and this time drill him clean, and he leaped, and there was the guy again, but this time Dox was a half second ahead, and his boot heels slammed into the near side of the pipe, and the guy didn't even get off his shot before the pipe went over with the guy halfway out the opening and shouting, "Fuck!" on the way down.

The falling pipe smacked into the one that had preceded it with the kind of clang that must have cracked the Liberty Bell. The guy's head and torso bounced violently on impact, and before he had any chance to recover, Dox had the Wilson's sights on him from above and put two rounds in his face.

Okay, but now what?

Repeat the operation on the other side? He'd have to kick over two more pipes just to reach the one the sniper was holed up in, which would take a lot of time. Besides which, the sniper would understand his tactics by now, and would react by . . .

By what?

Well, not by just waiting for his own pipe to go spinning off the edge, that was for damn sure. A picture flashed in Dox's mind, the guy easing out of the pipe on the river side, a pistol in hand, and having all the time in the world to creep up and aim carefully while Dox jumped purposelessly on one pipe after another—

He moved quickly to the openings of the pipes facing the trees and glanced over the edge. Nothing.

Goddamn it, which is it? Does he stay put, or move out?

They're good. What would you do?

No time to think it through further than that. If

the guy was good, and he was, he would get off the X. One way or the other.

Okay. Dox dropped to his stomach along the top pipe on the far side, where he'd kicked the two over. He darted his head down and then back, and in the instant during which he'd glanced, he'd seen nothing, no one clambering up the tree-side openings. He grabbed the edge of the top pipe with his free hand and swung down so that his feet were on top of the one at ground level.

Employing a weird sideways shuffle he sensed would be characteristic of a pigeon on LSD, he bobbed his head right, saw the pipe to that side was empty and that no one was trying to climb past it, then scooted in that direction and repeated the process. Everything was still moving in slow motion, but it couldn't have been more than a couple of seconds before he'd reached the opening of the pipe where the sniper had his hide. He flash checked it—empty.

Fear gripped him. *Where the hell is he?*

He pictured it an instant before it happened. Yeah, he'd been thinking these guys were good. And they were thinking it about him, too—the sniper especially, who understood now what had become of his spotter partner. So the sniper hadn't done the smart thing, the expected thing, which would have been to climb up. Instead, he'd done the risky thing, which was to jump down. If Dox had stayed on top, the guy would have been in a bad position. But now Dox realized the guy had outthought him and was circling around right now while Dox clung to the side of a bunch of rusting pipes like a dumb kid on the world's most awkward monkey bars—

He didn't think. If he had, he would have realized it was too high risk and second-guessed himself. Instead, he just let go and dropped to his back onto the weeds, his feet toward the side where he sensed, for no reason he could articulate, the guy would be coming from. If he had sensed wrong, he was dead.

But he wasn't wrong. The guy popped from around the side, his gun up in a two-handed grip, and aimed high, at about the point where he expected to see Dox clinging to the pipes. Except Dox wasn't clinging to the pipes. He was on his back, his knees up and the most beautiful Wilson Combat Tactical Supergrade God ever made steadied between his crossed ankles. The guy realized his mistake, and for a split instant Dox saw fear and horror in his expression as he tried to adjust. But too late. Dox put three rounds in his chest. The guy staggered back, let loose two rounds that went way high, tripped on something, and fell to his back, losing his pistol on the way down.

Dox sprang to his feet and closed on the guy, the Wilson up at chin level and zeroed on the guy's face. He walked in slowly, careful not to trip on whatever underbrush had just cost the guy his own footing, then stood close, the muzzle of the Wilson pointed directly at the guy's face. He did a quick scan and confirmed they were alone.

"Doctor," the guy said with a burbling gasp. "Call . . . a doctor."

"You bet," Dox said, still sighting down the Wilson. "Just as soon as you tell me all the things you know I'm interested in."

The guy seemed to rally a bit at the possibility of a doctor. His eyes rolled, then focused on Dox. "Who are you?" he said.

"No sir, you have it wrong. There's only one person asking questions here and that person ain't you. What outfit are you with? Spit it out and I'll have the paramedics here faster than you can say 'Help me, I'm dying from a sucking chest wound and bleeding out besides.'"

The guy nodded, seeming intent on signaling his willingness to cooperate. "OGE."

"Yeah? Why'd they send you?"

The guy wheezed for a moment, then said, "To kill the woman."

"Yeah, dumbass, that much I figured out on my own. I'm asking you why her. Why OGE wants her dead."

"How the fuck should I know? Come on, I'm just a contractor."

Unfortunately, that had the ring of truth. This guy was nothing but a trigger puller. Why would anyone tell him anything not need-to-know?

Well, there wasn't much time, anyway. That was a whole lot of shots fired. Even if Bob hadn't alerted the authorities, they'd sure as shit be getting alerted now.

His silence must have made the guy nervous, because he gave a weak cough and said, "Come on, man. I can tell you get it. Whoever she is, it's just business."

Dox looked at him. "Yeah?" he said. "Well, your shit luck, asshole, 'cause it ain't just business for me." He put a round into the guy's forehead.

The guy jerked and then was still. Under other circumstances, Dox might have savored the moment. But he had to beat feet. Damn, how the hell was he going to get to Labee's place? He knew from the maps that he could go overland from here to the bridge and not have to retrace his steps. But the bridge was a long, exposed walk for a guy fitting the description old Bob might have given, covered in gunshot residue, and whose prints were going to match the shell casings and a dropped magazine the cops were soon to find all over a gruesome crime scene.

He heard the first siren, then a second, and thought, *Well, I won't lie to you, it looks bleak for our hero.*

CHAPTER TWENTY-FOUR
GRAHAM

After Treven left, Graham had Curtis close the door, with orders of no disturbances barring emergencies.

He sat on the couch and looked out at the Blue Ridge Mountains. He loved this view. Not just for its beauty, but for the way it helped him focus on the big picture. The less parochial concerns. The things that would outlast him.

Treven, he thought. *What a waste.*

The man was an exceptional operator. Trained, experienced, with top-of-the-food-chain urban-combat judgment and reflexes.

A warrior, no doubt. But fundamentally a solo operator, not a leader. And for God's sake, not a salesman. The notion of Treven selling a group of cynics and survivors like Hort, Larison, and Rain . . . well, it would have been laughable if it wasn't so sad.

Whatever Treven told them, they'd never buy it. They'd assume it was a setup.

Which wouldn't make Treven's efforts useless. Far from it. Believing Treven was setting them up wouldn't stop Hort and company from coming at Graham. They'd just come around the setup. Which would, of course, be the real setup.

For a moment, he was bothered that Treven seemed to believe Graham would actually blow up a civilian airliner just to cover up a child-pornography ring. It was insulting, really. What kind of values did Treven think Graham had? He would never do something so monumental for stakes so small.

He sighed and poured himself a cup of coffee. It was all right. It wasn't really Treven's fault. The man simply didn't understand that the stakes were far, far larger.

CHAPTER TWENTY-FIVE
DOX

Dox followed a trail under the First Street South Bridge, the foliage thick around him. When he was sufficiently concealed from the road and felt safe for the moment, he immediately got the shakes. He crouched and breathed steadily in and out until they started to subside. Then he took the sat phone from the pack and called Labee.

She picked up instantly. "Are you okay? I'm hearing reports of shots fired and officers on the way."

"I'm fine, darlin'. Now the bad news is, there were two guys waiting for you across the river—a sniper and a spotter. The good news is, they're dead now. The bad news is, I can't get out of here because, right, there are sirens all around and it would be better if the local gendarmerie didn't see me walking away from the crime scene."

Two cop cars raced over the bridge above, their sirens howling.

"Where are you?" she said.

"Crouching in the underbrush near a homeless encampment under the First Avenue South Bridge. West side of the bridge, by a stream, if that means anything to you."

"South Park. Highland Parkway Southwest. I know exactly where you are."

"Well, that's great, because if asked, I would describe my current circumstances as 'in need of a rescue.' "

"I'll be there in ten minutes."

"Ten minutes? Not to be ungrateful, but I thought you were going to be close by."

"I am. But I need to stop at my loft first."

"My lord, whatever you need, it can't be that important. K. can deliver you pretty much any weapon you—"

"It's not a weapon."

"What, then? Look, I was expecting only one shooter across the river, and instead I found two. I don't know for sure there won't be another at your loft. Or inside it. At least let me come with you."

"There are cameras all around the perimeter of the building. We can't let you get recorded by them."

"I don't care about that. Why are you—"

"I'll explain later. Just stay put. I'll be by in ten minutes. Maybe less."

"Damn it, Labee, would you just listen to me for a minute?"

But he was talking to a dead line.

"Shit," he said aloud. "Why does she have to be so stubborn?"

He heard footsteps moving through the underbrush to his left. Nothing stealthy about the approach—in fact, it was pretty damn noisy—but juiced as he was from his recent near-death experience, he shot to his feet, his hand going under the fleece and around the grip of the Wilson.

But it wasn't a problem, just a skinny old dude who must have been one of the people sleeping in the tents under the bridge. His hair was white, he was missing most of his teeth, and the skin on his face was as brown and wrinkled as tobacco dried by the sun.

"Hello, my friend," the old guy called out to him with the trace of a Mexican accent. "I thought I heard someone back here."

"Well, hey there," Dox said, releasing the Wilson and sliding the phone back into the pack. "Sorry for disturbing you. My lady friend and I had an argument, and I needed to walk it off to cool down. You look like a man who's acquired some wisdom over the years. Can you tell me, why are women so difficult? I mean, I love them, but why?"

The old guy shrugged. "Because they're people. It's not women who are difficult. It's people."

Dox looked at the old guy, perplexed. He'd just been trying to throw out a little distraction. He hadn't expected to receive actual insights in return. Shame on him for underestimating the man.

"Well, sir, I have to say, I think that's profound. We haven't known each other long, but you've given me a lot to consider, and I'm grateful."

The old guy gave him a smile, sunny even though it was mostly gums. "Just imagine how difficult we seem to them. It's hard to walk in another person's shoes. If I've learned anything, I've learned that."

Dox nodded, feeling both humbled and impressed. "Say, I hope you won't consider it rude for me to ask, but if you find yourself temporarily short on cash, it would be my pleasure to share a bit of my good fortune, just as a way of thanking you for opening my eyes now."

The old guy straightened a little and shook his head. "You don't have to."

Damn, the dignity of the man, to refuse charity he so obviously needed.

"I know that, sir. But I'd like to. Would you be kind enough to oblige me?"

There was a pause, and the guy nodded. "All right."

Dox pulled out his billfold and peeled off ten twenties. "I hope this'll make things a little easier," he said.

The old guy stared at the bills, his eyes wide. Then he looked at Dox and nodded. "Thank you."

Dox shook his head. "I'm sorry I can't do more. But what I have left, I think I might need."

More sirens sounded. The old guy cocked his head as though listening. "All these sirens. My ears aren't what they once were, but I thought I heard shooting. I guess I was right."

Dox suppressed a smile. The old guy's ears had certainly been good enough to hear Dox on the phone earlier.

"Yeah, I heard it, too," he said. "Thought it was fireworks, but maybe you're right, with all these cops racing around."

"They're just doing their job. But I'll tell you, I make it a habit not to talk to them. They do their thing, I do mine. You are going to be okay?"

Dox appreciated the man's message—both its subtleness and its apparent sincerity. "Appreciate your asking, sir, but I'll be fine. In fact, my lady friend will likely be by to pick me up any minute now."

"She'll forgive you?"

"I think it was more a matter of my forgiving her, but . . . well, maybe you're right. I need to think about it in light of what you've shared with me today."

The old guy gave him the sunny, toothless smile. "Just don't be afraid to let her know you love her. Love really does conquer all."

"No, no, it ain't like that. I mean, I'm very fond of her, of course, but . . . well, anyway, it's complicated."

The old guy gave him another smile, this

261

one a little on the knowing side. "People are complicated. Thank you for the help just now." With that, he gave a little bow and disappeared back into the foliage.

Dox shook his head, trying to clear it. Two mysterious oldsters in one day, both of them philosophers. It made him less concerned about growing old himself. Hell, at the moment, he was glad just to be alive.

A few minutes later, he saw a car pulling over and moving slowly along the shoulder. A Jeep. He crept through the foliage, and saw it was her. Labee.

He moved out briskly, not running, but sure as shit not taking his time, either. She saw him coming and popped open the passenger door. The second he was inside, she was smoothly pulling away.

"Labee, darlin'," he said, overwhelmed by the sight of her. He'd almost forgotten how beautiful she was, he supposed because he'd been trying to. No makeup, hair back in a ponytail, jeans and a fleece—not working it at all, and still, there was just something about her that could make his head spin.

She reached over and squeezed his knee—a major display of affection for her, he knew—while keeping her eyes on the road. "What happened? Are you all right?"

"I told you, I'm fine. What about you? You went to your loft?"

"Yes."

"Any problems?"

"No problems. Whatever problems there were, you already took care of them."

Seeing that she was safe, he was suddenly angry at her. "Well, you were lucky, then. What the hell do you need that was so important that you risked walking into an ambush for it?"

She glanced at him and frowned. "Don't."

"Don't what? How do you think I was feeling, hiding in the underbrush after you hung up on me, imagining you walking into who knows what?"

"Probably the way I was feeling when I didn't hear from you, and was picking up reports of shots fired."

That set him back, though not in a bad way. "Is that your way of telling me you care?"

She glanced at him again, and he couldn't tell if she was pissed, or trying not to smile. Maybe both.

"Anyway," he said. "If that old philosopher hadn't distracted me, I would have been beside myself."

"What old philosopher?"

"Ah, never mind."

"Did someone see you?"

"Hell yes, someone saw me. The eponymous Bob of Bob's Automotive Repair and I are practically friends now. Plus a bunch of workmen who watched me strolling by before that. And oh, of course, the old philosopher I got to chatting with while I was waiting for you just now."

She nodded. "That's why you couldn't go to my loft. It's one thing for the police to have a description. It's another to have video to show witnesses."

He considered. Ordinarily, he'd be all over that kind of thing, wouldn't even have to give it a thought. He realized, not for the first time, that concern for her was making him forget himself. He had to watch that. He wouldn't be much use to her if he were dead. Though the thought that she might miss him did give him a warm feeling.

"You're right," he said. "But shit, are those bodies I left going to be a problem for you? I mean, under the circumstances, it's obvious it had something to do with you, right? Two dead guys, a sniper rifle, line of sight across the river to your domicile. Shit, I hadn't thought of it until just now, but aren't you going to be some kind of suspect?"

"When the shots were fired, I was in a place called the Hangar Café, less than a mile from my loft. I'm there all the time and know the owner, Justin. I used a credit card. And I'm now logged and time-stamped five minutes later by the cameras around my building. I couldn't have had anything to do with the shooting. At least not directly."

He smiled. "You thought all this through in advance, didn't you?"

She glanced at him. "What do you think?"

"I hope that didn't come across as condescending. I meant it as sincere admiration."

"Just being careful. But you're right, Seattle PD is going to make those bodies as part of whoever's trying to assassinate me."

"Is that good or bad?"

"I'm not sure. Good, I guess, because right now I'm being investigated as part of an officer-involved, and at this point it's going to be pretty unequivocal that it was clean self-defense. But bad because . . . I just don't want this attention."

"You know, most of your major police-detective types might have said 'Bad, because it means for sure some capable people are intent on killing mc.'"

"Yeah, that too."

He didn't press, but he'd only been half joking. It was odd that she was concerned more about attention than about being killed.

"Anyway," he said after a moment, "I hope what you got from your place was worth all the gray hairs you caused me."

She nodded. "It was."

"Would it be overly intrusive of me to inquire as to what might be more important than my generally youthful hair color?"

"The laptop I was using in connection with the

Child's Play investigation. And a case. A serial rapist from out of town. He works parks. Twice in Seattle in the last few weeks, and another one is coming. Probably next time it rains. There's a pattern, and I'm close to figuring out a way to preempt him. My notes were in the loft."

Part of him wanted to say, *You went back there. You risked your life. For some notes.*

But on the other hand, it fit everything he knew about her. Everything he sensed, anyway. And everything he admired.

So instead he just said, "You know if I can, it would be my pleasure to help with that."

She glanced at him again, nodded once, then looked back to the road. He had the sense she was suddenly fighting tears. It was one of the things that moved him so much about her. She was one of the toughest women—one of the toughest people—he'd ever known. But she felt things so deeply, too, and it was a lot closer to the surface than he thought most people would realize.

"Okay," he said. "You ready to go on a trip?"

She glanced at him and gave him a small smile. "Where are we heading?"

"Well, the friend I told you about—John Rain's his name, by the way, though he prefers it not to be mentioned even in encrypted phone calls, he's paranoid that way—he's currently in the DC area. Along with some friends I think you ought to meet. Plus Kanezaki's out there, too, and he's ready to help. All in all, I can't think of a safer group for you to be with."

He hoped it was true. He wanted to believe it was. But as good as he knew John and he and all the rest were, they didn't have the resources to bring down planes or send helicopter gunships or move trained snipers around on the board like they were no more than pawns. Dox had been through some shit before, some hellacious shit, in fact, but this felt worse to him. Maybe because of what OGE was capable of. Maybe because this time, the target wasn't him.

Well, whatever they were capable of, he hoped it was worth dying for. Because he was going to kill a whole lot of people before he let anything happen to Labee.

CHAPTER TWENTY-SIX
RAIN

The night after the three of us had braced Treven, there were two slow knocks on our motel-room door, followed by three fast ones. Horton and Larison took up positions behind the double beds, guns drawn. I had the slightly less enviable task of standing alongside the door. "Who is it?" I called out.

"Who the hell do you think it is?" came the unmistakable Texas twang. "You tell someone else to stop by at midnight and knock like that?"

I turned and glanced at Horton and Larison. They both nodded.

I opened the door and there he was, holding a cardboard box and wearing a big grin, a wary-looking midthirties Asian woman beside him.

The woman keyed instantly on Horton and Larison and the guns. She tensed.

"It's all right," Dox said. "These are my friends. They're being careful, same as we would. They're just less charming, that's all."

They came in and I closed and locked the door behind them. Horton and Larison stood and lowered the guns.

"Well, John Rain," Dox said, still grinning. He

set down the box and straightened. "Come on, bring it here."

He gave me one of his bear hugs, which I'd become accustomed to but which I didn't think I'd ever enjoy quite the way he did.

"And Larison," he said, walking over. "I won't lie to you, back in the day I never thought I'd say this, but it sure is fine to see you."

Larison got a hug, too, and even hugged back, albeit patting Dox awkwardly and saying, "All right, all right," when it had gone on too long.

"And Colonel," Dox said, shaking Horton's hand. "Lot of water under the bridge. Glad to find us standing on the same side of the stream for a change, if I may indulge an extended metaphor."

"It's a pleasure to see you, son," Horton said. "As far as I'm concerned, that water's all behind us now."

"That's gracious of you to say, sir, given everything that happened."

Horton nodded. "Why don't we just call it the Late Unpleasantness, and focus on the future instead? Life is short. Let's find a way to make it longer."

"Amen to that," Dox said. He gestured to the woman. "Everyone, this is my friend Livia Lone. Livia, this is John Rain, Daniel Larison, and Colonel Scott Horton, retired. Not that you'd know it." He gestured to each of us in sync with the introductions. "The kind of people you want on your side when you've gotten on the wrong side of someone else. And gentlemen, I hope you'll believe me when I tell you, because I wouldn't be here if it weren't true, that the same applies to Livia."

There was a round of handshakes and pleasantries, all feeling hesitant, watchful, wary.

"Okay," Dox said. "Livia and I brought in some wings and a couple six-packs of Dos Equis from a restaurant up the road. Figured y'all might not be getting out much and could use the grub. Hey, what is this place, anyway? The woman at the front desk told me it's a lake to cool a nuclear reactor—say what?"

Horton, who had suggested we meet here, filled him in. The place was called Lake Anna Lodge, located on the lake for which it was named. Apparently in 1972, the government built a dam on the North Anna River to create a reservoir to cool the nuclear reactors it was planning for the area. A few small towns grew up around the eastern shore, which was open to the public for swimming, boating, and fishing. The public side became known as the "cold side" because the private "hot side" was warmed by the reactors the water circulated to cool. And because the fish preferred the warmer waters, authorized users of the private side got the better fishing grounds.

It interested me that Horton knew so much of the local history and lore. It was obvious he loved the area. And it was obvious, too, that he sensed the feeling was somehow reciprocated. I wondered what that would be like. The closest I could imagine was Tokyo. But that love had never been requited.

"Hmm," Dox said. "Better fishing for the fancy folks? There's a metaphor in there, I think." He pulled a six-pack from the cardboard box. Horton and Larison each took a beer. Livia declined. So did I.

"Too tired?" Dox said to me after draining half of his. "What have y'all been doing, sleeping in shifts?"

"Of course," I said. In fact, because we were all still wired from the attack at Horton's place, and probably even now not quite trustful enough of each other to do more than doze off in the same room, I doubted either Horton or Larison had slept any better than I had, shift or no.

"All right, don't worry, Livia and I will be doing the same. And she waited out back while I paid for a room. Yes, in cash." He turned to Livia. "John's paranoid and a micromanager besides. It saves time if I can preempt his inquiries. Hey, hope y'all did the same, with just one of you checking in and going out for supplies."

"That would be me," Larison said.

Since Horton was black and I was mixed Asian, Larison would be the least noticeable among us, and was therefore our designated public face.

"Ah," Dox said, "that explains how you wound up with this quiet room around back, facing the woods and not the road. I did the same."

"What are you driving?" I said, so I'd know which cars in the lot were ours and which might be a problem.

He grinned. "Had a feeling you might ask. We rented a passenger van in case we need room for all of us. Red Nissan, parked nose-out at the end of the lot. Good to go?"

I nodded.

"Okay," he said, "let's get caught up on what seems to be our mutual problem—Oliver Graham and OGE. Then I need to pass out for a while. I left paradise a day and a half ago, killed two men in Seattle today, and have had nothing but a little airplane sleep before or since."

Even for Dox, this was a lot of chatter. I wondered if he was doing it to make Livia more comfortable. She was notably quiet. But not out of nervousness, I sensed—more some sort of native reserve. There was something about her that seemed at home with silence, with watching and listening rather than performing and talking. I wondered how she and Dox could get along, and then I smiled, because I supposed the same might have been asked of him and me.

Over wings and beer for the other three and water for Livia and me, we briefed each other on everything. Unfortunately, at the end of it, we still didn't know much more than we had at the outset. OGE was protecting something, most likely some sort of child-pornography ring at the Secret Service. It also seemed likely that OGE was operating on behalf of someone else—maybe the Secret Service, maybe Homeland Security, maybe the FBI, maybe some combination. While of course, at this point, being motivated also to conceal their own involvement. The resources they had expended in trying to silence anyone who knew about the ring or OGE's part in the cover-up suggested a high degree of motivation, and a low probability that attrition alone would get Graham to stand down.

Livia told us she was waiting to hear from a source within Homeland Security Investigations who she trusted at least enough for intel. The last time she'd spoken to him was before leaving Seattle, when she briefed him about Graham and the snipers. He told her he was looking into something. That was good, because so far we hadn't gotten anything from Kanezaki. And though Horton was convinced Treven was going to come around, I thought he was being excessively optimistic.

"My cellphone's off and in a Faraday case," Livia said, "so I don't know if my contact has been trying to reach me." She looked at Dox. "What about your satellite phone?"

Dox looked at me, anticipating the objection.

"It's scrambled," he said. "Encrypted. Graham can throw a helicopter at us, yeah, but he doesn't have a damn AWACS plane, okay? And driving fifty miles to find a fast-food place with a Wi-Fi connection has its own risks, at this point chiefly that I'll fall asleep at the wheel. Things could be moving fast, and we need intel. Let's get it."

I'd learned a long time ago working with Dox that there were times in a partnership when you had to give a little. It seemed like this was one of those times. I nodded.

"Shit, don't look so glum," Dox said. He handed the phone to Livia, who walked over to the window to get a signal.

"We've been lucky so far," Dox went on. "Livia getting ambushed at her self-defense place, that helicopter attack at the colonel's house, and the sniper team I outflanked in Seattle. But Graham's got more resources than we do, and sooner or later, one of these attacks is going to get through. We need good intel, and you know it."

"I'm not arguing," I said.

"You were arguing with your eyes."

"I'm allowed to argue with my eyes."

He laughed. "I guess that's true. And when Livia's through, one of us should ping our intel friend, K. Not just to see if there's any new intel. Livia's got her duty weapon and I see some others have managed not to leave home without, but I myself am feeling distinctly underdressed at the moment without a proper firearm. K. won't be happy about it, 'cause I had to toss the one he got for me in Seattle before flying out here. But I'll find a way to make it up to him."

Horton said, "I should check my voicemail. I think you're all wrong about Ben. He's struggling with his conscience, like he always has. But he'll get it right."

Larison said, "I doubt it."

"You better hope you're wrong," Horton said. "Because we need all the help we can get."

CHAPTER TWENTY-SEVEN
LIVIA

"Hey," Livia said as soon as Little picked up. "It's me."

"Livia. Damn it, I've been trying to reach you."

It sounded like something was wrong. She pressed the phone tighter to her ear and pushed back a ripple of anxiety. "I've been traveling. Is everything all right?"

"I know you've been traveling. You flew from Seattle to Washington Dulles."

The ripple turned into a small wave. She glanced at the men. They were all listening intently—Rain in particular.

"How do you know that?"

"ICE records. Which anyone at Homeland Security can instantly access. What are you doing out here?"

"Following leads."

"Never going to trust me, are you?"

"No more than I have to."

There was a pause, and she sensed he was tamping down his frustration with her. It wouldn't be the first time.

"I suppose it doesn't matter," he said. "I have information for you. Where can we meet?"

"Better over the phone."

She noticed Rain was looking at her closely. The man was obviously agitated by the idea that her contact had proposed meeting in person.

"Forgive me, Livia, I've about had it with your bullshit. I've gone out on a major limb for you, I've uncovered information critical to what you're up against, and I'm done with you disrespecting me and calling all the shots. And think hard about hanging up on me again, because this time I will not be calling back."

Shit. On the one hand, she didn't think meeting him would be a problem. But she knew it would be for Rain, and maybe for the others. And regardless, she hated that Little had taken her measure and was calling her bluff. Hated feeling he was in control of her.

"I'll call you back in five minutes," she said.

"Fine."

She clicked off, trying to find some satisfaction in not having capitulated, and in his acquiescence to her refusal to give him an immediate response.

But it was just a salve. She knew he had won. She tried to focus on the substance, which was his assurance that he had valuable information.

She looked at Rain, knowing he would be the one with the strongest objections. "He says he has information," she said. "I have to meet him."

But Rain didn't respond. Carl did. He said, "Why would that be necessary? I told you, the phone's encrypted. Anything he can say in person, he can say over the phone."

"There's no time to get into my whole history with him right now. His information has always been solid before. I trust him enough to meet him."

"All right," Carl said. "It's your call. But if you don't mind, I'd like to be there with you. Can't hurt to have someone watching your back."

Even as tense as she was, she couldn't help appreciating how carefully he'd phrased it. She didn't know if it was conscious or if he just had great intuition, but Carl knew not to tell her what she needed to do, and when he screwed up he always found an instant way to fix it. And maybe on some level his approach was manipulative, but what mattered most was the way it made her feel. Like he understood her, without ever having to be heavy-handed about it.

Rain shook his head. "I don't like meetings generally. I especially don't like ones that are unnecessary and proposed by someone else."

"No one else has to come," Livia said. "I'll hear what he has to say and share it with all of you. But whether I meet with him isn't up to you. It's not a negotiation."

Rain raised his eyebrows, apparently a little taken aback. That was fine. So many men had a way of just assuming they were in charge. She'd learned the most efficient way to disabuse them was clearly and up front.

Rain started to respond, but Carl cut him off. "Hang on, everyone, hang on. Let's not start throwing down and fucking up our teamwork before it even gets started. We all have the same problem and the same objectives. But being different people, we'll occasionally differ on tactics. That's not a bad thing—it's good. It means we can put our heads together, pressure check each other's ideas, and do things smarter together than we could alone."

Larison was looking at Carl and smiling, and Livia had the sense he'd seen Carl smooth over some rough patches before—and that he appreciated it, or was amused by it, or both.

Carl looked at Livia. "Now, Livia says she trusts her contact's intel and his intentions. And because she's the only one in a position to say, it's only logical that we would trust her judgment on that. But at the same time, Livia, there's no reason for you not to go into this meeting in a way that's calculated to mitigate whatever risks might be in play. Does that make sense?"

She didn't like it—she knew all about creating a framework that sounded reasonable to a suspect but that was in fact designed to box him in. But she didn't see a way to argue with Carl's proposal, so she gave him a reluctant nod.

Carl turned to Rain. "And John, I don't know anyone better than you at setting up a meeting in such a way that the good guys walk away from it as healthy as when they went in. Can you help with that?"

Rain gave a nod that looked as reluctant as Livia's felt.

Carl looked at Horton. "And Colonel, you seem to have a lot of expertise about the local terrain. Maybe you could suggest a venue we could control, maybe where John and the inimitable Mr. Larison could set up countersurveillance, that kind of thing?"

Horton smiled, obviously recognizing what Carl was up to. "The Lake Anna State Park right here would be ideal. There's an overflow parking lot at the trailhead. And a campground a half mile up the trail. This time of year, in the middle of the week, it'll all be empty." He looked at Rain with an *Over to you* expression.

Rain looked at Horton, then at Carl, and Livia had the sense that he was exasperated but didn't see a way out. A control freak? Maybe. Well, it took one to know one.

"All right," Rain said after a moment. "Livia, if you tell your contact to meet you at the campground, Larison and I could position ourselves at the trailhead. See when he arrives and whether anyone follows him in."

Carl smiled. "Say, that's a good idea."

Rain shot him a look. "Don't gild the lily."

Carl's smile broadened. "It's not that. It's just that I love it when a plan comes together."

"Here's what you tell him," Horton said. "The meeting will be in the parking lot at Cooper Vineyards at nine o'clock tomorrow morning, two hours before they open. Town of Louisa, Virginia. When he gets there, you can call again and give him the actual location, which will be the state park twenty minutes away. He'll enter the park and follow Cabin Road to the overflow lot. At which point, he gets out and follows Fisherman's Trail. It's all well marked. And the area is heavily forested. Plenty of places for John and Daniel to set up along the route early. Dox and I can accompany you to the meeting itself."

"There's one more thing," Livia said. "Carl, my contact said he knew I'd flown to DC because of ICE records. Which means he could track you, too. Last-minute ticket, that kind of thing. It could put us together."

Larison said, "Carl?"

Carl looked at him, then at the others. "No one else gets to call me that."

Livia couldn't tell if he was joking or not. And no one else asked.

"Anyway," Carl said after a moment, "I'm currently traveling with ersatz identification, courtesy of Christians In Action. And yeah, for someone clever enough and with enough to go on, that layer could be breached, too. But I don't care. I'm wanted for plenty of nefarious things by even more nefarious people. Being a known associate of yours would be the least of my offenses. And as for you, if anyone ever asks, you can just deny that you know me. You sure wouldn't be the first."

That was a relief. Though she hoped she hadn't screwed up, calling him *Carl* in front of the others. She realized she should have picked up on how he had switched to *Livia* when they were no longer alone.

She called Little and told him the plan. She was expecting some pushback, or at least a comment about her paranoia, but there was none. Apparently he hadn't been completely confident she was going to give in, and had no desire to push things any further than he already had.

"One more call," Livia said when they were done. "My lieutenant. She told me to get out of town, but those men Carl took care of outside my apartment . . . I need to know what's going on. And just to let her know I'm okay."

She called Strangeland. As soon as the lieutenant heard her voice, she said, "Jesus, Livia, where are you? Are you all right?"

"I'm fine. I got out of town, like you said."

"There were two shooters across the river from your loft this morning. Snipers, from the look of the scene. Both shot to death. Livia, please. If you had something to do with this, tell me. Someone is obviously after you in connection with this Child's Play thing, and it'll look like another case of clear self-defense. But not if you run from it. You have to come clean."

"LT, I was on my way out of town when I heard the reports about shots fired. But I had nothing to do with it."

"Please tell me you can prove that."

"I was at the Hangar Café, talking to Justin, the owner. I paid with a credit card. I went to my loft from there to pick up a few things. A half dozen workers in the building saw me there. And there are cameras, too. And then I drove to the airport. I had my phone with me, so all this would be further corroborated by cellphone-tower records. If the shots I heard about are the ones that happened across the river, it would have been impossible for me to be there. So yes, I can prove I wasn't involved."

There was a long pause. "Let me tell you a couple things, Livia. First, that much proof—multiple eyewits, credit-card receipts, surveillance-camera footage, cellphone data— might strike some people as so good it had to be planned. Second, next time someone brings this up—someone like Detective Phelps or Chief Best—you should act a little more surprised and concerned. You know, along the lines of 'What? Snipers across the river from my loft, shot to death? Good God.' That kind of thing."

Livia didn't answer. She realized that with everything else going on, she had focused too much on the proof and not enough on the performance.

"That said," Strangeland continued, "I'm glad you're all right. I'm not even going to ask you where you are. In fact, it's probably better if I don't know."

Livia smiled, relieved. "Any news from Phelps?"

"Some. He was noncommittal about slowing down his investigation, but I think he's okay with it. The theory now is that there was a third party at the martial-arts academy—a driver, because all the vehicles we checked in the neighborhood have been accounted for."

Livia had wondered about that. If the attackers had driven their own car, it would have been left somewhere nearby, maybe with evidence inside it.

"Bad luck," Livia said.

"Yeah. The good news is, video from the parking lot corroborates your story."

At this point, the officer-involved aspects of what she was up against felt remote. Still, Strangeland was right. It was good news.

"As for DNA matches," Strangeland went on, "the DOD database came up empty. But that doesn't prove anything, because military personnel can request destruction of their samples upon leaving the service. Here's something that feels relevant, though. We're getting all kinds of static from the Bureau about access to the IAFIS. Usually we're able to cut a few paperwork corners there for a priority case. Not this time. This time, they're making us dot every i and cross every t."

The IAFIS was the Integrated Automated Fingerprint Identification System, a huge database of criminal and civil prints maintained by the Bureau.

Livia considered. "So the likely inference—"

"Is that your attackers are in the system. And the Bureau knows it. And the Bureau doesn't want us to know. Which suggests that whoever else might be involved in trying to suppress this Child's Play thing, the Bureau is part of it."

"Well, that's reassuring."

"Yeah, I'm having trouble processing it, too. We've got detectives working the South Park snipers now, and my guess is there's no car there, either, and that they're going to run up against the same bureaucratic nonsense from the Bureau. But you never know. Maybe we'll get lucky on the DOD database—people leave the military all the time and don't bother or forget to request destruction of their samples. Or they request it, and the DOD never gets around to it, or loses the paperwork, or whatever. What about you, any progress on your end?"

From the careful way the lieutenant was phrasing it, Livia again sensed she might be concerned about what she said over the phone. Maybe they were all getting paranoid. Well, not without reason.

"I think so," Livia said. "I'll know more tomorrow morning. Can you cover for me a little while longer?"

"Well, you're still on administrative leave. Phelps is going to want to interview you about those dead snipers, but I can get him to focus on the physical evidence for now. And the chief . . . I think she'll give you a little time, too. I mean, two runs at you at known locations is two too many. I don't think anyone could reasonably dispute that you need to lay low for a little while."

It was nothing but good news, really. But the attention all this was bringing made Livia feel sick. With enough angles to investigate, Phelps could stumble across something.

Stop. You're okay. You know every gap in the building's camera coverage. You've never been picked up coming or going at night. You leave your cellphone in the loft. There's nothing for Phelps to investigate and there's nothing for him to stumble across.

She knew it was true. But the feeling persisted.

"Thanks, LT."

"Do I need to tell you to keep me posted?"

"No."

"Can I reach you?"

"I'm keeping my phone off. But I'll check in."

"Good. Don't make me wait too long. I've got enough gray hair as it is." She clicked off.

Livia handed the phone back to Carl. He said, "Everything copacetic at the office?"

She looked at the phone as though to confirm the call was done. In fact, she needed a moment. Strangeland's confidence in her, the risks she was willing to run . . . it was all producing a roiling mess of emotion she couldn't deal with right now.

She managed to push it away and handed the phone to Carl. "Copacetic enough."

Carl nodded. "And now, if nobody objects, I'm going to call Mr. K. Maybe he's got something we can work with. And even if not, if I wind up in another gunfight I intend to be properly armed. John, I assume you feel the same?"

Rain nodded.

"And Colonel, any suggestions for another appropriate venue?"

"I'd say the Lake Anna Winery, in Spotsylvania, Virginia. All the wineries are quiet this time of year, especially in the morning."

Carl punched some numbers into the phone and walked over to the window for reception. "Hey there," he said after a moment. A pause, then, "Yeah, everything's fine. I'm here with John now. The bad news, though, is that the hardware you provided me is now at the bottom of a river the name of which I can't pronounce.

The good news is, it saved my life, and reduced the opposition's numbers by two." Another pause. "Yeah, I'll tell you all about it, plus a few other things I've learned. But why don't we do it in person for a change? Since we're in your neck of the woods and all." A pause. "Oh, we're in some trouble all right, you don't have to be a CIA officer to know that. Which is why I'd be grateful for a couple more of what you were kind enough to lend me last time. Now, let me save you the trouble of telling me how hard it'll all be. I really do need the help and I really will make it up to you. I mean, hell, if you don't want to know everything we learn about a child-pornography ring operating out of the Secret Service and a cover-up that involves a downed commercial liner, that's fine, we won't burden you with the knowledge." Another pause. "Okay then. How about in the parking lot of a place called the Lake Anna Winery, in Spotsylvania, Virginia? Straight shot down Ninety-Five for you, and if we do it at sunup, you won't even hit any traffic." A pause. "Hah, consideration is my middle name. Thanks, amigo. I appreciate it, no shit."

He clicked off. "All right, we're set."

Horton said, "One more call to make. My voicemail. Let me see if Ben checked in."

Carl glanced at Rain and, seeing no objection, handed the phone to Horton.

Livia was intrigued by their dynamic. On the

one hand, Carl was freewheeling and obviously delighted in tweaking Rain. On the other hand, on at least some issues, he seemed implicitly to defer to Rain's judgment. Whatever their relationship, they'd obviously known each other a long time, and had developed a sense of when to push and when to back off.

She wondered why Carl hadn't mentioned that Rain was part Asian. It wasn't relevant, exactly. But she hadn't been expecting it, either. She wondered if he had grown up in the States. His English was native. But there was something about him that seemed . . . not quite at ease. Which made her wonder if he was an outsider, like her.

Larison said, "Treven's a dead end."

"Who's Treven?" Livia asked.

"Someone I've worked with," Horton said, walking to the window and punching in numbers. "Who I trained, just as I trained Daniel here. And who I think wants to come in from the cold."

After a moment listening, he smiled. "He called me. Just like I told you damn cynics he would."

He started to input a number. Rain said, "You mind putting it on speakerphone? It'll be more efficient."

Livia thought Horton would object to being the only one Rain challenged about a private conversation. She certainly would have.

But Horton finessed the issue. "That's a good

idea," he said. "And a good practice for everyone going forward."

He finished inputting the number. A ring, then a man's voice: "Yeah."

"I got your message, son," Horton said.

There was a long pause. Treven said, "Are the others there?"

"They are."

Another pause. "Graham's going to be in Paris two days from now. He knows you're after him. He put me in charge of his personal security because I know your faces and I know your moves. That's your opening, if you want it."

"Yeah?" Larison said. "What caused your sudden conversion?"

Livia wasn't surprised by the reaction. Whoever Treven was, Larison had already made his antipathy clear. It seemed there was some sort of history there—maybe professional jealousy, given that Horton said he had trained them both, maybe something else. Beyond which, of the four men, Larison struck her as having the most attitude. There was something about him that radiated danger, like a coiled snake, and she wondered how Carl had come to trust him.

"You don't want the intel?" Treven said. "Fine. Handle Graham on your own."

"It occurs to me," Carl said. "Perhaps speakerphone might be less efficient than advertised."

"Dox?" Treven said.

"That's right. How are you, Treven?"

"I'm fine. Now, if you or anyone else has something to say to me, say it. I've got things to do."

"I think what Daniel meant," Horton said, looking intently at Larison, "is, thank you."

"No," Larison said, "that's not what I meant. A couple of days ago, Treven, you were saying we had nothing more to talk about. That if you saw any of us again, it was going to get lethal. So I'm asking you. What changed your mind? And do me a favor, don't act like my question offends your honor or some other bullshit like that. In my position, you'd want to know the same. Or you would if you had half a brain."

"Yeah," Carl said. "Ixnay on the eakerphonespay."

"My reasons are none of your business," Treven said. "I'll have details soon. You want me to share them? Ask. Not interested? Not my problem."

He clicked off.

Horton looked at Larison. "Damn it, Daniel—"

"Come on, Hort," Larison said. "You know I'm right."

"It was a fair question," Carl said. "But I can think of a few different ways you might have put it."

"It doesn't matter how it was put," Rain said.

The other men looked at him, obviously waiting for him to continue. Again, Livia was struck by their deference. Horton was a colonel, or at least a former one, and had trained Larison. And yet it was Rain who, in his unassuming way, seemed to be in charge. Not by rank or position, so apparently by some sort of implicit . . . recognition. She wondered what it was about him that would make a colonel, and especially a man like Larison, accept him as a leader in a situation like this one.

"What matters," Rain went on, "is whether the intel is trustworthy. If Treven can't account for that, then Horton, respectfully, what he's feeding us is as likely to be a setup as it is actionable intel."

"More likely, I'd say," Larison added.

"I have an idea," Carl said. "Colonel, why don't you follow up with Treven yourself tomorrow. We can always suspect and even reject whatever else he tells us. But it can only help to have more intel to assess, even if all it does is give us more lies to tease apart. And I'll call K. again, tell him about Graham going to Paris, see if there's anything to what Treven told us. Maybe in addition to whatever else he has, K. can give us something we can use to corroborate. That make sense to everyone?"

Larison and Horton glanced at Rain. Rain nodded.

"Okay," Carl said, "I'm glad we have a plan. Because I have a meeting early tomorrow and I badly need a few hours' rest."

"We'll meet your guy K. together," Horton said. "John's right. Private conversations are just going to lead to suspicions."

Carl looked at Rain.

Rain shrugged. "Well, it's not as though K. has never sprung a surprise on us."

CHAPTER TWENTY-EIGHT
LIVIA

Livia and Carl left and went back to their room, Livia scanning the parking lot and the woods beyond as they walked, her hand on the grip of the Glock. The night was quiet, nothing but the crickets in the grass and the wind in the trees, not even the sounds of any distant highway traffic. The three cars she saw had all been there when she and Carl had arrived, their hoods dewy with moisture.

It had been tense at times with the others, but she'd gotten used to it. And now that they were separated, she felt nervous again, far from home and out of her element. She was glad to be with Carl.

He unlocked the door and started to open it, but she stopped him. "Let me," she said, the Glock out.

He looked at the gun. "Well, if you put it that way."

He swung open the door. The light was on, the closet door open, just as they had left it. She moved in, the Glock up. By the time Carl had closed and bolted the door behind them, she had cleared the bathroom. Carl checked under the beds. Everything was okay.

"Well," he said, sitting on one of the beds and unlacing his boots, "what did you make of the gang?"

She sat on the bed opposite, still feeling tense. "They seem a little . . . fractious."

"Hah. You should have seen us last time. It was some kind of miracle we didn't all just kill each other."

"You and Rain?"

"No, not John. He and I got past all that nonsense years ago and have worked together well ever since, though he does sometimes have a tendency to micromanage. But last time, Horton was on the other side of the table. And that Larison is like nitroglycerin—you have to handle him carefully. And the other guy you heard about, Treven, he's difficult, too, and conflicted in his allegiances."

She nodded.

He got off his boots and flexed his toes. "Are you feeling all right?" he asked. "This is a lot, I know, even for a certified badass such as yourself."

"Just feel a little . . . I don't know. Disconnected. Surreal."

"I think I get it. But on the plus side, here we are, sharing danger and adventure, back in a hotel room together . . . it's like old times."

She smiled. "Don't even think it."

He smiled back. "Too late for that. But I'll try not to."

"Good."

"Hey, I only promised to try."

She couldn't help smiling. She'd never known someone who made her smile the way he did. Sean, she supposed. But that was so long ago.

"Anyway," he said, getting his socks off now, "you mind taking first watch? I feel bad asking, but I'm going on forty-eight hours at this point and in danger of hallucinations. I don't need more than an hour or two, just a while to shut down and reboot."

"I don't mind at all. Okay if I just take a quick shower first? It's been a long day."

"Sure thing. I might do the same when you're done, or I might pass out instantly, it's fifty-fifty. Leave me the gun while you're in there?"

She handed him the Glock, grip first. "Hey," she said, "should I not have called you Carl in front of the others? You've been calling me Livia, so . . ."

"Ah, it doesn't matter. They'll probably just give me a hard time. Rain especially, because he doesn't get many opportunities, so when he does, my God, the man is merciless. Anyway, it's not a security thing. Dox is just a nickname, a nom de guerre, if you will, and no one but my folks calls me Carl anymore. Well, my folks and you, that is."

She nodded. "I like calling you that." She didn't add that she liked that no one else was allowed to.

"I like it, too. And I like knowing you as *Labee*. But I thought you'd prefer *Livia* in front of the others."

"I do. Only you get to call me *Labee*. Okay?"

He nodded. "Go on, go take that shower before I start saying things you'll regret, all right?"

She looked at him, and it was the strangest thing. She wanted to touch him. Just his hand, or his face. Something.

But the feeling was so unfamiliar it unnerved her. She nodded and headed to the bathroom.

In the shower, she tried to piece together everything that was happening, everything she was feeling. But she quickly gave up. There was just too much. She knew from working cases that sometimes you had to step back for a while and let go. And come at it later from a fresh angle.

She'd checked the weather in Seattle earlier. The city was in the midst of an unusual string of dry days. But that wouldn't last forever. She needed to wrap this thing up fast. And not just so she could get back and focus on the park rapist. But to find a way to restart the Child's Play op as well.

Things could have been worse. After all, only a day ago she was practically alone. Now she was with Carl and the others, all of whom had access to sources a cop wouldn't dream of. Only a day ago she had nothing but a vague idea of who was behind the attack at the self-defense academy. Now they knew about OGE's involvement.

As for Carl, the only thing she knew for sure was that he made her feel safe.

Though of all the frightening things that had been happening to her, that felt the most unsettling of all.

CHAPTER TWENTY-NINE
RAIN

Per the plan, we met Kanezaki in the parking lot of the Lake Anna Winery. Dox had given him a heads-up that it wasn't going to be just the three of us. And while Kanezaki had indeed been discomfited by the slight change of plans, it seemed the opportunity to expand his informal, off-the-books intelligence-and-action network was too good to pass up.

Kanezaki was standing next to a gray Toyota Camry when the five of us pulled up—Larison, Horton, and I in the car Larison and I had rented at Dulles; Livia and Dox in the passenger van. Having long ago come to accept that Kanezaki was no threat to me, I was able to admire him for having learned that the person earliest to arrive to a meeting was also the one most likely to leave it.

We stepped out in front of what looked like a converted barn. The morning air was cool enough to fog our breath, but the sky was already blue in the east, and daylight was beginning to peek through the treetops behind the building. All around us were green fields and woodland and birdsong, and the breeze smelled of earth and cut grass. It was a quintessential Virginia morning, and I thought I could understand Horton's attachment to the region.

We walked over, our footfalls loud on the gravel in the early stillness of the day. "Tom," Dox called out. "In the flesh and more handsome than ever."

Kanezaki held out a hand, which Dox shook while pulling him in for the customary hug.

When Dox had released him, I shook his hand. "I heard you're running the place now," I said.

He smiled, which made him look more like the Agency greenhorn I'd met so many years back, and less like the seasoned—and blooded— operator he'd become. "Not quite. Just a division chief."

I nodded. "Tatsu would be proud."

Tatsu had been a friend of mine, a formidable cop with Japan's Keisatsuchō, the national police force. Before his death from cancer, he had taken quite a shine to Kanezaki, treating him in some ways as a substitute son. And the affection, I knew, had been mutual.

"Thanks for that," Kanezaki said. "I miss him."

Livia, who had been notably guarded in the hotel room the night before, was surprisingly warm with Kanezaki. "I feel like I should call you K.," she said, shaking his hand.

Kanezaki smiled. "I've been called worse."

She smiled back. "Thank you for all your help. Now, of course. But before, too."

I wondered if she understood that the help wasn't a favor. And that at some point, Kanezaki was likely to request some form of help in return.

With Larison, it was also warm. The two of them had come to respect each other while Larison and I had been part of the detachment—Kanezaki's backing of which had been critical.

With Horton, it was a little stiffer. Horton must have realized it had been Kanezaki backing Dox, Larison, and me during what Horton now preferred to refer to as the Late Unpleasantness. And Kanezaki of course knew that Horton's political heroics from the time were tainted, to say the least.

When the greetings were done, Kanezaki extended a gym bag to Dox. "I hope this isn't like school, where I'm supposed to have brought enough for everyone," he said.

Dox took the bag and unzipped it. "Nope, some of the kids brought their own chewing gum. It's just John and me who are light." He looked inside and smiled. "Thank you, Santa, it's always fine when Christmas comes early."

He pulled out a bellyband holster and tossed it to me. I secured it inside my waistband and under my shirt and said to Kanezaki, "Anything on Graham?"

He nodded. "The Paris angle was a big help. And it sounds real."

Dox handed me a Wilson Combat .45. I

checked the load and eased it into the holster. "Real how?" I said.

"Graham bought his plane tickets over a month ago," Kanezaki said. "First class, round-trip, Dulles to de Gaulle. So if his presence in Paris is nothing but a setup, he put it in motion before even reaching out to you. Which seems unlikely."

Horton glanced at Larison. "What'd I tell you?"

"This isn't corroboration," I said, looking at Horton. "Graham's not stupid enough to feed us something we might confirm was cooked up yesterday. He'd weave the false intel into an existing tapestry. Just like you would."

"Just like you *did*," Larison added, staring at Horton.

"Hey," Dox said quickly, "we're going to focus on the future, remember?"

I kept my eyes on Horton. "We need to be dispassionate. We all have our own motivations for believing or disbelieving. But we're going to set that shit aside and evaluate the patterns. Okay?"

"All I'm saying," Horton said, "is that it looks good. But you're right, it's not dispositive."

I turned to Kanezaki. "Why Paris?"

"Graham does business development all over Europe. And the Middle East. These days even Beijing and Moscow. But Paris is a thing for him. He's in Paris several times a year. You might say he likes Paris."

He obviously wanted me to bite, so I did. "Okay, what's the special draw?"

"As far as I can tell, there are a number of things. There's the business development, as I mentioned. And he has a million-dollar Burgundy collection, and always sets aside a few days to acquire more while he's in the country. He seems to love the Ritz hotel, because he stays there every time he's in town."

"With that much money," Dox said, "and so much time in-country, why doesn't he just buy himself a fancy pied-à-terre?"

"You'd have to ask him," Kanezaki said. "But my guess is, he likes the convenience and the prestige. The hotel keeps his things for him, and when he arrives, his room is always ready, with his clothes laundered and pressed, the refrigerator full of his favorite local cheeses, and a selection of some of the Burgundies the hotel stores for him. He always stays in one of the prestige suites, usually the Mansart on the top floor with 'a magical view of the rooftops of Paris,' at seven thousand euros a night."

"Interesting," Dox said. "If he's got a view of the rooftops of Paris, the rooftops of Paris have a view of him, too."

"How do you know all this?" I said.

"Good lord, don't ask him," Dox said. "It's just an opportunity for him to feel smug about his 'sources and methods.' "

Kanezaki smiled. "Well, in this case, I wouldn't be giving away anything that hasn't already been reported based on the Snowden revelations, and accurately speculated on in some of the more informed spy fiction. Mostly it's about credit-card receipts and cellphone location records. Things like that. Now, if you want to know about the programs that give us access to everything a person buys other than with cash, and everyplace a person goes, and who he meets with unless he and everyone associated with him leaves their cellphones at home, and everything a person searches for on the Internet, and everyone a person knows and interacts with through social media . . ."

He paused, obviously for dramatic effect. For whatever reason, Livia was looking at him intently. Maybe she didn't know about these programs or hadn't imagined how far-reaching they could be. I wondered if she was horrified at her first glimpse of what most civilians preferred to pretend didn't exist.

". . . then I'll just have to say those programs are either classified," he went on, "or that they don't even exist."

"What did I tell you?" Dox said.

"Don't complain," Kanezaki said. "I haven't even gotten to the best part."

Dox smiled. "I love when there's a best part."

"He has a mistress. Dominique Deneuve.

Forty-one, former fashion model. He brings her to his business meetings."

"Why his business meetings?" Larison said.

Kanezaki shrugged. "Some men like to conduct their business in the presence of beautiful women. In Japan, it's a big thing—the geisha houses of old, the hostess clubs of today. John can tell you all about it. And some of the clients Graham wines and dines in Paris are from the Middle East, where sophisticated blondes are considered particularly desirable."

"Interesting," Horton said. "I was part of a meeting with Graham some years ago in London. And another in Brussels. On both occasions, he had quite a stunning blonde on his arm."

Dox gave me a look. "So he's got a thing for blondes," he said, as though just musing.

I ignored the look.

Kanezaki nodded. "It sure sounds like it."

Dox continued looking at me. I continued to ignore him.

"Anyway," Kanezaki said, "Graham being in Paris looks legit. But whether your intel about his presence there is fundamentally a leak, or he wants you to know it as part of a setup, I can't say."

"Maybe it doesn't matter," Larison said. "Put Dox up on one of those rooftops with the right hardware, problem solved."

I shook my head. "Only part of the problem.

I doubt in the end that Graham is more than muscle."

Larison looked at Horton. "Helicopter gunships are the kind of muscle I'd prefer not to have to fight."

"If it comes to that," I said. "First the intel. Then the action. Tom, anything else we can work with?"

"Maybe. He likes the Hemingway Bar in the hotel. His drink is the clean dirty martini. And he uses the private dining room of the restaurant to entertain."

"Can you get his schedule?" Horton asked.

"I'm working on it," Kanezaki said. "But it's one thing to put together credit-card receipts, cellphone locations . . . things that have already happened, already been logged. For things that haven't happened yet, I need to get into other networks. It becomes more of an interagency thing, so harder for me to do without leaving fingerprints."

"Well," Horton said, "as you've noted, worst case there's the Dominique Deneuve angle. Assuming she's just a civilian, wherever Graham is, at some point she should lead us right to him."

"That's fine work, Tom," Dox said. "We're all grateful. And no, you don't have to ask, as soon as we figure out what this is all about and where it's coming from, we'll let you know. Also, sometime down the road, when you want a bad person deniably removed, I know you'll feel free to call on us."

Kanezaki nodded, probably pleased that we no longer had to haggle about these matters. "You need to be careful," he said. "Graham has a lot of powerful friends in and out of government. Don't assume that the kinds of programs I used to put this intel together aren't available to him, one way or the other. Speaking of which, I need to go. My phone's been off since I left this morning. I want to get it back on before people start wondering where I am."

We waited until he was gone, then drove off in our separate vehicles. We hit a McDonald's drive-through for coffee and breakfast, and then continued to the state park. Livia's contact, Little, would be arriving soon, and I wanted plenty of time to get in position with Larison in case he wasn't alone.

CHAPTER THIRTY
LARISON

Larison and Rain were proned out under the leaves on a ridge in Lake Anna State Park, looking down on the overflow lot. Larison was glad to be working just with Rain again. He trusted Rain's intentions, and he trusted his abilities—which wasn't something he could say about anyone else he knew. Dox came close, he supposed. But as much as he'd reluctantly grown to like the big sniper, Dox was always going to be too brash and ebullient for Larison to ever really be comfortable with. Rain's quiet confidence and meticulous planning were more Larison's speed. And beyond that, he could tell that, like himself, Rain felt like an outsider, detached and alienated from the world but still seeking some kind of connection. Well, he'd made one with Larison, and Larison wouldn't forget it.

The other three were a half mile up the trailhead, waiting for Livia's contact, a Homeland Security Investigations agent named B. D. Little. Livia had described him as black, midforties, maybe six-two and 220, built like a former football player, probably wearing glasses and a suit, and looking like the federal law enforcement he was. The question was whether anyone would be with him or, more worrying, behind.

Even though Little was expecting the meeting to be at the winery, Rain wanted to get in position at the park early. That suited Larison fine. It was always good to get a feel for the rhythms of a place. It made spotting incongruities easier.

They'd been silently watching for close to twenty minutes when Rain said, "How are . . . things with you and Nico?"

Larison tensed. He knew Rain and the others knew, though he also preferred them to pretend they didn't. But . . . in any other context, it would have been a normal question, right? It might even have seemed rude not to ask. Maybe that was all Rain was doing. Just being . . . normal.

Still, he wasn't sure how to respond. After a long pause, he said, "Good."

They were both quiet again, watching the parking lot. A minute went by. Rain said, "You're lucky."

This was a lot of talk coming from Rain. And on an uncomfortable subject. Larison tried to puzzle it out. He couldn't. Finally he said, "You don't . . . have someone?"

"Not anymore."

"What happened?"

"Long story."

Larison glanced at his watch. "We've got fifteen minutes."

Rain sighed. "We had a dumb fight. But that wasn't the cause, it was a symptom. She was in the life and wouldn't leave it."

Larison tried to think of how to respond. Before he could come up with anything, Rain added, "How do you make it work with Nico? With a civilian?"

Larison considered. "That's what makes it work. This fucking life . . . Nico's so innocent, he almost makes me feel innocent again."

Jesus, had he really just said that? He hadn't thought about it, it just came out. But it was too late to take it back.

"I wish I could feel like that," Rain said. "But I can't. Not with her."

Larison had to laugh a little at that. "I'm not saying it lasts. You and I are never going to feel innocent. Not really. You should settle for her making you feel good. And you doing the same for her."

They were quiet again. After a minute, Rain said, "It's probably too late anyway."

"Well, why don't you go see her? Where is she?"

Rain glanced at him, his expression rueful. "Paris."

It took Larison a second to connect the dots. "Wait a minute, is that why Dox gave you that look when Kanezaki and Hort were talking about blondes?"

Rain nodded.

"You said she's in the life. Could she help?"

"I . . . shit, I don't want to talk about this."

Larison laughed. "Look, nobody's ever going to confuse me with Dr. Ruth, but hell yes you want to talk about this, you brought it up."

"Yeah, but I don't . . ."

Rain stopped talking and gestured with a finger to the lot.

A dark sedan had just pulled in. It stopped. A man got out, fitting Livia's description perfectly.

"Little," Larison said.

Rain nodded.

"All right. We'll talk about the other thing later."

"We really don't have to."

"Up to you. I'm probably not the best guy to give advice to the lovelorn. And I know you're afraid Dox will give you shit about it. But my opinion, for what it's worth? Talk to someone. There's too much room for regret if you get it wrong."

They watched as Little read the sign at the trailhead, then disappeared into the woods.

Rain glanced at Larison. "I think you might be better in the advice department than you think."

Larison laughed again. "I'll keep my day job. Just in case."

A minute later, another dark sedan pulled into the lot. It stopped on the side opposite from

Little's car. Two large men in gray suits got out. No ties. They started walking briskly toward the trailhead.

Rain was smiling. "One of my favorite surveillance tells," he said.

Larison nodded. "The in-between garb."

"Exactly. These guys are tailing Little. But they don't know where they might wind up. Maybe in a business district. Maybe in a diner. Maybe a shopping mall. So they dress at the low end of formal for some environments, and the high end of casual for others."

"But a walk in the woods was something they just weren't ready for."

Rain glanced over. "So you make them as tailing Little, not as working with him?"

"Yeah."

"Why?"

Larison considered. It was hard to articulate, but he knew he and Rain were seeing the same thing. "The way Little was walking, he seemed not to have a clue. A cop, not an operator. No sense of what might be behind him, whether opposition or his own people. And if they were with him, they wouldn't have been following so closely. He would have told them where he'd be, and they could have drifted way back before moving in. Those guys . . . they lost visual contact for a moment, and they didn't like it. So they moved in a little quickly."

Rain nodded. "Agreed."

Larison understood what that "agreed" entailed. Nothing else needed to be said.

A few minutes later, Little came around a bend in the trail and passed their position. Larison couldn't imagine walking an actual marked trail in the woods as instructed by someone else. Unless he was suicidal and just wanted to end it all. He reminded himself Little was law enforcement. A good investigator, Livia had said. But not even a street cop.

As soon as Little was past, the two of them took up positions behind trees on either side of the trail.

The two men following Little came around the bend. Neither was holding a gun.

Okay.

Larison and Rain stepped simultaneously from behind cover, their guns up. "Not even a twitch," Larison said. "Or you're done right there."

Both men froze, their eyes wide, their arms out slightly and shaking with tension from the conflicting *freeze* and *go for the gun* signals shooting through their brains.

"Easy," Rain said. "All we want is to ask you some questions. Answer them and you can walk out of here. Anything else is an instant bullet in the brain. Fair enough?"

"What the hell is this?" one of the men said, maybe thinking he could bluff his way out.

313

But their body language was all wrong. They were scared and they were pissed, but they were definitely not experiencing the kind of *tilt* reaction a civilian gets when confronted by two men insisting on having questions answered at gunpoint.

"That'll be your last question," Rain said. "The rest come from us. Do you understand?"

The men nodded. Larison was 90 percent sure Rain was just giving them something to hope for. You couldn't very well expect men to cooperate if they were convinced they were going to die no matter what. But even if Larison was wrong, it didn't matter. Part of the reason he'd lasted so long was his insistence on killing everyone who ever tried to come after him. Treven was the one exception. And he was pretty sure it was the exception that proved the rule.

"Follow my commands now," Rain said. "Hands over your heads. Higher. All the way. Splay your fingers. Good. Now turn and face the other way. Good. Now keep your arms up, and slowly—and I mean fucking slowly—get down on your knees. Good. Now bring your arms down straight out in front of you, and lower yourselves onto your faces. If your hands get anywhere remotely near your bodies, you won't get a warning, you'll get a bullet in the back of the head. Do you understand?"

The men nodded and carefully lowered

themselves onto their faces. Larison wondered if Rain was serious about talking to them, or if he just wanted to give Little time to move far enough along the trail to possibly be out of earshot. It was hard to tell with Rain. Larison had seen him talking to men one second and killing them the next, without noticeable variation in affect along the way.

"Good," Rain said. "Now, arms all the way straight out to your sides. Palms facing the sky and lifted off the ground. Now spread your legs. Toes out. Now both of you turn your heads right. Left cheeks to the ground. Good. Now each of you slowly—*slowly*—put your left hand against the small of your back, palm facing the sky."

The men complied. Rain approached the one on the left. He planted his left foot on the ground next to the left side of the man's head, then got his right knee under the man's wrist and swept it up higher along the man's back in a kind of chicken-wing hold. The man yelped. With his free hand, Rain pressed the man's head firmly into the dirt, immobilizing him. Larison, more accustomed to killing people than restraining them, stepped to the front so he could shoot both men in the head unimpeded.

Rain pressed the muzzle of the gun against the back of the man's neck. "Why are you following that man?"

Neither of them answered.

Rain looked at Larison and nodded.

"We're going to play a game I like," Larison said. "It's called 'The one who doesn't answer the question first dies.' "

Rain looked at Larison's gun and shook his head, then glanced at Larison's boot and nodded. Larison nodded back.

"Why are you following that man?" Rain said again.

Neither of them answered.

Larison stepped in, raised his foot, and stomped his heel into the near man's neck as though trying to break a log. The man's arms flew up. Cartilage and vertebrae shattered. The man's body spasmed and Larison stomped again to be sure. And again. After the third blow, the man's fingers were still twitching, but otherwise he was still.

"Damn," Larison said, "that was actually a tie. So you have to play again."

The man Rain was restraining started breathing hard. "Fuck," he said. "Oh, fuck."

"Take it easy," Larison said. "You're the only player now. You have a better chance of winning."

"I don't know why we were following him," the man said quickly. "We were told to."

Rain gave Larison a *Hold on, we're making progress* look. "By whom?"

"OGE."

"We know about OGE," Rain said. "What does Graham want with that man?"

"I told you, I don't know. We were just supposed to follow him. Observe who he might be meeting with. Jesus Christ, who are you guys? Why are you doing this? This is some kind of mistake. We were just following him, that's all."

"How were you following him?" Rain asked, overlooking the fact that the guy had violated Rain's *Only we get to ask the questions* policy. Not that it really mattered.

"Someone at headquarters is dialed in to his cellphone," the guy said. "They were giving us step-by-step instructions."

"Who at headquarters?"

"I don't know everyone at headquarters, okay? It's a big operation. There are people there who just do that stuff. Or who know people who do that stuff. Or whatever. And who get the data to field people like me. Look, I'm really trying to cooperate here. I think this is just a mistake, okay?"

Rain looked at Larison, his eyebrows raised questioningly. Larison shook his head—nothing more to be learned here.

Without another word, Rain raised the pistol and smashed the butt down into the guy's neck over the carotid artery. The guy went limp. Rain slid his gun hand onto the guy's right shoulder, pinning it to the ground, reached under the guy's chin with his free hand, and ripped the guy's head back at a diagonal as though yanking the starter

317

rope on a lawnmower. There was an enormous *crack!* as the guy's neck broke. Rain stood and stepped back, the pistol at the ready, but there was no need, the guy was already dead.

They searched the bodies and recovered cellphones, wallets, and a pair of SIG Sauer P229s and spare magazines. Rain wasn't interested in the guns, having been provisioned by Kanezaki, but Larison was always looking to improve his various stash sites, and so took both. They moved the bodies off the trail and covered them with leaves. They'd be found before long, but before long would be time enough.

CHAPTER THIRTY-ONE
RAIN

An hour later, the five of us plus Little were sitting in the rental van behind a supermarket on the outskirts of Spotsylvania. At the park, Larison had called Dox using the satellite phones and told him what had happened. Little needed to ditch his cellphone immediately. And they all needed to get back to the lot and the hell out of Dodge.

To his credit, Little kept cool when we confronted him. He insisted he hadn't known there was a tail. I found myself believing him. There had been his observable demeanor along the trail, of course, and that of his pursuers. But beyond that, if OGE had known he was on his way to meet the rest of us, they would have sent a lot more than just two guys—who hadn't even had their guns out when Larison and I intercepted them.

"Where are they now?" Little wanted to know.

"They're no longer a threat," Larison said.

Coming from a man with Larison's bearing, there was pretty much only one way to interpret that. Little said, "My God, you killed them?"

"They're no longer a threat," I said. "Which

319

is good, because in the last few days, Livia had four people come at her, the rest of us had four plus a helicopter gunship, and just now there were two more on you. You think those men were following you to make sure you'd be safe in the woods? Have they given any indication they look at law enforcement as untouchable?"

Little didn't respond.

"So how about if you just say thank you," Larison said, "and be glad we believe your story that you didn't know they were behind you."

Livia said, "Enough. Little. We need to put our heads together about why they were following you. Was it because you and I talked on the phone, and they connected us that way?"

Little was quiet for a moment, his jaw set. He was collecting himself, I knew. Whatever experience he had, it didn't involve people making the sorts of decisions Larison and I had made at the park and acting on them. This was a guy who thought he was comfortable swimming in the open water, the turbulent, dark water, and was only now learning just what kinds of creatures lurked in those depths.

Finally, he blew out a long breath. "It could be that," he said. "But I'm pretty sure it's something else. I think the problem is coming from the Bureau. What I don't yet know is why."

Livia extended a hand in a *please continue* gesture.

"Here's how I approached it," Little said. "After the first time you and I talked, I asked myself, 'How do you wind up with six predatory pedophiles in the Secret Service?' And not just your garden variety, either, but the worst, the hurtcore specialists. I mean, statistically speaking, that's a lot for a relatively small organization."

No one said anything, and he went on. "And then I thought, 'Okay, let's say there are that many. Unlikely, yes, but I suppose not impossible, because statistics don't get evenly distributed. Flip a coin a thousand times and it doesn't go heads, tails, heads, tails, all the way down the line. You get improbable runs—five heads in a row, maybe even ten. So okay, let's accept that, as unlikely as it seems, the Secret Service is home to six predatory pedophiles.'"

He paused and, seeing there were no questions, continued. "Well, if so, there must have been a prior indication of a problem. At some point, someone got caught using a work computer to access child pornography, or a victim came forward, or a past violation came to light. Something. *Something.* Not just a blank canvas with six predatory pedophiles and their ongoing vileness on the other side of it. No. That would be borderline impossible.

"Now, when there's a serious federal crime committed by a federal employee, SOP is to report the matter to the Justice Department. So I made it a point to stop by. Talked to a fellow in records there, made sure to inquire about a variety of matters to obscure the nature of my actual interest. And when I mentioned, 'Oh, one other thing . . . any reports filed about child-pornography charges against a Secret Service agent in the last five years or so?' You know what he said?"

We were all silent.

" 'That's funny,' he said, 'you're the second one to ask about that. Is something going on?' I asked him who was the first, at which point he got nervous, maybe thinking he had already said too much. He told me he wasn't authorized to say more, and that regardless, the records had now been sealed. Meaning that to access them, I would have to go through hell's own interagency process, and maybe even get a court order. And even after all that, I might find that the records had somehow been accidentally misplaced or destroyed."

"Who was asking before you?" Livia said. "And what did they find?"

Little looked at her. "Ever heard of J. J. Arrington?"

"Yes," Livia said. "The head of CID. My chief has a call in to him because Agent Smith was head of VCAC, and she reported to him."

Dox said, "CID? VCAC?"

Livia nodded. "The FBI's Criminal Investigative Division. And the Violent Crimes Against Children program, which is part of CID." She looked at Little. "What about Arrington?"

"Well, I'd already been thinking of Arrington as a person of interest because he was Smith's immediate superior and was ultimately in charge of the Child's Play joint task force. And then, when the records person at Justice told me someone else had been asking about Secret Service agents referred for investigation and possible prosecution for child pornography, I knew it had to be someone from Justice, if whoever it was got access and then had the records sealed. It didn't have to be Arrington, but it certainly could have been. And since you'd just gotten through updating me about OGE, I wondered if there might be some connection between Arrington and Oliver Graham."

He paused for dramatic effect, and though I badly wanted to hear the rest, I couldn't blame him for the pause, either. He'd been smart and diligent, and had obviously sensed patterns the rest of us hadn't.

Larison was less patient. "What the fuck did you find?" he said.

"That the two of them go way back," Little said. "They were in the same unit, SEAL Team 8. They trained together at Coronado and were both deployed to Operation Uphold Democracy in Haiti, and Operation Noble Anvil in Kosovo."

Dox laughed. "My lord, why won't someone hire me to name America's military actions? I'd be so much better at it. Operation Mine's Bigger. Operation No You Don't. Operation—"

"What's Arrington's interest?" I said, before Dox could build up a head of steam. "I mean, I get the Child's Play thing is a Secret Service scandal, and that Homeland Security and especially the Secret Service itself would want to cover it up. But why would the Bureau care? Why would Arrington?"

"That I don't know," Little said. "Arrington's part of the Justice Department, so he had access to those files, and therefore now knows who was referred to Justice from the Secret Service on suspicion of involvement in child pornography. But as I said, those records are sealed now. And I'd call it a safe bet they no longer even exist."

"Let me ask you something," Larison said, leaning in toward Little. "You're putting your ass way out in the wind on this. You could face charges, maybe a lot worse. What's your interest, anyway?"

Most people would have shriveled from Larison's danger vibe. But Little leaned right back, his eyes narrowing. "None of your fucking business," he practically spat.

"Back off," Livia said to Larison, the command tone something she must have learned as a street cop. "I know his reasons and I trust his reasons. And if you have a problem with that, then you have a problem with me."

There was a long, tense pause. I thought Dox was going to say something funny to defuse it, but he didn't. He just stared at Larison, and there was no good humor at all in his expression. His gal had thrown down, and he was going to follow her wherever that led.

Finally, Larison leaned back. He nodded and said, "Okay."

Strangely enough, Larison didn't look embarrassed at having backed down. He looked . . . comfortable. Satisfied. I wondered if what he had been looking for, consciously or otherwise, was less substantive information and more a sign of what Little was made of and maybe Livia, too. I'd known people like that, most of all Crazy Jake from a long-ago lifetime. There were men who could respect only the few people they couldn't frighten. Larison, I realized, was like that. I was surprised I hadn't seen it sooner, and supposed the explanation was obvious: I was one of those few.

"Anyway," Livia said. "It tracks. My lieutenant told me SPD has been trying to get access to IAFIS—the Integrated Automated Fingerprint Identification System run by the Bureau—to see if they could get a match on the prints of the two people who attacked me at the martial-arts academy. Ordinarily, the access is routine. This time, we're getting a ton of static. It sounds like someone at the Bureau, maybe Arrington, is anticipating someone learning what he's learned, and deleting the leads he followed."

"I don't doubt the Bureau is behind this," I said. "Most likely in the person of Arrington. But again, the question is why. In my experience with what passes for interagency cooperation, the Bureau would be more likely to make popcorn and laugh at another agency's scandal than to try to cover it up."

"That's true," Horton said. He paused, then added, "Unless the scandal is bigger than just the one agency."

CHAPTER THIRTY-TWO
RAIN

We headed north to a town called Culpeper—Horton, Larison, and I in the rental car, Livia and Dox in the van ahead of us. We'd sent Little off with the dead men's phones and wallets so he could see what might be learned from them.

Larison called Kanezaki from his satellite phone, leaning forward from the back seat and holding the unit up so we could all be heard over the speakerphone.

"Tom, we have something for you," I said. "You ever hear of a J. J. Arrington?"

"Are you kidding?" Kanezaki said. "Arrington is mixed up in this?"

Horton, in the passenger seat, glanced at me. "That sounds promising," he said.

"He's former Agency," Kanezaki said. "And a total nutjob. We managed to offload him to the Bureau. He was head of counterintelligence at the Agency and was ripping the place apart with his conspiracy theories. Everything was controlled by Russia, the Agency had been penetrated, the Kremlin had *kompromat* on every American politician . . . all that. Seriously, there's nothing that happens of any geopolitical significance anywhere in the world this guy doesn't think is a Kremlin plot."

"How did you get the Bureau to take him?" Horton said.

"We didn't share his psych evaluations," Kanezaki said, "I can tell you that. But when the top counterintel position opened up at the Bureau, we sold him to the Bureau as a seasoned expert, cross pollination, interagency cooperation, that kind of thing. And we sold the Bureau to him as a chance for greater latitude to work domestically, where naturally the Kremlin was doing its worst meddling. He knew his days at the Agency were numbered anyway and was happy to make the switch. But within six months, the Bureau had wised up that this guy should be nowhere near counterintel, and they moved him to head of the Criminal Investigative Division, where he couldn't do any harm."

Larison laughed. "The Bureau must love you guys."

"Believe me," Kanezaki said, "they've fucked us plenty of times and just as hard."

"One of the things we recently learned," Horton said, "is that Graham and Arrington go way back."

"Right," Kanezaki said. "Now that you mention it, Arrington's a former SEAL. What, did they serve together?"

"Exactly," Horton said.

"So the inference," Kanezaki said, "is that Arrington is the brains behind whatever's been happening, and Graham is just the deniable-action arm?"

Horton nodded. "I'd say it looks that way."

"But I don't get it," Kanezaki said. "Why would Arrington care about a Secret Service scandal? Let me tell you, the guy's not an altruist. He'd have zero interest in protecting another agency from scandal. If anything, he'd look for a way to exploit it."

Horton said, "That is our question exactly—why would Arrington even care? But exploit it . . . that's interesting. Exploit it how, I wonder? What would someone like Arrington want from the Secret Service? I don't see it."

Larison looked at Horton. "That's easy. You said it yourself. This isn't just about the Secret Service."

Kanezaki told us he would keep digging and we clicked off. We drove on, and a little while later, we followed Dox and Livia into the parking lot of a Walmart at the edge of Culpeper. Everyone went in to use the bathroom and buy food, and then we all got into the van. Horton briefed Dox and Livia on what we'd just learned from Kanezaki.

"I'll check in with my lieutenant," Livia said. "I wonder if Chief Best ever got through to Arrington, and what he might have said."

"Maybe this is a little audacious," Larison said, "but if we're reasonably sure Arrington is the brains behind this thing, whatever it is, and Graham is just muscle, we might be able to end it instantly by taking out Arrington."

I saw advantages and disadvantages, and wanted to think them through before saying anything.

But Livia didn't wait. She said, "I really appreciate everyone's involvement here. But I think you're missing something incredibly important."

No one spoke, and she went on. "At the heart of this thing is a child-pornography ring operating out of the Secret Service. Even if we eliminate the people who are trying to cover it up—the people who blew up a plane and who've been trying to kill us, too—would that take down the ring?"

Again, no one spoke. Larison was looking at her like she was speaking a foreign language. Horton was looking at her respectfully. And Dox . . . he was looking at her with an expression I'd never seen on him before. Like he would do anything for her.

"You're right," I said, searching for a way to navigate all the different reactions I saw, while also articulating my own. "But . . . there might be some tension in play between what we can do to take down that ring, and what we have to do to protect ourselves."

"I see that," she said. "And I'm just telling you, if you're willing to let a group like Child's Play continue to prey on children just to protect yourself, you're no friend of mine. And even though I'm grateful for your help, I'm done with you."

Dox looked at me, and I could see he had no inclination to try to bridge the divide, or even just smooth it over with some outburst the way he usually did.

Shit. We were going to fracture. And just when we seemed to be making real progress, too.

"If you see a way we can do both," I said, "I'd love to hear it."

We were all quiet again. Dox said, "I have an idea."

I thought, *Thank God.*

He turned to Livia. "Livia, all of us have had our share of horror. But I know the rest of us haven't seen what you described to me on the flight out here about the pictures and videos those Child's Play people trade in. And create. You called it hurtcore, isn't that right?"

Livia nodded grimly. "Yes."

Dox returned the nod. "Why is it called that?"

"Because the point is to cause so much pain the child is ruined by it. Left alive, but psychically crippled. For the people who get off on it, it's not enough to dominate a body. They have to destroy a soul."

Dox looked at the rest of us, then back to Livia. "And can you describe for these gentlemen some of what gets posted on that site, the way you did for me?"

Livia looked at the rest of us. "I can do better than that."

She pulled a laptop from her bag, found a store Wi-Fi connection, then worked the keyboard, saying, "Hang on, I need to do this through a VPN or it'll look suspicious to anyone at the site with admin privileges. The Bureau canceled the operation, but I still have my fake credentials, so . . . yeah. Here we are. Okay. Okay. Okay."

The last words were spoken almost ritualistically, like someone trying to self-comfort. She exhaled forcefully, turned the laptop around, and pressed the "Play" button.

Horton turned away instantly. Even Larison managed no more than a few seconds, which was maybe a second less than I could stand. I held up a hand and said, "You've made your point. Please, stop it."

Livia hit a button and the child in the video was cut off in mid scream. She looked at me, her nostrils flaring with her breathing, heat in her eyes.

In my life, I'd known many killers. And all at once, it hit me.

This woman was not just a cop.

"You wanted it to stop, and it did," she said, her

voice rising. "Even though it was just a video. Even though you were just watching. But the children in those videos *don't get to say stop*."

Her eyes filled and she brushed the back of a wrist against them furiously. She blew out a long breath, and then another. "So any plan you come up with that doesn't involve taking down this ring, has nothing to do with me."

A long, silent moment went by.

Larison spoke first. "I wouldn't mind . . . doing something about that," he said.

Horton looked at Livia and nodded.

Dox looked at me. "John?"

For a moment, I felt ashamed for having overlooked the issue. And not just for the sake of the kids those Child's Play monsters were preying on. For myself, too. Hadn't I tried to sell Treven on the idea of getting some positive points on the karmic ledger? Did I mean that? Or was it all just bullshit?

"You already know the answer," I said.

"I need a minute," Livia said. She pulled open the door and got out.

Dox hesitated, then said, "I'll be right back."

CHAPTER THIRTY-THREE
LIVIA

Livia walked toward the side of the building. She heard someone get out of the van behind her—Carl, no doubt, but she didn't wait or look back.

She turned the corner and headed down farther, then stopped and leaned against the wall. She closed her eyes and breathed deeply. She'd felt sick for a moment in the van. But it was cool over here on the shadowed side of the building, and quiet, and she started to feel better almost immediately.

She heard Carl come around the corner. She opened her eyes and looked at him.

"Hey," he said. "If you'd rather be alone, you know that's fine. I just wanted to check."

For anyone else, the answer most certainly would have been *Yes, go away.* But Carl knew about her past. He knew . . . he knew her.

She gave him a weak smile. "Thanks for checking on me. It's nice that you do that."

And then her eyes filled up again, and she looked away, furious. For the most part, she was so in control of herself. And then a small thing would happen, and it would dissolve her.

Carl said, "If you were anybody else, this would

be the moment where I put my arms around you and hold you tenderly."

She laughed and wiped her eyes. "It's a bad idea."

"Would you mind terribly if I did it anyway? Just to be sure?"

She didn't know what she wanted, from him or anyone else. She wished for the thousandth time that she could just be normal.

He came over and brushed the back of his fingers against her cheek. "You know," he said, "I've never seen someone take control of that band of killers and cutthroats the way you just did. Please don't think I'm being condescending saying this, but you just make me so proud. I mean, Larison, I think he's in awe of you now. And Larison's the damn angel of death, he doesn't do awe, not in my experience."

She laughed again, and cried more.

His fingers were curled against her cheek. "Labee?"

She sniffed. "Yeah?"

"I think you better hit me with one of those judo throws. Because if you don't, I'm not going to be able to stop myself from kissing you."

She shook her head. "It's a bad idea."

"Because we're in a Walmart parking lot? All the best romances happen in places like this. I read it somewhere once."

She laughed. "You did not."

"I did. Okay, I wrote it down first. Then I read it. But still."

She laughed again. She loved the way he made her laugh. But it also always made her sad.

"I'm sorry I'm so . . . weird," she said, her eyes filling up again.

He shook his head. "You're not weird. You're beautiful."

And he leaned in and kissed her very softly. It didn't bother her. It was actually nice. She liked the way he smelled. Which only confused her and made her cry harder.

He pulled back. "Was it that bad?" But he was wearing a cute, dopey smile and she knew he was joking.

"It was nice," she said.

"Really? I honestly think that's the best thing I've ever heard."

She reached out and brushed her fingers against his cheek. The gesture felt strange, but she liked when he did it to her.

"Be careful," he said, smiling. "I could get used to that."

That made her sad again. "I don't think you should."

"I'll take the chance if you will," he said, and kissed her again, softly like the last time, but also a little longer.

She felt herself getting aroused, but it confused her, because this wasn't ever how she liked it.

She liked it the way it had been between them in that Rayong beach place in Thailand, when they'd been on the run and barely knew each other and she'd been completely in control.

She broke the kiss. "We should . . . we should go back," she said.

"Yeah, you're right," he said quickly. "I'm sorry."

"No, it's not you, it's not that. I just feel . . . a little overwhelmed."

"I get it. I'm sorry if I was pushing. But when I'm around you? I can feel a little overwhelmed myself."

They were quiet for a moment. She looked down, afraid to meet his eyes, afraid of what she might see in them or how it would make her feel.

"Tell you what," he said. "Let's table this conversation until the next time we're in a romantic Walmart parking lot. For now, we'll get back to the van. I have an idea for how we can get the intel we need to dismantle this Child's Play atrocity, while also killing every last creature behind it. But John's not going to like it."

"Why not?"

"It involves working with a woman in Paris. An old flame of his. And let me tell you, he can protest all he wants, but those flames are still plenty hot."

CHAPTER THIRTY-FOUR
RAIN

Larison, Horton, and I were working out the advantages and disadvantages of going after Graham first versus Arrington first. Larison, in keeping with his general approach to the world, still favored cutting off the head, meaning Arrington. Horton favored attacking the flanks, meaning Graham.

"We have more intel on Graham," I said.

"Some of which might be tainted by Treven," Larison said. "And besides, we haven't even started focusing on Arrington yet. He might turn out to be a soft target."

Horton said, "Former SEAL, former CIA counterintel, now FBI, involved in some extremely shady goings-on, and aware of potentially formidable opposition. Does that sound soft to you?"

Larison nodded. "Point taken. But absent the intel, we still don't know."

There was a rap on one of the windows. Dox. Horton slid open the door. "All good?" he said.

Livia nodded and got in. "All good."

Dox remained outside. "Hey, John, could you and I talk for a minute?"

Larison gave him a suspicious look.

Dox shook his head. "It's nothing nefarious, amigo. If it were, why would I have asked for a private moment right in front of everyone else?"

Larison didn't respond. But he didn't look happy, either. On the other hand, when did Larison look happy?

I got out and followed Dox around the corner to the side of the store.

"Everything okay with Livia?" I said.

"She's fine. She takes child abuse more personally than most."

I nodded, sensing that to ask more would be to intrude. And besides, his meaning was clear enough, and it tracked with what I'd already seen.

"She's impressive," I said.

"Partner, you've barely seen her in action. Did you know she's a judo badass, too? Olympic alternate when she was in college. I bet she could give you a run for your money, and then some."

"I wouldn't take that bet."

"Well, here's the thing. Y'all have been talking about whether to go after Graham first or Arrington, is that right?"

I wondered where he was going with this. I had some idea, and didn't like it.

"That's what we've been talking about," I said.

"Well, obviously, there are advantages and disadvantages each way. For a variety of reasons,

I favor what might best be described as the 'kill Graham first' approach. For one thing, Kanezaki is dialed all the way in to Mr. Graham's Paris proclivities."

I realized I'd been right about where he was heading. I said nothing.

"So you know where I'm going with this," he said.

I shook my head.

"Look, man, it's obvious. If all we want to do is kill Graham, the way Kanezaki described his hotel room, I can probably just turn his head into the proverbial fine pink mist. But if we want a chance to interrogate him—if we want intel, and I think we do—then we're talking about Delilah."

I shook my head again. "No."

"She could really help us," he said. "And you know it. And if you won't take advantage of that, just out of some kind of misplaced wounded pride, you should at least admit that protecting your ego is more important to you than protecting the kind of children Livia showed us in that video. Not to mention protecting Livia herself. I can't say I'd take kindly to that, in part because it's not something I'd ever do to you if the shoe were on the other foot."

"Goddamn it, are you really going to play that card?" But I knew he was right.

"Come on, man, it doesn't get any better than this. A Mossad honeytrap specialist, and Graham

340

has a thing for blondes on top of it. She could have him wrapped around her little finger after the first one of those clean dirty martinis he likes, and you know it."

"No," I said again.

"Why the hell not? She's in Paris right now."

I shouldn't have been surprised. She'd been living in Paris the last time we'd been together. But for some reason, I thought she would have moved on.

"You've been in touch with her?" I said.

He shrugged. "Now and again."

Jesus. First Larison, now Delilah. "Why?" I said.

"Because we're friends, dumbass. Friends stay in touch. I won't lie to you, you're so good at reading people, but sometimes you assume everyone else is just like you, and that ain't the way the world works. Most people don't prefer to go months without talking to another human. That's unusual. I'm not saying there's anything wrong with it; in fact, there's not. I'm just saying you shouldn't be surprised to learn that the people in your life who care about you also care about each other, and might like to reach out from time to time."

Sometimes I hated talking to him. Not because he was full of shit. That would have just been irritating. But because he was so fucking insightful. And that was intolerable.

I looked away, not wanting to ask. But he just kept on waiting, silent and patient as the sniper he was.

Finally, I sighed. "How is she?"

"She's fine. She misses you."

"She told you that?"

"No, of course not. She's too proud. Hmm, why does that sound familiar?"

"Then how do you know?"

"How do I know how much you miss her, even though you refuse to say so? Just by the way you're talking right now. Well, it's the same with her. Each of you is pining so hard for the other, and pretending so hard not to be, it would be comical if it weren't so sad. Do you really not know this? My lord, do I have to run your entire personal life for you?"

We were quiet for a moment. I knew he was trying to get the silence to work on me again, and I realized it probably would. I tried to squeeze out of it by saying, "What's up between you and Livia?"

"My feelings for her are pure, but our relationship is complicated. And you can make fun of me for that if you want, but you'll have to do it later, because right now I'm not letting you change the subject."

I shook my head. "I'm not going to make fun of you. I'm sorry I did it earlier, when you called her 'my gal.' I didn't realize it was serious."

"Yeah, it is. And it hurts at times. Just like you and Delilah."

We were quiet again. I said, "Okay. Call her."

"No, partner, you call her."

"You're the one who's been in touch with her."

"Yeah, but now you get to correct that."

I shook my head. "I don't even know what to say to her."

He clapped me on the shoulder. "Come on, you're smart. You'll figure it out."

We went back to the van. As soon as we were inside, Dox said, "Okay, here's the deal. We have an asset in Paris. A Mossad agent, name of Delilah, extremely experienced and capable, and gorgeous and blonde, just how Graham likes it. This could be a game-changing advantage for us. The only complication is, she and John here are erstwhile lovers and still carry a torch for each other. But I know we're all professionals and will find a way to deal with that."

I looked at him, horrified and pissed. But all he did was shrug. "Hey, man, you're the one who said the speakerphone was the way to go. Now everybody knows why I wanted to talk to you privately first, and they'll understand why you're going to be all twitchy about meeting with Delilah."

"Thanks," I said. "That was good of you."

He grinned. "What are friends for?"

Horton said, "If your . . . lady friend is as good

as all that, she could provide a way for us to interrogate Graham, not just kill him."

Dox nodded. "That's what I told him."

"Look," I said, "let's not get ahead of ourselves, all right? I told Dox I'd call her. But I don't know how she's going to react. She might just tell me to fuck off."

Dox shook his head. "She's not going to tell you that. Not when you explain what this is all about. And even if she did, which she won't, Paris still makes sense to me. Especially if someone can get me a rifle with a night scope, for just in case and when all else fails."

"I have contacts in Paris," Horton said, looking at me. "Men I've worked with closely. DGSE, DGSI, GIGN . . . even a few former legionnaires. They should be able to get us anything we reasonably need, including commo. So in the hardware department, I'd say we're good to go."

Larison said, "Kanezaki told us Graham bought his ticket a month ago. Meaning if Paris is a setup, he only just came up with the plan. So if we're going to do this, we should do it now. The longer we wait, the longer Graham will have to position his forces."

Dox looked at me expectantly. After a moment, I sighed and gave him a reluctant nod.

"Oo-rah," Dox said. "We're going to Paris."

PART 3

CHAPTER THIRTY-FIVE
LIVIA

Livia and Rain caught a cab from the airport, having arrived before the others. Too many last-minute tickets all on the same flight might have looked suspicious, and besides, they were all mindful that OGE had recently brought down a plane to silence two of its passengers. It seemed unwise to present anyone with a single target.

The idea was that in Paris, where apparently the faces of Asian tourists would generally be lumped together as *Chinois*, Livia and Rain would look natural traveling and checking in to hotels together, and could act as needed as a front for the rest of the group. Carl, Horton, and Larison would present a somewhat more unusual grouping, so only one of them would reserve the second hotel room they needed, with the rest ghosting in later. Out of an abundance of caution, they'd change hotels every day, creating a rotating series of ad hoc safe houses.

Carl had been right about the micromanaging—Rain had them all develop and practice an extensive cover story for how they knew each other and why they were in Paris, drilling them on the details repeatedly until he was satisfied.

Strangely, she didn't mind. She was a cop, so why would anyone expect her to be familiar with the concept of cover for action? Though in fact, she had been instructed on the topic by experts from both the CIA and the FBI when she was working with SPD's anti-gang unit. And, of course, she had extensive practical experience as well from hunting rapists in a non-law-enforcement capacity.

She liked Rain. Unlike Horton, who had an avuncular confidence, and Larison, who was overtly dangerous, and Carl, who liked to distract people with his banter, Rain had a stillness she sensed must be the perfect cover for the formidable qualities Carl had briefed her on. He didn't have Carl's patient empathy—though really, had she ever met anyone who did?—but he was a good listener, and the way he respectfully considered everyone else's ideas took the sting out of his occasional pushbacks and critiques. She sensed from the way he sometimes looked at her that he was seeing more than she would have liked. But she also sensed that no judgment came with it—and, thank God, no pity. He had asked her little about herself beyond the obvious, but this struck her not as a lack of interest, but rather as deference to her privacy. It also spoke of his bond with Carl, because Rain didn't come across as someone in the habit of trusting others based solely on third-party recommendations.

They had both slept during the first half of the flight, and when she woke she saw him reading a book in Japanese. She had used the moment to try to draw him out, asking him a bit about his past. The matter-of-factness of his replies reminded her of how she fielded similar inquiries, and suggested similar childhood trauma, or at least a lot of buried pain. The book itself, he told her, was a collection of haiku by the seventeenth-century poet Bashō. He joked that he used the poems to help him sleep, but of course he had been reading the book after sleeping, not before, and the absorption she had witnessed in his posture and expression suggested that to Rain, poetry was anything but soporific.

She asked about his judo background—Carl had told her about the Kodokan, which was mecca for all serious practitioners. Rain acknowledged training there for decades, but claimed to have nowhere near her competition experience. His approach to judo, he said, was more about combat, and the techniques that interested him most, including a variety of neck cranks mostly lost to the modern art, would have been horrific to Jigoro Kano, the founder of "the gentle way." Livia told him that when this shit was over, she hoped they could roll together, and that he might show her some of how he used judo off the tatami. He looked at her for a long moment then, and she had that uncomfortable sense that he was seeing more than she had meant to show. But then the moment passed, and he told her he would enjoy the opportunity, graciously adding that he hoped she would offer any refinements she saw in the approaches he had developed.

He was watchful at the airport, which made sense—if Treven's information was part of a setup, CDG was a potential choke point. But their departure was uneventful, and after about twenty minutes of peering into the cab's side-view mirrors and turning to look behind them, he seemed to relax. They had checked their bags, and so were armed at least with knives—a Somico Vaari fixed blade secured in a pocket of her cargo pants and a Bowie neck knife by a designer named Fred Perrin that Carl had turned her on to, and an Emerson folder for Rain. But she felt exposed without her duty weapon, which Larison had stored along with the other firearms in one of his stash sites before they flew out of Washington. Well, if Horton's confidence was justified, she wouldn't have to feel naked for long.

She had checked in with Strangeland before boarding, and there was no word from Arrington. According to Chief Best, someone in the Criminal Investigative Division office had explained that Arrington was dealing with the loss of a senior agent and a valued contractor, both of whom had been on the doomed flight. And was therefore more backed up than usual. Strangeland agreed that the statement, while certainly not dispositive, was at least a little weird. Typically, when the Feds blew off local law enforcement, they didn't bother to provide reasons. And Strangeland was pissed, and concerned, that Best still wouldn't escalate—not even with the runaround they were getting about fingerprints from the IAFIS. The lieutenant sensed Best was irritated that Livia had used her administrative leave to get out of town and was therefore unavailable to the SWAT operators Best wanted watching her.

"How's the weather out there?" Livia had asked. She'd checked online, of course, but still wanted to hear it direct.

"Clear skies," Strangeland said. "Stop worrying about the park rapist, okay? For now, you've got bigger fish to fry. You nccd to focus."

Livia filled her in on what she had learned, and was relieved that the lieutenant didn't ask how she had acquired her information. Livia didn't want to lie to her.

Livia had talked to Little, too. The phones and wallets Rain and Larison had taken confirmed the two men they killed were with OGE. No other useful information.

It was a bright, crisp autumn morning, and she enjoyed the ride into the city. She had never been to Paris, and despite everything, she found herself excited to be there, smiling as they passed the Arc de Triomphe, and again at her first glimpse of the Seine. Rain had explained that while he had been living here with the woman they were now hoping would help them, Delilah, he had enjoyed exploring the city's best bars, many of which were located in hotels. So as an artifact of the interest in bars, he had become something of a local hotel expert, as well. The place he had in mind was called L'Hôtel, in Saint-Germain-des-Prés. It was only about a mile and a half from Delilah's neighborhood, he said, but on the opposite bank. She wondered if he wanted to put the river between himself and Delilah out of respect or fear, or in some more symbolic way. But maybe she was overthinking it. Maybe he just liked the hotel, or its bar, or the neighborhood. Regardless, she couldn't help but be curious about what this woman was like.

Rain had the cab drop them off at a different hotel—a precaution she was familiar with—and they walked with their packs to their actual destination after the driver had pulled away. While Rain saw about a room, at the reception area in the tiny lobby, Livia went deeper into the hotel and immediately liked it. There was a central circular column rising five or six stories, surrounded by balconies on every level and with a glass dome at the top through which sunlight poured all the way to the ground floor. The space was compact without feeling cramped, and aged without feeling old. She saw the bar he liked so much, and was intrigued by what his attraction to it might reveal about him. It was snug, with room for not much more than a dozen patrons. It had a low, softly lit ceiling, and though it felt private, even intimate, it was also quietly inviting. She wondered if it was one of the places he had enjoyed with Delilah, and thought it probably was.

They were in luck, and Rain was able to book them something called a grand junior suite, which turned out to be quite small. Still, the room was bright and comfortable, with eclectic flowered wallpaper and a wonderful claw-foot tub, and though Livia had little basis for the impression, it all seemed somehow appropriately European. Of course, it would be way too tight for five, and they would have to get an additional room somewhere later. After what had happened in the Walmart parking lot, she felt nervous at the thought of another night with Carl. Not because of anything he might do. But because of her uncertainty about what she might do in response.

When they were done examining the room, Rain said, "We've got some time before the others arrive. Would you like to see a little of the area?"

"I'd love it," she said.

They headed out. It was interesting. Inside, when he'd been dealing with the hotel staff, his posture had changed, becoming stiffer, somehow more formal. She had even seen him bending slightly at the waist as he spoke, a mannerism that struck her as somewhere between a nod and a bow, and that she sensed was an element of his Japanese persona. But as soon as they were on the street again, it was gone.

He took her on a brief walking tour, down narrow streets lined with art galleries and antique shops, and onto a bridge over the Seine called Pont des Arts, with the Louvre on the other side and spectacular views of all of Paris left and right. And then down a wonderful narrow street called Rue de Buci, bustling with pedestrians basking in the late-morning sun and lined with sidewalk tables filled with diners enjoying coffee and delicious-looking pastries. The air was perfumed with food smells—baking bread, brewing tea, savory aromas like roasted chicken with rosemary. Outside of television and movies, Livia had never seen anything like it, and for a moment, she just stared at it all, openmouthed. But then, as seemed always to be the case when she found herself hit by a wave of happiness, or joy, or delight, there was an immediate undertow of sadness. The first time she had tasted ice cream, the first time she had come, and now her first time in Paris . . . firsts always made her think of Nason, of everything that was done to her and taken from her and of all the things Livia's little bird would never do or have or see.

They came to a corner restaurant called Bar du Marché. "Let's grab that table," Rain said, pointing to one under the edge of a bright red-and-white awning. "It's usually packed."

Rain ordered her the cappuccino she had asked for and an espresso for himself, along with a basket of bread. As soon as he switched to French with the waiter, she saw that interesting transformation again—a persona that was subtly different from what she'd seen before. And focusing on that helped her shake off the weight of the past.

"Your French sounds really good," she said when the waiter was gone. She knew that complimenting men was a great way to get them to talk—interrogators called it *ego up*—and she wondered if she could get him to open up a little.

He shrugged. "I lived here for over a year. And all I really did was study the language, and watch French movies, and chat with bartenders."

No mention of Delilah, who she assumed must have been instrumental in his progress. She had expected him to call the woman as soon as they landed—they were carrying Carl's satellite phone—but maybe he wanted to wait until everyone else arrived.

"Still," she said, "your accent just now sounded authentic. You must have a gift for languages."

"I don't know about that. What about you? Do you speak any French?"

"*Un peu.* I studied it in my senior year of high school."

"Just your senior year?"

It was interesting, how deftly he had flipped the conversation so the focus was on her. Well, she had given him the opening. And anyway, sometimes you had to give a little to get a little.

She nodded. "When I got to the States, I spoke no English, so I had to concentrate on that."

"Where did you come from?"

"Carl didn't tell you?"

He smiled, probably at the way she called him Carl. "He's told me almost nothing about you, other than that you're a Seattle sex-crimes detective, that you can handle yourself—which is a compliment Dox does not give lightly—and that you saved his life in Thailand."

She nodded. As close as these two men were, Carl treated her business as her business. It didn't surprise her. It just made her feel . . . grateful.

"He saved mine, too," she said.

Rain didn't respond, so she went back to his question. "Anyway. I grew up in a little village in the hills of Chiang Rai province in Thailand."

"And then where in America?"

"A town called Llewellyn. In Idaho." Where she would never go back.

"That must have been some culture shock."

She nodded. "You could say that."

They were quiet after that. Some people

would have kept pressing. Rain, she could see, sensed not to. She wondered again what kind of childhood he'd had. But if she asked him, she couldn't very well object to his asking her.

The waiter brought their coffees and bread. He spoke with Rain for a moment, chuckled, and moved off.

"What was it?" Livia said.

"He wanted to know where I'm from."

She laughed. It was a kind of in-joke among Asians in the States, whites constantly asking them where they were from, as though they were some alien, exotic species that couldn't have been born and bred in America like anyone else.

"What did you tell him?"

"That I like to pretend I'm Parisian."

She laughed again. "Can I ask you something?"

"Sure."

She poured two generous portions of brown sugar into her cappuccino, stirred, and took a sip. "Wow," she said. "That's good. And Seattle's no slouch when it comes to coffee."

Rain took a sip of his espresso and waited.

"I could be wrong about this," she said. "But I noticed you're carrying yourself differently here. In the hotel, you seemed foreign. Not American foreign. I think . . . Japanese. And walking around here, and talking to the waiter . . . again, not American. But not Japanese, either. Maybe that's why the waiter asked you."

He nodded and took another sip of espresso, and she realized he wasn't going to respond to an implied question. Whether out of discipline, or some native reticence, or both, she wasn't sure.

"Am I just imagining it?" she said. "And on the assumption I'm not, what is it?"

He set down the espresso and picked up a croissant. "It started as a game for me," he said. "A long time ago. I'd watch people and see if I could guess where they were from. And then I'd ask what I was going on. Clothes? Shoes? Eyeglasses? Accessories? Haircut? Posture, body language, gait, expression? If you pay enough attention, it's amazing what you can see."

She was intrigued. "So you watched for the details."

He nodded. "And then started trying to imitate. To see if I could fool people. I'd make up whole stories about my past—my parents were rich. My parents were poor. I grew up here. I grew up there. And see if I could bring off the role convincingly."

"It was a game?"

"Well, it was a game for high stakes, given the things I was mixed up in. But you know how Dox can just disappear sometimes, even though he's a big guy?"

She nodded. She'd seen it, if that was the right way of putting it, in Thailand, when he'd shot the last two men she'd been after.

He tore off a piece of the croissant. "He's

better at that than I am. My thing is more about blending. Just making myself part of the scenery. I give people . . . what they expect to see. And what people expect to see, they don't notice or remember."

For a second, she flashed on what it was like growing up in the Lone house. Doing everything she could to make Fred Lone not see her. Looking down. Hardly breathing. Pretending to be a chair.

But none of it had worked.

He started chewing the piece of croissant he'd torn off. Then he smiled. "That is just . . . so delicious. There's great food in Tokyo, but you'd be hard pressed to find a croissant like this one."

She barely heard him. "The thing you said, about imitating . . . do you think it's something anyone can do?"

"I wouldn't say anyone. But I think . . . people with a talent for acting. I think it's something like that."

She nodded. She wondered why she had never broken it down before the way he had just described. She did some of what he'd talked about, she knew. But not so systematically.

"So you have to be . . . a chameleon?" she said.

"Yes, but it's more than that. A chameleon just changes on the surface. What I'm talking about . . . it has to come from inside. Because if only the surface changes, incongruities seep through. You have to feel it, you have to be convinced by it. It has to seem real. There's still this place inside you that knows the truth, but that place is sealed off way down deep. It doesn't touch anything else."

Livia knew all about sealing things off down deep. She wondered if Rain ever felt as . . . different as she did. As cut off.

As fucked up.

And she wondered why he was telling her so much. Certainly this was more than she'd ever heard him talk before. Did he feel a connection? Did he sense the dragon inside her? Could he see what others overlooked, because a kindred creature dwelled in him?

He took another bite of the croissant, then chased it with the last of his espresso, smiling a little at the pleasure of it.

"You really love it here, don't you?" she said.

The question seemed to catch him off guard. He started to answer, then stopped and just said, "Yes."

She wondered if whatever he loved about the city was tied up with Delilah. Meaning maybe she should drop it. But instead she said, "What is it about Paris?"

The waiter came by. Rain ordered another espresso, then gestured to her cappuccino. "Another?"

She looked at the waiter and said, "*Oui. Un cappuccino, s'il vous plaît.*"

Rain laughed. "You're picking it up already."

They were quiet. If he didn't want to answer, it was okay, she wasn't going to press more than she already had.

But after a moment he said, "A friend who loves Paris once told me, 'There aren't many things we humans need to do. We need to eat, we need to drink, we need to make love. And the French attitude is, okay, we should do those things very well.' "

She found the notion lovely, and before she could stop it, it invoked Nason again. She blinked back the tears and laughed to cover her reaction, but she knew he'd seen it anyway.

"Sorry," she said. "I've just been dealing with . . . a lot."

He shook his head quickly. She liked that he did nothing beyond that to reassure her. It was so minimalist it felt genuine. And, of course, respectful.

"Can I ask you something else?" she said.

He smiled. "Are you this polite when you're interrogating suspects, too?"

She laughed. "No. But I'm not interrogating you." Which wasn't completely true.

He didn't respond, so she said, "Was the friend Delilah?"

The waiter brought their coffees and moved off. Rain said, "Yes."

She looked at him. "Thank you for agreeing to get in touch with her."

He nodded. "I should have done it a long time ago. So thank you for giving me a reason. Let's just hope it works out."

He took a sip of the fresh espresso. "Can I ask you something?"

She thought, *Payback is a bitch.*

"Of course."

"What's up with you and Dox?"

She didn't like the question. And though it wasn't fair after how relatively forthcoming he had been with her, she said, "Why are you asking?"

He didn't get irritated that she had refused to answer and had instead asked a question of her own. He just sipped his espresso. He was very . . . patient, she realized. In control of himself. She couldn't help but admire it.

"I've known Dox for a long time," he said. "He loves women. Loves them. But I've never seen him the way he is with you."

She shook her head, stymied for a response.

"He's one of the toughest men I've ever known," he went on. "I mean, he likes to play the clown and all that, but he's been through shit that would have broken most people—really, broken them, okay?—and all it's done is increase his joie de vivre. But that's just the surface. You know how it is. The worst bruises are down deep. Where no one else can see them."

She nodded. Yes, if there was one thing she knew, it was that.

"You know that Yeats poem?" he said. " 'The Cloths of Heaven'?"

She shook her head. "I don't."

He glanced up for a moment, then said:

"Had I the heavens' embroidered cloths,
Enwrought with golden and silver light,
The blue and the dim and the dark cloths
Of night and light and the half light;
I would spread the cloths under your feet:
But I, being poor, have only my dreams;
I have spread my dreams under your feet;
Tread softly because you tread on my
    dreams."

He stopped and sipped his espresso. She waited, then said, "That's a beautiful poem."

He nodded. "I like it, too."

"Another one you read to fall asleep to?"

"Be careful with him," he said. "He's not unbreakable. At least not with you."

She felt paralyzed. Ordinarily, someone telling her what to do or not do made her want to push back. But it wasn't like that with Rain. He wasn't being territorial. He wasn't trying to dominate her. He just cared about his friend.

The problem was, she did, too. She just didn't know how. Or what to do about it.

At the same time, it was interesting that he wasn't criticizing her for getting Carl involved in all this. He seemed to take that as a matter of course. It was as though he accepted the risk of getting killed as just a potential cost of doing business. His concerns weren't primarily matters of the body. They were matters of the heart.

"I don't want to hurt him," she said. "And . . . I don't want to get hurt, either."

He smiled—an exceptionally sad smile. "It would be nice if there were some guarantees in these things, wouldn't it?"

He finished his espresso and stood. "I guess that's as good a segue as any," he said. "I'll be back in a few minutes, okay?"

"Where are you going?"

He took Carl's sat phone from the pack he was carrying. "Probably to go get hurt."

CHAPTER THIRTY-SIX
DELILAH

Delilah was enjoying a cappuccino at La Caféothèque, a place she liked not far from her apartment in Le Marais. The café was best in the morning, when it was quiet and she could linger at one of the wooden tables in a window seat and read for as long as she wanted. There were a number of others she sometimes visited— Le Peloton, Strada Café, Le Barbouquin in Belleville, and of course when she was in the mood for a stroll, there was always Dose in the Latin Quarter and especially Numéro 220—but La Caféothèque was her favorite, and more and more, she enjoyed starting her mornings there.

Once upon a time, she'd needed to be careful about a predictable routine, but these days security was no longer so much of a concern. She was still on Mossad's payroll—technically still part of the service, technically still an Israeli. But they didn't want her home, and she couldn't really blame them. She'd been good, yes, she'd been part of a succession of ops that had entrapped or led to the elimination of numerous terrorist financiers and other enablers. But she'd caused a fair amount of trouble, too. For a while, there had been intemperance and acrimony, even some threats. But all that seemed over with now, replaced by a kind of cold peace.

Which on balance wasn't bad. The legend she lived, as a local fashion photographer, was self-sustaining, with real clients and real referrals. Her expenses were minimal. She had a weakness for some of the local designers, and when she traveled, she stayed in the best hotels. But those were her only real indulgences. Her apartment was comfortable but modest. She didn't even own a car, or want one. The monthly stipend they sent her all went to a retirement account, which was funny because come on, in every way that mattered she was retired already.

But retirement was fine, really. She was realistic. She was in her forties now, and while she still got a lot of attention, over time it had become more a matter of manner and sophistication, which could be managed, than of raw beauty, which was an elemental force. In some ways, it was a relief. Ten years earlier, she couldn't have read a book in a café without a half dozen men interrupting her. These days, there were fewer distractions.

She supposed she should be grateful for the way things had turned out. The cold peace, and the stipend, and the security and freedom she had. But it was hard not to feel some bitterness, too. She had slept with the enemy—literally, and repeatedly, and she had done it well. And her reward was suspicion and distaste, a sense among the men who ran the organization that she was dirty, and tainted, and fundamentally a whore. A necessary evil to be used for the greater good, and then disposed of at some unspoken expiration date.

She took a sip of her cappuccino and smiled, knowing she was being silly. What did she want, a management position at headquarters? Would she rather be trapped in a windowless office in Tel Aviv, or free, here in the city she loved more than any other? The last time she'd been back, for her father's funeral, she had felt like an alien. And since her mother had predeceased him, and her only brother had died in Lebanon when Delilah was just a girl . . . what was there to go back for? Paris was her home now, and she was a country of one within it.

John had once mentioned the parable of a Taoist sage, who awoke from a dream of being a butterfly and wondered if he was not then a butterfly dreaming he was a man. It was on one of those nights in her apartment, their lovemaking done and overtaken by languor, the large windows open, the breeze cool on their skin. He felt like a killer, he had told her, who had awakened from a beguiling dream of being a weightless, innocent young man. But when he was with her, he'd said . . . that weightlessness sometimes felt real again. He would always look away when he told her things like that, as though he was embarrassed or ashamed or afraid to see how she might react. And she would listen, and reassure him with a touch, or a kiss, and sometimes they would make love again. And now it was those nights that had become a dream.

She was still in love with him, she knew. She hadn't thought it was something she was capable of, not after everything she'd done in her work with Mossad. She'd been so shocked by it that for a long time, she'd been in denial. And when she'd finally acknowledged it to him, it had been good. They'd lived together, here in Paris. He'd changed. His paranoia seemed to subside, his combat reflexes began to relax.

But they couldn't find a way to meet in the middle. There was never any stasis. As soon as he felt he'd gotten out, he started pressuring her to do the same. And she couldn't. She wasn't ready. She hated the work, she hated the people, but she knew what she did saved lives. Her brother had died for that, she'd told John. She wasn't going to quit just because a few people were mean to her at the office.

And then he'd issued an ultimatum, and they had a stupid fight, and then he was gone. And she'd be damned if she was going to beg him to come back.

Besides, it wasn't as though she didn't have

distractions. She still saw Kent from time to time. He was usually able, and always willing, to drop everything and meet her somewhere if she wanted company. But that was part of the problem. He was too attached. Kent was a player, she knew, and probably had a dozen women he saw when he traveled on his official duties with MI6. The strange thing was, she didn't mind. In some ways, she wished he would fall for one of them. It would be an easy and elegant way for their own increasingly tenuous relationship to come to a dignified end.

But still, she missed John. She had almost broken down and called him after that disastrous op with Fatima. There was no one else she could talk to, no one else who would have understood. Certainly not Kent, who had been part of it. That weight John had talked about . . . Delilah had her own to carry, and what happened to Fatima would always be part of it.

Her mobile lit up. She glanced at the screen and saw the call was blocked. She didn't get many calls. A wrong number? She almost ignored it, but then for no particular reason picked up anyway. "*Allo*?"

There was a pause. Then John's voice: "Hi, Delilah."

She actually froze. Was he calling her? Was it really him? It was as though she had summoned him with a random thought.

Flustered and wanting badly not to show it, she said, "Is . . . everything all right?"

"Yeah, yeah, everything's fine. Well, the usual complications, but . . . it's good to hear your voice."

She wanted to say it back. But she wouldn't. Instead, careful to keep her tone neutral, she said, "Why are you calling?"

There was a long pause. He said, "I'm sorry."

"For what?" She was pleased the perplexed tone she was trying for sounded genuine. But she was worried, too. What had moved him to call? And to apologize?

"For a lot," he said. "For . . . more than I could explain in just a phone call."

She realized her heart was pounding. She'd told herself so many times that if he ever called, she would show him she didn't care. That he hadn't hurt her. That she had moved on.

Instead, she heard herself say, "Then you should apologize some other way."

There was a long beat. He said, "You mean . . . would in person be okay?"

"I don't know. Would it?"

"I think so. I mean, I'd like that. If you would."

"Yes. I'd like to hear you apologize in person." Good. That seemed the right balance between receptiveness to his overture, and a demonstration that she was still somehow in charge.

"Delilah, there's something else."

Her worry escalated to outright fear. Did he have cancer or something?

"John, what is it?"

"I need your help."

She would have laughed, but she was too furious with herself. And here she'd been worried he was dying or something.

"Ah, of course," she said.

"It's not why I'm calling. Not exactly. I mean, I should have called a long time ago."

"But still. You're calling because you need my help."

"The one's not related to the other, but yes. Dox and I both. And a woman he's involved with. Maybe we could talk about that in person, too. But first, maybe we could just talk about . . . what an idiot I've been."

She felt an infuriating rush of hope and shoved it away. "If we're going to talk about you being an idiot, it would be a long discussion."

"I hope it will be."

"I guess we'll see."

"I can meet you anywhere you want. I'm here in Paris."

"You're in Paris?"

"Yes."

"From when?" She didn't want to seem like she cared, but it came out before she could stop it.

"From about an hour ago. I flew in this morning."

She was angry at herself for being relieved that he hadn't been here for weeks without telling her, but she couldn't help it.

"Wherever's good for you," he said. "I'm not far from your neighborhood."

Knowing John, that probably meant the Latin Quarter or Saint-Germain. She thought about just telling him where she was, and that he could come meet her if he wanted. But . . . maybe better to go back to the apartment first to change and put on some makeup. Nothing obvious or overdone, of course. She didn't want it to seem as though she was trying to look good for him. But she knew how to look good without seeming to have tried. And why shouldn't she look good? He should know what he lost.

"You know that place you liked?" she said, reflexively slipping back into oblique references, not that anyone was listening. "With the back room with all the dark wood, that you said was your favorite haven?"

The place was called La Palette, in Saint-Germain.

"I know it."

"I'll see you there in an hour."

"Delilah."

"Yes?"

There was a pause. "Thank you."

"I don't want your thanks," she said, and clicked off.

She sat there for a moment, looking out at the passersby. She felt surreal. A roiling mix of anger, hope, fear, and confusion.

But most of all, anger. Anger at him for hurting her. Anger at herself for letting him. Anger at how vulnerable she felt from one stupid phone call, after all this time.

He hadn't even called her because he missed her, because he was sorry, because he wanted her back. Not really. Or even if he felt those things on some level, they hadn't been enough. What it took to get him to actually pick up the phone was whatever help he needed.

She would have called him back if she could. Told him that on second thought it was better if they didn't meet. She was seeing someone, and didn't want to complicate it.

Well, she could say much the same in person. That might be even better. Say it, and just walk away.

But how would she feel later, if whatever trouble he was in ended badly?

And what about Dox? She knew if she ever needed him, he would come running. How could she not do the same?

She hoped she wasn't rationalizing. Inventing reasons to see John when really she should stay the hell away.

She didn't think she was. Whether missing her would have been enough to call her or not, he never would have asked for help if the trouble weren't serious. And whatever trouble was so serious that men like John and Dox couldn't handle it alone had to be very bad indeed.

Well, she would learn more in an hour. She couldn't very well decide what to do until then, could she? Maybe he didn't just need her help. Maybe he needed her also in some better way.

But if she was wrong? And all he wanted was some kind of professional favor, after which she would never hear from him again?

She was going to kill him.

CHAPTER THIRTY-SEVEN
RAIN

Larison called as soon as they had cleared customs at CDG. Everything was fine.

"Good," I said. "We didn't have any problems, either. And the hotel I mentioned worked out. Dox and Livia should take it."

It was a good room, and I'd seen the way Livia looked at it. Life was short. Let them enjoy themselves if they could. The rest of us could deal with something more spartan.

Or maybe the second room would be for just Horton and Larison. Maybe I would wind up at Delilah's. I tried not to hope for it, but I could picture it so clearly. The simple wooden bed frame. The white sheets. The large casement windows, the curtains around them rippling inward, the sounds of distant traffic drifting in with the breeze. The feeling of moving inside her, her legs around my back, her breath hot on my face. Touching her the way I knew she liked to be touched. The sounds she would make. The words she would say. The way she would kiss the sweat from my shoulders after. How she would look in my eyes and need to say nothing, and I would wonder at how she could know me so well, and accept me so much, and how, after all the mistakes I'd made and the horrors I'd inflicted and endured, I could ever have earned such a reprieve.

Being back in Paris was whipsawing me between delight at a city I'd grown to love, and regret for how stupid I'd been, for how much time I'd wasted, for how I had probably blown it with her irrevocably. Tokyo was filled with so many ghosts for me. I had no idea how much I needed Paris to be for the living.

"The hotel sounds fine," Larison said. "And Hort has already set up a meeting with some of his local contacts. We're on our way to that now. No word yet from Treven, though."

"That's all right. I like that we got here beforehand. You said it yourself, less likely Graham will have time to position forces this way. Listen, we need to be careful with the firearms. I've seen guards examining bags at a few checkpoints. Aftermath of November 2015. I haven't seen any pat downs, but bags are definitely getting opened."

"No problem, I'll relay that to the others."

"Good. Why don't we meet at the primary at fifteen hundred?"

The place we had agreed on in advance was in front of the Grande Galerie de l'Évolution, alongside the greenhouse overlooking the Jardin des Plantes. There was a library there from within which we would have a view of anyone attempting to approach through the garden. Of course, we had preset fallback locations and backup approaches as well. Encryption or no, I didn't want us to ever have to say more over the phone than necessary, and besides, phones get lost, or don't get reception, or any of a dozen other problems for which the solution is always preparation and redundancy.

"Works for me," Larison said. "Any word from Delilah?"

"I'm on my way to meet her now."

"You and Livia?"

"No, she wanted to wander around. Get acclimated. She's never been here."

"So just you."

"Yes."

"Good. Just so you know, everyone's counting on you."

"Great."

"I'm joking. Well, not really."

"I think you've been spending too much time with Dox."

"He says good luck, by the way."

"All right, I should go."

"He says don't be an idiot. Tell her you care. Look, don't get mad, I'm just passing along a message."

I clicked off. I should have known Larison wouldn't sober up Dox, and that in fact Dox would rub off on Larison.

The sidewalk tables of La Palette were mostly full, but the back room I had liked so much was occupied by a single patron: an elegantly dressed older woman with a demitasse and a book open in front of her, who from her clothes and her ease I made as one of the nearby gallery owners enjoying her morning espresso before opening the store. I walked in and took the corner table in back, pleased at the feeling that the place had been waiting for me. Billie Holiday was playing quietly from unseen speakers. The acoustics were hushed. And it was pleasingly dim, even on this sunny morning, the walls all of dark wood, the ceiling painted ochre, the spare tables and chairs deep and comforting shades of brown. When the weather was good, the sidewalk tables were much more the draw for passing tourists and Parisians, but I always liked La Palette best from inside.

The pace of table service in Paris could be perplexing to Japanese, irritating to Americans, and unfathomable to, say, anyone accustomed to the almost supernatural speed of Hong Kong. But this time, I was glad no waiter disturbed me too promptly. It was my first moment alone since returning, and though I had enjoyed Livia's reactions to the city, and her questions and what they revealed about her, I was also glad to finally have some solitude.

Which made sense. The majority of the time I had lived here, I'd spent by myself. Which I supposed made my demands on Delilah even more incomprehensible. In retrospect, I realized our balance had actually been good: she needed to travel for work; I needed time alone. So what had possessed me to push her and push her until something had snapped? Had I been trying to sabotage the best thing that had happened to me in longer than I cared to remember? Was I really that self-destructive?

Maybe I would ask Dox what he made of it. I'd been reluctant to before, fearful of the accuracy of his insights. But accurate insights might have helped me. Medicine isn't supposed to taste good—that's what candy is for. Medicine is supposed to make you better.

It was strange. I'd been alone for so long. And in an hour or so, I would be with her again, even if only briefly and badly. So for the moment, I relished the feeling of sitting in that dusky haven of a back room, a little relic from my recent past. I felt like Schrödinger's cat. She would come, or not come. She would take me in, or throw me out. She would forgive me, or tell me to fuck off. And in that narrow, purgatorial space, a feeling crept in, a kind of mourning for my younger self and all his terrible choices, and a wish that I could somehow tell him what I knew now and help him for both our sakes to get it right, and a grief that such a thing was impossible, the young man's blindness irreparable, his mistakes immutable, the consequences irreversible. And then I smiled, thinking of *mono no aware*, the sadness of being human, aware of the irony of having traveled all the way to Paris to feel something so quintessentially Japanese.

A half hour passed. The gallery woman left. Several more people, also looking like locals of one kind or another, drifted in. I ordered an *omelette aux champignons* and an *orange pressée*, and finished both. I had another espresso. At the end of the hour, she still hadn't come.

Maybe I should have given her the satphone number. Maybe something had come up, and she couldn't reach me. Maybe I should call her again. I wondered why she had chosen this place, rather than one of her Marais haunts. I had always liked the Left Bank more than she did; was the choice an attempt to accommodate me? Or was it a way of saying, *I'm going to keep you away from my neighborhood, from my life?* Or was I missing something entirely?

Finally, over ninety minutes after we had first talked, she showed. She stood for a moment in the doorway, probably letting her eyes adjust from the sun outside. She was wearing jeans and suede boots, a combination I always liked on her. And a leather bolero. Her hair was down, and her beauty wasn't just moving—it was also a stinging rebuke.

She saw me and walked over. I stood, my heart pounding.

"John," she said. "It's nice to see you."

Whatever I'd been expecting, it hadn't been that. "It's good to see you," I said. I wanted to add *really good,* but thought it would come out wrong.

We stood there awkwardly for a moment. Then I gestured to the table. "Do you want to sit?" I had selected the corner table so we could sit ninety degrees from each other and both have a view of the entrance.

She nodded. "Sure."

We sat. Up close, and without the light outside silhouetting her, I could see a few new lines. I didn't care. She looked more beautiful than ever, and it hurt.

There were so many things I wanted to say. *I missed you. I'm sorry. I'm an idiot.*

I love you.

But none of them came out.

"So," she said after too long a silence. "What is this help you need?"

Tell her, you fucking idiot. Tell her.

But I didn't. Instead, for the next forty minutes, I briefed her on everything that had happened, culminating in our trip to Paris this very morning.

When I was done, she said, "This is bad. I know OGE. Mossad uses them."

"Apparently, everybody uses them."

"Exactly. Graham doesn't really have enemies. Only clients. Some of them quite powerful."

"Well, you know me. I only piss off the best people."

I thought she would at least smile at that, but she didn't. She said, "And what is it you hope I can do for you?"

I was aware on some level that we shouldn't be talking about the plan yet, that business first was the wrong approach here. But business was also the more familiar terrain, the less fraught topic, and I didn't listen to whatever voice was telling me I was getting it wrong.

"I'm not sure yet," I said. "I won't be able to propose something meaningful until we have more detailed intel from Treven. But the general idea is, if you can lure Graham into a position where he's detached from his bodyguards, it'll be an opportunity for us to interrogate him. With the intel we have, we probably could just kill him, despite his protection. And it might still come to that. But what we really need is information. Why is this guy Arrington so hell-bent on covering up a child-pornography ring? What's he using the information for? Who does this really involve? If we don't know those things, just killing Graham might not end the threat. And it won't dismantle the ring."

She looked off to the side and drummed her fingers on the table. Then she said, "When did fighting child pornography become a thing for you?"

It felt at least as much a provocation as a question, but I thought for a moment anyway. "When it was right in front of me," I said. "And I realized I was in a position to either do something about it or just pretend I don't care."

"I see."

"What are you getting at?"

"I just want to make sure you're clear in your mind why you're doing all this."

"If you saw that video Livia showed us, you'd understand."

"I'd like to meet her. She sounds quite special."

"I think she is."

"You trust her?"

"I haven't known her long enough to say. But Dox trusts her."

"He trusts more easily than you."

"You're saying he's the weak link in the chain?"

"I'm saying it sounds like this woman has drawn four people, and now possibly a fifth, into a war she's fighting. Her war."

"I told you, Graham came after me before I'd even heard of Livia."

"But do you have more need of her, or she of you?"

"I'd say it's mutual. It was her intel that led to our breakthrough on Arrington. Until then, we knew Graham was probably just muscle, but we didn't know for whom."

"Is her intel anything you can verify?"

I looked at her. "Am I missing something?"

"That's what I'm trying to understand."

"Why are you so . . . cynical on this?"

"If you think my questions come from cynicism, it makes me even more concerned."

"Dox knows her. He says she saved his life. And I've had a chance to observe her up close and under pressure. I haven't encountered anything inconsistent with what he's told me, or anything that feels off to me. So again, what am I missing?"

She was quiet for a moment. Then she said, "I've made a career out of getting men to trust me. To believe utterly all the things I want them to believe. And now you tell me this woman's effect on Dox, and the war she's involved you in. How can I not wonder if the four of you aren't being as gullible as all the men who were so sure about me?"

I looked at her. "I was sure about you."

She shook her head. "No, you weren't. You left. And you were the one man who should have been sure of me. My God, the irony. It's nauseating."

"I was sure about you," I said again.

"Then why did you leave?"

"You wouldn't give up your job. This life."

"This life," she said, her voice rising. "This life that, now that it suits you, you're trying to drag me back into?"

A few people in the room looked up, then went back to their own conversations.

I looked at her. "I'm sorry."

She shook her head, her expression incredulous. "You had years to call me and tell me that, John. Years. And even this morning, you could have told me. But you didn't. All I've heard up until this moment, the only reason you're even here, is because you're in a jam and you need me to help you out of it. You want all the benefits and none of the responsibilities. And the worst part? You're so fucking blind, you can't even see it."

"No, that's not—"

"Don't argue with me when I'm berating you. You think I care what you tell yourself you feel in your heart? What does it matter to me? What matters to me is your actions, John, and your actions are that you gave *me* an ultimatum, that you left *me* without looking back, that you're here today only because you need something from me, and if you're telling yourself that oh, no, you missed me, you longed for me, that's why you're really here, then you're not just lying to me, you're lying to yourself, because you can't face what a selfish, manipulative asshole you really are, and you have to create a pretty fiction to hide from yourself the pathetic, ugly truth."

I looked around. The people staring went back to their conversations.

"That stings," I said.

"And why would I care about your feelings?"

"But you know what makes it tolerable?"

She didn't answer.

"That you're wrong."

The waiter came by, probably to check on what all the fuss was. I thought, *Well, that's one way to get a little table service.*

"Bring me a glass of Syrah," Delilah said to him in French. "No, make that a vodka. Belvedere, up, very cold, no garnish."

"Two," I said.

He looked at us for a moment as though doubting the wisdom of our order, then nodded and moved off.

She shook her head. "Only an hour, and you've driven me to drink."

"I've driven both of us."

"Yes, it's you who did that. Do you see how in all these things you make your problems mine?"

I couldn't tell if she was joking. I decided not.

She looked impatiently at the interior window to the front room, beyond which was the bar. "What if I told you it's too late for us?" she said.

I looked away, feeling something tighten in my chest. "Then I'd live with that sadness forever. And I'd never stop missing you. And what we had together. And I'd never stop regretting what an idiot I must have been to fuck it up."

"You're not going to make me feel guilty about that. You caused it. It's yours to live with."

The waiter brought our drinks. Delilah lifted hers and, without bothering with any kind of toast, promptly drained half of it. She closed her eyes and shuddered, a reaction that reminded me—unfortunately, given the fraught moment—of the way she sometimes looked when she came.

I drained half my glass as she had. Three espressos and a vodka, on jet lag and not a lot of sleep. Especially under the circumstances, this was probably a science experiment I didn't want to conduct. And yet I didn't care.

I set down my glass and blew out a long breath, the warmth of the vodka blossoming in my gut. "I'm not trying to make you feel guilty," I said.

She shook her head. "I'm not even in the life anymore, you idiot. Not really. What you said you wanted . . . all you had to do was wait. But you wouldn't. How can a man who has such patience in his work be so impatient in his personal life?"

"I don't know," I told her truthfully.

"But there has to be an answer. Were you just looking for a way out because you were bored?"

"No."

"Then what? Were you trying to sabotage yourself? Sabotage us?"

"I don't know. All I can tell you is that . . . all the patience I've developed in my work, and my life . . . and all the precision, and logic, and self-control . . . it's just not there with you. I wish it were, but it isn't."

We were quiet for a moment. She finished her vodka, closed her eyes and shuddered again, and said, "What if I told you I'm seeing someone?"

For whatever stupid reason—fear or denial or narcissism—I hadn't anticipated that. I felt the tightness in my chest again.

"I'd ask if it was serious."

"And if I told you it is?"

Once upon a time, I would have wanted to kill whoever it was. Literally. Eliminate the threat.

But suddenly, I felt only sad. Of course she was seeing someone. Had I really expected this vital, cosmopolitan, gorgeous woman to be waiting around for whenever I was done sulking?

I finished my vodka. "Then I guess I'd say I deserved it. And . . . I would try to be happy for you."

We were quiet again.

"Are you?" I said.

"Am I what?"

"Seeing someone."

"Yes."

Fuck.

"And . . . is it serious?"

She waited a long time before saying, "Not like you and I were serious."

The contours of the room had picked up a nice patina. The conversations around us were cocooned in a gentle hum. I realized I was quite buzzed. And maybe it was the vodka, or maybe it was the last thing she had said, or maybe I just didn't give a shit any longer about circumlocutions or protecting myself or dignity or whatever. I looked in her eyes and said, "Take me to your apartment."

She shook her head. "Oh my God, the nerve of you."

"I don't care. Make love to me. This morning. On your bed. With the light coming through those gauzy curtains. The way we used to."

"I don't think so."

"Why not?"

"I'm too angry at you, for one thing."

"Take your anger out on me."

She looked at me, and I could see she wanted to. The warmth in my gut got hotter. I felt a pleasant stirring somewhere south of that.

"This much anger I don't think you could handle."

"But you said it yourself. It's my fault. So it should be my risk."

She shook her head, her eyes narrow, her nostrils flared. Then she grabbed me by the back of the head and pulled me in and kissed me passionately, even savagely. I kissed her back just as hard, my hands on her face, gripping her tightly, holding her close, determined not to ever let her go again.

She broke the kiss and looked at me. "I hate you," she said.

"I love you," I said back.

There was a quiet round of applause around us. I looked up and saw the other patrons smiling and clapping.

I wanted her so much I didn't even care. "Come on," I said. I threw down some euros, grabbed her by the hand, and pulled her from behind the table.

Out on the sidewalk, she said, "Wait. Where are you staying?"

"Around the corner. L'Hôtel."

"Take me there. My apartment is too far."

What the hell, I thought. *We'll find something else for Livia and Dox.*

CHAPTER THIRTY-EIGHT
DELILAH

After they had made love, John passed out almost instantly. "But wake me in an hour, okay?" he'd said, lying on his back while she looked at him from her side. "I have to meet the others."

She watched as he struggled to keep his eyes open, trying and failing not to feel tender toward him. "You should sleep longer."

He shook his head. "After the meeting. I don't know where I'll stay, though. With five of us, it's going to be crowded."

She punched him lightly on the shoulder. "You're an idiot."

He was asleep a moment later.

She set an alarm, and for a while, she dozed herself. She felt peaceful. She wasn't angry at herself for giving in. It had been too good for that, so good that for the moment, she didn't even care what it meant or what would come after.

You'll figure it out, she thought. *What, did someone tell you it was going to be easy with a man like this? And come on, be honest. You're not always the easiest person yourself.*

She heard a key slide into the door lock. But

they'd locked the door from the inside. The person tried again.

Delilah got up, grabbed a robe from the bathroom, and went to the door. She looked through the peephole and saw an attractive Asian woman, midthirties, casual in cargo pants and a flannel shirt over a tee shirt. It had to be this Livia.

"Yes?" Delilah said quietly, wanting to be sure.

"Oh," the woman said, obviously confused and playing catch-up. "I'm—I can come back."

Delilah smiled. No question.

She unlocked and opened the door. "It's okay," she said softly. "It's your room. I'm sorry for intruding." She held out her hand. "I'm Delilah."

The woman nodded. "Livia," she said, and they shook. "But it's really no trouble, I can come back."

Delilah glanced back. John was still sleeping. Which was extraordinary. He had always been one of the lightest sleepers she had ever known. For him to be out this cold suggested an exceptional level of exhaustion.

And, she supposed, an exceptional level of trust.

"It's okay," Delilah said. "He told me to wake him soon anyway. The meeting. Come in, you probably want to freshen up after the trip. I don't think he'll be disturbed. I've never seen him sleep this deeply."

"I can just splash some water on my face downstairs," Livia said. "You two . . . you could probably use some time alone."

"We'll have a chance for that later. Come on, I don't want to feel like I'm keeping you out of your own room. Why don't you use the bathroom if you like, and I'll get dressed out here?"

Livia took her bag in with her, and less than ten minutes later opened the door wearing a new tee shirt, her hair wet and combed back. The mirror was fogged from the shower. "Thanks," she said quietly, stepping out. "It's all yours if you want it."

She was pretty, Delilah thought. Not quite beautiful, but that might have been because of the shapeless clothes and the complete lack of makeup. If she'd been working any kind of con on Dox or the others, she wasn't doing it by playing to her looks, though she probably could have if she'd wanted to. But there was something about her, no doubt. A strength, or an intelligence . . . a quality of intensity. It would be interesting to see how she interacted with the others.

"Thank you," Delilah said. "I'll just be a minute. You should stay not too close to the bed in case he wakes."

"What do you mean?"

Delilah had once made the mistake of waking John by shaking him. His reaction had been instantaneous and violent. He'd pulled back

393

somehow, and hadn't hurt her, but he'd been horrified by what had happened. He blamed himself, but in fact, Delilah realized afterward that she should have known. With the kind of life John had led, a surprise when he was vulnerable would of course produce an extreme defensive response.

Delilah glanced over to him, then back to Livia. "He can wake badly."

"Ah," Livia said, and Delilah had the strange sense that the woman knew exactly what that was like, and what might cause it. Then she added, "Are you coming to the meeting?"

Delilah looked at John again, then gestured that Livia should join her in the bathroom. Livia stepped inside and Delilah closed the door behind them. "Sorry," she said. "I don't want to disturb him."

And I might as well take the opportunity to get to know you a little better, too.

"Of course," Livia said.

"Anyway, the meeting. Yes, I think I ought to be there."

Livia nodded. "Rain and Dox speak very highly of you."

Delilah wiped the mirror with a washcloth. Their lovemaking had been intense, and a few minor touchups to her makeup and hair wouldn't have hurt. But she didn't want to do it in front of this woman.

She turned to Livia. "And John of you. He told me this is about a child-pornography ring."

"And the people trying to cover it up."

"He said you showed him a video from the site."

Livia looked at her, a touch of wariness in her eyes. "That's right."

"I'd be curious to see it, too."

"I can show you right now if you like."

"No, later is fine."

"Are you sure? It's easy to lose sight of what's at stake in these things."

Was that a challenge? "Yes, it sounds like you've done well at keeping everyone focused."

"I'm just a Seattle cop," the woman said. "Not a global-intelligence operative. But I always appreciate when people have the balls to say what's really on their mind. Is it not the same for you?"

Delilah watched her, and couldn't help feeling a degree of grudging respect. Along with a measure of resentment.

She glanced at the door, behind which was John, presumably still passed out on the bed. "I hope I won't sound callous in saying this," she said. "No, actually, I don't care how I sound. What I care about is that man out there. It's been a difficult road for us. An improbable one. For a while, I lost him. And now he's here again, and maybe we have another chance. Maybe. And the first thing I learn is that he might be risking his life in someone else's battle? Someone I don't know, who I've never heard of? Do you think that makes me happy? Do you think it makes me feel like some sort of ally to you? Grateful to you?"

Livia didn't respond, and Delilah went on. "I understand there's a threat," she said. "To all of you. All right, eliminate the threat, it's what John does. But don't complicate the mission. Don't turn it into something these men have no experience in and no stake in. Don't turn your own battle into someone else's."

Livia remained silent. Her respiration didn't pick up, her color didn't change, she didn't even blink. Again, Delilah felt the grudging respect. Whatever else might be true, this woman was tough.

Finally, she said, "It's sad you think of child rape as my battle. Not as yours. Not as everyone's."

"I meant—"

"I know what you meant. And it's okay. If the cruelty and depravity traded in on sites like Child's Play don't concern you, then they don't."

"No. I didn't say they don't concern me. I said they're not my war. There are many things that concern me that I don't go to war over. And I've been at war. A real war. But do you hear me demanding that you join me and fight in it?"

"I'm not talking about geopolitics. I'm talking

about children. For me, the war to protect children from predators is a war everyone should fight."

"No. Not John. He's fought in enough wars. And almost died in them."

"Look, you know him better than I do. But the way you talk about him, it's like you think I used some Jedi mind trick to cloud his brain. I told him—I told all of them—straight up that for me this wasn't just about saving my own skin. And if that's all it was for them, and they didn't care about the people who were making and trading videos of children being raped and tortured, then I was out. I put my cards on the table. I didn't manipulate anyone."

Delilah could have pointed out that in some circumstances, putting your cards on the table could be the most powerful manipulative technique of all. But what would have been the point? The woman was obviously a zealot.

"And one other thing," Livia said. "Dox, Rain, all of them—they've done a lot for me. Dox especially. But it's not a one-way street. Oliver Graham tried to blow up Rain with a helicopter and rockets before Rain had ever even heard my name."

"Yes, John pointed that out, too. But it was because Graham wanted *you* dead. And John wouldn't go along with it."

Livia smiled. "Do you think he should have?"

Delilah didn't respond. She realized the woman had been leading her to this point. She'd anticipated it several moves back and set it up nicely.

"Do you *wish* he had?" Livia said.

The truth was, there was a part of Delilah that did wish it. But then, she supposed, John would never have contacted her. And they wouldn't have been presented with this unlikely second chance.

But it wasn't just that. Wishing John had killed this woman, who seemed innocent of everything except an excess of self-righteousness . . . no. It was one thing to feel the shadow of such a thing. To give over to it completely would be perverse. And irrevocable.

"You must be quite an interrogator," Delilah said.

"I do all right."

"Why don't you show me that video?"

"You don't have to. Especially if you're going to claim later that I used it to manipulate you."

"I'm not going to claim anything. I'm going to help you. It's not in me to ignore it when John and Dox are at risk."

"Thank you."

"I'm not doing it for you."

"But I stand to benefit."

"And so do a lot of children, I suppose."

"I didn't say it. You would have thought I was laying it on too thick."

"You didn't say it because you didn't want to sell past the close. Anyway. Show me the video. I should know what this is all about."

Livia took a laptop from her bag. She set it on the counter and spent a minute configuring it. Then she rotated it so the screen was facing Delilah and held her finger over the "Play" button. "I've watched it too many times already," she said. "I don't need to see it again."

She pressed "Play."

For a moment, Delilah couldn't believe what she was seeing. Literally, couldn't believe it, was sure it must be something else. Then she realized it was her mind, trying to defend itself from horror, looking for a way to believe this was anything but what it obviously was. The reality of it hit her like a blow to the stomach. She threw a hand over her mouth, lurched to the toilet, dropped to her knees, and threw up.

Livia hit "Stop" and the child stopped screaming. Delilah breathed heavily for a moment, then retched again, thinking *My God, my God . . .*

Her stomach did a slow roll, but then seemed to achieve some stability. When she was sure it wasn't going to happen again, she spat, stood, and flushed.

"Well," she said. "You certainly proved your point. You must have enjoyed it."

Livia looked at her, and it was the oddest

thing—the woman seemed to be fighting tears.

"There is not one thing I enjoy about those videos," she said. "Except punishing the people who make them."

There was a knock on the door. "Everything okay in there?" John said.

"Fine," Delilah said. "Just Livia and I, getting to know each other."

"Oh. Okay, good. When you're out, maybe I could take a quick shower."

"Yes. And then we should go."

There was a pause. He said, "Are you coming?"

"Yes."

Another pause. Then, "Thank you."

Delilah looked at Livia. "I'm glad I can help."

CHAPTER THIRTY-NINE
RAIN

Per the plan, we met outside the Grande Galerie de l'Évolution. Dox, Horton, and Larison were already waiting at the top of the stairs as the rest of us approached through the garden. As soon as Dox saw Delilah, his face lit up in a delighted grin and he started heading down.

"Hey there," he said, which for Dox was practically tongue tied. He gave her a hug—affectionate, certainly, but briefer and more deferential than one of his typical bone-crushers.

"Dox," she said, smiling at him. "You know in Paris, it's more the kiss." She mimed the double cheek kiss.

"Well, we can do that, too," he said, and promptly did so.

She laughed. I knew she didn't mind the hugs—on the contrary. The comment was more a *when in Rome* reminder. But good luck with that with Dox.

It felt right to be back with the two of them. More than right. What the hell had been wrong with me, to walk away from people who had my back the way they did? I needed to come to grips with that. And make sure it never happened again.

Horton shook Delilah's hand with a genteel "It's a pleasure to meet you, ma'am." Larison did so with only a wary nod. As soon as the introductions were done, Larison said, "I have a suggestion."

We all looked at him.

"Hort's people came through with five Beretta APXs and bellyband holsters. Extra magazines, too. Hort has one set and Dox and I are each carrying two, and we're starting to clank when we walk. There's a restroom next to the library inside. Single toilet stall. Why don't we use it one after the other to get you and Livia equipped. Quick drop, no public exchange."

I nodded to Horton. "Glad your people came through."

Dox said, "Partly came through. Still would be good to have a proper rifle on hand."

"Well," Horton said, "if you don't want the pistol . . ."

Dox shook his head. "Roger that, my bad. Didn't mean to sound ungrateful. Just want to make sure we have the full range of options."

Larison used the stall first, leaving one of the Berettas for Livia, then Dox repeated the exercise for me. Everyone was keeping one eye on the two approaches to the library, but no one followed us in.

When we were done with the hardware, we took a stroll down the long sand-and-gravel paths of the gardens, symmetrical rows of trees to our sides, the branches forming a canopy against the sun overhead. The benches beside the paths were occupied by tourists and Parisians—pensioners snoozing or reading; mothers with infants, chatting; young people, probably cutting classes, smoking and laughing and holding hands.

Dox took the opportunity to throw an arm around my shoulder. "Proud of you, son."

I glanced at him and said nothing.

"I mean, I knew the second I saw you two that you'd kissed and made up."

Still I said nothing.

"And thank God, too, 'cause I'll bet you haven't been laid since the last time you saw her. Not many women are as charitable as Delilah, and that's a fact. You're a lucky man."

Saying nothing seemed not to be working, so I tried "Thanks."

He laughed. "Okay, I'm done giving you a hard time. Seriously, man, I'm happy for you both. You two are made for each other. The only person who couldn't see it was you."

"I thought you were done giving me a hard time."

"What? That's not a hard time. It just feels hard 'cause it's the truth."

We paused by a thick cluster of trees. Between the six of us, we had complete coverage of every approach to our position. But the gardens were peaceful, just wanderers and daydreamers enjoying the sunny afternoon.

"Ben checked in," Horton said. "He and Graham arrive tomorrow morning. He says he wants to meet."

I nodded. "What do you think?"

Horton glanced at Larison. "You know what I think."

Larison said, "I think Treven's full of shit. How do we know he doesn't show up with an army of OGE operators in tow?"

I looked at Horton. "Why doesn't he want to just use a phone?"

Horton shrugged. "Would you?"

I glanced around the gardens and saw no problems. "Generally no, but I'd prefer a phone to a face-to-face I thought might be unacceptably dangerous."

"For what it's worth," Horton said, "I had the same misgivings, and expressed them to Ben. He told me he wanted to do it face-to-face, and if we had a problem with that, it was up to us, and we didn't have to hear what he had to say."

"I can't say I like the sound of that," Dox said.

Livia nodded. "Same."

"I understand how you feel," Horton said. "So I'll tell you what. Since I'm the only one who seems convinced Ben wouldn't double cross us, I'll meet him myself. The risk will be mine alone."

Larison glanced at him, and I could tell he

wasn't happy about the idea. Not because of an excess of concern about Horton's welfare. But because he distrusted Horton only slightly less than he distrusted Treven.

"There's another possibility," Delilah said.

We all looked at her, and she went on. "There are six of us. We can monitor the route. If there's a problem, we abort before Colonel Horton is even in position."

"Please, call me Hort," Horton said. "Or Scott, if you like. I haven't been a colonel in a long time."

Delilah nodded. "Hort, then. John, you remember Le Piano Vache, near the Pantheon?"

It was a jazz bar I had introduced her to—one of the places I had found during my explorations of the city. I nodded, having some notion of where she was going.

"It's a narrow street and there are only two approaches," she went on. "If they meet there, the rest of us can monitor the route. The Sainte-Barbe Bibliothèque side, and the Rue de la Montagne Sainte Geneviève side. That little restaurant, L'Écurie—it's right on the corner. I could sit at one of the sidewalk tables with a view of the entire approach. The Bibliothèque side would be a little trickier, but four of you could have the street covered."

I looked at Larison. After a moment, he said, "I like it. With one change."

"Yes?" Delilah said.

"Aborting is fine," Larison said. "But if Treven brings company, I don't see any reason we should let any of them just walk away. I don't mean to tell anyone else here how to protect yourselves, but what works for me is, you only get to come at me once. I don't let people walk away from that. I don't give second chances."

I had no problem with that. I looked at Horton. He said, "That's fair."

I nodded. "Tell him . . . you'll meet on the south side of the Pantheon at nineteen hundred. There are a bunch of hotels on that side, all with views of the whole Place du Panthéon. Shouldn't be hard to find a room. If we can't, we'll figure out something else. You'll be out somewhere on foot, someone else will be in the room watching the street. If Treven shows up and the spotter sees no problems, you come out from hiding. Then the two of you walk to Piano Vache, with the rest of us all already in position to see whether anyone is ghosting along behind you. And we don't have to worry about anyone setting up at the bar before you get there."

Horton smiled. "I like it."

"Seven o'clock is early," I said. "The bar won't be crowded. None of the nearby restaurants will be, either, and Delilah won't have a problem getting an outdoor table at L'Écurie. You'll walk right past her. If for some reason she can't get a table, there are a few other places nearby that would also work, though not as well. We should walk the route, though—now, and then again later, to note any time-of-day changes we might need to take into account. Also, I know not all of us are familiar with Paris, so we'll want to go over escape routes, bug-out points, and backup plans."

Dox nudged Livia. "What did I tell you?"

I knew he was ribbing me about the micro-managing. I didn't care. "Better to say it now," I said, "than regret it later."

Livia looked at me and inclined her head toward Dox. "He micromanages, too."

"I do not," Dox said. "I give appropriate instructions for the consideration and benefit of my peers."

"Well, for the consideration and benefit of my peers," I said, "let's go see the terrain we're talking about."

"One thing," Livia said. "I've noticed a good number of surveillance cameras around the city."

I nodded, glad she was pointing it out, since I'd been about to and it would have just become fodder for the micromanagement cracks. "Yeah," I said. "Not nearly as bad as London, but they're around. What are you thinking?"

She pulled a baseball cap and shades from a pocket in her cargo pants. "I picked these up while I was wandering the area around the hotel.

Wouldn't hurt for everyone to do something similar. And maybe when we get close, one of us can go ahead and see what kind of surveillance environment we're wandering into."

Once upon a time, I had a video-camera detector, courtesy of my late friend Haruyoshi "Harry" Fukasawa. But emerging technology had eventually outpaced it, and sadly Harry was no longer around to implement any updates.

"Good idea," I said. "I don't remember any cameras near the bar, but . . ."

"It's possible it's changed since you were last here," Livia said, "and if it has, it could only have gotten worse."

I would have expected a cop to have a more positive view of surveillance cameras. But I saw no reason to point it out.

"Agreed," I said. "We'll stop at a few tourist stores along the way for hats and shades for anyone who doesn't already have them. And why don't you make the initial pass? Seems like you have a good eye for where to look for the cameras."

Piano Vache was about fifteen minutes away on foot. Delilah walked ahead with Horton and Larison. I was unsurprised that she was taking the opportunity to get to know them, and to make sure everyone got comfortable and familiar with everyone else. Dox, perhaps recognizing the possibility of mutual assured destruction, didn't make any more cracks about Delilah and me.

Delilah was already carrying a scarf and sunglasses, but the rest of us picked up caps and shades in a handful of stores along the way. Near the end of Rue Descartes, with Piano Vache a couple of minutes away, I said, "Left here, then your second right—Rue Laplace. The bar will be on your right. Obviously, what's directly in front of the bar is most relevant, but make sure to have a good look up and down the streets on either end of Rue Laplace, too."

I looked at Dox. He held up his hands in mock surrender and said, "I didn't say anything."

The rest of us grabbed a couple of tables at a place called Le Petit Café. Everyone got coffees, but I was done with caffeine for the day and stuck with an *orange pressée*.

Twenty minutes later, Livia was back. "All good," she said quietly, sitting and pulling her chair in close. "Nothing on Rue Laplace, nothing up or down either of the streets running perpendicular to it. Of course, I could be missing something, but if so, it's well hidden."

"Okay, let's stagger it," I said. "Two by two. And regroup here in thirty minutes to compare notes."

A half hour later, we were back. Everyone was reasonably satisfied with the terrain and our ability to monitor the approaches to the bar. I saw one thing missing, and I was pleased that Larison brought it up first.

"What if Treven is carrying some kind of beacon?" he said. "It could be anything—his phone, a commercial GPS tracker, something connected to Wi-Fi. In which case, no one follows him. They just show up ten minutes after he arrives."

"Come on," Horton said. "What would be the point? Best case from their perspective, they'd drop me. Meanwhile, the rest of you would still be at large. And you'd all know Ben is a rat. They'd be showing their hand for almost no winnings. I appreciate the concern, but since it's my risk, why don't you just let me take it?"

"What about this?" Livia said. "The place directly across the street has a second-story terrace. Maybe twelve feet up, with a trellis on the corner, a streetlight, a concrete lip . . . I could be up and over in five seconds, with cover and concealment and an elevated position directly over the entrance."

Larison said, "What are you, some kind of monkey?"

She stared at him, and he added, "I meant it as a compliment."

"I was looking for places we could set up," she said. "Not just for cameras."

I glanced at Horton. "Can your local contacts get us any kind of body armor?"

"Maybe."

"Earpieces, lapel mics?"

Horton nodded. "I don't think that should be a problem."

I looked at Larison. After a moment, he shrugged. "It's up to you, Hort. You're the one who trusts Treven."

CHAPTER FORTY
DOX

The hotel room was nice, but Dox wouldn't have minded twin beds instead of the king. Not that he didn't want to share a bed with Labee— literally and otherwise—but he wanted her to be comfortable. And despite the crazy thing that had happened that night in Rayong, when they'd been stressed and on the run and she'd just taken him the way he guessed she needed to, she was still protective of her space.

On the other hand, he wasn't exactly consumed with regret that circumstances had conspired to force the issue. Although really, it wasn't like they'd be in the bed much together anyway. Dox thought it was excessive, but John wanted everyone to sleep in shifts, just in case they'd overlooked something in their security and the wrong people decided to show up in the wee hours. John had gotten them all a second room in one of the Pantheon hotels they were going to use for countersurveillance. And then, when in front of everyone Delilah had said, "John, why don't you stay at my place—three in one of these Latin Quarter hotel rooms is going to be very tight," Dox had been tempted to make a crack, something along the lines of *Oh, no, you know John, I'm sure he'd prefer to stay close to the rest of the team and watch the street through the curtains,* or maybe something about Delilah taking one for the team by shacking up with John. But instead, he'd just looked at her and smiled, because he was happy it seemed to be okay for them for the moment, and he hoped it would last. And she'd given him a subtle smile back, along with a small shake of the head, like she was saying, *You better not say anything smart,* and he just kept smiling and shook his head back, like he was saying, *Oh, no, I would never.*

He'd taken a shower, which was heavenly, then put on one of the hotel's fancy robes, to find the lights low and Labee looking out through the curtains. He would have liked to think she'd turned down the lights to create a romantic atmosphere, but he knew it was just so she wouldn't be silhouetted from the street.

He eased himself into the plush chair in the corner and sighed. "My lord, I needed that."

She nodded. "Why don't you crash first. I'm pretty wired."

She sounded tense—probably about sharing the room. That was all right. He figured he'd just keep talking until she felt reassured.

"Nah, that's okay," he said. "I'm a little wired myself. What'd you think of Delilah? Glad you two finally met."

413

She kept looking through the curtains. "She doesn't trust me. She thinks I've manipulated all of you into a war that's not yours."

"Hmm," he said. "I'm very fond of Delilah, but I don't believe her view is fair or accurate."

She looked at him. "You don't think I've manipulated you?"

"You asked me a favor. Where I come from, we don't call that manipulation. Especially when the person asking is someone who saved your life."

"Yeah, but the favor was just to help me. And then I told you I didn't want your help if . . . you know. If it didn't involve taking down Child's Play."

"Sure, I suppose that might have been manipulative, if I wasn't already determined to help you in that regard. I mean, not to sound selfish or anything, but helping you kill Sorm and those other traffickers in Thailand was about the best thing that happened to me all year. Besides meeting you, that is."

He was trying to make her smile with that, but she didn't. "What about the others?" she said. "Do you think I manipulated them?"

He considered for a minute. "I think 'manipulate' in this context isn't a helpful word. Sure, you were hoping for an outcome, but you didn't do anything nefarious to achieve it, did you? I mean, if I say to you, 'Labee, would you be kind enough to please pass me the sugar,' instead of 'Hey, Labee, pass

414

the fucking sugar,' am I manipulating you? Or am I just being sensible about trying to get you to agree with what I want?"

She went back to looking through the curtains. "I take . . . a lot of risks in what I do," she said, and he had the feeling she was talking about more than just the risks she took as a cop. "Protecting people who can't protect themselves. It's . . . a big deal for me."

"I know. It's one of the things I . . . respect about you so much."

Good lord. He was so jetlagged that his mouth had almost said *that I love about you* without any prior meaningful input from his brain.

But if she noticed, she didn't say anything, and after a moment, she went on. "What I told you about in Thailand. My sister. It's all tied up with that. But knowing the cause doesn't really do much to change the . . . the obsession."

He watched her for a long moment, but she kept staring resolutely through the curtains. Then he said quietly, "Darlin', I think you underestimate yourself."

She looked at him, and he saw she was crying. Lord, the amount of pain this woman carried around inside her.

But it wasn't like before, where she would turn away or wipe her eyes as surreptitiously as she could. And he realized that was something. That she was letting him see her like this.

"Have you ever thought that maybe this is just the way you are?" he said. "Not all of it, not the obsessiveness, maybe. But losing Nason . . . I don't think that took you in some direction that was the opposite of the one you would have been going in anyway."

Her face contorted for an instant at the mention of her sister. He supposed at the invocation of her memory, and maybe because she was unaccustomed to hearing anyone ever say her name.

"What I mean," he went on, "is that I think . . . losing Nason probably just intensified what was already there. And what was there was a fierce, enduring instinct to protect people weaker than you are. And that's a lot of people, because you are almighty strong."

His voice cracked before he could finish, and he was embarrassed and almost made a joke about how he must be more tired than he'd realized. But then he thought fuck it, she wasn't afraid to cry in front of him, why should he be afraid to cry in front of her?

She let the curtain close and walked over to the chair. She knelt and touched his cheek. He covered her hand with his, and she didn't pull back.

"I like when you do that," he said. "It always feels like a big gesture, coming from you."

"It is."

"You mind if I do the same?"

She looked at him for a long moment. Then she said, very quietly, "You can if you want."

He did. Just with the back of his fingertips, as softly as he could.

She looked in his eyes, not trying to hide the tears in hers. "I'm sorry I'm so fucked up," she said.

"I'm not," he said. "And I don't think you're fucked up at all. I wish there were more people like you. And besides, I told you to never apologize for that."

She shook her head. "I don't know why you're so nice to me."

Come on, you told John to tell Delilah how he feels. Are you too chickenshit to do the same?

But no. Maybe he was rationalizing, but this was different. Opening up too much with Labee . . . it would just make her feel pressured.

"Hey," he said. "Are you really still wired?"

She nodded.

"Okay," he went on. "I think I could sleep for a while. Probably not long, due to the overall jetlag, but if I don't wake up of my own accord, then you do it for me anytime you feel yourself starting to nod off."

She nodded again.

He smiled. "But first, you have to do me a favor."

"Sure."

"You have to tuck me in."

"Tuck you in?"

"Well, lie down next to me for a minute. And touch my cheek the way you do. I won't pretend, I would really like that."

She shook her head. "You're a strange man, Carl."

"I suppose. I won't deny that despite my reputation in certain quarters as a hardened mercenary who lives for nothing other than to get paid and laid, I actually have a tender side."

"Yeah, I've noticed that."

"Well, I'd be grateful if you could indulge it, even if just for a minute."

She looked at him for a long moment. And then she nodded.

He got on his side under the comforter, staying close to the edge so she could have as much space as possible. She sat in the middle, looking uncomfortable.

"I'm concerned you might not be able to reach my cheek from there," he said.

She laughed awkwardly but didn't move.

"Let's try this," he said. "Why don't you just lie down facing me, on top of the comforter. And I'll look in your eyes and try to think of something funny to say to make you laugh."

She smiled. And then stretched out on her side, facing him, albeit from a pretty good ways off. But he didn't care. It was wonderful to just lie on the same bed with her.

"How bad is it?" he said. "I mean on a one-to-ten scale."

"You mean with one bad, and ten really bad?"

He laughed. "Sure, like that."

"Maybe . . . a two. Or a three."

"Well, shit, that's not bad at all. I was afraid you were going to say an eight, or maybe even a nine. I mean, a ten would have killed me, I know you'd never say that even if it were true, but still, a two or three? You just made my night."

She laughed. God, he loved the sound of her laughing.

"I'll tell you what," he said. "Tonight I already feel like a winner. So you don't even have to touch my cheek, if you don't want to."

She didn't say anything. She just looked at him. And then she reached out and cupped his face.

Her fingers were so warm and felt so nice. "That's not taking it up past a five or so, is it?" he said.

She shook her head.

"Okay, good. Let me know if it gets bad. If it does, you can always stop."

She took a deep breath, then blew it out. And surprised him by pulling herself closer, and leaning in, and kissing him, very softly. And then she pulled back, but not that far, and their faces were still only a few inches apart.

"Wow," he said.

Her eyes filled up. "I'm scared."

He wanted to hold her so much it made him almost dizzy, but he knew he had to be careful. "Don't be," he said. "We don't have to do anything at all, and I'm sorry if I've already made us do too much."

"You know, I had boyfriends in college."

"Okay. Well, I'm happy for them, whoever they were."

"What I mean is, I learned to, you know, do some of the things they wanted. Not everything. Some things I can't . . . ever do. But I never liked it. I only liked it the way you and I did it at that Rayong beach hotel. And I don't think . . . I don't know if I ever will like it. If I can. The way normal people do it. Kissing. And, you know. Things like that."

"Now, you listen to me. First of all, there is no normal. Anyone trying to sell you on normal is also trying to sell you on abnormal, and that's a load of shit. Just a bunch of boring people trying to make exceptional people as boring as they are."

She laughed a little, but she was still crying.

"Maybe there's typical," he went on. "I mean, how could there not be? So okay, fine, you're not typical. But did you not get the memo? You've been through things that would have shattered almost anyone. How could you have endured what you did, and come out typical?"

"Rain said . . . you've been through a lot, too."

"He did? What, was he telling you not to monkey with my delicate feelings or something?"

She nodded.

He chuckled. "He's a good friend, I'll tell you that. A little taciturn at times, but his heart's in the right place, even though he has a hard time understanding that."

"Is that why you are the way you are with me?"

"I don't know. How am I with you?"

"I don't know . . . kind? Understanding? And . . . patient."

"Oh, well, that's just me being me."

She laughed.

"But honestly," he said, "I haven't really been through that much. John's just being protective. I got held and tortured once by some pretty nasty folks, including a guy I called Uncle Fester and who I'll admit I still have the odd nightmare about because he was fixing to castrate me when, thank God, old John saved the day."

"That's horrible," she said. "Is that what you were talking about when I first called you? The jam with those maximally unpleasant people?"

"Yeah, that was the one, and it was a pretty bad time. But I stopped John from killing Fester and had the satisfaction myself, which definitely saved me a whole lot of therapy afterward. Did killing Sorm and those men in Thailand help you?"

She was quiet for a long time. Then she said, "For a while."

"I'm sorry, Labee. I don't have to tell you, it's just a whole different ballgame when you're a kid. Which is part of the reason I'm happy to be helping you with the Child's Play thing. And why it didn't take any masterful manipulation on your part. Okay?"

She nodded.

"And now that you've kissed me," he said, "would you mind if I kissed you back? I mean, it probably won't be as good as the last one, because this is a fancy Paris hotel and that was a Walmart parking lot, but if we go into it with realistic expectations, I think it could be all right."

She laughed, and again he loved the sound of it.

He leaned in and kissed her. Just softly, with his lips barely parted, but he let it linger, and so did she. And then she surprised him by opening her mouth a little. And he was afraid she was just doing it for him, and he almost said something, but maybe she wasn't, maybe it was really okay, and if so, he didn't want to spoil the moment. And then he realized he was overthinking, and then he stopped thinking entirely, because her tongue had touched his lips and his head swam and he opened his mouth and let his tongue touch hers, and then she pulled back as though she'd received a shock or something and looked at him, her eyes wide.

"I'm sorry," he said quickly. "Did I . . . was that too much?"

She shook her head. "No."

He was afraid to ask. Afraid of the answer. But he said, "Was it . . . okay?"

She nodded.

"Do you want to . . . try a little more?"

She nodded again. And then she leaned closer and, even though she was trembling, she really kissed him.

They wound up doing a lot more than a little. At some point, he realized no one was keeping watch. *What the hell,* he thought distantly. He'd never really thought they'd need to bother with all the security tonight. And he doubted John and Delilah were steadfastly manning the guard posts themselves.

CHAPTER FORTY-ONE
HORTON

Horton strolled along Rue Descartes. The evening was cool and dry, and the sidewalks were lively, crowded with diners at an eclectic scattering of restaurants—Chinese, Italian, and Vietnamese; coffee and ice cream and pastry places. He'd always liked Paris, but every time he'd been here on official business, he'd stayed on the other side of the river, near the Arc de Triomphe. His then-wife, who had accompanied him on some of those trips, had enjoyed shopping on the Champs-Élysées, and some of the restaurants they'd been taken to, Michelin-starred and apparently celebrated, were certainly delicious. But there was an earthiness he liked on this side of the river—the winding cobblestone streets; the soft lighting, which sometimes bordered on dim; the overall smaller scale of things. It was as though on those previous visits, he'd been presented with a carefully curated selection of Paris, and not the city itself. He supposed he should have realized at the time, but he'd had his preconceptions, and his hosts had been happy to fulfill them. Well, now he knew better. And if they all survived this thing, he'd be sure to come back and see the city with new eyes.

"There he is," he heard Larison say. They were all wearing the commo gear he'd picked up from his contact at GIGN—earpieces and lapel mics. They were also each equipped with a prepaid burner, but that was only for backup. No body armor, unfortunately, but when it came to a friend disappearing inventory from an armory or an evidence room, you couldn't really expect more than catch-as-catch-can.

"Just him?" Horton said.

"He's not walking side by side with anyone," Larison said. "Beyond that, I couldn't say."

"Horton, why don't you start heading toward him," Rain said. "No hurry, give us time to observe first."

"I'll take it nice and slow," Horton said.

"Dox," Rain said. "Time for a drive-by."

Livia had hotwired and stolen them one of those motorcycles with two front wheels—a skill Horton wouldn't ordinarily have associated with a cop. Dox was wearing a full-face helmet, and Ben would have no way of recognizing him.

"Already on my way," Dox said. "On my three-wheeled motorcycle. I'm telling you, this thing is an abomination before God."

Livia said, "Crime of opportunity. Dark cul-de-sac, no cameras."

"It doesn't matter if they're abominable," Rain

said. "What matters is that they're all over Paris. We want you to blend."

"Shit, if you wanted me to blend you should have just got me a damned beret. Or a Gauloises cigarette. The only thing that makes the shame tolerable is that no one can recognize me."

"Hmm," Rain said. "It's almost like that's the point."

Dox laughed. "Yeah, yeah. Okay, I'm riding past Treven now. Don't see any suspicious-looking types so far. Larison, can you see me?"

"Yeah, the dork on the three-wheeled motor-cycle."

"The ignominy!" Dox said. "How'd I wind up on this monstrosity? Larison, you should have ridden the damn thing, and I should be up there in that hotel room."

"I would have," Larison said. "But I have too much dignity."

"Enough," Rain said. "Circle the Pantheon. If it's all clear, we'll move Horton in."

Two minutes later, Dox said, "I haven't seen anything out of order. If he brought company, they're hanging way back."

"Okay, then," Rain said. "Horton, go say hello."

Three minutes later, Horton turned onto the Place du Panthéon. He was surprised that his heart was pounding so hard. He trusted Ben. He did. But was he being objective? Could Daniel have been right?

Ben saw him immediately and nodded.

Horton walked over and held out his hand. "Good to see you, son. I'm glad you called."

They shook. Horton started to feel a little calmer.

Ben said, "Just you?"

"Yes, it seemed like it would be more comfortable this way." That was vague enough to encompass a variety of meanings, none of which it would have been productive to acknowledge explicitly.

Ben nodded. "I assume we're going somewhere else."

"There's a little place I had in mind. Just a short walk."

Again, there was nothing to be gained by acknowledging what the procedures were really about.

They set off. Three minutes later, Delilah said, "I've got you." In his peripheral vision, Horton saw her sitting at one of the tables in front of L'Écurie, her blonde hair held back under a thick headband, a pair of stylish reading glasses perched on her nose while she played with a mobile phone.

"Livia," Rain said, "you might want to ease back for now. In case he looks up."

"Already done," Livia said.

"Livia," Dox said, "how are you doing over there?"

It was obvious the big sniper had some kind of crush on the quiet cop. It didn't seem to interfere with their focus, so Horton considered it none of his business. Likewise for Rain and Delilah.

"All good," Livia said. "The apartment behind me is still dark. If a light comes on, I'll climb down. But for now, this position is perfect. It's dark up here, but I can see the bar entrance clearly."

Horton and Ben turned the corner. Ben said, "You mind if we stop here for a second? I didn't see anyone tailing me before we met, but let's just see."

"I was going to suggest the same thing myself," Horton said. Then, for Larison's benefit, he added, "Glad you're being surveillance conscious."

"Or just pretending to be," Larison said.

They waited three minutes. No one came around the corner behind them. Horton said, "I'm good if you are."

Ben nodded. "Yeah."

"The place a few doors down. How about if we get a beer?"

A minute later, they were heading inside. Rain said, "Okay, we're going to cut the chatter to a minimum. If we see anything, we'll holler. And if you need anything, you do the same."

"This ought to work, am I right?" Horton said to Ben, for the benefit of the others.

"Seems fine," Ben said.

In fact, Horton thought it was more than fine. Piano Vache felt both unpretentious and like an institution—the walls covered with overlapping posters advertising music and jazz acts, some of them dating back to the fifties, the support columns in the two interconnected rooms covered with chalk drawings, the lighting soft and the acoustics crisp. The decorations were eclectic—an old radio here; a guitar hung from the ceiling there; an antique piano with a stuffed cow's head over it, from which Horton supposed the bar took its name. The place was on the ground floor, but it had a subterranean feel, like something hidden or secret or frequented only by initiates. Rain had been right—given the early hour, it was only about half-full, mostly with hipster and student types. There was a pleasant buzz of conversation mingled with French pop from a stereo—the kind of background chatter that would allow two people to talk privately and not have to shout. They had no trouble finding an open table all the way in back that gave them both a view of the entrance.

"Beer?" Horton said.

Ben nodded. "Pint of whatever."

Horton went to the bar and returned a minute later with two foaming-over dewy mugs. He set them down, and before he'd even sat, Ben had picked up one and taken a swallow.

Not feeling terribly convivial, Horton thought. But that was all right. *Just because someone else is rude,* his mother had always told him, *doesn't mean you should be.*

He lifted his mug. "*Santé.*"

Ben grunted. "Chin-chin."

They drank, then were quiet for a moment. Horton said, "You wanted to meet."

Another pause. Ben said, "Yeah. For some reason, I was expecting to see the rest of them."

Horton nodded. "Everybody's just being extra cautious."

"Yeah."

Ben took a swallow of beer, then set down the mug with a sigh. "He's using me," he said. "To set you up. It doesn't make me feel good to admit it, but I don't want to be a sucker about it, either."

"I'm not sure what you mean."

"I'm supposed to tell you about a meeting he has, day after tomorrow. Lunch at Le Grand Véfour. Super-fancy restaurant in the first arrondissement. I'm supposed to tell you this like it's a leak, so you'll recon the place and try to hit him there. Except it won't work. He'll have people waiting for the recon and waiting for the hit. The whole thing is just an ambush."

"Why are you telling me this, son?"

Ben drummed his fingers on the table. "You know, Hort, I'm not really sure. You've fucked me. Why shouldn't I fuck you back? And maybe

430

one day, I will. But right now . . . I'm not going to let Graham make me his patsy. If he wants to kill you, he can. Or you can kill him. All I'll say is, think twice about Le Grand Véfour."

"If we don't show up there, what happens to you?"

"Nothing happens to me. Graham figures you all sniffed out the ambush and steered clear. He's disappointed. He doesn't give me a pat on the head or another bullshit promise. What difference does it make?"

Horton hesitated, mindful of the man's pride, then said, "How's it going for you over there? I mean, at OGE."

Ben looked at him. "Why do you care?"

"Because it's partly my fault that you wound up there."

"That's right. So if you care, you're caring a little late."

"Maybe we can find you something better."

"Save it, Hort, okay? You're starting to sound like Graham."

"Look, give me something. If Le Grand Véfour won't work, then where?"

"I don't know where. He told me his executive assistant is still working out the details of his schedule. I think that's bullshit, and that the idea is to give you just the one, shiny, irresistible bit of intel. But either way, I don't have anything else."

"No other meetings? No places he likes to go?"

"He likes the hotel. The bar especially. But that's not going to help you. Part of the reason he always stays at the Ritz is because the security is extensive, inside and out. Half their guests are VIPs—celebrities, politicians, Saudi fucking princes, that kind of thing. So they've got cameras everywhere. Guards. And on top of the hotel's own security, the Ministry of Justice is next door, with its own armed contingent. And then there's Graham's own detail. I've met them. They're good. Don't even think about making a run at him there. You'd have better luck inside a bank vault."

Delilah said, "We may have a problem."

Horton's heartbeat kicked up a notch. He took a sip of beer as though considering, wanting to pause the conversation so he could focus on the update.

"I've got two large men," Delilah went on, "dressed for surveillance—gray clothes, everything average, comfortable shoes—and looking like former military or national police to me. Bulky jackets that would be good for concealed carry. I just watched them go into the second restaurant in a row on my street."

Larison said, "I'm on my way. Three minutes out."

"Same," Dox said. "Say the word if you want us to come in."

"Not yet," Rain said. "Delilah, how sure are you?"

"Sure. They're way too focused to just be trying to find the right spot for dinner." There was a pause, then she said, "They just went into my restaurant. Hort, you should leave. Turn right onto the street as you leave the bar. And be careful. There might be others closing in from that direction."

"I'll head that way," Dox said. "In case you run into a problem."

"That's where I'm coming from, too," Larison said.

Horton shook his head. "It doesn't make sense."

Ben looked at him. "What doesn't?"

Horton set down his beer, his heart kicking harder now. "Did you bring anyone with you tonight, son?"

"No."

"I need the truth."

"That's funny, coming from you."

"Goddamn it, tell me if you did. And tell me why. Things are going to go sideways otherwise."

"Why do you think I brought someone? Is someone coming?"

"Yeah, someone's coming. But I don't know why. Are they after you, or me? Or both?"

Ben turned and started scanning the room, his right hand drifting over to the edge of the table.

"They're leaving my restaurant," Delilah said. "Turning onto Rue Laplace."

"I see them," Livia said. "I'm pulling back for a minute so they don't make me."

"Hort, stay put," Delilah said. "If you leave now, you'll walk right into them."

"Did Treven have a beacon?" Larison said.

"I don't think so," Delilah said. "If it were a beacon, they wouldn't be checking other places. They'd head straight in. My guess is, they had mobile surveillance in a wide grid—keeping way back, and falling in or turning off so that no one was ever on Treven for more than a single city block. Now he's been gone for ten minutes, so they assume he's stopped. They're closing the net and going place by place to determine where he is."

Rain said, "Horton, what do you want us to do? Your call."

"Stay outside," Horton said. "Ben and I can handle this."

"Handle what?" Ben said, still scanning the room. "Who are you talking to? Is that Rain?"

"They're looking in the window now," Delilah said. "Just like they did in the last three places. I'd say you've got thirty seconds before they come in."

"I see them," Larison said. "I'm coming down the other side of the street. And it looks like . . . yeah, pretty sure those are two more ahead of me, closing in on the bar."

Horton looked at Ben. "If you came here to kill

me, you can do it now. It'll be a lot less messy than if you wait."

"What the fuck are you talking about?" Ben said, still scanning. "If I'd come here to kill you, I would have dropped you in the dark in front of the Pantheon. Or the second you told me no one else was coming."

Horton believed him. Maybe it made sense, but still, on some level, he knew it was an act of faith. He didn't care.

"I believe you," Horton said. "Now listen, son. I'm armed. I assume you are, too. In a second, my hand is going to disappear under the table. Once it's down there, it's going to have a gun in it. That gun is not for you. It's for the two men who just came through those doors, if they show any hostile intent."

Ben had already made them, and his hand had already vanished under the table, same as Horton's.

"What the fuck are you up to?" Ben said, glancing back and forth from Horton to the two men.

"I'm not up to anything. Think about what you just told me. If I wanted you dead, why would I do it this way?"

The two men reached the connection between the two rooms. They made Horton and Ben. One of the men started forward, his hand moving toward the opening of his jacket. But the other guy stopped him with a hand on his shoulder and a few words in his ear. Followed by a few words into his lapel.

"Do you know them?" Horton said.

Ben shook his head. "No. They're not part of Graham's security detail, anyway. Maybe local auxiliaries."

"They made us," Horton said. "For the moment, it's a standoff. I think they're waiting for reinforcements."

Through the earpiece, Horton heard two pistol shots. Then Larison: "The reinforcements are going to be late."

The man who'd spoken into his lapel a moment earlier did so again. His brow furrowed. He spoke again. A pause, and then he spoke urgently. Much more urgently. He and his partner slipped back behind the support column. Maybe they were being generally cautious; maybe they'd been briefed on what kind of a shooter Ben was. Either way, Horton realized the table he and Ben had chosen was a mistake. He hadn't envisioned a standoff like this one, and had been focused less on cover and more on spotting a threat before it got too close.

"Oh, hell," Dox said. "We've got three motor-cycles, each a tandem, all turning onto Rue Laplace from the Bibliothèque side. I think somebody just called in an emergency or something. Larison, best find some concealment beaucoup quick."

"They had two backup on the way," Horton said to Ben. "Larison just capped them. But six more will be here any second."

"I'm at Delilah's position," Rain said. "Livia, you ready?"

"Eyes on the front entrance."

"*Merde*," Delilah said. "Three more motorcycles, all tandem. So twelve incoming."

"Here I come," Dox said, the rev of the motorcycle engine audible through the ear-piece. "Feeling stupid and deadly on this damn contraption. Larison, I don't know where you ghosted to, but you'll see me in a second."

"I'm right here," Larison said. "Pick me up."

Ben must have realized the same thing Horton had about their position, because he said, "They have cover, but they're clustered. I'm going to slide left. You go right. But be ready. As soon as they spot the pincer, they're going to run, or fight."

"Go," Horton said. They both moved out. The men, apparently having failed to anticipate the move, waited a second too long. Then the one on the right yelled, "*Tout de suite*!" And brought up a pistol from behind the column.

He hadn't even finished fully extending it before Ben put two rounds in his face. The buzz of background conversation stopped so abruptly it was as though someone had hit a giant "Stop" button, and for a moment there was no sound but the music from the stereo. Then someone screamed, and there was another scream, and people started scrambling from their tables. The guy on Horton's side moved left to clear his gun hand from behind the column. Horton kept moving laterally and put three rounds into the man's torso. The guy got off two wild shots anyway and Horton kept moving in, his gun up, walking up his shots until he'd put two in the guy's face and he was down.

It was pandemonium now. Everybody out of their seats, screaming, running in panic for the exit. It didn't look like the stray shots had hit anyone, but Horton wasn't sure.

"I think they're wearing body armor," he shouted. The lapel mic would have picked it up without the extra volume, but he was juiced with adrenaline. "You need headshots. Headshots."

"Is there another kind?" Larison said, and Horton heard two reports through the earpiece. Then an eruption of gunfire just outside the restaurant.

"Come on," Horton said, hustling toward the exit. "There are twelve more out front. Or ten, anyway. Sounds like Larison just dropped two."

They got closer, and then had to stop—the crush in front of the door was too much. The people in back were trying to stampede out, while the people in front, trying to escape the gunfight in the street, were fighting to get back in.

A girl about his daughter's age tripped and

stumbled into Horton's arms, crying hysterically. Ben shouted, "Hort!" and fired two rounds. Horton looked up and saw someone in a full-face helmet and riding leathers who had made it through the door. The man staggered, but the crush behind him kept him from falling. Horton pushed the girl away and fired. He was no longer the shot he'd once been, and with all the people and tumult he was afraid to go for the head. But he hit center mass. Once. Again. Ben put two rounds through the facemask of the helmet and the inside of it erupted in red.

There was more gunfire outside, but the people who'd made it out of the bar must have been dispersing left and right now, because the crush was suddenly gone, with maybe a dozen shaking stragglers hiding under tables and quaking in terror. Reflexively, Horton and Ben swiveled from one of them to the next, their pistols up, causing sobs and moans of terror. Horton looked through the door and saw another rider, his pistol up, apparently engaging Livia. He heard her shots through both the door and the earpiece, and the man went down.

"Go," Ben said, turning to check their six. "Help the others. I'll make sure—"

Another rider popped up from behind the bar. He must have slithered under it during the commotion and then waited until he sensed his moment.

"Ben!" Horton screamed, bringing his gun around. He fired at the man. He hit him, center mass. A second time. A headshot. And another to be sure. The man went down.

In his imagination, in the reality he expected and still clung to, that was all that happened.

But burned into his retinas was a different sequence. The man had fired before Horton hit him. Ben had staggered back.

Horton looked. Ben's back was to the support column. His left hand was pressed to his chest, his gun hand covering it.

Blood was coursing through his fingers.

"Ah, fuck!" Horton said. "Fuck!" He raced over and got an arm out just before Ben starting sliding down. He tried to hold him up, but the angle was too awkward, and Ben's legs had given out. All he could do was keep him from sliding past the column on one side or the other, and stabilize him in a sitting position at the bottom of it.

"Ben's hit!" he yelled, not even caring if one of the people cowering under the tables heard the name. He scanned the bar and, seeing no threats, fumbled for his burner with shaking fingers. The damn thing was off, a security precaution. He pressed the "On" button, and waited while the screen gradually brightened . . .

Come on, come on, come fucking ON

"I'm coming in," he heard Rain say.

"Negative," Horton shouted back. "Just get everyone out. I'm calling a friend. A medic."

Jesus, was it possible for a phone to take this long? He looked down. Ben's color was bad, very bad. The floor was soaked with as much blood as Horton had ever seen. And Horton had seen his share of blood.

"Hold on, son, hold on," he said, and he realized he was crying. "Do you hear me? I have a friend, he's right here in Paris. A former medic. Legionnaire. I've seen him patch up wounds way worse than this. Way worse. You're going to be fine, do you hear me?"

Ben groaned. He said, "You used to be a better liar."

"It's no lie. Come on, you fucking phone!"

"I'm coming in," Rain said. "Don't shoot."

And a moment later, Rain was kneeling alongside Ben. He glanced at Horton, but Horton wouldn't look at him. He didn't want to see what was in Rain's eyes.

Ben's breathing was getting extremely shallow.

"You're going to be fine," Horton said again, a battlefield reflex.

Ben groaned. "How stupid do you think I am?"

There was nothing more to say. Horton took Ben's hand and held it tightly. Shot in the chest, and this much blood . . . it was a matter of seconds now.

"What can we do?" Rain said.

441

"Just go," Ben said, his speech slurring now. "Maybe you'll believe me now."

"I do believe you," Rain said. "And for what it's worth, Hort always has."

"Yeah?" Ben said.

Horton squeezed his hand. "Always," he said.

Ben's skin had gone dangerously white. He murmured, "Fuck."

"Is there anyone at home?" Rain said. "Anything you want anyone to know? Tell me. I'll make sure it gets done."

Ben looked at him. "My brother. Alex."

"What about him?"

"Tell him . . . I'm going to be with Katie. And that . . . I'm sorry I was always such an asshole. Shit. I can't believe—"

Then his eyes closed and his head lolled to the side.

"Oh, no," Horton said. "No, no, no."

He felt Rain's hand under his arm, the grip like a steel hook. "Come on," he said. "We need to go. Now."

CHAPTER FORTY-TWO
RAIN

An hour later, the six of us were clustered in a tight circle on chairs and cushions around the living room in Delilah's Marais apartment. The curtains were drawn, the lights low, and though there was a thick rug underfoot, we were speaking softly to take no chances on disturbing the people in the apartment below.

Per the plan, we had met at the bug-out point, a dim and graffiti-covered underpass at the intersection of Rue Jean Calvin and Rue Mouffetard. Dox and Livia had gotten away on Dox's motorcycle. Delilah and Larison ghosted away on foot. Horton and I requisitioned one of the dead riders' bikes and, being the last to leave, were chased by two police cars. Horton laid down suppressive fire, and I lost them by gunning the bike through a series of alleys. Eventually, we ditched it near a park farther north on Rue Mouffetard and walked the rest of the way.

But we stayed at the bug-out point only briefly. There were sirens everywhere, and Delilah insisted the safest place would be her apartment. I didn't want to agree—we had made enough trouble for her already—but I knew she was right.

443

Witness accounts were apt to be fragmentary and confused, but we couldn't count on that. We needed to debrief, and doing it anywhere in public, or in one of our hotel rooms, where we would have to get past a front desk and security cameras, would be risky. So we split up and headed separately to Delilah's place.

It might have felt strange to be back in her apartment with so much company, but I was too concerned about what had happened at Piano Vache to be much struck by that. What mattered was that it was a quiet building on a quiet street. There were no security cameras, and we had drifted up the staircase one at a time without so much as running into a neighbor.

Horton was being stoic, but I could tell he was shaken. He had trained and molded Treven, mentored and promoted him, and viewed his prodigy with justified pride. But there had also been a complicated paternal dynamic in their relationship, with Horton a manipulative and exploitive father as well as a protective and caring one. He was grappling with grief, of course, but it was grief marred by guilt.

Figuring out how it had happened was easy. Everyone agreed with Delilah's initial assessment, which was bolstered by the number of operatives who had converged on the bar. With a bench of sixteen, they could have had people at all times on the streets parallel and perpendicular to Treven's position—a kind of roving mesh. And every time he stopped or turned or doubled back, the mesh could have reconstituted around him. And then, when it became clear he was no longer moving, the mesh began to tighten.

And figuring out what had happened was mostly a matter of stitching together our individual perspectives. The more difficult question was why. I had agreed with Horton's initial assessment—that it wouldn't make sense for Treven or anyone else to use the meeting for an ambush because it was unlikely more than one of us would have been there. And as someone whose survival had always depended on an outsized ability to put myself in the shoes of the opposition and predict their next move, I was more than perplexed that I'd gotten it wrong this time. I was spooked.

As it happened, Livia supplied the winning insight. Looking at no one in particular and speaking so softly the rest of us had to lean in to hear better, she said, "I think we got lucky. Well, the rest of us, obviously."

I shook my head, not sure what she meant. "Sure, but . . ."

"What I mean," she went on, "is that what happened was almost what was supposed to happen."

Dox looked at her. "How do you mean?"

She waited a moment, as though still puzzling

it out, then said, "I think Horton and Treven were supposed to see the first two, and see them calling for backup. And I think seeing that the opposition had just called for backup was supposed to make Horton and Treven call for their backup, too."

Everyone was quiet for a moment, processing that. I said, "Because they knew we almost certainly wouldn't risk a meeting with more than one, or at most two, of us."

Livia nodded. "Right."

I was starting to see it. "But they could also be confident that the rest of us would be deployed nearby. And that if we thought we'd miscalculated—and Horton and Treven were in danger—we'd come running."

Dox said, "That's why they had so many. It wasn't just the mesh surveillance. It was also they knew if things went as planned they'd be engaging all of us."

I was seeing it now. But I'd learned it was better to let other people contribute. I said, "So what went wrong?"

Dox glanced at Larison. "A little something called the angel of death, I'd say."

"That's right," Horton said. "That's it. Ben and I were supposed to see the first operative talking into his lapel. I wondered about it at the time, but only half-consciously because so many other things were happening and so fast. But you don't need to dip your head for these mics, they're already sensitive enough to pick up a damn whisper. We were supposed to see that man calling for backup. And if that alone didn't get us to call for our own backup, the next two bad guys showing up would have. But they didn't show up. Thank you for that, Daniel."

Larison nodded once in acknowledgment.

"There's something else," Livia said.

We all looked at her. Everyone was attentive—she was obviously an exceptional tactician—but with Dox it was more than that. It was pride. And pleasure. And devotion.

It was love.

I hoped he was going to be okay. There were depths to Livia, obviously. Dark depths. Lovestruck as he was, I wasn't sure Dox could see them. Or, even if he could see them, understand what they were.

But one worry at a time.

Livia looked at each of us. "They weren't that good," she said. "At least, not all of them."

Larison nodded, and I knew he'd had the same impression. And now that we were talking about it, I realized I'd been vaguely conscious of the same thing. But I was so relieved that we'd come through a serious ambush with only one loss that emotion was occluding my insight.

"I think you're right," I said. "But tell me what you saw."

She shrugged. "As soon as it wasn't going the

way they'd planned, they panicked. Most of their shooting was spray and pray. It was lucky the civilians coming out of the bar were behind them, or there would have been a lot of casualties. But they weren't hitting us, either. Now, some of that is because we caught them off guard, with Dox and Larison moving in from the sides while I engaged from above. But I've seen gangbangers shoot. And those guys—at least the ones outside the bar, I don't know about the ones who went in—were amateurs, not pros."

It occurred to me that Livia, who had dropped four of the attackers, seemed not terribly troubled by it. Most cops might have felt their involvement had crossed a line. Apparently, wherever Livia lived in relation to that line, she was accustomed to both sides of it.

"The ones inside were good," Horton said. "It's just that Ben was better."

"Not quite better enough," Larison said.

"He was looking to make sure none of the civilians had been hit!" Horton hissed, rising half out of his seat. "About the last thing in the world you would ever give a damn about!"

"Maybe," Larison said, eyeing him coolly. "Then again, I'm still around to be criticized for it."

"You're a goddamn sociopath is what you are," Horton said, coming to his feet. "And I'll tell you something else—"

"No," I said. "That's enough."

"He's not a sociopath," Dox said quietly, eyeing Larison with a look no one would ever want to be on the wrong end of. "He's just rude. And callous at the wrong time. And I for one would appreciate it if he would knock it the fuck off."

There was a tense silence. Horton returned to his seat.

Larison looked at him. "Treven wasn't my favorite guy," he said. "But . . . that wasn't fair. I'm sorry."

Horton nodded.

Livia, probably recognizing it would be useful to move the conversation along, said, "Delilah, you made the first two as former military or police."

Delilah nodded. "Of course, I can't be sure. But the way they were checking out the restaurants . . . there was an air of authority. Like these were men accustomed to clearing rooms, or going into residences to arrest suspects and collect evidence. Criminals look like they're casing a place. Cops and soldiers look like they think they own it."

"So a mix," Horton said. "A few pros, and a lot of amateurs. Why?"

"Graham's bench might not be that deep out here," I said. "Maybe he didn't want to risk his own security detail. And maybe the pros he managed to assemble wanted a few expendable hired guns in the mix. More firepower on their side, and a few pawns to be sacrificed as needed."

"They did manage to get two more in while we were engaging the others," Larison said. "Presumably, those second two would have been pros, because they were trying to help their comrades." He looked at Horton and added, "Also, they must have been good if they got Treven."

We were quiet again.

I considered. Horton had already briefed us on what Treven had told him, but we were missing something, and I wanted to recap. I said, "Treven told you the 'intel' about the lunch at Le Grand Véfour was a setup."

Horton nodded. "That's right."

"Okay," I said. "But now it seems the real setup was the meeting itself."

Horton nodded again. "Agreed."

"Graham didn't trust Treven to sell us on the restaurant," I said. "Or, even if Graham did trust him, he knew we wouldn't."

They were all quiet, waiting to see where I was going with this. I wasn't sure myself. But . . . it felt like something.

"The point is," I said, "Graham didn't trust Treven. The things Graham told him, he didn't care if we knew. Or he wanted us to know."

We were quiet again. I said, "So . . . what didn't Treven know? What didn't he tell you? What was Graham keeping from him, because Graham doesn't want us to know it?"

Dox said, "You mean like a known unknown?"

I nodded. "I'm hoping we don't have any unknown unknowns."

"The hotel," Horton said. "He didn't have anything specific on that. Just that Graham liked the bar and did a lot of business in the hotel. But he also warned me not to try anything there because there's too much security. Now, ordinarily, the more cynical among us"—he glanced at Larison—"might have surmised that Ben was employing some kind of reverse psychology there. But I'd have to say that Ben has now tragically proven his bona fides."

"Agreed," I said. "The hotel's not a dangle. As you say, what Treven offered was just what he knew generally, nothing operational. Beyond which, Treven's general observation tracks with Kanezaki's more detailed information."

"On the other hand," Dox said, "if Treven was right and the hotel really is that tough to crack, we might now be in a plan-B situation. Especially with Graham on high alert after his failed ambush. But no matter how careful he's being, I doubt he'll be able to resist at least a brief look at the beautiful skyline from his fabulous suite. So if one of Horton's contacts or Kanezaki can get me a rifle, I'm sure I can find an appropriate rooftop of Paris from which to send him our best."

Delilah said, "Can Kanezaki get us anything more specific about the hotel?"

I looked at her, hoping she could help, feeling guilty at the notion. And worried, as well. She hadn't engaged at Piano Vache. She hadn't even been armed. Her cover, and everything it offered, was too important. But anything could have happened there. And the more involved she became, the more likely "anything" would become, too.

"What do you have in mind?" I said.

"We know how much Graham appreciates blondes," she said. "And we know about the mistress. Dominique Deneuve. Whatever business Graham has in the hotel, according to Kanezaki, she would be part of it, is that correct?"

I nodded.

"Well," she said, "what would happen if Ms. Deneuve were unable to play her customary role? And Mr. Graham were to meet another blonde, instead?"

"Oh, Delilah," Dox said. "I think you might be even more devious than you are beautiful."

Delilah gave Dox a smile, which quickly faded. She looked at me. "There's just one small complication," she said.

CHAPTER FORTY-THREE
DELILAH

The following evening, Delilah was in the Hemingway Bar at the Ritz. She preferred the Ritz Bar, which in her opinion was better lit and infinitely more chic, directly across from it. But this was work, and her preferences didn't matter. What mattered was that for whatever reason, Graham was a devotee of the self-consciously masculine atmosphere of the Hemingway Bar, with its heavy pancling and hunting trophies and eponymous memorabilia all over the walls. And she had to admit that Kent, louche in his perfectly tailored camel-hair jacket and sipping his Gordon's martini, certainly looked at ease there. But looking at ease was only part of it. He had a role to play, too, and he was playing it just a little too well.

He'd been happy enough when she'd called and asked him to visit her in Paris. "I could be there tomorrow," he'd said, a hint of lasciviousness present at the edges of his otherwise impeccable British boarding-school accent.

"In fact," Delilah had said, "that's when I need you."

"Need me? Hmm, scratch tomorrow, I'm on my way now."

"Kent. It's not like that. It's professional. A professional favor."

"Ah. I see. Well, why don't I help you with the business, whatever it is, and dinner at my hotel afterward?"

She never let him stay with her when he visited, preferring the control—and, she knew, the lesser intimacy—of confining their time to his rented spaces and away from the one she lived in.

"I can't. I need you for just a few hours, and I can't see you after that. Not this time. I'm sorry."

He was quiet for a moment. Then he said, "That's all right. I'm happy to help. Just don't apologize, all right? Unless you're trying to make me feel pathetic."

She felt a pang of remorse at that. The problem was, she liked Kent. He was intelligent, he had a rakish charm, and, though in some respects he could be self-absorbed, in bed he was anything but. But he had never been more than a convenience for her, while increasingly, for him, Delilah was a priority. And now she was taking advantage of that unstable dynamic, to his detriment.

She didn't want to tell him more than what was operationally necessary, but she had to be realistic, too. He was a professional; it was possible he would use MI6 to find out if anything was known about what VIPs were staying at the Ritz, in which case he would learn Graham was the target. Or he might recognize Graham without any input from the organization. It was even possible he'd worked with Graham, in which case the op would have been compromised before it even got started.

She'd floated the idea with the team, and they all agreed that to get the theatrics right, they needed a man. Since all of them were known to Graham and his security team, that meant an outsider. Kent, who was both a professional and someone she knew personally, would do nicely. His MI6 affiliations were a risk, and so was briefing him on the identity of the target, but the alternatives were worse.

John, she could tell, had been struggling with the decision. He'd gone along with it because nothing else made sense. But later, when everyone else had curled up on her two couches or on the living-room floor, and she and John were alone in her bedroom, he had asked if this Kent was the man she had told him about, the one she was seeing. She acknowledged he was, to which Rain responded with a silent nod.

"Are you jealous?" she asked.

"What do you think?"

"I can't tell with you. You hide your feelings too well. Or else you don't have any."

"Yes. I'm jealous."

"Good. It's been a long time since you appreciated me."

He shook his head. "No. I've always appreciated you. I was just too stupid to show it."

"Don't be sweet with me. I haven't forgiven you yet."

He smiled. "Do you have any more anger you need to get out?"

She tried not to smile back, but couldn't stop herself. "Come here, idiot," she'd said, and they made love again, quietly, so as not to disturb the others.

But now Kent was being petulant, demanding to know where things stood between them, and whether they were going to see each other after this, and a dozen other items she didn't want to talk or even think about.

Delilah glanced at the entrance. They were sitting beside each other on one of the cushioned benches at the back of the bar, with a nice view of both rooms. "I can't tell if this is part of tonight's performance," she said, "or if you mean it."

"Perhaps it's both. Perhaps I'm a method actor."

"Just don't forget your lines."

"No need to worry about that. This role you've assigned me has come to feel like second nature. And what about you? You look ravishing, and you know it. But is it for my benefit, or for your quarry?"

She had worn a slim-fitting, short-sleeved black lace midi with a scooped back, along with a gold cashmere shawl for the cool evening air. The outfit was keyed to casual with minimal jewelry and makeup: Mansoor & Gore opal-and-gold earrings, a vintage hammered-gold bracelet, a touch of eyeliner and lipstick. The look was still more than she would ordinarily have chosen for a bar, but it was important for Graham to see what she might look like at an elegant dinner. So yes, of course tonight it was for Graham's benefit, and Kent ought to have known that. She still couldn't tell how much of what he was doing was real, and how much the role.

A heavyset man in a dark suit walked in, stopped, and scanned the room. He was wearing a wire-line earpiece. Security, obviously, but for whom?

His eyes lingered on Delilah for a moment, then moved on. It was all right. Bodyguards stared at her all the time. They just never saw what they should have.

The guard spoke into a lapel mic. A minute later, Oliver Graham strode in. She hadn't needed any special research to recognize him; the man was in the news often enough, giving regular interviews about how much more efficiently America could fight its wars if the Pentagon would turn them over to the private sector. He looked fit in a tailored navy blazer with a cinnamon windowpane, and, she couldn't deny, he was attractive, with a good jaw and cheekbones and sandy hair fading to silver at the temples. He was with another man, older and heavier, who looked more corporate, his jacket of good material but hanging lifelessly off his shoulders.

The bartender saw him and said, "Welcome back, Mr. Graham, always a pleasure to have you here."

"Colin," Graham said, walking over and shaking the man's hand, "good to see you."

"The usual?"

"For both of us, thanks."

Interesting that Graham ordered for both himself and his companion. Did he like to be in charge? Did he enjoy showing off his knowledge and familiarity? She hoped his companion liked martinis, because she knew from John's briefing that the bar's signature thirty-euro clean dirty martini was Graham's tipple of choice.

Graham and his companion sat at a corner table near the bar—a little far from Delilah and Kent, but still workable. The bodyguard took up a position near the doorway.

"I need the ladies' room," Delilah said. "I'll be right back."

She saw Graham looking her up and down as she passed his table. He was subtler than most, but not as subtle as he probably imagined. Outside the bar, there were two more guards. And it was possible Graham had a pair of advance people positioned in the bar even before his arrival—Delilah hadn't made anyone for sure, but if they were pros, she wouldn't necessarily know. All right. Not the definitive answer to what Graham's detail would be like outside the hotel, but if he had at least three men inside, he'd probably have more when he was moving around the city. Especially given what had happened at Piano Vache, and knowing that John and the others were in the city somewhere and gunning for him.

Graham eyed her again when she returned, but she didn't even glance in his direction. The best way to attract powerful men, she knew, was to ignore them. They took it as a challenge, sometimes even an affront.

She sat. Kent had finished his drink. A bit loudly, he said, "That took a while."

"What are you talking about? It couldn't have been five minutes."

"It's been like that all night," he said, still too loudly. "And I'm getting tired of it."

This time a few people looked over.

"Really? Well, maybe you're not the only one getting tired."

"Fine. I'll be more than happy to take you home."

"Why don't you just leave? I'll find my own way home."

"I came all the way out here to see you, and

I'll be damned if you're going to just dismiss me because you're in one of your moods."

A lot of people were looking now. Including Graham. He was looking quite keenly.

"I was in a fine mood," she said, "until you started acting like you own me. I told you, go. I'm happier here by myself."

He stood and held out his hand. "Come."

"No."

He grabbed her wrist. "I said come!"

She threw her drink in his face and said, "*Cochon*!"

There were gasps and murmurs from all around the bar.

He wiped his face, then flung the liquid from his fingers.

Instantly, one of the waiters was beside him. "Sir, perhaps you would like a taxi?"

Delilah had to hand it to the Hemingway Bar staff—they knew how to tell a guest it was time to leave.

"No," Kent said. He picked up one of the little linen napkins and wiped his face and hands. Then he took several twenty-euro notes from a pocket and dropped them on the table. "You know what?" he said. "I'm bored with you anyway." He walked out.

Everyone stared at him on the way. Except Graham. He was staring at Delilah.

She apologized to the waiter in French and

thanked him for his timely intervention. He told her it was nothing, and asked for a moment to clean up the table. "Please," she said. "I think I'll just have a seat at the bar."

She got up and said in French to all the people who were now pretending nothing had happened, "I apologize for disturbing your evening." Then she repeated it in English.

She took a seat at the bar. Colin the bartender said, "Something sweet to kill the taste?"

She gave him a little laugh. "That would be perfect."

From behind her, she heard, "Please, put that on my bill, Colin."

She turned. Graham said, "Would you like to join me?"

The trick was to always make them work for it. "That's very nice of you, but no, thank you."

"Are you sure? My companion is just leaving, and I hate to drink alone. Are you a local?"

She looked at him as though trying to gauge his intentions. "Yes."

"Then I'd be grateful if you could tell me what it's like to live here. The real Paris. I visit several times a year, but it's always the Ritz and Michelin restaurants and a chauffeured Maybach."

As lines went, it wasn't a bad one. Especially for anyone likely to be swayed by money and power, which, in her experience, was most people.

"You should get out more often," she said.

He laughed. "I'm trying to. Won't you join me? I really would love to hear your impressions of the city."

"All right," she said. "Thank you."

Though he hadn't even finished his drink, Graham's companion said a quick good night, offering Delilah his chair and claiming an early meeting the next day.

Over the course of the evening, she and Graham wound up having two drinks each—the clean dirty martini for him; the French 75—gin, lemon juice, sugar, and champagne—for her. She told him about her work as a freelance fashion photographer, which was an opportunity for him to say, "Ah, that explains that beautiful dress." He told her his company consulted with governments to help improve their security, and seemed pleased rather than disappointed when she pretended not to know who he was. He wasn't a bad companion. As promised, he asked a lot of questions about Paris—not terribly informed ones, but still it was always refreshing to chat with a powerful man who didn't think a conversation was simply an opportunity to soliloquize. He did have a way of dropping too many hints about his wealth—the suite at the hotel, the Burgundy collection, why Lorenzo Cifonelli was the best tailor in Paris. But all of that was good. He was clearly bent on impressing her, and compared to that, whether he actually knew how was irrelevant.

At a little past midnight, Delilah glanced at her watch. "Well," she said, "thank you for a lovely evening. I have a shoot in the morning, so . . ."

"Of course," he said. "Can I have my driver take you home?"

She hadn't anticipated that, but it was easily handled. "You're very nice, but no, I can get a taxi easily enough."

"Are you sure? My car is probably nicer than a taxi."

She smiled. "I imagine it is. Another time?"

She'd closed off tonight. But opened the door to the future. Now to see if he would walk through it. Or, more likely, how.

"I'd like that," he said. He paused, then added, "This may sound odd, because it's last-minute, but . . . I'm giving a dinner here tomorrow night. Low key, in the smaller private dining room. A business gathering, with some important clients. I have a friend in Paris who ordinarily helps me host these things, but she's come down with some sort of stomach bug and is completely out of commission. These men are all quite successful, but some of them can be surprisingly shy. And I can't imagine anyone who could draw them out and make them comfortable the way you could. Would you care to be my guest?"

The stomach bug was in fact a quite nasty staph

463

infection. Kanezaki had given them a month-deep map of Dominique Deneuve's mobile-phone movements, and then pinpointed her that very day at Le Baromètre, where she was having lunch at a sidewalk table with a girlfriend. It hadn't been difficult for Livia to pop a Kanezaki-supplied staph squib over Deneuve's wine while Delilah distracted her and her friend with a few confused questions about directions.

"Your guest?" she said, still playing it reluctant. "It sounds like you're looking for another host."

"Well, both, honestly. But I wouldn't expect you to do anything other than what you've done tonight—which is to just be an exceptionally charming, engaging person to talk to."

"Ah, now I think you're flattering me."

"I would if it would persuade you, but really, I'm only telling the truth."

She paused. "Would I be the only woman there?"

"No, not at all. Most of the guests will have companions."

If the companions were wives, Graham would have said that. So she imagined they would all be courtesans and mistresses.

"It sounds interesting," she said. "But . . . I don't know that I'm really so charming as you seem to think."

"Shouldn't I be the judge of that?"

She laughed and said nothing.

"I know these people," he went on. "And I know how they'll respond to you. You'll make them feel successful, witty, charming . . . exactly what they want to believe about themselves, but tend to doubt without a little outside encouragement."

She thought that was actually a pretty astute observation of how women like Delilah ingratiated themselves with men. It was interesting that Graham was able to recognize the dynamic with regard to others, but not as it applied to, say, their own interaction here tonight. Interesting, but not so terribly surprising, either. After all, men like Graham knew all about a thing called a honeytrap. But knowing of the thing's existence rarely seemed to save them from getting ensnared in one themselves.

"What time?" she said.

He smiled. "Eight o'clock."

CHAPTER FORTY-FOUR
DELILAH

It was a little past eleven the following evening, and the last of Graham's guests had left the small but sumptuous private dining room, shaking Delilah's hand effusively on the way. Graham closed the door behind him. Then he turned to Delilah and his face broke out in a delighted smile.

"Delilah. You were . . . fantastic."

She shook her head. "Please."

"No. Don't even try to be modest. You were captivating! And you know it. My God. Mr. Liu, the Chinese defense attaché? You got him to talk more in five minutes than I've ever seen him say in an entire evening."

"Stop. I think he was just lonely and enjoying a night out."

"Yes, that's exactly the point! You might not realize it, but compared to his usual reserve, Liu was practically bubbling over."

"Well, I'm glad."

"I put together some major deals tonight. Major. That can't be done if the mood isn't right. And you made the mood . . . perfect. What can I do to show you my appreciation?"

She shook her head. "You don't owe me anything. It was a delicious dinner, and you weren't the only one who did some business. Several of your clients told me they were looking for a photographer for corporate events and gave me their cards."

Depending on how things went, she might even tell Mossad about the contacts she had made—they could be useful. But on the other hand, maybe she wouldn't. Let sleeping dogs lie.

"That's not nearly enough," Graham said. "How about this? The hotel keeps a portion of my Burgundy collection in a private section of its wine cellar. Why don't I have them bring a 2003 Denis Mortet Chambertin Grand Cru to my suite, and you and I can open it? It's the least I can do to say thank you."

It was almost funny to hear him describe what was obviously a plan to seduce her as a means of expressing his gratitude. She smiled and said, "It's an enticing offer."

"It was meant to be."

"But can I suggest something even better?"

"I can't imagine what that would be, but . . . sure."

"You said you wanted to experience more of the real Paris. Not just the fancy hotels and restaurants, no? So look, while I have no objection to Domaine Denis Mortet—no sane person does—it's also nothing new for you. Why don't I take you someplace I like, instead? Where I bet you've never been."

He cocked his head. "What do you have in mind?"

"A special bar close to my apartment in the Latin Quarter. Prescription Cocktail Club. A wonderfully private and intimate place, like a speakeasy."

She had once seen a Gary Larson cartoon about what dogs hear when their owners talk to them—just their names and "blah blah blah." She knew it was like that for Graham now: "close to my apartment . . . private and intimate . . . blah blah blah." She could have said, "A sewage treatment plant, close to my apartment." Or "An abattoir, close to my apartment." Or "A toxic-waste facility, close to my apartment." His reaction would have been the same.

"You're right," he said. "I think that is better. Hmm."

She knew what he was thinking. On the one hand, the failed attack at Piano Vache. And doubtless, the advice of the bodyguards, a breed that always preferred the principal to be kept on lockdown.

On the other hand, quite a lot of wine with dinner. The flush of successful business. And a beautiful, obviously interested French woman right in front of him, who had just said the words *close to my apartment . . . private and intimate.*

He smiled and pulled out his cellphone. "Why not?"

Five minutes later, they were getting into the back seat of Graham's Maybach, with one of the bodyguards riding shotgun. The windows were smoked for privacy, which was perfect. Behind them was a follow car—a Mercedes, four men inside it.

In retrospect, it was funny. The part the others were most worried about—whether Delilah could persuade Graham to leave the hotel and take her to a place she herself had suggested—was the one that had concerned her least. After that was where Murphy's law was most likely to make an appearance.

John had been the one to propose Prescription. "If Graham's people check it out," he said, "they'll see it's a legitimate place—a classy, intimate bar, the kind they'd expect you to propose. And it's on Rue Mazarine—a one-lane, one-way street. And that block has only one street leading onto it—Rue Guénégaud, another one-lane, one-way—because farther north, Rue Mazarine is closed for construction. From Rue Guénégaud, you either have to make a left onto Rue Mazarine, or go straight on Rue Jacques Callot. There's no way to turn around, and no way to pass because the sidewalks are narrow to nonexistent. So no matter what route the security people might want to take, in the end they're going to have to come all the way down Rue Guénégaud from Quai de Conti and then make a left on Rue Mazarine. They can stop or they can go forward, but those are the only options."

"This is the part where a map might be helpful," Dox said. "You know, for those of us less familiar with the local terrain."

While Delilah fired up a map application on her laptop, John said, "The point is, we know Graham's hotel won't work—the security's too tight, and it's where Graham's people will be most alert, especially after Piano Vache. But okay, they get him safely into his car at the Ritz and drive together to the club. Someone riding shotgun, probably a follow car, too. They'll drive all the way—there's no chance Graham's people are going to drop him off anywhere but right in front of the club. That means if Delilah can get Graham to Prescription, we already know the last three hundred yards of the route, maybe more. And I don't have to tell you, a lot can happen in three hundred yards."

Kanezaki's intel had been critical. He was able to track down the purchase of Graham's Mercedes-Maybach and confirm that it was armored and equipped with bullet-resistant glass. The other car Graham kept parked at the Ritz was an ordinary Mercedes. Kanezaki was even able to identify a networked video camera inside

Prescription, and had people capable of shutting it down at the critical time.

And he'd come through on equipment, too. For communication, a transmitter integrated in the buckle of a reasonably stylish leather purse. They judged an earpiece too risky, but with the purse, the team would be able to hear everything Delilah heard. And for the follow car they expected, something called an RFVS— a radio frequency vehicle stopper. Apparently, the Pentagon's Joint Non-Lethal Weapons Directorate had dreamed up the device, which used high-powered microwaves to stall a car engine. Its existence had already leaked, Kanezaki said. What the public didn't know was that CIA had a much smaller version, which it was using in Paris and elsewhere to help foil the kind of vehicle-rampage attacks that had been occurring all over Europe for the last several years.

The one thing Kanezaki was having trouble with was a rifle. But Hort's local contacts had delivered: a suppressed FAMAS G2 with a thirty-round magazine and three-in-one telescopic sight, thermal sight, and laser range finder, all of which Dox had assembled as lovingly as a child with a new Christmas toy.

Now, as they pulled away in the Maybach, the bodyguard turned to Delilah. "I'll have to ask for your mobile phone," he said. "Standard security procedure."

Graham turned off his own phone. "Magnus, it's okay. Delilah, if you could just turn your phone off. No need to hand it over."

The guard said, "Mr. Graham—"

Graham shot him a look. "I'll confirm it's off myself. Delilah, if you don't mind. There have been some threats recently. Nothing to worry about, I'm sure. But out of an abundance of caution, these gentlemen want to make sure no one has a cellphone that could be tracked when I'm outside the hotel. Would you mind?"

"Threats?" she said.

"Just the sort of thing people in my line of work get all the time. But these gentlemen are the best. They're just doing their job, taking even remote possibilities seriously."

"Okay," she said, showing him as she powered down the phone. She had switched off the purse transmitter a moment earlier—it had already done its job of keeping the others informed of developments, including the moment they were leaving the hotel. John was concerned Graham's team would be equipped with detectors that could pick up a transmitter once the devices around it had been switched off. Not that it wouldn't have been convenient to have a mobile phone or other device to track remotely, but they didn't need it. Livia and John were already on motorcycles nearby—stolen, courtesy once again of Livia, who, whatever else she might be, was obviously no ordinary cop. In full-face helmets, able to anticipate the route because they knew the destination, and tag teaming when they needed to follow, the two of them would be difficult if not impossible to spot.

Graham's driver took them over Pont Neuf. Turned right on Quai de Conti. Rush hour was long past, and traffic was moderate. Delilah didn't allow herself to think about what would happen next. If she had, it could have affected the vibe she needed Graham to feel. She was just his guest, attracted to him, pleased he had agreed to her proposal, excited to show him a bar she liked, flush with the uncertainty of what might happen after.

Left on Rue Guénégaud. She glanced casually through Graham's window and saw the truck with the RFVS equipment parked directly to their left, at the very end of the street where it met Quai de Conti, Hort at the wheel. Dox was in a room they had taken in the Hôtel Prince de Conti, or, with luck, maybe even on the roof, either way with a view of the street. Larison would be at Prescription. Rain and Livia should be pulling past the follow car now. Any second, and Hort would—

The bodyguard touched his earpiece, then turned and looked behind them. He said, "There's a problem with the other car."

CHAPTER FORTY-FIVE
DOX

It was too bad about the Prince de Conti, really—
it was another nice hotel, and Dox wouldn't have
minded a night there with Labee. Well, there were
lots of nice hotels in Paris, he'd be happy to visit
all of them with her if she liked, when this was
done. But this one they'd needed operationally,
so Dox had burned yet another debit card and
fake passport to get a room there.

He'd thought he might need to find a way
to get up on the roof, but his room was high
enough, with great coverage of the street. He'd
zeroed the rifle using a construction dumpster
as a backstop, and everything was good to go.
The only difficult angle, really, would be right
under his windows, but he didn't expect anyone
would make it that far, unless they were faster
than bullets.

John and Labee had kept him and the rest of the
team apprised of Graham's approach, so he was
already in position when the Maybach turned
onto the street. The lights were off in the room,
and Dox had set up a bureau so he could use the
rifle's bipod and not have to fire from standing.
Not that it would have been a problem—he could

probably have thrown rocks from this close—but the bipod was better.

The follow car turned the corner behind Graham's Maybach . . . and stopped. That was Horton, inside the truck they'd parked that morning at the end of the street, zapping the engine with that RFVS thing Kanezaki had acquired for them. Dox was not a fan of the CIA's fancy millimeter-wave ray guns and the like, having been on the wrong end of one once in Singapore, but on the other hand, the thing had saved his life. That one had been small, being that it was designed just to boil your skin. This one was for jamming car engines, and weighed several hundred pounds. Well, luckily Kanezaki had left it waiting for them, truck and all, with the key hidden under one of the wheel wells. Kanezaki had made them promise to return it—*intact, please* to the same spot where they had picked it up, and Horton had assured him they would.

Graham's Maybach kept going, past Dox's position and toward the corner, which they had expected, because if the bodyguards suspected that the follow car's engine trouble was anything nefarious, their first instinct would be to keep the principal moving, get him off the X. Unfortunately for them, in this case, the principal was already in a funnel, and the X was at the end of it, exactly where Graham's driver was taking him.

Dox watched the follow car through the integrated scope. Everything was lit up beautifully, and magnified, too. He was ready to go. All he needed was the word from John.

CHAPTER FORTY-SIX
DELILAH

"The bar is right around the corner," Delilah said. "We can walk from here."

Graham ignored her. "What kind of problem?" he said to the bodyguard.

"Engine trouble," the guard said. "They stalled. Out of the blue. I don't like it." He turned to the driver. "Keep going. Don't stop." He reached into his jacket and came out with a machine pistol.

"Wait a minute," Delilah said. "What's going on?"

"Put that away," Graham said. "Let's not over-react."

The guard grimaced. "Mr. Graham—"

"Put it away," Graham said again.

The guard complied. But he had good instincts and was obviously on edge.

The driver turned left—the only direction possible—onto the rough cobblestones of Rue Mazarine.

"That's the bar," Delilah said, pointing to the left side of the narrow street just thirty meters ahead. "Are we going? What's going on?"

"Everything's fine," Graham said. "Magnus, what are they saying?"

The bodyguard touched his earpiece and listened. "Just . . . that the engine died."

"No blown tires? Nothing like that?"

"No."

"Then let's just relax. The bar's right there. Kyle, pull up close, past those motorcycles. Okay, perfect. Magnus, you go in and make sure everything's okay. Get the other guys out here on foot. By the time you're done clearing the bar, they'll all be in position."

The driver checked his rearview. "If I stay here, we're going to create a hell of a traffic jam."

"That's okay," Graham said. "It'll be just a few minutes."

"Oliver," Delilah said, "maybe this wasn't a good idea."

Graham patted her knee. "No, no, it was a great idea. I should have given you a heads-up about the security. This is just the way I travel around Paris. To me it feels completely normal, but of course it wouldn't to someone else. I'm sorry for that."

"Javier," the bodyguard said, looking behind them as though hoping to see the follow car. "You stay with the vehicle. The rest of you, get out now and double time it on foot. Take your first left. The bar is thirty yards up on the left from there. We're parked right in front of it."

He scanned the street. It was empty of traffic ahead of them now, the left side clogged with parked motorcycles and a few cars. The sidewalk ahead was thick with pedestrians queuing up at restaurants. Behind them, as the driver had noted, was a lengthening queue of traffic—cars, scooters, and two motorcycles, the riders in full-face helmets and leathers.

The bodyguard got out, his hand inside his jacket, and headed into the bar.

Delilah thought, *Here we go.*

CHAPTER FORTY-SEVEN
RAIN

I saw Graham's car stop in front of the bar. That was good—it was what we had expected, but there was a chance his bodyguards would be insistent enough, or he would be paranoid enough, for them to abort on the bar and just keep going. If so, Larison would have emerged to engage while Livia and I skirted around the car and dropped our bikes in front of it to form a roadblock. But happily, it seemed we were still dealing with plan A.

The bodyguard got out. "Larison," I said. "Bodyguard's coming in."

I revved the engine of the bike and rode up onto the sidewalk to the right of Graham's car, flipping off the driver as I passed, as though irritated at whoever had stopped there and stranded everyone behind him. I had to force myself not to look more closely—losing the commo link with Delilah had been the right call, but I hadn't been prepared for how anxious it would make me. *She's fine,* I thought. *Everything's going according to plan. Graham doesn't suspect her. In a minute, she'll just open the door and get out. You and Larison will handle the rest.*

Livia followed me into a parking garage three entrances up from the bar, where we dismounted. We'd leave the bikes here. There was no way for anyone to connect them with us.

Livia nodded to me and walked out to the street. We had parked a stolen moving van there earlier in the day, having waited almost six hours for the space to open up. It wasn't as close to Prescription as I would have liked, but it was close enough.

"We've got three guys coming out of the stalled Mercedes," Dox said, with that supernatural calm he got when he was behind a rifle scope. "Running toward your position and soon to be past mine. Now would be a good time for me to engage."

"I see the bodyguard," Larison said. "Coming up the stairs. Give me the word and he's done."

I took a deep breath and tried not to think of Delilah, twenty feet away in the back of Graham's Maybach.

"Go," I said.

CHAPTER FORTY-EIGHT
LARISON

Larison was sitting at a corner table next to the bannister of Prescription's second floor. A waiter had been by, and Larison asked the man if he could hold off on ordering for a little while until his friends arrived. The guy didn't seem thrilled about someone keeping the table if no one was drinking at it, but he nodded and moved off. People tended not to argue with Larison.

Some of the other tables would have offered a better view of the stairs, which led down to a landing and then around to the ground floor in front of the entrance. But they were all taken. Anyway, Larison didn't need a view, because Rain had alerted him when the bodyguard came in. The guy headed straight for the stairs, probably figuring to start his sweep on the second floor and complete it below to make sure no one had slipped in behind him.

Well, too bad someone was inside already.

"I see the bodyguard," Larison said. "Coming up the stairs. Give me the word and he's done."

Rain said, "Go."

Larison stood. He eased the pistol from the bellyband and moved it behind his back, then started down the stairs. The bodyguard was already above the landing and made him instantly—Larison's demeanor, the right hand concealed behind the back. His reactions were good, too: he dove to the left and went for whatever was inside his jacket. But all that took way too long, and before he'd even reached the opposite bannister or gotten his hand on a weapon, Larison had put a round through his left eye. The guy crumpled backward and hit the deck, his legs going over his head and his body flopping down the stairs all the way to the landing.

The bar was suddenly silent but for the background music, the patrons no doubt asking themselves, *What the hell was that? A firecracker? A blown fuse?*

Larison didn't even break stride. He just stepped over the body, saying, "He's done, I'm coming out," and continued on his way.

The waiter he'd sent off earlier raced up the stairs past him, no doubt to check on whatever had just happened.

Larison pulled on a ski mask, pushed open the front door, and stepped out onto the sidewalk—directly in front of Graham's driver's window.

CHAPTER FORTY-NINE
DOX

The three men who had just exited the follow car were running up the street, toward the corner where Graham had made his left. Dox heard a gunshot through the earpiece—that would be old Larison, dropping the bodyguard in the bar. And yes, a second later he heard Larison say, "He's done, I'm coming out."

Dox sighted through the integrated scope, exhaled, and—

Crack! Dropped the first man.

Crack! Dropped the second.

The third guy was the only one who had time to realize they were taking sniper fire. He dashed for a position behind a parked car, and almost made it, too. But unfortunately, the last part of him to reach said cover was his head, and that was the part that got blown off by Dox's third shot.

"So close, but so far," he said softly to himself.

He tracked back to the follow car just in time to see the driver diving out and hauling ass on foot in the other direction. The guy might have dropped down and relied on the engine block to protect him, but then he would have been a sitting duck for anyone approaching on foot. This

484

way, though, he was exposed while he searched for new cover. Not a great range of alternatives either way.

On any other occasion, Dox might have let him go—he was out of the battle now, and no longer mattered.

But directly or indirectly, these people had come after Labee. And they weren't going to get a second chance. Dox exhaled, paused, and put a round in the back of the guy's head.

"Thank you for playing," he said softly. "Next contestant. Oh, wait, there are no more contestants. Colonel, this would be an excellent moment for you to get out of Dodge. Too bad you have to leave, too, there's a nice Mercedes sitting right there, I'll bet with the keys still in the ignition."

"Good shooting," Horton said. Dox saw the truck lights come on, and then it was backing up onto Quai de Conti. There was a ton of traffic south of Rue Guénégaud, with everyone wanting to make a left from Quai de Conti stuck behind the stalled Mercedes. But the north side was clear. Horton laid on the horn and backed up into the nearest car, shoving it sideways. There was a cacophony of answering horns, and suddenly whoever was in the car in his way decided he didn't need to make that left turn so much after all. The car lurched right and then ahead onto Quai de Conti, clearing a space. Horton screeched into the gap, then raced north and out of Dox's field of vision.

"Well played, sir," Dox said. "John and Larison, Graham's follow-car cavalry will not be arriving as they were planning. Over to you."

CHAPTER FIFTY
DELILAH

The Maybach was well soundproofed, but still Delilah could make out the crack of a pistol shot from inside the bar. It was muffled enough to have been something else, but Graham must have been on edge, because he said, "Was that what I think it was?"

The driver said, "Magnus? Everything all right in there?"

Rifle shots rang out to their rear. Dox.

"Son of a bitch," Graham said. He reached behind his waistband and came out with a Baby Glock.

"What the hell is going on?" Delilah said, staying in character.

"They're taking fire!" the driver shouted.

"Get us out of here," Graham said, remarkably cool. "Now."

The driver popped it in gear. But a white van was suddenly racing in reverse ahead of them, screeching to a halt just in front of their front bumper and stopping them in place.

"Fuck," Graham said, scanning left and right. The driver pulled a machine pistol.

"That's it!" Delilah shouted. "Let me out! Let me out!" She went for the door handle.

"Wait!" Graham shouted, grabbing her hair and pulling her back. She stretched her arm for the door lock, but Graham was pulling too hard, and she knew instantly from the desperate strength of his grip that he'd put it together, he knew she was a plant.

Larison fired a round into the driver-side window. It bounced off the glass. But it drew the driver's attention.

Delilah tried again for the door lock and Graham hauled her back. But she'd been expecting it, and used the force to ricochet toward him, twisting counterclockwise as she moved, jamming the pistol back with her left forearm and snapping the thumb side of her right hand up into Graham's nose. His head rocked back and she tore the pistol from his hand. The driver started to turn, and she put a round in his head just behind the ear. He slumped forward onto the steering wheel, and the car's horn sounded.

Delilah barely heard it. She scrambled forward into the passenger seat, keeping her head down and her face averted from the windshield. Graham grabbed at her, but what he got was the shawl, and she shook free. She hit the unlock button. Instantly John was inside the back passenger-side door, his helmet still on, his pistol pointing at Graham. Larison hauled open Graham's door. He butt-stroked Graham in the cheek and dragged him out onto the pavement.

John tossed Delilah a ski mask, then bolted out and around the back of the car. She pulled it on and got out. If no one captured any of this with a mobile-phone video camera, it would be a miracle. But now there wouldn't be much to film.

Livia, also still wearing the full-face helmet, threw open the hatch of the van and raced back to the front. Delilah scrambled in. John and Larison hauled Graham up from the pavement. He started to struggle, and John kneed him in the groin. Larison hit him in the liver. He started to go down again, but they caught him and dragged him into the van. As soon as they were inside, Delilah slammed the hatch. "Go!" she yelled. Livia floored it and they all lost their balance, but there were padded moving blankets all over the floor and no one got too banged up. The street ahead was empty—Graham's car had stopped all the traffic—and in a few seconds, they had reached Boulevard Saint-Germain. Livia turned left, then right on Rue Saint-Jacques. She slowed, joining ordinary traffic, and suddenly they were just another white van, like the hundreds of others in the city.

Larison was kneeling on Graham's back. He pulled off the ski mask, took out a pair of flex-cuffs, and secured Graham's wrists behind his back.

"Everyone okay?" John said, taking off the helmet and setting it on the floor. They were out of range of Dox and Hort now, and the comment was just for the four of them.

"All good," Livia called out from the front.

"Fine," Larison said. He was searching Graham now, looking for tracking devices.

John looked at Delilah, and the naked concern in his eyes, the vulnerability, moved her. "I'm fine," she said, pulling off the mask.

All at once, the character she'd been playing was gone. And into the vacuum of its disappearance rushed the knowledge of how close it had been. And what had just happened. What she'd just done.

She started to shake. John didn't say anything. He just came over and put his arms around her.

"I'd say you worry too much," she said, a quaver in her voice. "But it's not true, you worry too little."

"I'd argue," he whispered in her ear, "but I know that's a mistake when you're berating me."

She laughed, feeling a little giddy. She realized if he kept acting like this, she wouldn't be able to stay angry at him. Well, maybe that was all right. But it was unsettling, too.

After a moment, John disengaged and kneeled alongside Graham. He took one of the moving blankets and slid it under Graham's head. "Sorry about roughing you up," he said. "I didn't think you'd come if we just asked nicely."

Graham looked up at him, his face already

swollen and purple from the blows he'd received. "What do you want?" he said.

"That's really up to you," John said. "Right now, we want you dead. But maybe you can change our minds."

CHAPTER FIFTY-ONE
LIVIA

An hour later, they were all in the van, parked at the bug-out point—a lightless cul-de-sac between a sprawling train terminus and a place called the Pavilions of Bercy, which looked like some sort of fairground art museum. Behind them was a graffiti-covered stone wall; all around were dumpsters, earth-moving equipment, and a profusion of construction detritus and weeds. Rain, who in addition to his expertise with local bars and jazz clubs seemed also to be a specialist in what might be called "lonely, abandoned, nocturnal Paris," had suggested the spot, and Livia had to agree, it was a good one. They ought to have all the time they needed with Graham here.

Still, in case they were disturbed, Delilah was behind the wheel, keeping watch through the windshield and via the mirrors, and the men all had their guns out. Graham was propped against one of the wheel wells, some of the moving blankets folded under him into an impromptu cushion, and Livia was kneeling next to him, holding an ice pack against his swollen face.

"What is this," he said, "good cop, bad cop?"

492

"Believe me," Livia said, setting the ice pack on the floor, "if I'm the good cop, you don't want to meet the bad one."

Graham looked around the van. "Am I missing something? I thought I already had."

"That depends on you," Livia said.

"It's actually pretty simple," Rain said. "Arrington's done. You can show us you're with us on that, or you can go down with him."

Livia gave Rain a look. She respected him, but she didn't know him or his moves nearly well enough to have him tag teaming her subject. Well, the man was a bit of a control freak, as Carl had said. She'd find a way to manage him.

If Graham was surprised they knew about Arrington, he didn't reveal it. "How can I show you something like that?" he said.

"I can suggest a few ways," Livia said. "But under the circumstances, I think you might want to get creative yourself."

Larison added, "Because if you don't, tomorrow they'll find your body in a dumpster."

Livia gave him the same look she'd given Rain. She realized she should have been more explicit about how this interrogation would be conducted. Initially, she'd been relieved when everyone agreed she would lead it, that there had been no need for an argument. But she hadn't counted on all of them wanting to chime in.

At least so far, no one had said anything stupid.

The trick now was to make Graham understand they knew a lot, and to make him believe they knew even more than that. A healthy appreciation of how things would go for him if they found him uncooperative wouldn't hurt, and in fairness, Larison's comment, along with the man's overall deadly vibe, was useful in that regard.

"Arrington pulled records," Livia said. "And then had them sealed. The names of Secret Service agents who had been referred to Justice for using their devices to access child pornography."

The referrals she was sure of. The precise reason for the referrals, she wasn't. But she'd dealt with enough instances of predators getting busted for using their work computers to access illicit materials that she felt confident in the bluff.

Graham looked down. He seemed to be struggling with something—possibly the realization that he'd been outplayed and had run out of options. This was the point where suspects started to think about what they could offer in exchange for some kind of deal.

After a moment, he looked up. "If you think about it," he said, "this whole thing was nothing but a cluster-fuck. Just a giant misunderstanding."

Neither Larison nor Rain spoke. Thank God. There was a time to press, and a time to back off.

"Anyway," Graham went on, "I'm . . . sorry it all happened. I really am."

Larison said, "It's a little l—"

Livia silenced him with a furious stare. She kept staring until he'd nodded. Then she looked back to Graham.

"Talk is cheap," she said.

He nodded. "I think I know what you want. But I'll need certain assurances."

Even before becoming a cop, Livia had known that you had to ease off slightly as your opponent went to his back—trading pressure, which you no longer needed, for more control, which you did. People fighting from their backs were desperate, liable to do almost anything to get free, and needed to be managed carefully. So she stayed cool. She'd been at this exact moment, and in fact had heard Graham's exact words, countless times in police interrogation rooms. A potential deal was on the table now, yes, but it wasn't yet closed. And closing was an art unto itself.

Again, Larison and Rain kept their mouths shut. Slow, but not ineducable. She said to Graham, "I'm listening."

He looked at her, then at the rest of them. "I know Arrington is finished. But I don't want him prosecuted. Do you understand?"

Livia said again, "I'm listening."

"I want immunity," he said. "And the only kind of immunity I want is the kind that doesn't get to implicate me or anyone else—not in a confession, not in testimony, not in leaks to the press. Not at all. I'll show you my bona fides, as long as we agree that once I do, either you or I will take out Arrington."

"We're supposed to just let you walk out of here on your say-so?" Horton said.

Livia gave him the look she'd given Larison. What was it about men that always made them feel they had to add something, and wouldn't let them just watch? Delilah was up front, ready to drive if there were a problem, but even if she'd been in back, Livia sensed the woman wouldn't have interfered the way the men did.

Horton nodded and shut up.

"What I can give you," Graham said, "would be more than enough to prosecute Arrington. Blow up the Secret Service ring . . . everything. So the person who should be having trust issues right now is me, not you. What's to stop you from killing me right after I've told you what you want?"

"Maybe you can't trust us not to kill you if you tell us," Rain said. "But I guarantee, you can trust us to kill you if you don't."

This time, Livia didn't bother to stare him down. Part of her wanted to, on principle, but in fact it was more or less what she had been planning to say herself, and a pretty succinct summary of where things stood for Graham. Still, she hoped it wouldn't encourage the others to keep chiming in. It occurred to her that Carl, who was ordinarily the most loquacious of the group and then some, was the only one keeping quiet now.

"I get that," Graham said. "So let me just say this. All of this was business. And none of it was necessary. Rain, I was prepared to respect your no. But then you and Larison went to see Hort, and it felt like a security breach. Maybe I overreacted, but still."

"What about me?" Livia said. "That was just business, too?"

Graham nodded. "That was the beginning of the business. You know what happened. You uncovered a child-pornography ring at the Secret Service. The contractor you were working with told his supervisor. His supervisor told Arrington. At which point, Arrington decided the toothpaste needed to go back in the tube."

Livia almost asked why. It was the one thing they had never been able to understand—why was Arrington so intent on protecting the Secret Service?

And then all at once it hit her, one of those cop insights that could remain so frustratingly out of reach in the dark, and then reveal itself in a spontaneous burst of clarity. Probably what had triggered it was just that simple word—*protect*—which for whatever reason she'd been looking at the wrong way up until this very moment.

She'd always thought of rings like Child's

Play as a disease. One that, like all diseases, had vectors. A patient zero, who then infected others, who in turn infected others.

She'd been so focused on Secret Service agents infecting each other. After all, the encryption app Trahan had uncovered on Child's Play was the one he had designed for the Secret Service.

But who else did Secret Service agents come into contact with? Who else could they infect?

Not just each other. Also . . . their *protectees*.

She let nothing show in her expression. The excitement. The satisfaction. The exultation. Nothing.

"Stop pretending this is about the Secret Service," she said, leaning close and getting in his face. "How fucking stupid do you think we are?"

She could feel the others looking at her. *I swear to God, if one of you interferes with my play now, I will kill you.*

But none of them did. She let the silence work on Graham, then said, "Arrington found it in the Justice records, didn't he? We had six instances of Trahan's encryption app being used on Child's Play. But not six previous referrals to Justice. And Arrington had a hunch: the agents who'd been referred to Justice had shared Trahan's encryption app with someone else. Someone outside the Secret Service."

Graham blinked, and she knew she was right.

He'd been hoping to bullshit them. To hold something back. Now he realized he couldn't, and was trying to recover.

"So Arrington braced the agents in those Justice files," she went on. " 'There's no statute of limitation on these crimes,' he told them. 'The FBI is going to prosecute. We're going to expose you. Send you to prison. Ruin your life.' And they all shit their pants, and begged him, and offered to cooperate any way he wanted. And he said, 'Tell me who you shared this encryption app with. Give me names, and I won't prosecute you. I'll protect you.' "

Graham was impassive. But his pupils were dilated, and a bead of sweat rolled down his swollen face.

The men were all silent. Well, it was never too late to learn not to interfere with someone else's interrogation.

Livia sensed she had another bluff, and decided to play it. "I want your copy of those Justice Department files," she said.

Graham blinked. "Why do you think I have a copy?"

He sounded like a guy trying to conceal that he was sucking wind after being gut-punched, and she felt a surge of excitement.

"Because if anyone else ever got hold of those files," she said, "they'd learn the same things Arrington had. And if what he'd learned ever

499

became public, he wouldn't be able to use it to blackmail the people those Secret Service agents had shared the app with. So he didn't just have those files sealed. He destroyed them. But he still needed his own copy to hold over the heads of the people he was threatening."

"I suppose that's possible," Graham said, and she knew, she fucking *knew,* he was at the end of his bluff, "but why would you think Arrington would share any of that with me?"

"Because you guys go way back," she said, her voice rising. "SEAL Team 8. Haiti. Kosovo. Because you weren't going to kill a cop and an FBI agent, you weren't going to *bring down a fucking plane,* without seeing the proof yourself. Without having access to it. So you better get smart right fucking now, and prove to us which side you're on, or Larison is going to jam the muzzle of a gun in your ear and pull the trigger and we're going to leave what's left of you out on the sidewalk. And prosecute Arrington anyway, because—you know what?—I already have enough. In fact, fuck it. I'm sick of this. Larison. Kill him."

Larison raised his eyebrows in surprise—and evident pleasure. He looked at Rain. And Rain, finally deferring to her on this the way he should have from the beginning, nodded.

Larison took one of the moving blankets and spooled it around his gun hand—an expedient way of muffling the sound of a shot. Then he grabbed Graham by the collar of his jacket. "Outside," he said. "I don't want to have to ride around in this thing with your brains all over the walls."

"Hold on," Graham said. "Hold on. Okay, my bad."

Larison hauled him up. "Too late, asshole."

Livia held up a hand to Larison and said to Graham, "Last chance. Get it right, or we're done."

"I have the files," Graham said. "They're on an encrypted site. I can give you the log-in credentials. You can see for yourself."

Carl pulled Livia's laptop out of a bag, handed it to Rain, and fired up his sat phone to use as a Wi-Fi hotspot.

Larison shoved Graham back down, but kept the grip on his collar. Graham intoned the credentials. Rain punched them in, then handed the laptop to Livia. She suppressed a flush of triumph. It was exactly what she needed—Secret Service referrals to the Justice Department. Three agents. Accessing child pornography from work computers, just as she'd suspected. She moved a copy to another site, forwarded it to Little and Strangeland, then handed the laptop back to Rain.

"Three referrals," she said. "But six Child's Play members were using Trahan's app. Now, maybe some of the remaining six had just never

501

been caught accessing child porn from their work devices. But at least some of them were protectees. And I can go after them now, I can uncover them, exactly the way Arrington did, because now I have the Justice Department records and I know the initial vectors. So all you'd be doing by telling me the rest is saving me a little time and effort. Which, if you think about it, is a pretty good deal for saving your own life. So tell me. Who were the other three Child's Play members who were using the Secret Service encryption app? The ones who aren't named in those Justice Department records."

A long moment passed. No one interrupted the silence.

Finally, Graham said, "You're not going to believe me."

She looked at him. "Try me."

He sighed. "All right. Walter Barkley, for one."

Only years of professional discipline kept Livia from showing her astonishment at the mention of a senator—and presidential front-runner on top of it. To conceal her reaction and keep him talking, she downshifted to something secondary. "Which of the agents shared the app with him?"

"It wasn't an agent who shared it with Barkley. It was another senator."

Livia realized that, in her excitement, she'd made an unnecessary—and mistaken—assumption. She should have asked a wider-aperture version: *Who shared the app with Barkley?* She hated that kind of misstep. But okay, no harm, no foul.

"One of the agents shared the app with a senator he was protecting?" she said.

Graham nodded, his shoulders deflated. She'd seen the posture before, on suspects who realized as they bargained that their position was getting steadily weaker, while the cops' position hadn't been affected at all. But once the dynamic started, it was difficult to stop.

"Which senator?" she said.

"Fenwick."

It was beginning to feel surreal. But she pushed the feeling aside and reminded herself to stay matter-of-fact. The suspect needed to feel like the revelations were routine, nothing the cop didn't already know, and therefore neither much of a betrayal nor particularly valuable, either.

"Garrison Fenwick?" Horton said, his tone incredulous. "The Senate majority leader?"

Oh my God, what is wrong with these people, I swear I should have duct-taped their mouths shut

This time, Livia didn't give Horton the *Shut the fuck up* look. She gave him a disgusted one. He held up his hands in a *Sorry, my bad* gesture.

She turned back to Graham. "Why would the Senate majority leader get Secret Service protection? I thought that was mostly presidents and vice presidents and their families."

"They also do special assignments," Graham

503

said. "Case by case, depending on security concerns. And a few years ago, Fenwick was dealing with threats in the face of some contentious legislation, and someone made the call that the usual Capitol Police detail wasn't enough. An Agent Crocker—one of the three in those Justice files—started shadowing him, spending nights in the senator's Potomac home, while the senator's wife and children were traveling. They got to know each other, the hints got increasingly brazen, they realized their mutual interest . . . and they started sharing material. Crocker wanted to curry favor, so he told the senator, 'Don't use Tor, you know the Bureau and NSA are doing everything they can to crack it—here, check out this super-secure app the Secret Service itself developed.' "

"All right," Livia said. "So Fenwick shared the app with Barkley."

Graham nodded. "One senator to another. Your tax dollars at work."

"Who else?" Livia said. "Remember, I'm going to find out anyway. Don't make me think you have conflicted loyalties here."

"One other. Fenwick shared the app with Charlie Hamm, the chairman of the Armed Services Committee. Three senators, all in Arrington's pocket. That would be quite a thing no matter what. But on top of it, Barkley is poised to become the next president of the United States.

Can you understand why this was a big deal?"

"I can understand why it's a big deal," Livia said. "What I can't understand is why the head of the FBI's Criminal Investigative Division didn't prosecute."

"Look," Graham said, "it's not just that Arrington is power mad. Not exactly. He also figured that if *he* could have learned about this child-porn ring in the Senate, the Russians could have learned of it, too. And can you imagine what the Russians would be able to do if they had this kind of *kompromat* on the president? Not to mention the chairman of the Armed Services Committee and the Senate majority leader."

That tracked with what Kanezaki had told them—that Arrington was obsessed with the notion of Kremlin plots. Okay, it seemed Graham was being forthcoming.

"If he was really worried about blackmail," Livia said, "he should have sought indictments. If it's out in the open, no one can use it."

Graham smiled. "Well, that's where it starts to get a little complicated. I mean, first, can you imagine what it would be like to try to prosecute men like Barkley? Between those three senators alone, you've got a fortune of probably two hundred million dollars. And then there's the Secret Service. They'd fight like hell. The Agency would try to disassociate itself from Arrington. They'd leak his psych file. There would be a coordinated campaign by some of the most powerful members of the government and the deep state to destroy him. Why fight that battle—and probably lose it—when you can do something easier and more effective?"

She looked at him. "Which is?"

He shrugged. "Take control of the Russian assets. Double them. Run them. Have them do your bidding, for the good of the nation, not Russia's to the nation's detriment."

"What kind of bidding did Arrington have in mind?" she said.

Graham sighed. "Himself as CIA director, for one thing. For him it would feel like Steve Jobs returning to Apple. He'd have guaranteed confirmation support from Fenwick and Hamm in the Senate, and an unlimited black-ops budget after that."

"So Arrington had a lot to gain," Rain said. "Personally gain."

Livia didn't mind the interruption now. They obviously couldn't stop themselves, for one thing. But more importantly, she'd gotten what she needed. The rest was mostly mopping up.

Graham looked at Rain. "I suppose so."

Rain nodded. "But aren't you leaving out what was in it for you?"

"What do you mean?" Graham said.

"The president?" Rain said. "And the Senate majority leader and the chairman of the Armed

Services Committee? You would have finally gotten all those privatized wars you've been agitating for. It would have made you a billionaire."

Graham shook his head. "I already have more money than I can spend."

Carl laughed. "The only people who say that are the ones who have more than they need and not as much as they want."

"Regardless," Graham said, "look at our endless wars. Are you really going to try to argue they've been effectively prosecuted by the government? Can't you see the private sector would do better?"

Carl laughed again. "That's what I like, an argument for the effectiveness of the private sector by its chief representative, who is currently zip-tied on the floor of a van with his face beat up and surrounded by a bunch of irritated people pointing guns at him."

"That's one way of looking at it," Graham said. "Another is, you're the private sector, too. And you've done pretty well for yourselves."

"Well, that's fine," Carl said, "but you don't hear any of us saying it means we should take over entire wars, do you?"

"My point," Graham said, "to go back to the beginning of this conversation, is that our interests—yours and mine—aren't naturally adverse. I've given you what you wanted. You have nothing to gain from killing me. And a lot to gain if I'm still alive. I need good people. Especially after all the ones you've recently removed from my employ. Now, I've shown you my bona fides. Let me go, and I'll show you more. I'll kill Arrington myself."

"Lord," Carl said. "I thought you two went way back."

"We do," Graham said. "But this is business."

"I don't think so," Horton said. "How could anyone ever trust someone like you?"

"You can always trust me to be smart about business. And all of us working together is obviously smart business."

Livia looked at Rain. He shrugged as if to say, *Your call.*

She knew what that call was. But Larison got there ahead of her. He raised the blanket-wrapped pistol and shot Graham in the head. Everybody jumped, startled at the report, which was loud in the confines of the van even with the padding around the gun. Graham slumped to his side, blood running from one of his ears, an expression of perfect surprise frozen on his swollen face.

Larison looked at them. "What? You weren't serious about letting him go, were you?"

No one said anything, and Larison added, "For fuck's sake, he killed Treven."

Horton said, "You didn't even like Ben."

Larison shrugged. "That was when he was

alive. Anyway, sorry if I got a little ahead of things there. Hope I'm not out of sync with anyone else's sensibilities."

"If you hadn't done it," Livia said, "I would have."

Carl said, "Hear, hear."

Rain looked at Livia. "Can you really use those files to bring down Arrington? And the Secret Service ring? And Barkley and the other senators?"

She considered for a moment. Then she said, "No. But Homeland Security can. And B. D. Little will make them."

CHAPTER FIFTY-TWO
RAIN

I was standing naked in front of Delilah's bedroom window, looking out at the sky, now pink with the rising sun, the eastern glow silhouetting the somnolent rooftops of Paris.

We'd dumped Graham's body, then torched the van in a separate location, using a jug of petrol we'd bought earlier. And then rendezvoused here. Delilah was on the bed behind me. The others were in the living room, probably still too juiced to sleep.

Delilah got up and put her arms around me. "That was . . . okay," she said.

I turned my head and kissed her. "It seemed like you were still angry at me."

"I'm always going to be at least partly angry at you."

I looked at her. I couldn't tell if she was serious or joking. "Really?"

She paused, then said, "Yes."

"Why?"

"I don't like the power you have over me."

I nodded. "I think I get it. I don't like yours over me, either."

"Yes, but you didn't come back to me because

510

you wanted to. It was because you needed something."

I paused, then said, "Maybe what I need from you isn't as obvious as what you think."

She gave me a small smile. "We'll see."

We were quiet for a moment. I said, "What's . . . going to happen with Kent?"

"Kent has a dozen women all over Europe. He'll find a way to comfort himself."

I looked at her. "There aren't any women like you."

She laughed. "What, do you feel sorry for him?"

"No. But . . . I can sympathize. I know how I'd feel if you found someone you preferred over me."

"For a long time, I wished I could."

"I don't want you to wish that anymore. I'm glad you're out of the life. And that I'm retired. I'm glad it's not too late."

She laughed again.

"What?" I said warily.

"Is this what you call retirement? Danger, and intrigue, and killing?"

"That part is done."

"Yes? And how many times have you told yourself that?"

Not for the first time, her intuition made me uncomfortable. "You know, Dox once made a similar point."

"He did? Well, I'm not surprised. He's much more insightful than he likes to let on."

"Do all the people who know me, know me better than I know myself?"

"John. It's not that you don't know yourself. It's that you won't *admit* to yourself what you know."

My discomfort increased. "Which is?"

"You look for ways to balance your karma. To alleviate suffering where before, you caused it."

I supposed her words wouldn't have been so disquieting if they hadn't been true. I tried to come up with something to say. Finally, I managed, "I'll . . . think about that."

She shrugged. "Well, Paris is a good place to think. It's where Rodin sculpted *Le Penseur*, no?"

I smiled, thinking I didn't deserve her. I wondered if that was why I had pushed her away. I'd have to think about that, too.

But with her. Not by myself.

"I'd have to give up my place in Kamakura," I said. "It's a *minka*—an antique Japanese farmhouse. I had it reconstructed, all from the original timbers. I think you'd like it."

"Why don't you show it to me? You've seen my Paris. Are you afraid to show me your Tokyo?"

"I can't tell if you're being literal or figurative."

She frowned. "Why don't you answer as if I'm being both?"

512

I nodded, feeling I was on the edge of a precipice, excited to leap but also afraid.

"I'd love to show you my Tokyo," I said. "But . . . it's a labyrinthine place. I've spent most of my life there, and I still don't understand it."

"Do we not have time?"

"No, we do. We do. Just don't think this means you're done showing me Paris, okay?"

She looked at me for a long moment, then said, "Paris can be labyrinthine, too."

I nodded. "I know. It's one of the things I love about it. One of the things I missed."

She didn't say anything in response. She just took my hand, and led me back to the bed.

CHAPTER FIFTY-THREE
LIVIA

They dispersed one at a time the next morning, having agreed it would be safer to leave Paris separately.

Livia had checked in with both Little and Strangeland. Little told her he was going to press for indictments, starting with the three Secret Service agents referred to Justice, and working his way up from there. The same route Arrington had taken, but with public prosecution as the goal, rather than private exploitation. And Strangeland said she had a way of backing up Little's play. Livia didn't like the two of them closing the loop, but there wasn't a lot she could do.

"Phelps told me you're all but cleared in the officer-involved," Strangeland had said. "But no progress on the identities of your attackers—not the two at the Ravenna-Bryant academy, not the two South Park snipers, either. We finally got access to the IAFIS, and guess what?"

"No matching prints?"

"Correct. You ask me, if there ever was a match in there, somebody deep-sixed it. But I'll tell you what. You and I know who the assassins were working for. Maybe we can't prove it, but the way I see it, they're dead and you're safe. For now, I'll settle for that."

So much had happened in the last week. The park rapist, the attack at the academy, Phelps and the FIT investigation . . . it felt surreal, like something she'd dreamed more than something that had actually happened. "And the chief?" Livia said. "The two of you . . . it's all right?"

"Well, like I told you, she wasn't thrilled you weren't around for her SWAT bodyguards to monitor. But what could she do? You were on administrative leave. And she's going to be even less happy in a day or so, but I'll tell you about that when you're back. Speaking of which, your leave is about to end, and I'm not going to be able to cover for you anymore."

"I'll be there tomorrow."

"Good. Take a little time to get caught up. And then you and I are going to have a long talk."

Livia had known that was coming. Strangeland already knew a lot, and seemed inclined to keep it between the two of them. But some of what she was likely to ask about would lead to more questions, which could in turn lead to areas the lieutenant might feel she couldn't look away from.

But there was nothing to be done about that now. "How's the weather?" Livia said.

"Still dry. No attacks in any parks. Let's just get you back here. And back in the saddle."

And then it was time for the goodbyes.

Larison was the first to go. He shook hands with everyone—except Carl, who he hugged, and of his own volition, too.

"Thanks for having my back outside Piano Vache," he said to Livia.

"Thanks for having mine," she said. She realized she had come to like Larison a lot. She was glad they'd gotten past their rough patches.

He nodded. "I don't forget. Ask these jokers. If you need me, say the word."

He turned to Delilah. "He might not show it," he said, inclining his head toward Rain, "but he's crazy about you. It was tormenting him so much he tried to talk to me about it. Me. Can you imagine?"

"Thanks," Rain said. "Appreciate that."

Delilah laughed, then kissed Larison on both cheeks.

"Come out to Costa Rica," he said. "That goes for all of you. It's peaceful there. You'd be amazed."

Livia didn't see that ever happening. But she was also surprised to realize she didn't want to rule it out.

Horton was next. He had already collected Larison's gun, and now he took the others, too, along with the commo gear—his contact had told him the hardware was a loan, not a gift.

"Time to go," he said. "And see whether my

homeowner's covers helicopter rocket attacks."

"You going to be okay?" Rain said.

"I expect the police will have some questions about my whereabouts at the time of the attack, and my knowledge of what happened. But I have a good lawyer, and a bad memory. And I have a feeling there's going to be a whole host of reasons the government will prefer to overlook what happened, and attribute it all to a mysterious fire or other natural disaster."

Livia had some experience with government decisions to overlook the obvious. And efforts to publicize it as something else.

"What about Treven's brother?" Rain said. "You want me to follow up on that?"

"I'd rather do it myself, if you don't mind. I owe him that much."

There was another round of handshakes. And then Horton, too, was gone, and it was just Rain and Delilah, and Livia and Carl.

Livia wanted to talk to Kanezaki. There was something she needed from him—needed so much she was afraid to even ask for it. But she didn't see an alternative.

"Hey," she said. "We haven't checked in with Kanezaki since just after Piano Vache."

"Right," Rain said. "I was going to update him via the secure site."

Livia nodded. "Can we try calling him anyway?"

She thought Rain was going to ask why, but he

glanced at Carl and then just nodded. Carl put the sat phone on speakerphone and called.

"It's about time," Kanezaki said by way of a greeting. "I really don't like to get my information about what you've been doing in Paris from CNN. They're reporting Oliver Graham as kidnapped."

"Hey, Tom," Carl said. "That's why we're calling. CNN is way behind, you can't rely on those guys at all. I mean, kidnapped? That's ancient history. He's dead now, too."

They filled Kanezaki in on everything that happened and all they'd learned, including that Little was going to blow it all wide open. Kanezaki seemed glum at the prospect, saying only "I see."

"Tom," Livia said, her heart kicking up a notch as she got closer to what she needed to ask for. "Can I call you that, Tom?"

"Of course. It's what all the people who drag me back and forth across this side of the law call me."

She considered mentioning that it wasn't always so clear who was doing the dragging, but decided to let it go. "I know you're in the intelligence business," she said. "And I know what we learned would have been powerful intelligence for you—if it stayed secret. Can I ask, is that what you were thinking just now? Because you sounded a little down when we told you about Little."

"Well, it's academic at this point," Kanezaki said. "Little and Homeland Security Investigations have those Justice Department files. I expect it's only a matter of time before indictments start coming down. But yes, none of what you've told me is particularly useful to me now. Still . . . for what it's worth, it's not a hard thing for me to look on the bright side about."

"You're a good man, Tom," Carl said.

Kanezaki laughed. "Whenever you say that, you always ask for something."

Livia swallowed. "I do have something to ask you," she said.

Kanezaki didn't answer right away. Maybe he'd been joking, and was surprised by the gravity in her tone. "Okay," he said.

"I've got a case," she said. "A serial rapist. He's in Seattle now. And the next time it rains, which in Seattle will be soon, he's going to do it again."

Carl was looking at her, unease in his expression.

Kanezaki said, "What do you need from me?"

She was encouraged that he said *need* instead of *want*. But they weren't there yet.

"You mentioned some programs. Programs that give you access to everything a person buys, everything he searches for on the Internet, everywhere he goes."

Another pause. "You know I can't confirm or deny—"

"Come on, Tom," Carl said, and though he still looked uneasy, Livia realized that whatever doubts he might have had, he must have decided to back her play. "I heard the scuttlebutt a few years back. Some program called God's Eye. Stupid-ass name if you ask me. They might as well have called it 'Government Looking Down Your Throat and Up Your Ass.' Just going to scare people when the news leaks, instead of lulling them. But whatever."

"In fact," Kanezaki said, "there was a program called God's Eye. But it was shut down."

"Uh-huh," Carl said. "And in my experience, programs your 'intelligence community' loves but that public pressure forces you to shut down, don't get shut down, they just get renamed."

A long moment went by, and Livia had the sense that Kanezaki might be smiling. "Well," he finally said. "Again, I can neither confirm nor deny, but I might have heard something about a program called . . . Guardian Angel."

Carl laughed. "Glad to see you people finally hired a decent marketing team."

"I can give you a lot," Livia said. "I know what this guy does. What he searches for. What he buys. How he moves around. I know everything about him, but it's all parameters, I don't have the specific data. Eventually I'll have that data, and I'll catch him. But only after he's ruined who knows how many more lives."

Kanezaki said, "Unless."

Livia gripped the phone, hoping and trying not to. "Yes."

"I'm not promising anything. But . . . give me the parameters."

She told him about the likely fetishes—the running gear, the trauma shears, the zip-ties—and possible online purchases. The likely searches— parks on the water. The dates in which the man probably rented a place through Airbnb or a similar rental service—first in or near Bridgeport, currently in or near Seattle.

"One thing," Kanezaki said when she was done. "Whatever case you're going to make against this guy—and I assume you're planning to make a case—it's got to be done with parallel construction."

Parallel construction referred to the law-enforcement technique of reverse engineering a case to conceal the true origin of the investigation behind it. Sometimes the practice was legitimate—for example, protection of a confidential informant. Other times, what was being concealed was a civil-rights violation or some other illegality. And while Kanezaki had a point, of course, it would be academic if Livia were inclined to deal with the park rapist . . . off the books.

But she recognized she couldn't do that now. She was already under too much scrutiny. And she had already asked too many people for too much help. Besides, going off the books wasn't necessary. She was confident that if she could identify the guy, she could get the system to work.

"Whatever case we build against him," Livia said, "what I learn from you won't have anything to do with it."

"All right," Kanezaki said. "Give me an hour."

"I'll be back in Seattle tomorrow," Livia said. "Anything you can get me before then, and especially before the weather changes out there, I'd really appreciate."

She clicked off. Carl said, "I wish you'd told me why you wanted to talk to him. Tom's a good man, but he doesn't do freebies. When he gives, he expects to get. Maybe not today, but at some point."

So that's why he'd seemed uneasy. She looked at him and said nothing.

He nodded. "I know, I know, it's worth it to you. I just would have preferred to warn you first."

She knew he meant well. She even knew he might be right. But she didn't care. She'd have to worry about it later.

Livia turned to Delilah, not entirely sure how their goodbye would go. She'd certainly come to respect the woman. And she was glad Delilah and Rain had gotten past whatever had divided them.

But she hadn't forgotten the woman's initial suspicions, or her initial reluctance.

Livia gave her a nod—perhaps not warmly, but with some recognition of what the two of them had been through together. And what they'd achieved. "*Merci*, Delilah," she said.

Delilah returned the nod. "And to you. We could have gotten off to a better start, but . . . I think that was my fault, not yours."

Livia was surprised by her graciousness, and realized she'd been expecting something laced with some lingering resentment. She shook her head. "I know I was . . . pushing pretty hard. How could you not have been suspicious? I would have been, too."

Delilah smiled, and though Livia sensed there might have been a touch of effort behind it, she also appreciated that the woman was trying.

"Look," Delilah said, "let's not make that conversation in the bathroom the only one we ever have. Come back to Paris. And we can talk some more."

Livia nodded and held out her hand, and Delilah shook it. And then she surprised Livia by leaning in and kissing Livia's cheeks, and it wasn't bad, it didn't make Livia want to wince the way being touched usually did.

"I know we shouldn't go to the airport together," Carl said. "Things are likely too hot."

Rain said, "You shouldn't go to the airport at all."

Livia shook her head. "I have to get back. My lieutenant can't cover for me anymore. And I have to stop in DC first, to pick up my gun where Larison stashed it. I don't have a ton of time."

Rain sighed. "Well, maybe just you. Dox, stick around for a few days. Or take the train to Brussels and fly from there."

"No, sir," Carl said. "I'm not going to be a third wheel. You two need some time together. But we'll have other opportunities. You haven't had nearly enough of a chance to make fun of me for riding a three-wheeled motorcycle. Hell, old Larison beat you to it and made all the best jokes."

Rain laughed. "Yeah, whoever thought the angel of death had a sense of humor?"

Carl hugged them both, then picked up his bag and Livia's. "Okay, you two. Enjoy Paris. And this time, let's not wait so long before we see each other. And let's not wait until a bunch of people are trying to kill us, either."

CHAPTER FIFTY-FOUR
LIVIA

Livia was back in the office the next morning. It was official: the Force Investigation Team had issued an unequivocal report, and the Force Review Board had cleared her. Cops took turns congratulating her as she made her way through headquarters, in their good cheer even clapping her on the back despite her well-known dislike of that kind of contact.

She went straight to Strangeland's office. Strangeland, too, was unable to hold herself back. She came from around her desk and gave Livia a squeeze on both shoulders. "I never doubted it," she said. "But . . . still, Jesus Christ, what a relief."

"Thanks, LT."

"Have a seat. You know, the strangest thing happened yesterday."

"Yeah?"

"Yeah. An anonymous tip to Sex Crimes. We got a guy named Matthew J. Stroop, staying at an Airbnb rental in Queen Anne. The tipster said he's our park rapist—claimed to recognize him from the most recent attack. We were able to check out Stroop's credit-card records, and you'll never guess where he was staying during the Bridgeport attack you suspected he was behind."

"Tell me it was Bridgeport," Livia said.

"Bingo."

Livia nodded. It wasn't just Bridgeport, she knew. Kanezaki had been able to place Stroop in San Diego, Charleston, and Portland, Maine, too—all of which, Livia had quickly confirmed through ViCAP, had their own unsolved rapes during the relevant time periods. Stroop was some sort of day trader, with the money and flexibility to travel to new hunting grounds every few months. Part of the case against him would be his presence in the vicinity of five different crime scenes. But that would all come out later—parallel construction.

Yeah, Kanezaki had delivered, and then some. And at some point, Livia knew, he was going to demand something in return. She didn't want to think of what it might be.

"We got a warrant," Strangeland said, "and have physical surveillance outside his apartment and are all over his cellphone, too. Did you know it's supposed to rain tomorrow?"

Livia nodded. "I checked."

"Of course you did. Well, the idea is, we'll follow him to the park. Catch him as he leaves to go hunting. More for the prosecutors to work with. You want to be part of that? It's still your case."

She did want to be part of it. Very much. "Thanks, LT. Yeah, I'd like to be the one to put the cuffs on him."

"Done. Should be a good day tomorrow. And not just because we're going to take this creep down."

"What else is going on?"

"Well, let's just say there's a certain journalist I happen to know and the chief doesn't. Guy named Leopold. Some people call him the FOIA Terrorist because he's so unrelenting with the Freedom of Information requests. Anyway, it might be that he's about to publish an exposé on a string of Secret Service agents referred to the Justice Department for child-pornography charges—charges that Justice sat on, at the request of the Secret Service. Word is, the comparisons are going to be to the Catholic Church's child-rape cover-ups. There's going to be a ton of heat. A ton of follow-up."

She thought of the men Rain and Larison had killed at the state park. "It sounds good. But . . . still, could Little be in danger? I mean, they killed an FBI agent. They tried to kill me."

"Graham's dead, Livia, and his people are reeling. Besides, the stories I'm talking about are going to create the kind of climate where no one would dare impede Little's investigation, let alone try to take him out. Even if he goes after senators. Even presidential candidates. It's all going to come out. All of it."

It was enormously satisfying. But at the same time, it worried her. She'd had more than enough attention already.

"Good," she said. "But . . . the chief won't know the leak came from you?"

Strangeland waved a hand as though it was nothing. "Ah, she'll suspect. But it might have come from anywhere. Leopold's not local. And Little's going to work for those indictments. So who can say where the leak came from?"

Livia sensed the lieutenant was putting on a brave face. Chief Best liked to play it like a sweet aunt, and maybe it wasn't all an act. But she had also made it plain that she didn't care to be crossed. Making an enemy of the chief wasn't something any cop would wish for, and not for the first time, Livia felt the weight of what she might owe the lieutenant.

"The only bad news," Strangeland went on, "is that as soon as the word is out, the rest of the Child's Play rats will scurry for cover. But the five whose names you and Trahan uncovered will be arrested and prosecuted. So there's that."

Livia nodded. Another tradeoff she had already seen. And another there was nothing to be done about. But the rats wouldn't stay in hiding for long. Eventually, they always came out to feed. And when they did, Livia would be waiting.

"Here's the thing," Strangeland said, "I saw the news about Oliver Graham on CNN. I don't want to know where you were when all that went down. I don't want to know who you were with the past few days, or what you know about our anonymous tipster. Not today, anyway. At some point, you and I are going to have that talk I mentioned. But not today. Today, I'm just glad you're safe. Now go on. Get back out there, and be the great cop you are."

Livia thanked her and went back to her desk. She was grateful for the reprieve. But fearful of the reckoning.

There was already a paperwork backlog. She tried to get caught up. But she couldn't. She couldn't stop thinking about everything that had happened, and of everything that might happen still.

After an hour, she gave up. She walked downstairs, left the building, and headed over to the ferry terminal, where she stood for a while, watching the sunlight glinting on the water of Elliott Bay, listening to the gulls and the empty sound of the wind. She could smell rain in the air, and nodded in satisfaction at what was waiting for Stroop, the image of her taking him down and slapping the cuffs on.

But everything else was worrying her. How far would Little's investigation take him? Would investigators learn—would anyone believe—the downed plane was brought down not by ISIS, but by a private military contractor? And if they did, would it mean even more attention for Livia?

She watched the water and listened to the wind, and eventually, the anxiety dissipated. She found herself thinking of Carl, of that moment when they'd left Delilah's apartment and walked down the stairs, and how ambivalent and confused she'd felt by the coming goodbye.

When they reached the street, Carl had said, "Do you even know what flight you're taking?"

She'd shaken her head. "I was thinking I'd figure it out at the airport."

"Well, shit," he said, "you might be waiting there for hours. Plus it looks odd to show up at the airport and not already be booked on a flight. Tell you what. Delilah told me about a place she likes, less than a mile walk from here. Chez Prune. Good food and a view of a pretty canal. How about you and I get a table, order ourselves some cappuccinos and croissants, book you a flight online, and get you a cab when you need one. And if your flight's not until later, I can help you kill some time in Paris. If you like. Otherwise, I could just get lost. I know you like your alone time."

She gave him a small smile. "I don't want you to get lost," she said, hating that feeling happy always made her feel nervous.

She thought he was going to say something light in response, the way he usually did, but he didn't. Instead, he said, "I know you need to get back. You've got business to take care of. And you know me, I'm not going to press. But I'd sure like to see more of you, Labee. In Seattle, or in my little corner of paradise in Bali, or, hell, right here in the City of Light. But . . . if that's not right for you, I just hope you'll tell me. I don't want to have to wait by the phone like I was before."

For some reason, that hurt. "Were you really waiting by the phone?"

"Yeah, in retrospect I realize I was. Though at the time, I guess I was in denial."

She looked at him, wanting to ask, afraid of what it might mean. Their nights together . . . it had been good. They'd kissed. A lot. The first kissing she'd enjoyed since . . . well, since her first kiss, from Scan, all the way back in high school. All the others had been a reluctant accommodation on her part. But with Carl, it was different.

And they'd done other things, too. Not the way she usually needed to. More slowly. Gently. She hadn't come. But it hadn't been just an accommodation, either. It had been good. Good enough for her to want to try it again.

"What is it?" he said.

Before she could change her mind, she said, "Do you still have any more of those fake passports and burner debit cards you've been using?"

"More? I've got practically a shoebox full. One

of the benefits of working with a rapscallion like Kanezaki."

"Then . . . why don't we skip the café. We could . . . we could order room service. I could get a later flight."

Her heart was pounding. God, what was wrong with her? Why did trying to be normal . . . scare her so much?

He looked at her, his eyes a little wide. "Are you sure?"

She nodded. "Unless you don't want to."

He smiled. "Darlin', I'm always going to want to with you. For better or worse."

As it happened, it was better. What that meant, or what it might lead to, she didn't know. She would have to figure out things with Carl slowly. Gently. The same way they'd been making love. He'd spread his dreams under her feet, and while she wasn't yet ready, and might never be able, to do the same for him with hers, she would find a way to tread softly. She wanted at least to try.

EPILOGUE

Evening had come, and it was snowing in Kamakura. I sat by the *irori* with a pencil and paper, looking out at my rock garden, composing a poem. When it was done, I tried to capture the same feeling in English. It was all right, but not the same. Japanese is better suited to haiku.

I heard Delilah coming down the stairs. "What are you doing?" she said.

I considered folding the paper and tossing it onto the coals. Instead I said, "Just scribbling something."

She didn't answer. She pulled over a cushion, sat, and leaned against me. She knew I would show her if I wanted to. When I was ready. The way it had been for the last month, as I introduced her to more and more of my labyrinthine city.

It had been a good month. Good for us; good generally. The five Child's Play predators Livia's operation had initially identified had been arrested in joint FBI–local law enforcement actions. America was rocked by scandal: the Secret Service was being investigated by a special prosecutor; Barkley, Fenwick, and Hamm had resigned their seats to spend more time with their families; Barkley had ended his presidential campaign; and the future of OGE looked uncertain following the unsolved Paris kidnapping and assassination of its CEO, Oliver Graham. Police were looking for a "person of interest"—a mysterious blonde Graham had been seen with shortly before his disappearance. But she seemed nowhere to be found. There were rumors she was a Russian prostitute, perhaps even a Kremlin spy.

There would be more casualties, of course. The three senators were facing investigations, and resignations alone weren't going to stanch any of that—especially with Little maneuvering in the background and the journalist Livia's lieutenant knew digging up more damning evidence. But I thought OGE would survive. Its role in the downing of the flight over Lake Michigan was rumored, but not provable. The possibility of such a thing caused too much cognitive dissonance for the public to accept, or to want too closely examined. Instead, it was relegated to the realm of conspiracy theory, where it could be comfortably scoffed at by the people who benefited.

Besides, as Delilah had once said, the company didn't really have enemies—only clients. And those clients needed an OGE. The board, recognizing the importance of a break from the sordid allegations of the past, had already changed the company's name—Percivallian, a neologism adjective derived from Percival, one of King

Arthur's most loyal and intrepid knights. If Dox was right about the power of marketing, I expected Percivallian had a bright future, indeed.

Arrington was under indictment, but seemed determined to fight it. His lawyer claimed the whole thing was a plot cooked up by the Kremlin to destabilize America, carried out by an army of hackers and disinformation specialists, and that Graham's demise, too, was an attempt by Russia to weaken America. The amazing part was, a lot of people seemed to believe him. Which was useful to the powers that be, I supposed, and I wondered if they might prefer to lend credence to Arrington's fabrications via his own mysterious demise. I half expected someone to try to contact me about the possibility of Arrington expiring of natural causes. The contact wouldn't be easy—I had taken down the secure site—but it wouldn't be impossible. I wouldn't do it, of course. I was done with all that. But there was something vaguely tempting in the notion, because no matter how I went about it, it would be so easy to blame on the Russians.

Kent had contacted Delilah. He'd heard the news about Graham. He wasn't surprised, and wasn't inclined to tell anyone what he knew. He asked if they were going to see each other again. She told him she couldn't. He asked if that applied even if he ever needed the kind of professional service he had just rendered for her. To that, she had no answer. But that would be a challenge for another day.

I was leaving my satellite phone powered on after Paris, and Horton checked in. He was right—there was enough dirty laundry being aired already, and no one wanted to look too closely into what had really happened at his house. The five bodies found on his property, along with the helicopter wreckage, were quietly disposed of. There would be no investigation about who was behind the men's deaths, or of the weapon-filled tunnels and safe rooms under Horton's property.

Horton had delivered the bad news to Treven's brother, a Silicon Valley lawyer named Alex, who had taken it stoically. Horton's understanding was that the brothers hadn't been close, and that they were even estranged. But Horton had seen something in Alex's eyes at the mention of Katie—their sister, Horton explained, who'd died in a car accident when they were all teenagers. Maybe there was some element of closure for Alex in his brother's posthumous message. But there was no way to know.

Dox had called, too. He was going to visit Livia—in Portland, he said. Her caseload wouldn't permit a real vacation, and she wasn't yet ready to spend time together where she lived, or where he did. But I could tell he was giddy at the prospect of seeing her, and despite my concerns, I was happy for him.

For a while, Delilah and I watched the snow falling on the rock garden, our shoulders pressed together in comfortable silence.

"Will you show me what you were scribbling?" she said.

"Just a silly poem."

"Ah."

I knew she wouldn't press further. Which was what made it possible. I handed her the paper, and she read the English aloud:

Snow covering rocks
A moment of concealment
Shapes last forever.

We sat silently again, listening to the soft crackling of the *irori* embers. She said, "Do you think that's the way the world works?"

I waited a moment, considering.

"Probably," I said. "But that's not really what the poem is about."

"What, then?"

I looked at her. "Maybe it's about us."

She raised her eyebrows. "The shapes?"

"Yes. Because, you know, the snow melts. The garden emerges again. I just couldn't express all that in a haiku. I'm a dabbler, not Bashō."

She drew in close, close enough for me to feel her breath on my lips. "We'll find another way to express it," she said, and kissed me.

I didn't know if she was right. But I wanted to keep trying. I was glad I was finally retired. And this time, I was going to make it last.

At least for as long as I could.

But those were thoughts for another occasion. I put my arm around her, quietly overwhelmed at her presence, the unexpected conversion of my fortress of solitude into a nation of two.

NOTES

CHAPTER ONE

A beautiful video requiem about the rebirth of a *minka*—a traditional Japanese farmhouse like Rain's—and the love behind it:
  https://vimeo.com/20658635

CHAPTER TWO

Two articles on the real-world operation that's the basis for Livia's sting:
  "The Takeover: How Police Ended Up Running a Paedophile Site," https://gu.com/p/4m3dp/sbl
  "Australian Police Sting Brings Down Paedophile Forum on Dark Web," http://bit.ly/2y2LCxC

Pentagon $7600 coffee pots, $640 toilet seats, etc.:
  "Only the Pentagon Could Spend $640 on a Toilet Seat," http://bit.ly/2l4ihiN

For more on the power of mirroring:
  Chris Voss, *Never Split the Difference:*

Negotiating As If Your Life Depended On It,
https://www.amazon.com/dp/0062407805
More on cognitive dissonance:
  https://en.wikipedia.org/wiki/Cognitive
_dissonance

CHAPTER FIVE

Rain's reference to who, where, and how much is courtesy of Max von Sydow's Joubert, from *Three Days of the Condor*. "I don't interest myself in why. I think more often in terms of when. Sometimes where. Always how much."
  https://youtu.be/voPmfT09jlg

CHAPTER SIX

The "hurtcore" subculture Livia describes is real.
  " 'Sadistic' Paedophile Matthew Falder Jailed for 32 Years," http://bit.ly/2HsX6Pl

CHAPTER EIGHT

Additional information about the multiple Secret Service scandals Lieutenant Strangeland mentions to Livia:
  https://en.wikipedia.org/wiki/United_States
_Secret_Service#Misconduct

CHAPTER NINE

The adrenal stress training Livia puts her students through, including verbal intimidation and escalation, is modeled after Peyton Quinn's Rocky Mountain Combat Applications course. I highly recommend it.

http://www.peytonquinn.com

If you want to be safer in the world, reading Gavin de Becker's *The Gift of Fear: Survival Signals That Protect Us from Violence* is an exceptionally cost-effective measure.

https://www.amazon.com/dp/0316235024

CHAPTER TEN

The article Livia recalls, about how undersea mountains and trenches exert a gravitational effect on the water thousands of feet above them, detectable at the surface:

"Ocean Technology," http://econ.st/2FuOoCL

CHAPTER ELEVEN

While I was casting about for a good name for the front-runner presidential candidate, I happened to listen to this wonderful *Intercepted* podcast

episode—"Evening at the Talk House." One of the characters was named Walter Barkley, and it felt perfect, so I borrowed it.
https://interc.pt/2HscEpp

CHAPTER FIFTEEN

A video of the tunnel El Chapo Guzmán used to escape from a Mexican maximum-security prison:
https://www.cnn.com/videos/tv/2015/07/19/el-chapo-escape-tunnel-cost-blackwell-intv.cnn

George Carlin on the slightly nonintuitive concept of the "near-miss":
https://youtu.be/zDKdvTecYAM

CHAPTER FORTY-FOUR

The radio frequency vehicle stopper is real.
"The Pentagon Wants to Stop Marauding Vehicles with High-Powered Microwave Beams,"
https://bit.ly/2FI6I6K

CHAPTER FIFTY-ONE

If you were thinking I made up the idea of a mercenary corporation pitching the government to privatize a war . . . I didn't.

"Erik Prince's Plan to Privatize the War in Afghanistan," https://theatln.tc/2xbfF4q

"Trump White House Weighing Plans for Private Spies to Counter 'Deep State' Enemies," https://interc.pt/2kkwOHL

More instances of the Pentagon using off-the-book contractors to track and kill enemies:

"Contractors Tied to Effort to Track and Kill Militants," http://nyti.ms/2HHoUPf

"CIA Sought Blackwater's Help to Kill Jihadists," http://nyti.ms/2zOjth0

NSA collects Tor and VPN traffic on hundreds of thousands of Americans each day:

"The Senate Intelligence Committee 702 Bill Is a Domestic Spying Bill," http://bit.ly/2zL8L84

FBI efforts to hack Tor:

"The Tor Teardown, Brought to You by Goats, Giraffes, and Thor's Hammer," http://bit.ly/2CivVmC

CHAPTER FIFTY-THREE

Some background on "parallel construction":

"Parallel Construction Revealed: How the DEA Is Trained to Launder Classified Surveillance Info," https://bit.ly/1bYzJpi

ACKNOWLEDGMENTS

Thanks to the Legislative Drafting Institute for Child Protection—an organization that does work Livia would be proud of, and that deserves your support. https://ldicp.org.

Thanks to Michael Devine, Seattle Police Department, who opened the door for me with SPD interviews and ride-alongs, and who continues to patiently answer all my cop-related questions.

Thanks to Lori Kupfer, who knows Delilah and her moves better than I do.

Thanks to Micah F. Lee of The Intercept for giving me a primer on encryption and anonymization apps. Anything I managed to get wrong anyway is despite Micah's efforts.

Thanks to "FOIA Terrorist" Jason Leopold, who got me thinking in the right direction about the Secret Service and the Justice Department.

Thanks to Wim Demeere for helping me get the unarmed-combat sequences right. Of course, this means when I get anything wrong, it's Wim's fault.

To the extent I get violence right in my fiction, I have many great instructors to thank, including Massad Ayoob, Tony Blauer, Alain Burrese, Loren Christensen, Wim Demeere, Dave Grossman,

Tim Larkin, Marc MacYoung, Rory Miller, Clint Overland, Peyton Quinn, and Terry Trahan. I highly recommend their superb books and courses for anyone who wants to be safer in the world, or just to create more realistic violence on the page:

http://www.massadayoobgroup.com
https://blauerspear.com
http://yourwarriorsedge.com/about-alain
   -burrese
http://www.lorenchristensen.com
http://www.wimsblog.com
http://www.killology.com
http://www.targetfocustraining.com
https://www.nononsenseselfdefense.com
http://www.chirontraining.com
http://moderncombatandsurvival.com/author
   /peyton-quinn
https://conflictresearchgroupintl.com/terry
   -trahan
https://mastersofmayhem.info

Thanks as always to the extraordinarily eclectic group of "foodies with a violence problem" who hang out at Marc "Animal" MacYoung and Dianna Gordon MacYoung's No Nonsense Self-Defense, for good humor, good fellowship, and a ton of insights, particularly regarding the real costs of violence.

Thanks to Naomi Andrews, Jacque Ben-Zekry,

Phyllis DeBlanche, Grace Doyle, Alan Eisler, Emma Eisler, Bart Gellman, Brad Handler, Meredith Jacobson, Dan Levin, Genevieve Nine, Valerie Paquin, Matt Powers, Laura Rennert, and Paige Terlip for helpful comments on the manuscript. Special thanks once again to Mike Killman for never letting me get lazy about creating action scenes that are both dramatic and tactically correct, and for his fascinating, discursive editorial comments generally.

Most of all, thanks to my wife and literary agent, Laura Rennert, for being such an amazing daily collaborator and otherwise doing so much to make these books better in every way. For anyone else grateful for the increased pace of my writing, Laura's the one we owe it to. Thanks, babe, for everything.

BIBLIOGRAPHY

Matsuo Bashō's *The Narrow Road to Oku* (translated by Donald Keene and illustrated by Miyata Masayuki).
https://www.amazon.com/dp/1568365845

Robert Young Pelton's *Licensed to Kill: Hired Guns in the War on Terror.*
https://www.amazon.com/dp/1400097827

John Roderick's *Minka: My Farmhouse in Japan.*
https://www.amazon.com/dp/1616894512

Jeremy Scahill's *Blackwater: The Rise of the World's Most Powerful Mercenary Army.*
https://www.amazon.com/dp/B0097CYTYA.

Yoshihiro Takishita's *Japanese Country Style: Putting New Life Into Old Houses.*
https://www.amazon.com/dp/4770027613

ABOUT THE AUTHOR

Barry Eisler spent three years in a covert position with the CIA's Directorate of Operations, then worked as a technology lawyer and start-up executive in Silicon Valley and Japan, earning his black belt at the Kodokan Judo Institute along the way. Eisler's award-winning thrillers have been included in numerous "Best Of" lists, have been translated into nearly twenty languages, and include the #1 bestsellers *The Detachment* and *Livia Lone*. Eisler lives in the San Francisco Bay Area and, when he's not writing novels, blogs about torture, civil liberties, and the rule of law. www.barryeisler.com.

Center Point Large Print
600 Brooks Road / PO Box 1
Thorndike, ME 04986-0001 USA

(207) 568-3717

US & Canada:
1 800 929-9108
www.centerpointlargeprint.com